THE PRODIGAL

The Crockett Chronicles Book 3

JENNIFER LYNN CARY

Praise for the Crockett Chronicles

"This book is so good! If you like Christian Historical Fiction, you will love this book. It hooked me on the first page and I couldn't put it down." —Ann Ferri

"I thoroughly enjoyed the book! A big fan of Christian Historical Fiction, this one was absolutely great! Looking forward to the rest of the series!" —Amazon Customer

"I was drawn in by the idea that this series chronicles the descendants of Davy Crockett written with the fictional imagination of a direct descendant. The time period and a glimpse of the Huguenots made for an interesting story. I am excited to read more." —Jennifer Berry

"Exciting and grabs your attention from the first page! You find yourself there! A must read!" —Nova Forrest

"Excellent story of the Crockets. I could not put it down. The characters touched my heart." —Mary Rima

Also by Jennifer Lynn Cary

Available now:

The Patriarch: The Crockett Chronicles: Book 1

The Sojourners: The Crockett Chronicles: Book 2

Coming soon:

Tales of the Hob Nob Annex (May 2020)

Relentless Heart (July 2020)

Wedding Bell Blues (September 2020)

Relentless Joy (November 2020)

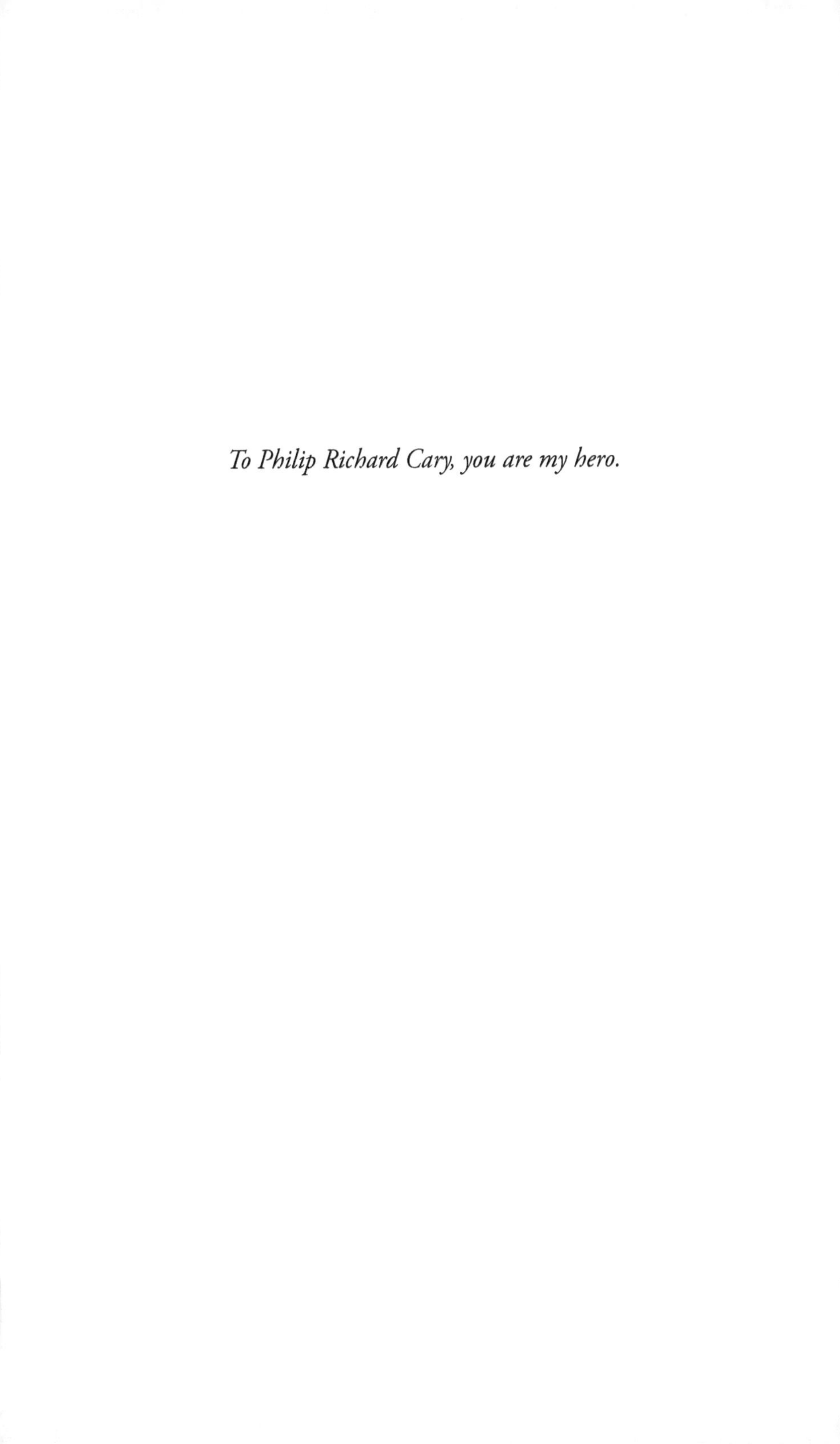

To Philip Richard Cary, you are my hero.

And His mercy is upon generation after generation toward those who fear Him.

— LUKE 1:50

Chapter One

Beaufort, North Carolina 1730

Willie!" The voice called from behind.

William increased his pace. Not now, please, not now.

"Willie! Mama says you are to help me!"

Five minutes. He only needed five minutes.

The voice now panted.

He really should stop. There was no way her little girl legs could keep up with his long full-sized strides. But William strode faster toward the summit.

"Willie, please wait for me!"

His conscience poked him, but his goal was in sight. He could not hold back. He needed this moment, the briefest of solitudes to take in what his soul craved.

Finally, at the top of the bluff, the panorama of the shore opened. The ocean's breeze smacked him in the face, and he smiled from the inside out. This is what he needed, what he'd missed. The scents, the atmosphere, it all fed him as he closed his eyes and stretched out his arms, embracing everything. He could feel the currents, ride the waves, soar the blue while the wind caressed his cheeks. In all his almost twenty years, this was the one thing that calmed the storms raging inside him. He inhaled one last breath of freedom when he felt the tug on his breeches.

"Willie, why didn't you wait? Didn't you hear me?"

William opened one eye and glanced down.

His youngest sister held on to him while gasping for breath. "Oh, Willie, I'm going to tell Mama!"

He scooped her up in his arms, though she was getting too big for him to do that anymore. "Aw, Janie, you don't want to tell Mama. See!" He pointed to the bay. "See all the ships? All the goods coming in? I'll bet Mama has something special for us before the day is out. That will make her happy. You wouldn't want to spoil that, would you?"

Sarah Jane's forehead squished into thinking wrinkles. She shook her head. "I guess not. But why wouldn't you wait for me?"

William hugged her and set her back on her feet. "I needed an alone moment, Janie. That's all." He couldn't help the sigh that followed his admission.

She seemed to accept his explanation because she dropped the subject and grabbed his hand. "So, will you help me with my sums, then?" Her earnest face reminded him how much he had missed this little pest.

He stole one more glance at his ocean before swinging her hand. "Sure."

Leading her to a sweet gum tree, standing tall in a lonely spot near the cliff's edge, they sat beneath its shade and cracked open the book Sarah Jane had lugged along. "Where are you having trouble?"

"Mama says I need to practice carrying over. She says I forget to add that in." She squished up her mouth and gave him a sideways glance.

Now he understood why she was sent to him instead of one of his other many siblings—that was a lesson his mother managed to get him to understand when he was the same age as Janie—seven. Truth be told, he still imagined Mama's voice in his head when he tallied up sums. *Willie, don't forget to include what you already have.* He set the book aside and grabbed a twig from the ground, scratching number problems in the dirt. "Try this one, Janie. Talk it out so I can hear what you are thinking."

She took the twig from him, using it like a pointer. "Seven hundred and fifty-six—"

"Don't say the 'and,' Janie. It means something different if you say 'and'."

"Seven hundred FIFTY-six plus three hundred an..." she glanced at him, "I mean sixty-nine. I need to add the nine and six first."

He smiled and nodded, trying to stay focused, but hearing the call of the ocean's waves.

"That's fifteen so I write my five and put the one over the top of the five in the next column. Then I add five and six, oh, and the one. That's the same as six plus six, so I know that is twelve."

Now she smiled, acting pretty sure of herself. "I write the one and put the two up on top of the seven...?"

He wasn't sure if she made the mistake to see if he would catch her or if she really thought that. His instinct told him she knew what she was doing, so he kept his mouth shut, curious what she would do.

"What do you think, Willie?"

"You can figure it out. Give it a try."

She sighed and fixed the placement for the parts of the twelve. "Like this, the two goes into the answer and the one goes over the seven."

He smiled and nodded again. She was a manipulator with more than numbers. But she was tenderhearted to a fault. He pointed to the final column. "Finish it."

She did. "Seven plus three plus the one I carried over comes to... eleven." She added that to her answer. "So, seven hundred fifty-six plus three hundred sixty-nine equals one thousand, one hundred twenty-five, right?"

"Right you are, Janie." He gave her a wink. "Ready for another?"

Just as she nodded another voice called. "Sarah Jane, William. Mother wants you! Now!"

Their fourteen-year-old brother, Jason, crowned the hill. He stopped before coming any closer than necessary. Fear of catching the infirmity that kept William forever in trouble with his parents was most likely what held him back. Oh, well. No need of Janie catching his disease. "You go on. I'll be along soon." He helped her. "You don't want to get in trouble along with me, Janie." He winked at her and sent her off with Jason.

As he turned, he spotted the arithmetic book still on the ground. "Oh, Janie girl, you are going to end up a black sheep like me." He bent to retrieve it when a small chunk of bark landed on the cover. He glanced up in the tree.

A rustle having nothing to do with the wind in the leaves brought a smile, and he shook his head. Little sister Martha must have finished her studies early and scrambled up the tree so as not to get roped into more chores. Still the tomboy at age ten, Martha preferred running and climbing to about anything else. His eight-year-old sister, Mary, on the other hand, would be too prissy to climb, but Martha didn't know the definition of prissy. "Time to come down, now, Martha. I'll walk you home."

No answer. No movement. She would make this difficult.

"Come down, lass, before I must come after you."

"Ye wouldn't!"

That wasn't Martha's voice.

But it was a lovely voice. An intriguing voice. "So, you are not Martha. Who are you?"

"It be none of yer business who I am, so away with ye. Leave me be."

Rather than intimidate William, the voice sent funny little tingles through his soul. "I don't think I can do that."

"And why, pray tell? Do ye mean me harm?"

Harm her? He wouldn't hurt a fly! "Oh! You cut me to the quick, miss… whatever your name might be. I do not mean you harm. It's just that you have aroused my curiosity. It would delight me to make your acquaintance." He paused, searching for the best idea. "Shall I come up and join you on a branch or would you prefer to come down?"

Rather than a reply, the leaves again rustled. She made her decision. Soon shoes and legs dangled overhead and then a full person appeared, dropping to the ground at his feet. She rose to her full height, standing no taller than his breastbone, her raven hair slipping in soft wisps from beneath her mob cap. Her back skirts were pinned at her waist from where she had pulled them between her legs, so she untucked them. She smoothed her clothes, transforming herself into a proper young lady of sixteen or seventeen years of age.

William held out his hand. "I am William Crockett, Willie to my sisters and brothers. With whom have I made the acquaintance?"

She placed her hand in his and made a small curtsy. "My— BEE!" In one motion she pulled her hand from his and flipped her apron over her head.

William couldn't stop the laugh that burst from him. "Maybe? Your name is Maybe?"

Indignation seeped through her linen apron, dripping chagrin all over him, even before she pulled the cloth from her face.

He stopped laughing.

"Is it gone?"

"Is what gone?"

"The bee! Oh, they terrify me! Please tell me it's gone!"

He glanced about. So that's what scared her. "I'm sorry. Yes, it's gone. I didn't realize. Shall we start again?" He bowed. "I am William the Oaf Crockett, and you are?"

"My name is Elizabeth Boulay." She curtsied again, paused and then snickered. "You thought my name was Maybe?"

William snorted, and they laughed together. "I didn't know what to think. Elizabeth is a pretty name, Miss Boulay, but I must confess, I prefer Maybe."

SARAH CONTINUED TO PUMP THE TREADLE OF HER spinning wheel, tugging the wool into a thin, tight string. If Da could see her now. She shook her head, wondering what he might think of the fine lady he had wanted her to be. She wouldn't trade her life, this amazing life she'd spent with Joseph and their children, for all the emeralds in the world. But a house full of children in a settlement situated between the wilderness and the deep blue sea meant she worked hard. The whole family did. They needed to pull together.

Why didn't William see that?

Oh, her Willie boy. Now he was a young man and should be finishing up his studies at William and Mary. Joseph worked hard to get him into the university. But it was William's job to stay there until they graduated him. Not that it was easy, but it was necessary. He needed an education.

Instead, he popped in here last evening saying he was done with schooling. It was not for him. Oh, the look on Joseph's face!

"Mama, you will pump your spinning wheel to death!"

Sarah glanced into the concerned eyes of her daughter, Mary. "I'm sorry, darlin' girl. Had me head in the clouds, I reckon." She chuckled, slowing the wheel as she did. "Now I know where your sister gets it." She leaned over and tweaked the child's chin.

"More like where Willie gets it. He always seems to be wondering about something out there somewhere." Mary wrinkled her nose as though "out there" was not a pleasant place.

She chuckled and found a stopping spot before going to the

fireplace. Using the tongs she pulled the kettle hanging from the hook where she might stir and check for doneness. "Yer father will be home soon, with yer brother. Ye need to be helping set the table for dinner."

"Yes, Mama. Shall I set places for Joseph Louis and Jeanne?"

Sarah shook her head just as William burst through the door. "I dinna think it took that long to follow yer brother and sister home."

He brushed a kiss on her cheek. "I'm a grown man now, Mama. Sometimes I need to be about manly things."

"You are a man when you show us you can behave as one and not go gallivanting around when you should be working with your father." She sounded sterner than she meant to, but if she could smooth things before Joseph came home, it would be so much better.

His sigh didn't escape her notice. "Mama, all I wanted was a day or so to just breathe in freedom before getting tied down to responsibility all over again. Is that too much to ask?"

"That depends. Have you gotten yer breath of freedom now so ye can start working with yer father in the morning?"

He stared at the floor. She'd seen this before, when he felt blocked. "Yes, Mama."

She caressed his face. "It isn't a bad thing to be a responsible adult, ye know. Now, go get washed for dinner."

He turned and left, tossing a towel over his shoulder as he exited. Her miracle baby, born during a storm at sea. Something about the ocean called to him, louder than all the love and guidance she and Joseph could give.

When God blessed her with baby William, Sarah had promised God that she would be the best mother she could be. The red-faced, bellowing snippet of a thing with a down of strawberry hair captured her heart. Since that moment, there were days where living with Willie amounted to living with a hurricane, but inside that storm beat a tender, loving heart that craved acceptance.

The sound of boots scraping caught Sarah's attention. She rehung the ladle just as Joseph entered, hanging the towel back by the door, followed by John and William. "Go call the others," she directed at Mary before greeting her husband with a warm embrace. "Dinner is ready to dip. I'm glad yer home."

Joseph returned her squeeze and placed a kiss on her cheek before getting out of her way. They knew each other's every move, and she knew that he understood that feeding their sizable, crazy family took maneuvering. In groups of two and three, the rest of her children still living at home found their way to the table—the large, family table Joseph had made for her when the family began to grow at a rapid rate. They had six sons, one she left in a grave in Ireland and another was still at William and Mary, where her William should be. The eldest, Joseph Louis, was a married man so, though she longed to see all her children around the table, there was always someone missing. The bittersweetness of that thought made it difficult to be too upset with William when he filled his chair at mealtime.

Everyone stood until Joseph asked the blessing. Both William and Jason grabbed at her chair, vying for the honor of holding it for her. William won the skirmish. Jason pouted. She'd have to speak with him after dinner.

Once she was seated, the girls brought the food to the table and dinner was underway.

"Tell us about your day." Sarah hoped this request of her husband might spark a desire in her son to help his father.

"Like any other day, I imagine. Between working the field and carving on the rocker for Jeanne, it was another day. Joseph Louis gave me some help with the steamer, and John worked on an order from Master Pratt." He paused and gave John a smile. "Oh, and I got the sideboard to the docks to sail back to Ireland. Should bring a pretty penny."

"That is wonderful. We had a lovely day of lessons. I think Janie is getting better at her sums." She winked at the child. "Mary, Lettie, and Martha are getting on so well with multiplying and dividing, I think they will need a better teacher soon enough. Beth and Jason, suppose you share with us what you've been reading."

Jason opened his mouth, but before he got out a word, his father cleared his throat. Jason pouted again, glaring at his food.

"Ladies first, Beth."

Beth's steady gaze on her plate was a telling sign that she hoped Jason would go first and take so much time that they'd forget her. Sarah could not comprehend the crippling shyness that attacked her daughter at every turn—Sarah had never had a shy day in her life—but she felt the pain. Even now, Beth's head dipped, her quiet words falling onto her plate. "I read—"

"Speak up, girl, we all want to hear." Joseph meant it kindly, and his tone was gentle, but the words still bruised.

Beth cleared her throat. "I read Shakespeare's *The Merchant of Venice.*" Her eyes began to search her plate as if something else captured her interest.

"What did you think of the story, Beth?"

"It… it made me cry." Again, her voice was soft. But as she raised her head, she began to quote from the play. "'The quality of mercy is not strained. It droppeth as the gentle rain from heaven upon the place beneath. It is twice blessed: It blesseth him that gives and him that takes. 'Tis mightiest in the mightiest. It becomes the thronèd monarch better than his crown. His scepter shows the force of temporal power, the attribute to awe and majesty wherein doth sit the dread and fear of kings, but mercy is above this sceptered sway. It is enthronèd in the hearts of kings. It is an attribute to God himself. And earthly power doth then show likest God's when mercy seasons justice.'"

William gave his sister a slow grin as he added to the monologue. "'Therefore, Jew, though justice be thy plea, consider this —that in the course of justice none of us should see salvation. We do pray for mercy, and that same prayer doth teach us all to render the deeds of mercy.'" He nodded to her. "You did well, Beth."

"So did you, son. I am glad you remember that from your mother's lessons." Joseph smiled and Sarah's heart swelled a mite.

She spotted the silent nods between William and his father. Whatever happened, it would work out.

JOSEPH STILL MARVELED AT HOW WELL SARAH GOT THE children to help. After dinner, Jason fetched water to heat for dishwashing while the girls cleared the table. John hung the chairs out of the way and pushed the table against the wall while Beth swept the floor. They all knew what to do, no one begged off, and quicker than Joseph ever imagined, they set the room in order. He had an inkling Sarah had learned this from Anne Fontaine over in Bantry Bay. That was a forever ago. Yet Sarah's eyes still flashed like emeralds when their gazes locked, just as they had back then. She still stood tall and lithe, and her auburn mane still thrilled him when she let it down to brush. He longed to watch her brush it all day. Even after all these years. Even after all their children.

Joseph found his heart mellowing with his thoughts. He wouldn't be as strict as he should with William.

But why was the boy home? James was still at college, at least according to Willie. What made him leave his younger brother and return? Joseph had an idea. Should he demand to know? Should he send him back straightaway? Should he let William find his own path? If Joseph ever needed wisdom, it was now.

"Willie, let's go for a walk." Hopefully that wouldn't make the boy too defensive. He didn't want to ignite that short fuse.

"Sure, Da." William stood, and Joseph was taken with how tall he'd grown. Even more since being away. Willie held the door for his father.

Joseph nodded, grabbing his hat from the peg by the door as he passed. Willie followed, pulling the door shut.

They walked, Joseph waiting for his son to say the first

word. Back home in Ireland they would have walked to the River Foyle. Here, it was safer not to venture too far into the wilderness. The docks were a busy place with the recent arrivals, so he headed in the direction of the center of Beaufort.

Once at the Commons, he found a tree with a good-sized rock near its base. He could sit on that and lean back, still waiting for William to speak.

Finally, after kicking at oyster shells and scuffing his toes in the sod, the boy found his voice. "I suppose you'd be wanting to know why I came home."

Joseph nodded. "That might be the place to start."

William sighed and began to pace. "I'm just no good at this school stuff. I thought Mama had taught me enough to make it, but it is like they speak a strange language."

"You are not stupid. What seems to be the problem?" He was in no hurry to push the boy. If he could hold his tongue, William just might use his to explain it all.

"Well, I feel stupid. And it is so boring! All anyone does there is study. Read. Read. Read. No one takes a break to see the town or just live. I felt so... confined." He stopped pacing, meeting his father's gaze. "Da, I'm not cut out for classes or classics or antiquated philosophies. I've got to move and breathe and experience things. Da, I want to travel, to see places, not just hear about them. I get excited when ships pull in, imagining where they've been. I want to go to sea."

"You do not understand what you are asking, son." The words were out before he could stop them. The look on William's face told him he should have tried harder. "Son." He reached for him.

William pulled away. "You don't understand! I'm trapped here." He raised his hands, palms out, as is to push back any arguments. Turning on his heel, he left in the bluff's direction.

The place called to his son. He'd seen him up there, allowing the sea breeze to pour over him. It was better to let him go. At least he wasn't heading for the docks. Yet his heart told him Willie would head in that direction soon enough.

WILLIAM HAD PROMISED HIMSELF HE WOULDN'T LOSE HIS temper. And he knew his father tried to listen. What an ignoramus he was! He didn't give his father a chance. His father, who worked so hard to pay for him and James to attend William and Mary College. His father, who took care of his family, loving each of his children. His father, the man he admired and wanted to emulate.

"I am so daft!" He shouted to the wind. Of course, his father didn't understand. He was solid, strong. The protector. Craving freedom wasn't in his father's blood. Perhaps the storm that brought him from his mother's womb left him bewitched, for if ever there was a person to embody a mix of thunder, lightning, and wind, that person was he. And right now, the storm within raged beyond his control.

Chapter Two

Elizabeth slipped in the back door, snatching a leftover biscuit on her way past the larder. To sleep outside wasn't a safe idea. As far from the center of town as they were, an Indian kidnapping or worse was still a possibility. If she chose closer to town, there were sailors to consider.

Yet, none of that was more dangerous than what she faced in her own home.

Or rather, her stepfather's home, as he often corrected.

She made sure the house remained clean, that he had food, and worked to accomplish those things while he slept or went out. Other than that, she gave him a wide berth. If he'd been to the tavern, there was no telling the condition he'd be on his return. He might stagger in and collapse into a deep slumber for enough hours to give Elizabeth time to sleep. Or he might come back angry that someone bested him at cards. Then he was more likely to take out his anger on her—with his fists or a leather strop. And then there were the times he claimed he was lonely, now that her mother had gone. Elizabeth reminded herself that her mother hadn't abandoned her to this. She had died. Unexpectedly. Her leaving seemed to unlock a door for her husband, a door that led to Elizabeth's bedroom.

After waking to find him standing over her one night, Elizabeth had added a bolt. Still, she never felt safe.

"Lizzy? Dat you girl?"

A chill slithered up Elizabeth's spine. "What do ye want?"

"C'mere, girl. I need yer 'elp."

Elizabeth took one, then two steps toward the front room.

"Get in 'ere, ya trollop."

She inhaled and stepped into the room.

He'd slid down the wall to land on the floor. It appeared he was part drunk and part pummeled senseless. His eyes were bruised, swollen. The right side of his mouth bulged. A trickle of blood ran from the corner, down his chin. When he parted his lips to call again, she spotted a new bloody gap where he once had teeth. "There ye be." His nose wrinkled, as if he were trying to squint his eyes but the swelling refused to cooperate. "Lizzie, need a drink."

She brought him a whiskey bottle, he snatched it with his left hand. She jumped back. That was when she noticed his right arm's strange angle.

He bit out the cork and spit it onto the floor before taking a giant slug.

"Yer arm, 'tis broken."

"Ye, dear girl, are a master of ob-ser-VA-shun, that ye are. Me arm's broke. Ye need to set it for me."

Had he lost his mind? What could he be thinking? "I know nothin' of settin' broken bones. I will get the bonesetter." She turned toward the front door, the one she noticed stood wide open.

"No!"

Freezing mid-step, she turned to him. "Ye need more help than I can give ye. I won't be long." Her heart tendered a smidge, as she knew he suffered.

"No," He hung his head. "There's n' money ta pay. Nuthin' left." He took a breath, raised his head, and tried to focus on her face. "Ye have ta do it, Lizzie." He tossed back another drink, his Adam's apple bobbing as he chugged.

She scanned the room for something sturdy for the setting. Perhaps a blown-off roof shingle courtesy of the last storm? Then she spotted it. Draped across the chipped basin in the corner. His strop. It would have to do—at least it wouldn't be used on her if it was holding his arm together. She added a stick from the fireplace that had yet to burn and found an old linen sheet of her mother's, and at last dumped her supplies on the table. A quick prayer might be in order, though it seemed hypocritical. Useless, although she thought *help me!*

She would have to get close enough to touch him. Goose pimples raced up her arms and her stomach twisted. But despite the bile at the back of her throat, she inched closer to look. "I need to be cuttin' away yer sleeve." She wouldn't call him Da, even now.

"Then be doin it." He slurred worse, except for the curses he muttered under his breath. Those were all too distinct.

"The knife be in the other room. One moment." She hopped up to get it.

"Lizzie, ye won't b' leavin' me lie this, will ya?" A tear made a track down his cheek to mingle in the blood pooled at his lip.

The thought had crossed her mind. Walk out the back door, never return. But who could do that? "I won't be but a stitch." She even offered a small smile, hoping he'd believe her.

The knife lay hidden at the back of the larder. Why leave an extra knife where he could get it? She pulled it from its hiding place and returned to the front room. "See, only an instant. Now, I'll check yer arm."

She cut the tattered cloth away as gently as she could.

He still moaned and finished the whiskey, letting the bottle fall to his side.

The bone was broken but had not punctured the skin. Her stepfather passed out before she could give him the stick to bite. She tore off a section of the sheet and then tore that into strips, binding them about his arm, working the two parts of the bone together. The next thing to do was to wrap the strop about to give body and support, keeping the bones from pulling apart. She added the stick, since it wasn't between his teeth, at the base of his forearm between the cloth and the strop. Once done, she fashioned a sling from the leftover linen.

There was no moving the man. He was much taller than she and weighed at least fifteen stones. So, she got bedclothes from his room and tucked the pillow behind him. A paper fell from his pocket. She placed it into her apron waist and draped the cover over him. He was out for the night. If God were smiling, a good portion of tomorrow, too.

She closed and bolted the front door, gathered a candle, extinguish the others, and made the back door secure before climbing the stairs to her room. The bolt slid into place, though she had little to fear tonight. She sat on the edge of her bed, stymied at the troubles her stepfather could find. The paper at her waist rustled, reminding her of its presence. Any bill needed to go through her, or it would most likely be lost or forgotten. She pulled the scrap free and unfolded the piece, reading the quill scratches. A bill of sale.

One girl, seventeen years of age, four and a half stones. Sold to Eleazar Ferguson in lieu of the thirty-pound debt. Delivery expected the twentieth of May in the year of our Lord 1730. Debt paid in full upon delivery of girl.

Sold to Eleazar Ferguson?

An icy wave poured over her. Elizabeth's hands shook. The paper fluttered to the floor.

Her stepfather had sold her.

JASON STARED OUT THE DOOR, DARING HIS BROTHER TO

come home. Willie's presence made life so haphazard. When he was gone, life was—

"What are you thinking about, Jason?"

He startled. "None of your concern, Janie. You wouldn't understand anyway." He closed the door and plopped on the bench.

Janie followed his actions, crossing her arms to match his. "What do you mean, I wouldn't understand? I'm not a baby anymore. I understand lots."

"Oh, you do? Have you noticed Mama crying or Papa more quiet than usual?"

Janie's eyes grew wide. "No! Why is Mama crying? Is she sick?"

"Sick at heart. William is breaking her heart."

She squished her face at him. "What do you mean? She's glad he is home. I am too! I miss Willie when he's gone."

"Don't you miss James?" Not that he missed him, but Willie couldn't be that special.

"Aye, only James would chase me away. He likes to study and says I interrupt him. Willie lifts me in the air, and he helps me." She scooted closer. "Don't you love Willie anymore?"

Jason sighed. "I told you, you wouldn't understand. You're a girl." He turned his back on her.

"Mama, Mama! Jason hates Willie! Jason hates Willie!" She ran upstairs to her mother.

Jason darted after her. "I didn't say that! Mama! I didn't say that!"

"Whoa!" Mama stood at the top of the stairs. "What a fuss! Tell me, what is going on?"

Janie tugged at her mother's skirts. "Mama, Mama, Jason hates Willie. He doesn't love him, and he wants him to go away!"

"Jason, is that what you think?" Mama's eyes tore into his soul.

"I never said that!"

Her hand went under his chin, making him peer in her eyes. "But is that what you think?"

He glanced down at Janie's smug little face.

She stuck out her tongue.

He sighed. "I just think he disrupts things. He's like a powder keg ready to go off. It's peaceable when he's not here. That's all." He stuck his tongue out at Janie.

"That's enough! Yer talking about me son. Me flesh and blood. I love all me sons, all me daughters too. I do not have a favorite. But each one of ye has a special place all yer own in me heart." Mama put her arms around both Jason and Janie. "I know life gets exciting with Willie. But I love him for that. How dull life would be without his exuberance!"

"And how less disappointed you would be if he'd only—"

"Only what, Jason?" The voice came from behind.

Jason swung toward the staircase. Too late to stop, he knocked Janie off balance. She flailed her arms, grabbing for the banister and missing. Mama leapt for her, grasping only air as Janie tumbled down the steps, one after another, with William catching her at the bottom.

"Quick, lay her on the bench." Mama was downstairs before Jason could even move.

"I got her, Mama. She's all right." Willie carried her to the bench. At first it appeared as if Janie wasn't breathing, but then she caught her breath and let out a howl. Willie and Mama comforted her while all Jason could do was watch. The horrified anguish and then relief on Mama's face crushed him. Just as much as Willie's heroics made his blood steam.

What if Janie were hurt? No doubt she'd have a couple bruises, but it could have been much worse.

It was Willie's fault. Jason crossed his arms, his mind made up. All of it. If Willie hadn't been sneaking in on private conversations, this wouldn't have happened. Jason charged out the door.

He hadn't gone far when something grabbed his shoulder, stopping him in his tracks.

"Jason, it's all right. Janie is all right. Don't beat yourself up about it."

Jason spun and took a swing at Willie, fist connecting with nothing but air.

"Whoa, wait a minute. What's that for?"

"For knocking Janie down the stairs, for one."

Willie's jaw dropped. Now was the time to hit him. Instead, Jason exploded. "You scared her, sneaking up on our private conversation. Who gave you that right? You don't belong here. Go back to school. We don't want you here!"

"You mean, *you* don't want me here."

"I mean WE don't. I am not alone." Jason felt like two different people—one who ranted and raved at his brother and one who stood by wondering who the mad man was.

"Well, brother Jason, if that's how you see it, perhaps I will have to oblige you. I can't stay where I'm not wanted." Willie turned on his heel and headed for his bluff.

Jason dropped to the ground, ownership of his words sinking in. What had he done?

❧

Elizabeth waited for the first rays of light. It was the dawning of the twentieth day of May. If she stayed here, she would be the property of one Eleazar Ferguson. If she ran away, providing she got away where no one found her, she'd be leaving her stepfather in a cruel fix. No less cruel than he left her, but would she sink to his level?

Could she become the property of a man like Eleazar Ferguson?

No, she could not.

She made a bundle—change of clothing plus all the money she had in the world. As she started to leave her room, she spotted her father's fiddle. If she left it, her stepfather would sell it. She added it to her bundle with a couple biscuits and slipped out the back door. Without a time listed on the bill of sale, she couldn't know when she was expected.

When her stepfather woke and she was nowhere to be found, Master Ferguson would most likely come calling, expecting his goods. She prayed she'd be long gone before that happened.

Prayed. She hadn't prayed since her mother was taken. Her mother wouldn't approve of her lack of prayer life, but what kind of loving God would do what He'd done to her family? Yet, old habits die hard. Perhaps this once He'd help her.

Elizabeth had paced all night, praying a plan would drop from heaven, but none came. She needed a place to hide until she had one. That old sweet gum tree up on the bluff. If she climbed it, no one would find her. Master Crockett wouldn't have known she was there if she hadn't knocked that piece of bark free. No one else went near the place.

At least she had a small step of a plan.

On approach of the rise, she noticed something beneath the tree. She slowed her steps, continuing with caution. It was a person. A man. He lay curled at the base of the sweet gum.

Her heart began to pound. What if he were dead? Worse, what if somehow someone had learned of her special place and set a trap for her? She scanned about for a weapon, lighting on a long stick. She weighed the feel in her hand before stealthily moving closer.

The man moved, and she got a good view of his hair, or rather wild red mane. It was that Crockett fellow. Probably had one too many. At least he didn't appear to be a mean drunk. She breathed again.

Drawing near, she dropped her stick, set her bundle on the ground, and nudged his knee with her toe.

He mumbled something, waved a hand in the air, and rolled away from her.

She nudged again. "Master Crockett, are you all right?"

He rolled to his back and cracked open one eye. She knew the instant she came into his focus. His jaw dropped, his other eye popped open, and he jumped to his feet running his hands through his mop. "Oh, Miss... Boulay. Ah, so sorry. I didn't see you there." He brushed at the grass and dirt still clinging to his clothes.

It started as a small tickle. Elizabeth put her finger under her nose to head it off, but there was no stopping it. The laugh burst from her toes. She dropped to her knees, trying to catch her breath when the thought of how crazy she was to be laughing at such a time crossed her mind. The tears of laughter running down her cheeks became tears of panic. Perhaps she was mad.

A hand came under her chin, drawing her to gaze into the face of Master William Crockett the Concerned. His expression convincing her she was mad.

"Miss Boulay, I am so sorry. How can I help you?"

She forced herself to suck in a breath. If she got her breathing under control, perhaps she might find her voice. Raggedy breath in. Raggedy breath out. In. Out. In. Out. She wiped her eyes on her sleeve and nodded her head. She would not be a weak, needy female. She would not.

"'Tis me what should apologize." Breath. "I am sorry. It has been a trying night." She glanced around, making certain no one else was in the vicinity.

"I can well understand. You have my sympathies, for what they are worth." He sat next to her, stretching out his long legs.

"Thank ye. Yer kindness is a salve. And ye have me sympathies, as well." She glanced at him from the corner of her eye. "For what they are worth."

He chuckled. "Shall we commiserate together? I am the family failure. You can add that to the oaf part. Oaf and failure. That's me."

"My, aren't we the tragic hero?" She didn't have time for his gloom and doom story. She needed to get hidden before she was found.

"Well what is your story? Has it more tragedy?"

Her heart stopped at the thought of everything that happened this last year and what she faced. "Ye do not have time to be hearin' me sad tale."

"Oh, I'm sure I do. I am not wanted anywhere today." He studied her face; she feared he read it all.

Perhaps she should tell him he wasn't so bad off. "Me stepfather..." No, she wouldn't tell him all. But she could tell him the immediate. He might help her come up with a plan. "I learned last night that me stepfather sold me to Eleazar Ferguson. He is to deliver me today."

If she had planned to shock him, she succeeded. His eyes grew so big, she feared they might roll out of his head. "Sold you? To Eleazar Ferguson? That man is..."

She nodded. "I know. Me stepfather owed him thirty pounds. This cancels the debt. But I just canna."

"They will take it out on your stepfather if you run."

"Aye. Someone already has. I had to set his arm last night." She glanced away, torn how to admit the next part. "I have no love for the man. He... I will not miss him. I dunna want to cause his downfall, but truth be told, he was slidin' down without me help. This will make things worse."

His hand covered hers. "What do you plan to do? Where will you go?"

"I dunna ken. I thought to climb the tree and think a wee bit." She almost pulled away, but she liked the feel of his hand. His touch was gentle, light.

"No one would see you there." He chuckled. "You know, you climbed that tree like a boy."

She laughed at that. Her mother had said the same thing. Another time. About another tree. "If I were a boy, I'd have a lot more options."

He withdrew his hand and sat straighter. "Why can't you be a boy?"

Was he that daft? A grown man and he dinna ken the difference between a boy and a girl?

"Now, wait a minute. Think about it. Who will they be searching for? A girl. But if you were dressed as a boy, your hair cut, in breeches and all that, you might fool them." He captured her gaze while the idea took hold.

She saw it play out in his eyes. "And I would hide right under their noses. Aye. No." She had another thought. "I would need work. Too much interaction might give me away."

A big smile played over Master Crockett's face. "Not if you go to sea. I've longed to go to sea from my first moment. You and I can go as friends. We'll sign on at the docks, be gone before evening." He stuck out his hand. "Shall we?"

She stared at his hand. She wouldn't be a weak female. But, with his plan, she wouldn't be a female at all. She'd have to stay strong enough to fool the rest of the crew. The trip onboard ship last year when they had come to America from Ireland had been exhilarating. She'd wanted to explore, but as a sixteen-year-old unmarried girl, she had kept her place. The idea bloomed. As a boy, she would be safe in ways a girl would not. And she would not be alone. They would be together. Could she trust him?

She gazed at his hand again and grasped it. "We shall." She smiled. "So where shall we begin, Master Crockett?"

"First, with names. You must call me Willie. I will call you..." He grinned. "I shall call you Maybe."

"Maybe?"

"No one would ever connect that name to Miss Elizabeth Boulay. We'll say you're called that because—"

"Because I was a foundling, and no one knows my name. Maybe it's this, maybe it's that. So... Maybe."

"Yes! And you need different clothes." He set his elbow to his knee and tapped his lips with his fingertips. "I have a brother about your size. I could borrow something of his." He rubbed his hand across his mouth, looking like he wasn't sure of the idea. Then his hand fell back in his lap, and he turned to her. "That's what I'll do. I can get his old clothes and other necessities. You go up the tree and wait. When it is safe, I will come for you."

"Mast__ah, Willie, there's another need."

He gave her a quizzical stare.

"I might dress as a boy, but the Good Lord gave me a woman's figure. I will need something to... bind myself." She felt the heat in her cheeks speaking it aloud.

Willie laughed. "You are right. He blessed you, that He did. I will bring something for binding. Now, up the tree with you, Maybe. I'll be back as soon as I can."

He turned his back while she gathered her skirts from behind, bringing them between her legs and tucking them at her waist. Then he waited until she had shinnied up a couple branches before lifting her bundle to her.

She watched him walk away before climbing higher into the leafy canopy. This was likely to be a long wait. She might as well get comfortable.

❧

Halfway home, the import of what he agreed to hit Willie. Did he want to leave his family like this? He'd always felt the pull of the sea, but leaving without a word, let alone a blessing, would deeply hurt his parents. But if he stayed to talk with them, they would not let go until he'd told everything about Maybe. He mustn't put her in danger. No one deserved to be purchased by Eleazar Ferguson.

Funny how he considered her Maybe and not Elizabeth. He shook his head and slipped into the house.

Mama was up tending to breakfast. An excellent cook, his mama cooked better than anyone he'd ever met. That he wouldn't taste her food again for a long time, possibly ever, crossed his mind, causing something inside to twist. He tiptoed over and kissed her cheek.

"So, yer wanting to make amends, is it?" She never stopped flipping the flapjacks to face him.

"Yes, Mama. I figured I best cool off." Which was somewhat true.

"And yer cooled off? No more hot head?"

He chuckled. "For now."

She finally peered up at him. "So, what happened? You were going to tell Jason that Janie wasn't hurt."

"I did, but me and my temper. I got angry and then later felt bad about it." Jason must stay here. He would not put this on the boy and leave him alone to defend himself. That much he would do.

She nodded. "Ye understand, I can tell when you are hiding something. And I ken Jason is making it rough for you."

"He's just a boy yet. He'll find his way."

She smiled, and he knew she was thinking the same thing of him. Would she ever view him a man? "Call yer brothers and sisters. Yer father is in his room. Ye can call him too."

He nodded and sidled off to do her bidding. For the last time.

After breakfast, they cleared away the dishes, but everyone remained at the table. His father opened his Bible and began reading to the family. Today it was from the book of Luke—the Prodigal Son. If his father wanted to stab him in the heart, he couldn't have done a better job. But he had no intention of asking for any inheritance or money. He wasn't leaving to live a life of debauchery. Yet, no matter how he tried to deflect the pinpricks of guilt, they still found their mark.

He glanced about at his brothers and sisters. How many would miss him? Maybe Janie and possibly Martha and Beth. Lettie and Mary were obedient little girls, doing what was expected. Oh, they were sweet and kind, but Martha and Janie had spunk, and Beth, well, Beth had a heart that was much too tender. As for his brothers, John and Joseph Louis might think of him. They watched out for him for as far back as he remembered. He doubted James, back at school, had pulled his nose from his book long enough to notice his brother was gone.

And then there was Jason. Somehow, he and Jason had never gotten on, though he didn't understand why. Perhaps it was how Jason took everything so literally, without a sense of humor. Willie had no memory of a time when the boy laughed for pure joy. Just always an undercurrent of discontent. Now it had grown from an undercurrent to full-fledged hatred on his brother's part. Willie would never hate him back, though. Something wasn't right, and he kept thinking if he figured out the problem he might fix it and they'd get along. Now he'd run out of time. He glanced at Jason. The boy appeared tortured. What did he think to cause him such pain?

The Scripture reading over, his father prayed for the family before they all went about their day. Everyone did their part to put the room in order and the older girls started washing the dishes while Mama took Janie and Mary to work on spelling.

Father stopped at the door. "Willie, you planning to come work with us today?" It wasn't as much a question as an expectation.

Something squeezed Willie's heart as he lied. "I'll be along. I must first take care of something."

His father nodded and pulled the door closed behind him.

The clock in his brain picked up speed. He hadn't crossed that threshold of no return, but he was dangerously close.

He crept upstairs to the room he shared with his brothers. There he borrowed a too-small pair of Jason's old breeches. Willie figured he wouldn't miss them, and they should (he hoped) fit Maybe. He grabbed a worn shirt and other things, including a hat his mother had knitted. Then he needed something to use for her binding. He was at a loss. Nothing upstairs fit the bill. As a last resort he checked in his parents' room. He rummaged about and found several things his mother had saved from when her children were babies. He'd no idea she'd kept all those things—like the stays he and his brothers had worn as toddlers to help improve their posture. Sentimental tokens. It pulled at his heart that he would leave Mama and the family.

He settled on an old scarf his mother had made when a thought struck. Perhaps if he left a note. He still mustn't tell them everything, but he could tell them to not worry. And he could promise to send word. Locating a pencil and a piece of foolscap, he left what he hoped would ease their pain and tucked the finished note beneath his mother's pillow.

As he left the room, he met Beth. "Oh, I didn't know you were up here."

"Mama wants to fix the tear in Da's blue waistcoat." The question shone in her eyes, but he knew she was too shy to ask.

"I see. Well, I will see you downstairs, Bethy." He lied yet again.

She nodded. As he walked past her, she touched his arm.

He turned and noticed she stared at the floor. "What is it, Beth?"

Her whisper stopped his breath. "I will miss you, Willie."

She was in their parents' room before he began breathing again. What did she know? Was she going to prevent him? Would she tell? Could she tell?

He ran down the steps and out the back door before anyone else could stop him.

Chapter Three

Why did Da pick that reading for today? Jason kicked an oyster shell from the path. Did his father see Willie as a prodigal? If so, what did that make him? The miserable son left behind?

Oh, he was miserable. Nothing would rid him of his misery. Nightmares plagued him when Willie didn't come home all night. But there he sat this morning. And before he'd considered being grateful for his brother's safety, he was grumbly again because Willie was still home. How bitter must he become? Not a good question. If he hadn't reached the pinnacle of bitterness yet, he didn't want to think how much worse it might get.

He was supposed to be reading *Richard III*. Mama would expect a report before the afternoon was out. However, misery made reading too much the chore. One more year and he could spend his time helping Father instead of helping with his sisters. It wasn't so bad before James left for school. Then he wasn't the only boy, they had done their studies together. But Willie couldn't go off to school by himself. Oh, no! He had to take James with him. And leave him at school to boot! Irritation burned his gut.

He picked up another shell, planning to send it flying when

he saw his nemesis slipping out the back door of the house. Perhaps he should pelt him. That would serve him right. Ha! But Jason's curiosity outweighed his irritation, and he dropped the shell to follow.

He hadn't taken but a few steps when Janie called from the front. "Jason! Mama wants you!"

Of course, she did. If he were Willie, he'd just pretend he hadn't heard. But he was Jason. Jason obeyed. Kicking a clod of dirt to smithereens, he sighed and stomped for the house.

⚜

ELIZABETH OBSERVED WILLIE FROM HER PERCH LONG before he crested the hill. He was alone but for the bundle he carried. She had plenty of time to think about their plan. Had she been rash? Yet each time the face of Eleazar Ferguson floated through her brain she knew. She would do whatever she must to keep from that man's grasp.

Willie's pace was steady, deliberate. He didn't hide his destination. Should that worry her? Did he tell anyone? Had she been foolish to trust a man she'd barely met?

She scanned the path behind him in case he'd been followed. No one else was in sight. Perhaps this might work. Just the notion made her heart thunder. Another minute and Willie would be there. She'd better decide now before it was too late for second thoughts, before either of them did anything that could not be undone.

⚜

"MAYBE, PSST! MAYBE, YOU STILL UP THERE?" A PART OF Willie hoped she'd gone, giving him a way out of the plan. He yearned to go to sea, but this was wrong. He would break his parents' hearts. And what if they got caught? There's no telling what Eleazar Ferguson would try to do to his father's business.

Yet if he got his clutches on Maybe... The idea made his skin crawl.

He heard a rustle from above and glanced up to see her peering down on him. Her face appeared paler than usual. "Stay up there. Come close enough to grab this bundle. I had trouble finding something for your binding and ended up grabbing an old scarf. My mother made it for me. If nothing else, it will keep you warm." Her hand reached down to accept his gift. "I will take a walk, you get changed. When I come back, you can hop down and I'll see what kind of barber I make." He nervously laughed at his own joke, hoping she wasn't sentimental over hair.

She nodded and scurried higher in the branches.

Willie shrugged and walked toward the edge of the bluff. In all that she hadn't said one word. Was he encouraging her into something she didn't want? Should he call this off? What if she were counting on him to call it off? Or was she counting on him to help her from this dilemma? He covered his ears against all the "what ifs".

He scanned the tree and noted movement in the lower branches so headed back. Maybe dropped to the ground at his feet, dressed in Jason's clothes and appearing more like a boy, but not completely. Her female clothes were wadded under her arm, but she still wore the mob cap. He knew the next part would be the hardest.

"Will I pass?" Both her smile and voice trembled.

Willie nodded. "Almost. We must cut your hair."

Her hand went to her head, as if she tried to hold her cap in place, and one tear dropped from her cheek. She straightened her back, tilted her chin and pulled the cap from her head. "Let us get it done."

All that raven hair tumbled down past her waist, long enough to sit on. And it was beautiful, framing her oval face, making her violet eyes flash. He suddenly hated himself for what he was about to do.

Drawing his knife from his boot, he had her turn her back to him. It was hard enough without gazing in her eyes. His hand smoothed her dark waves, tendrils wrapping about his fingers, before grasping a section and pulling the blade through. Now his hand held a hank of the softest hair he'd ever touched. He searched about for somewhere to put it.

"Just drop it. We can scatter it and the birds will find it for their nests."

In that moment, he knew Miss Elizabeth Boulay was the strongest woman he'd ever met. It made his hands shake.

"I am sorry, Elizabeth."

"I'm Maybe. And I ken. Let's jist be done."

Willie grabbed another section and sliced it free. Within a couple minutes, the hair was cut.

She tucked what was left behind her ears. "Now do I look like a boy?"

She did. Or more than she had. "Perhaps you could use some dirt streaks across your cheeks? And you need dirty finger-nails, too."

She stooped to the ground, scratched up sod, and rubbed it on her face. "There?"

"There." He nodded, and she smiled. He handed her the work cap his mother had made for him. It helped even more.

"What should I do with my clothes?"

Willie glanced around, then pointed up.

Maybe separated a fiddle from the rest of her bundle before handing it to Willie. She shimmied back up into the tree and he handed the bundle back up to her. She climbed out of sight momentarily, but then came back empty-handed. "If a strong wind comes, my clothes will be all over Beaufort. Hopefully, by then, we'll be far enough to sea that it won't matter."

"So, Maybe, are you ready?" He stuck out his hand.

"Ready, Mate!" She grinned and shook his hand.

The deal was set. She grabbed her fiddle, and they headed toward the harbor.

DANIEL O'MALLEY WINCED AND TOOK AN INVENTORY OF his pain. His face hurt, his ribs hurt, his right arm really hurt. Even his hair pained him. He cracked open an eye or tried to. It was swollen shut. He tried the other with only a slit more success. "Lizzie!" The exercise in voice choked him, and he began coughing. Which only made everything hurt more.

Remaining stone still, he searched for a way to breathe that would not bring about the coughing or make his head want to run from his shoulders. Once he'd gotten the pain to a level of bearable, he tried standing. His right arm wouldn't obey his command. It was useless and in a sling, so he put his left palm on the floor and attempted to push himself up. The throbbing waves washing over him killed that idea.

How was he to get up? Where was that girl?

He explored with his good hand for a bottle, finding short lived success. The bottle was empty.

Bit by bit, the last evening returned. The fickle cards that abandoned him. The look on Ferguson's face when he learned he could not pay. The blow that broke his arm. The kick that cracked his ribs. The paper shoved in his pocket after he pleaded and begged and bargained for his life. The paper.

His left hand groped for the pocket. No paper there. He pawed the floor beside him, nothing but the blanket... Lizzie must have put that blanket on him. Did she find the paper? Oh no, no, no.

Panic rose, as well as bile. He thought he would vomit. Fighting the pain with every ounce of strength he had, Daniel forced his body to stand. Then he leaned against the wall until his head stopped spinning. He slowed his breathing, waiting out the waves of pain. With the wall for support, he made it to the stairs, mounting them one measured tread at a time.

By the time he reached the top, his chest heaved and his cracked ribs screamed. He waited to catch his breath before pushing open her bedroom door. Tidy but for a wad of paper on the floor. She knew.

He was a dead man.

***

SARAH TOOK JOSEPH'S MENDED WAISTCOAT BACK TO THEIR room. Normally, she would have put it away and returned downstairs. There was too much work for dawdling. But for some reason she couldn't name, she straightened the pillows on the bed. Never mind that she'd made it when she and Joseph rose for the day. Never mind that all was in place. Her hands did what they did, causing her to find what she found.

A note.

Sarah opened the folded paper, and her knees grew weak. She'd know that childish handwriting anywhere. Dropping to the bed, she read her son's words a second and a third time.

> *Mama, Da,*
> *Plez do not wury for me. I am sory, but I canot*
> *ignor the sirun's call. I hav go to see. I mus get*
> *this out of my sistem or I wil nevr be fre. I love*
> *you both so verry much and I no this mus hert.*
> *I cont on yur pryrz for my retern. I wil com bak*
> *on day, I prmis. I wil evn sen werd to you*
> *wenevr I can. Untl I see you agin, I remane yur*
> *lovng, but detrmind son, Willie.*

"Jason!" She jumped up and ran to the head of the stairs. "Jason!"

"Yes, Mama?" He met her halfway.

"Go get your father! Tell him it is urgent!" She turned him and practically pushed him down the stairs.

He twisted around as she pushed. "What is it, Mama? What is the matter?"

"No time to explain. Just get your father!" She pushed him out the door and leaned against the frame, reading the note one more time.

How could she not have known. That niggle told her something was wrong this morning. He had that look about him. But going to sea? Without talking to her about it? She crushed the note in her fist. *Why, Willie?*

She sank onto her rocker, the one Joseph made for her to rock Willie as a babe, and began to weep.

Joseph burst through the door, and she ran to his arms.

"Sh-sh." He held her and rocked her in his arms. "What is it, love? What is the matter?"

Sarah pulled back and handed him the note. She felt his stagger as the words on the page bludgeoned him.

He pulled away but kissed her cheek. "Do not worry. I'm going after him." Joseph was out the door and running for the harbor before she could kiss him to send him on his way.

ELEAZAR FERGUSON PRIDED HIMSELF ON HIS COMMUNITY standing, or what he perceived as his standing. A part of him knew he was disliked, perhaps disdained, but no one said that to his face.

It was important he look the part of the successful businessman, so his frock coat, breeches and waistcoat always matched. The neck handkerchief, always neatly tied, sported the finest lace. Even his silk stockings, elegantly complimenting his suit, remained dirt free despite the natural dustiness or mud the streets of Beaufort produced. A few might call him dapper, but again, never to his face.

He smiled at the thought. Which brought him to his next thought. That lovely daughter of Daniel O'Malley. She would be a wonderful addition to his... habits. He remembered seeing her once when she paid for one of O'Malley's bills, though he couldn't recall ever seeing her in O'Malley's company. A tiny thing, she was. A new plaything. Again, he smiled and checked the time.

Now he frowned. O'Malley should have brought her by now. If he must retrieve the girl, it would not be pleasant. He paced to the window and peered into the street. No one of interest headed his way.

Then unpleasant it would be.

With a call to his assistants, Eleazar put on his hat, tugged on his sleeves, and headed toward the O'Malley cottage. His assistants followed. It was not a long walk. He'd watched while his assistants escorted O'Malley to his home last evening. However, it was irksome to go himself.

He rapped on the door with his walking stick. There was no answer, so he stepped to the side and nodded to his assistants. They opened the door in two shakes.

Eleazar stepped around the splintered wood and began a cursory search of the downstairs. An empty whiskey bottle rolled about the floor when his toe encountered it. An old worn blanket lay in a heap next to the wall. But there was no sign of O'Malley. Or the girl.

Eleazar nodded to his assistants.

They trudged the rickety staircase and returned moments later. Alone.

The back door stood ajar. Another nod sent the two to check. Less than a minute later, Eleazar heard the scream. Someone was in desperate pain.

He meandered out the back door toward the sound, which stopped as soon as it started. His assistants were dragging O'Malley between them toward the house. They dropped him at Eleazar's feet.

Folding his long legs into a stoop, Eleazar dusted off his shoes then used his walking stick to lift O'Malley's head. The man was unconscious.

Eleazar slipped off his leather gloves. He gripped them in his right hand, and tapped them against his left palm, contemplating his next move. O'Malley moaned.

"Where's the girl?" The gloves backhanded O'Malley's bruised cheek, causing the man's head to jerk. "Listen and answer, Master O'Malley. Where is my property? What have you done with the girl?"

O'Malley's head bobbled. He spit out a tooth, letting a bloody string of spittle dangle off his chin. "I dunno. I woke 'n' she gone. Was jist goin' fer her."

Gone? She had no right to be gone. She was his property. "Where might she go? Who are her friends?"

"Dunno. She ha' no frien. Ony me." Assistant number one grabbed O'Malley by the hair to keep his head from bobbling.

"You? You sold her to me. What kind of friend are you?" Eleazar stood and nodded to his assistants before turning and walking back into the house. He had crossed the threshold before the first outcry. He closed the door.

❧

WILLIE SCANNED THE SHIPS DOCKED IN THE HARBOR, searching for one that appeared about ready to leave. He didn't want to sign on and wait several hours or the morrow. They needed to be gone now.

This was a time where his height served him. He could see over the crewmen working, the cargo being loaded and unloaded, even the farewells from loved ones. That helped direct him. He pulled Maybe along, holding her arm so as not to lose her in the chaos while listening to conversations and hoping for a piece of helpful information.

"Master, found Meekle and Grue. You won't like it. They are in stocks in the center of town."

"We sail in the hour, and now I'm out two crewmen? I knew we should have kept them locked on board."

Willie turned to where he'd heard the speaker. "Excuse me,

sir. Do you need two hands? We're looking to sail. We'll work hard for you." Willie tried his most charming smile.

The master, an average-sized man with average brown hair and beard gave him more than an average passing glance. "We? Where's the other one?"

"Right here, sir. Master, sir." He spun Maybe around in front of him.

"Why he's just a lad. Too young and small." The master shook his head.

"But I'm healthy and strong. I will work hard." Maybe didn't hold back.

The master shook his head again. "No, you don't understand. Meekle's job was to man the top. It takes a brave man to climb to that height."

Maybe shoved the fiddle into Willie's hands and shouted over her shoulder as she ran up the gangplank. "I can do it!" Before anyone thought to stop her, she climbed the Jacob's ladder. Within a minute, she manned the platform on the mast.

The master who'd run after her, followed by Willie and the boatswain, called up. "So, you are up there. Can you climb down?"

Without a word, she started her return journey, dropping that last foot at his feet. "I can climb anything. Will you take us on?"

Willie wasn't sure at first. He watched the master's eyes. His expression said he was angry, but his eyes held esteem. "Never try a trick like that again!" He paused. "But, aye! Never seen the sight before! You're a natural monkey, you are!" He turned to the man who'd located the missing crew members in the stocks, Boatswain Johnson, and told him to get them situated. "We cast off in one hour."

Willie lost no time getting onboard. Boatswain Johnson showed them their immediate jobs and gave them the abridged version of expectations, letting them know he would give them the full listing of their responsibilities once out to sea. He then left them to their work.

Once they started, there was a moment. Maybe glanced his way, their gaze locked. That was when it all turned real. They were doing this. His heart began to thump. She flashed him a grin that trembled to the beat of his pounding heart. No turning back.

As the last bit of cargo was stashed below, the boatswain called out "Cast off!" Willie went to the side for one last glimpse of home, the only hometown he could remember. He would miss it, almost as much as he would miss his mother and father.

And there on the dock he stood, his father, searching for him. Willie watched as he grabbed a man's arm, saying words the wind carried away. But Willie knew what he said. He could see the urgency as he spoke with one person after another. Then one man didn't ignore or push him away. This one pointed toward the ship. Da turned in his direction as Willie ducked behind a barrel. Had he been seen? A new fear attacked, causing his knees to go weak. Was that the last time he would see his father?

Chapter Four

Maybe loved the sensation of wind in her hair. The last time she'd been on board a ship, she had to mind her manners as a young lady, traveling with her mother and stepfather. Her hair had remained proper beneath her cap. But now, with no female restrictions, she soaked in the joy of freedom. She pulled off her work cap and let her hair blow free.

"I see you like the sea life."

She startled to find Boatswain Johnson standing beside her. Had she done anything to give herself away?

"All is well. I only wished to go over our rules and responsibilities now that we're underway. You don't appear the type to become seasick. In fact, you quite enjoy this."

Maybe smiled. "Aye, that I do."

"There's a lilt of Irish in your speech, boy. Am I correct?"

She nodded, cautious not to reveal what must not be revealed.

"Where about in Ireland, lad?"

Maybe's mind whirled. The less she made up, the less she'd have to remember. "I left from Bantry Bay. Bare Haven."

"But what about your people?"

She remembered her mother and sister. "No, no people."

He pulled out a pencil and paper. "Well, I should get your name down for the record, that is you and your friend. Where is he?" Boatswain Johnson glanced about.

"He took something below. Said he'd be back in a thrice."

The boatswain seemed to accept that. Truth was it had been a bit since Willie said he'd be back. She was wondering herself.

"Well, I can start with you and will catch him when he comes back. I need your name and a next of kin."

The words she'd rehearsed in her brain fled for escape, but she caught them in time. "Me name is Maybe. No family name. Dinna know me family nor me name. Someone said they should call me Maybe because whenever I looked for me family I would say 'Maybe that's them.' Seemed better than 'hey, boy.'"

Boatswain Johnson smiled, but it was a sad smile. She hoped that meant he believed her.

"So now I answer to Maybe."

He stuck out his hand. "Well welcome aboard the *Frances Pearl*, Maybe."

She shook his hand, and he went his way, presumably searching for Willie. She hoped he found him soon. He'd be back, either way. He never finished the rules and regulations.

⁂

WILLIE FOUND A QUIET CORNER BEHIND SOME CARGO where he would be alone with his thoughts. Swiping a tear from his cheek, there was no wiping away the memory of his father at the dock. He knew, without a doubt, Da searched for him, like the shepherd who went after the lone sheep. But Willie wasn't alone. Maybe was with him. And since he'd been the one to suggest this foolhardy idea, and she had no other recourse, he also had no other recourse. His heart had gone out to Maybe. So small and alone. Her fate with Eleazar Ferguson would have been worse than death. His father always taught him to be kind, but he also taught him to guard his heart. One meant saving Maybe at the risk of losing all he held dear, the other meant turning his back on her plight and leaving her to... He shuddered.

He saw nothing else to do. So why did everything feel so wrong? Because he was an abject failure.

An absolute abject failure.

How could he help Maybe when he couldn't even help himself?

He wiped away another tear.

❦

IT WAS FUTILE. JOSEPH HAD REPEATEDLY ASKED, ONLY TO have people irritated by his interruptions. Still, he must find Willie. He could not go back to Sarah and tell her that her boy was gone to sea.

There was a moment he thought he'd seen him, a flash of that curly red mane peeking up over the rail of a ship pulling out from the harbor, but then it was gone. Surely it was his imagination. Surely, he'd still find him here.

But he knew better.

With a sigh of resignation, he turned and started the long walk back to his home to his Sarah. He would hold her and remind her they had placed all their children in God's hands. His hands were huge enough to span the ocean. And all the teaching they had poured into their lad would guide him back in God's hands.

He rehearsed the words in his brain, praying they would make it to his heart too.

❦

ELEAZAR FERGUSON WAS NOT A MAN WITH WHOM TO trifle. He had money, he had power, and he would use it however he desired. That some ignorant drunk and a slip of a girl could thwart him left a sensation to which he was not accustomed. Nor did he care to become accustomed. This must be rectified. Another person might get ideas.

He'd sent his men to make discrete inquires after the girl and her habits. Sadly, the O'Malleys had not lived in Beaufort long. However, if an offer of money didn't help with recall, the threat of physical violence jogged the memory.

Taking a seat in his parlor, Eleazar rang for his maid. A timid thing, she scurried in and curtsied.

"Tea, Aphra. Now."

"Aye, Master." She curtsied and flew to do his bidding. He liked that about her.

He was growing weary of her terror of him, though. A little fear added to the excitement, but it was becoming a bit of a chore to deal with it all. Besides, there was no surprise left. He knew exactly how she would behave. It was time for his new girl. And he wanted her. Now.

◈

BETH WALKED THE PATH TO THE BLUFF. MOST DAYS SHE stayed closer to home, but this afternoon she had an urge to visit her brother's favorite spot. She'd known when she'd met him by their parents' room that he was about to leave. She didn't know where, but something told her he was leaving.

Shade beneath the old sweet gum tree called to her, and she sat. Should she have told her mother? What would Beth say? She had a feeling? She shook her head. No, without proof, she couldn't say a word.

She picked up a twig and began scratching at the dirt. It was hard feeling so locked inside, so afraid of one's own shadow. Well, that wasn't exactly the truth. It wasn't her shadow that she feared. What terrified her was making a mistake. What if she said the wrong thing? Did the wrong thing? Caused another pain or worse? Given the time to put everything in order in her brain, she could sort it out, give a thoughtful reply, and hope she had gotten it right. Willie, though, seemed to process everything aloud, like arranging all the words and thoughts in front of his face while the world gazed on.

That was something she could never do.

A robin lighted on the ground a few paces beyond her reach, pecking at the dirt and then flying off with something stringy and long in its beak. Busy bird. It didn't allow the cares of the world to dictate its purpose. It just did what a robin should and kept to its business. What must it be like to be a bird? What cares filled its mind? Building the right nest? Laying the correct number of eggs? Protecting its babies from cats and winds and storms? Beth imagined the freedom to fly away from the weight of worry and care. Fly and not worry about perfection again.

The robin returned to the same spot.

"So, Master Robin Redbreast, what is on your little mind today? What worldly cares plague you?"

The robin cocked his head as if he understood her words. He blinked twice, then pecked up more stringy stuff from the ground and flew away.

Beth's curiosity got the better of her. She stood and walked to where the bird had pecked, stooping to examine the spot. Strands of what appeared to be black hair lay windblown over the grass. She scanned beyond to larger clumps. Someone cut his hair, though the strands appeared long enough to be a woman's.

"Beth! What are you staring at?"

Janie, with Martha behind her, ran up the hill.

"Something I saw in the grass. What are you doing here?"

Janie appeared about to cry. "I miss Willie. This is where he helped me with my arithmetic." She rubbed her arm under her nose.

"And you, Martha?"

"I am just watching out for Janie." Martha walked to the

sweet gum and peered up into the branches. "This is a good climbing tree."

"I wouldn't know about that." Beth watched as Martha circled the trunk, continuing to stare at the leaves. "You aren't going to climb it now, are you?"

"Why not?"

"Well, because—" But Beth was too late. Martha grabbed the lowest limb and hoisted herself up. "Martha! I think you should come down."

"Willie would have climbed with me. Why don't you come up, Beth? This is fun."

Why indeed! "No, I don't think so."

"Beth, Janie, there's something up here."

"A little robin is building a nest. Someone cut his hair and Master Robin is taking advantage of the nest-building supplies."

A bundle dropped, nearly hitting Beth on the head. "I don't think it was a he. I think it was a she. Look!"

Beth stooped to investigate. A dress, an apron, a mob cap, undergarments. A complete outfit for a young lady. Someone about Martha's size, maybe a tad bigger, though Beth doubted she herself could fit into the clothing.

Martha dropped from the tree. "This is strange. I know this is Willie's special place. No one comes up here except him, unless Mama sends one of us to fetch him. Why would there be girl clothes here? And why would she cut her hair?"

Martha asked all the questions that popped into Beth's mind except the biggest one. What did this have to do with Willie?

❧

SARAH'S TEARS WOULD NOT STOP. SHE CRIED WHEN WILLIE and Jamie left for college, but that was planned, and she knew it was what they should do. She prepared herself for that. But this? Nothing could prepare her. This was wrong, all wrong.

Joseph assured her it would work out for good. He said that

God needed to get her boy where he would hear Him, and that they needed to trust God to do what He needed to do. Her head agreed. Her spirit understood. But her heart would not be consoled.

"Mama, someone has been in my things."

"Oh, Jason, now is not the time. Please." Sometimes he could be just petty, and she was hurting too much to help him find his way.

"Son, your mother can't deal with that right now." Joseph understood. He hadn't left her side since returning with the awful news.

"But I think it was Willie. I think he took my waistcoat and some breeches."

"Why must ye always blame Willie! He's not even here to defend himself. Canna ye find one piece of sadness in your heart for our family's loss? We may never see him again, and here yer blaming him for things ye probably misplaced."

Her son's face grew red, and his eyes grew wide. She had not meant to be so blunt, but her pain ate at her patience.

Just then, Janie and Martha burst into the room, followed by Beth. "Mama, look what we found in Willie's tree!"

"Willie's tree?" Sarah shook her head, trying to make sense.

"There is a big old tree up near the bluff where he loves to go." Martha filled in the gaps. "He sits under it when he helps Janie with her sums. Well, when Beth got there, she found lots of black hair on the ground. Long like a woman's. Then I went up in the tree—"

"Ye were climbing the tree?" Why was she not surprised? "Go on."

"Aye, Mama, I climbed the tree, and this bundle was up there. I sent it down to Bethy, and when we opened it we found all these girl clothes inside."

"Girl clothes? What are you talking about?" Sarah stared at each face. Pieces of a puzzle stared back. Cut hair, girl clothes all at Willie's tree. Then Jason's missing clothes. Somehow, she knew this was all connected. And it had to do with Willie. But what?

&2%3

JOSEPH WALKED THE HALF MILE TO THE HOME OF THOMAS Miller, the Constable for Beaufort. Despite the assurance in his brain that it was futile, he still felt compelled to make someone in authority aware what his girls found. He'd probably be laughed at, or at least he would've been had he not previously held the office of Justice of the Peace. Most who held that office used it as a stepping-stone to higher political aspirations. However, Joseph saw it as an opportunity to serve, which he did before returning to his ordinary life once his term completed. That aside, the information was flimsy, with no conclusion of a crime. But if something had happened, and this information helped find the guilty party, then he was duty bound to share.

As he drew near, he noticed several people milling about, including the current Justice of the Peace, Henry Waddington. The cacophony of voices announced their presence before Joseph came in sight of the property. Something big was afoot.

Joseph slowed his steps, trying to make sense of what the crowd said. He caught phrases, here and there. "Drunken lout" and "had it coming" and "terrible fright." Then, he heard what made his heart stop mid-beat. "Murdered."

Murdered? Who? What happened? He spotted Henry Waddington speaking to someone over at the side and caught the man's attention.

"Ho, Master Crockett. So, you've heard of our great mystery."

"No, only snippets. Made me wonder about the to-do."

Waddington cleared his throat. "Since it is you, I'll tell you what we've found. The Widow Attwater came home to a ruckus behind her home and asked her neighbor, Master Freely, to see to the problem. He found some wild dogs tearing at what used to be Daniel O'Malley, or what was left of him. Most grizzly sight I've ever seen, I can tell you. Can't say if he fell down drunk, and the dogs got him, or if he met with foul play and was left for the animals. Some call it murder, but until we have facts, who can know? The thing is, they say he has a daughter, and no one has seen her. Just a wee slip of a girl, they say. I haven't had the pleasure. But that is what we have. Care to help with the investigation?"

No, he didn't care to help with the investigation. However, if this somehow involved Willie, even remotely, anything he might learn might help him help his son. Joseph paused before finally answering. "If you need my assistance, I am available. I doubt it is something anyone would relish."

"You speak the truth, sir, on that score. I will not sleep well tonight after seeing those remains. Ghastly."

"What would you have me do?" The sooner it was over, the better.

"I still need statements from the Widow Attwater and Master Freely. With all the neighbors clamoring about, I haven't been able to get them alone to make a record of anything. Then we must question those at the places frequented by the deceased, to determine when he was last seen, and anyone with whom he might have spoken."

"Shall I invite them to your house, or shall I make a place in Thomas Miller's home?"

Master Waddington waved Thomas Miller over, explaining that Joseph was to use a room in his house to interview the witnesses. Joseph almost corrected him—there were no witnesses--but he kept that to himself and followed the constable into his home.

"I don't suppose you have paper and ink, do you? I didn't come prepared to do this." Joseph felt bad for the man whose home was now the center stage of this macabre circus. The job of constable was thankless and many times dangerous. Now the one place he found solace was overrun by higher authorities dictating what went on there.

"Aye, I suppose you didn't. Sure, I have paper and ink. You'll have to sharpen your quill, though. I haven't one at the ready."

Joseph nodded, and pulled the knife from his boot, putting it on the table until all the implements could be brought. Minutes later he was ready and summoned the widow.

A stout woman of about forty years, the Widow Attwater still shook from the grizzly news. "I was coming home from my sister's house. She just had a baby boy, bless him. The sweetest little baby ever, too. Lots of hair and you know what that means." She nodded as if they shared a secret.

"Yes, Widow Attwater, I understand. Might you start with how you came upon Master O'Malley?"

"The drunken lout. It isn't kind to speak ill of the dead, and him having died so horribly, but he was not a nice person, if you understand my meaning. He was loud and rude, swearing and yelling. I don't know how that daughter of his tolerated him. I think she feared him. I know I did." She nodded emphatically at that.

"But how did you find his remains?"

"Oh, I didn't! I was coming home from my sister's when I noticed the ruckus. It was monstrous and frightening. Well, I wanted someone to check to see what the problem was, and I wasn't about to stop at Master O'Malley's for fear of what he might do. He was more frightening than the noise behind the houses, I tell you!"

Joseph's patience was ebbing fast. He took a breath and nodded, hoping she'd get to where he could start writing facts.

"So, I hurried to the Freely home and Mistress Freely—she is such a lovely woman! So warm and kind. Wonderful neighbors, just wonderful. Well, she asked me in and said she would send her husband out to see."

"And did she?"

"Why, yes, that is how we found him."

"So you saw the remains?"

"Of course not. Do you think a lovely gentleman like Master Freely would allow a lone woman like me to see such a sight? He told us to remain in the house, and he fetched the constable." She sat back in her chair, putting the punctuation on her narrative.

Joseph finished writing her words, thanked her for her time, and escorted her to the door where he asked Master Freely to join him.

Jonathan Freely was a tall, thin man who appeared to be paler than usual. Joseph was sure that chasing off the dogs and finding the body had left images in his mind he'd rather forget. The man sat and wept.

"I cannot unlook. This will ever be in my mind."

"I am sorry, sir, especially when I must ask you to recount it all again."

Master Freely closed his eyes. "I investigated behind the houses on our row. As soon as I opened the door of the house, I witnessed the commotion. The dogs were snarling and fighting each other for him. They had already torn open his belly and his intestines were a bloody mess. His face, what was left, was disfigured. I only knew it was he because of his clothing. He always wore the same waistcoat with patches on the sides. My dinner did not remain in place, I confess. When I could again breathe, I demanded the ladies stay in the house and tracked down the constable. After I took him there, he sent me for Justice Waddington."

Joseph recorded the man's account before asking for more. "I understand there was a daughter. Where might we find her?"

Master Freely shook his head. "I am sorry. I understand he shamefully yelled and screamed at her. I am sure there was worse that happened, but I cannot attest to that."

"Did O'Malley have friends or known associates? Were there places he spent time away from home?"

"Any place with disreputable air, I imagine." The man shivered.

"I thank you for your help, Master Freely. This was distasteful but very necessary. We appreciate your service." Joseph stood and escorted the man to the door before coming back and putting his pages in order.

Nothing pointed to Willie as being involved. Both mentioned the deceased had a daughter. If she were small enough to fit into Jason's clothes, then perhaps it was her hair and clothing the girls found.

Yet he still had not one shred of proof. How was he to help his boy if he couldn't learn anything? Or was it better not knowing? Was this a coincidence? Or had Willie gotten himself mixed up in a murder?

Chapter Five

❧❧

"W here've ye been?" Maybe pushed from the rail. Something was different, he wasn't his normal self. But then, she only met him yesterday. Perhaps this was his normal self.

"I needed to think." He didn't or wouldn't meet her gaze. Instead, he faced the wind, letting it whip his curly mop straight back.

"About what?"

"Things."

Her ire rose. She'd put herself in his hands, trusted him, and now he closed himself off like she was a perfect stranger. She shook her head—she was a perfect stranger to him and he was to her. How could she become attached to him so fast?

"Good, you are both together."

The boatswain had come up behind them, making her jump. "Oh, I dinna see ye there, sir."

"Shall we walk? I will show you the living area and go over the work." He motioned and Maybe and Willie followed, taking a tour of the ship. It differed from what brought Maybe and her mother. Not as large, with nowhere for paying passengers. There was barely space for the crew to sleep. That part caused Maybe's pulse to increase, hoping the close quarters wouldn't give away her secret.

Once back on deck, Boatswain Johnson took them to the wheelhouse. "Mr. Stewart, you will take your turn at the wheel when Mr. Brighton goes off. You will work for four bells and then be relieved. I will take the helm with you, to make sure you understand. Maybe, I do not have you on this schedule as you will be taking your turn on top. The master was impressed with your agility. You will take your turn at first light. Questions?"

The questions dancing through Maybe's brain were ones that would give her away. She'd just have to hope Willie would be more talkative with her and help. She shook her head.

Willie mumbled, "No, sir."

"Very well. If something comes to you later, I'll be here in the house. Mr. Stewart, you have—" he pulled out a watch on a chain and popped it open— "thirty minutes until your first shift."

"Aye, sir."

Maybe glanced up at Willie—Stewart? She waited, hoping he might say more, but Boatswain Johnson nodded and returned to view the vastness of water lying ahead.

Willie nudged her elbow and nodded toward the door. She walked the way he'd indicated. He followed.

Once away from other ears, Willie touched her shoulder.

She stopped and turned toward him. He must start this conversation. She'd tried once.

He shoved his hands in his pockets, staring at the toe of his boot while scooting his foot back and forth. He cleared his throat. "I guess... I'm sorry."

"Ye are now? And for what may I ask?"

"Oh, Maybe, I really am sorry. It hit me all at once that I didn't understand the price I was paying, that is until we were gone."

She narrowed her eyes. "The price you were paying? What do you mean?"

He sighed. "As we were pulling out, I spotted my father on the dock. He was searching for me."

"How did he know where to search?"

"I left a note."

Was he an imbecile? "A note? Ye left a note to say... what?" Blood pounded in her ears.

"Stop. Do you really think I would talk about you? I told my parents not to worry, that I was going to sea. I did not mention you. They know nothing of you."

Maybe's knees grew weak.

Willie put his hands under her elbows and steadied her. "Maybe, you are safe. I am sorry I frightened you. I am sorry I was rude earlier. And I'm sorry I have hurt my parents and my family. I had a choice: help you and hurt them, or—"

"Leave me to Eleazar Ferguson. Oh, Willie, now I am sorry. I never thought about what helping me might cost you." She threw her arms about him.

He returned the hug, but then pulled back. "Uh, two men wouldn't do that." He winked at her. "Looks like I must teach you how to be a rough and tumble boy." He grinned.

"That you will. Am I forgiven?"

"You? The question is, am I forgiven? What say we just forgive each other?" He stuck out his hand. "Friends?"

She shook it, remembering to give a proper shake and not to add a curtsy. "Friends."

"I best be getting back to the wheelhouse. I will see you in —" he held up four fingers— "four bells."

"Aye, Mr. Stewart." She winked. "By the by, why Stewart?"

"It is my mother's maiden name."

Maybe nodded and waved as he headed to his post.

THE NEW MORNING ONLY BROUGHT MORE QUESTIONS. Joseph left his two eldest sons to keep the business going while he set out to learn more about Daniel O'Malley. He had yet to speak to anyone with a kind word to say about the man. One person mentioned that his wife had died so suddenly that the question of foul play had arisen, though nothing more than gossip ever bloomed.

Joseph thought it too early to investigate more thoroughly into the places where O'Malley was known to frequent, places called disreputable in polite circles. But he could visit the victim's home. Perhaps he could get a better sense of his life there. Stopping by the constable's home, he convinced Thomas Miller to go with him to the house.

"But what if the girl has returned?"

Joseph wondered how a man as timid as Miller ever became a constable. "Then we will knock first and enter only if no one answers."

After a bit more cajoling, they left, walking the half mile to the home of Daniel O'Malley. The house had belonged to the Smythe family until they all came down with smallpox while visiting other family members somewhere in South Carolina. The surviving family chose not to return and abandoned the house. Which meant the town now owned it and rented it to the O'Malleys. Thomas Miller had gathered a lot of information due to his position. Joseph quietly listened, filing it for later, in case he needed it.

The town's ownership also meant Thomas had a key, should they need it. They didn't. The front door stood open, having been broken in. "Hallo in the house!" Joseph waited before calling again. "Is anyone home?" Still no answer. So, he stepped in.

The first thing he noticed was the empty whiskey bottle on the floor, next to a wadded blanket. A streak of something, maybe blood, smeared down the wall near where the blanket lay heaped. The next room held the larder and a cook fireplace. Nothing in there looked out of place. Even the back door remained closed. A narrow staircase opened from the front room. Joseph mounted the steps finding two bedrooms at the top. One was minimal but neat. The other was a disgusting mess. Multiple whiskey bottles in various stages from half-empty to completely drained lay scattered about the room with spillage marks spotting furniture and bed clothes. The bedding smelled and was tossed and clumped. Joseph left the room, wiping his hands on his breeches.

"Did you learn anything?" Knowing the house was empty seemed to give Constable Miller more backbone.

Joseph shook his head. "Not really, other than O'Malley was the slovenly one. The daughter appears neat as a pin."

"Then let's be done with this place." The new-grown backbone wasn't all that stout yet.

Joseph headed for the door. "No one seems to know much about the daughter, other than she existed."

"True. I don't think they lived here long enough for folks to get to know them well. That and the wife dying so soon after their arrival and all."

"Perhaps a shopkeeper or someone like that might have done business with her? It is obvious she was the civilized one. Everything in the cooking room and her bedroom has been organized and put in place. Most of the front room is like that, other than where it looks like O'Malley collapsed after a binge. He must have hurt his head at some point." Joseph caught Thomas looking at him and realized he was starting to think aloud. "Just some observations." He shrugged. "Perhaps we could go speak with some shopkeeps before we question those at the taverns by the dock."

Thomas shook his head. "I have a day full of things to do. You will have to make those inquiries on your own."

Though Joseph didn't say it aloud, he was sure his expression shouted "coward" as Thomas cringed and took off toward his house at a brisk pace.

Never mind. He didn't need to share his thoughts with anyone but Sarah. His fears, though, he sent straight to God.

MAYBE WANDERED ABOUT THE DECK, NOTING THOSE NOT busy with something specific gathered into groups of two and three finding ways to keep busy. Two men played a dice game on top of a barrel. Two others practiced knot skills. Further on, three men sat on crates, whittling. Every so often, one would stop and hold up his project as if searching for the hidden shape starting to reveal itself in the wood. The others commented and then all was silent but for the lapping of the water while they continued their creative work.

The cook came around looking for someone to peel potatoes and turnips. Maybe was chosen and didn't fight it. The ship took on fresh vegetables at Beaufort so they would eat well for the beginning of the trip. When they reached their next destination, she hoped they could take on more. She knew it wouldn't be long before they'd be craving these bits of civilization.

Cookie seemed surprised at her knife skills. She made quick work but worked harder to hide that she knew her way around a kitchen. But, Cookie's gruffness eased, though he seemed to prefer silence. That suited Maybe just fine.

"Anything else I can do?"

"I'm good for now, but yer welcome anytime, boy. Yer gonna fit right in, ye are." Cookie gave a gummy smile and shooed her away.

By the time she got back on deck, Willie was waiting for her, gazing over the rail. She joined him.

"How was the wheel?"

"Exhilarating!" The grin on his face punctuated his words.

"Of that I'm glad."

"And you? How did you pass the time?"

Maybe shrugged. "I wandered the deck a bit, working at my sea legs. The cook called out for some assistance, so I helped peel potatoes and turnips. It passed the time."

Willie nodded, appearing more interested in the wind on his

face. "We've set sail for New York, then Boston. Then after that, we cross the water to Ireland and England." He closed his eyes and tipped his head back. Perhaps he dreamed of all those places. She should tell him they aren't all that wonderful. Yet anything was better than what she left.

Maybe's dream was to survive another day. Now, away from the clutches of Daniel O'Malley and Eleazar Ferguson, she might see her dream come true. Perhaps.

Eleazar Ferguson's information grapevine informed him that the O'Malley creature's body had been found with only a fuzzy notion regarding foul play. Though he worried not about anything pointing to him—he'd acquired more than enough contacts to protect himself—it was a comfort to know it wasn't much of a concern.

Nothing had been discovered about O'Malley's brat, however. And that did not bring him comfort. Rather it stoked his wrath. Some fellow who fancied himself important enough to investigate was poking into things. If this Crockett person learned anything, perhaps he might be persuaded to share his information. At the moment, it was Eleazar's only clue.

His assistants were sent on to Charlestown until life returned to normal. Less likely they could be captured that way and convinced to talk.

"Mama?"

Sarah glanced up to see Jason standing in the doorway. His woebegone face pierced her heart. Perhaps she had been too hard on him. "Yes, Jason?"

"May I speak with you?"

"Of course, love. What do ye need?" She patted the seat next to her and waited for him to take it.

Instead, he paced in front of her. She couldn't help but glimpse the man he was growing to be. "No, I need to stand." He continued to pace, now running his hand through his auburn curls. "You were right. I've been picking at Willie. I am just so jealous of him. He always has a joke, a ready wit. Everyone likes to talk with him, laugh with him. Only I am so often the butt of the jokes. It becomes wearing. I'd thought while he was at school with James, I might find my place. Without being the butt of anyone's joke. But he came back. And it started again. And then when he rifled my things... I reached the end of my rope." He stopped and faced her. "I am worried about him, though. And I love my brother, Mama. I do. I fear something terrible happening to him. I... well, it just took some time, and I guess you getting so upset with me, to realize I do love him. If he needs my clothes, he can have them all."

"C'mere, lovey." Sarah again patted the seat, then reached for his hand, pulling him next to her. "I worry for him too. But praying is the answer. Have you tried that?"

He hung his head and shook it.

"That might be an idea." She lifted his chin to peer in his eyes. "You've been well taught. Now make faith your own. And, Jason, I do not know what need Willie had with your clothes, but I am sure he wouldn't have taken them without a good reason."

"I realized that. Willie isn't a thief or a liar. I just feel like something important cornered him."

Sarah nodded. "I agree."

"I saw him that morning. He was headed for his bluff. I think my things were tucked under his arm."

She looked in his eyes. He wasn't trying to incriminate his brother this time, only wanting to be honest. "Thank you, love, for telling me, I'll inform your father. I'm hoping he learns something to make sense of this."

JOSEPH SMILED AT THE TINKLING BELL AS HE ENTERED THE shop of Master Edward Moseley, whose political fame in the region grew more with each passing day. However, he was also a merchant and Joseph hoped he'd had dealings with the young Miss O'Malley. "G'day, Master Moseley."

"G'day Master Crockett. How can I be of service?" It was unusual for him to be there alone. He had the means to have employees running his business. Perhaps this was his way to stay in touch with his constituents?

"I am helping to investigate about the death of Daniel O'Malley. The body was found yesterday, and it has yet to be determined if it involved foul play. My search discovered the man's daughter has yet to be located. I grasp at straws, here, sir, but I wondered if she might have done business with your establishment."

The man's right eye narrowed as if he were trying to put a memory into focus. Then, he smiled. "Aye, I can help you. She did not come here to purchase. I believe she needed cash. She brought in a few very nice volumes of books and asked if I would like to buy them. Returned a second time with more. Told me that was all she had. That her mother died, and she needed to handle the finances as her stepfather could not do it."

"Stepfather?"

"Aye." Master Moseley nodded. "She made a point of letting me know the man was not her father."

"I see. Then her name was not O'Malley."

"No. Hmm. Let me see. I should have it in my ledger." He pulled a book from beneath his counter and began flipping through the pages. "I had her sign for the cash. She did not want a bank draft. Insisted on cash. Ah, here is her name. Miss Elizabeth Boulay."

"Boulay, is it? Funny, I remember a lad back in Ireland with that name. A bit younger than myself, we worked for Jacques

Fontaine in Bantry Bay." Joseph hadn't thought of the lad in years.

Master Moseley nodded. "Well, he might be a relative as her accent reveals she is also an Irish lass. I believe she and her mother came over not quite a year ago. I'm not sure about the stepfather." He slapped the counter. "A mystery for another day, what?" And with a chuckle, he slipped the ledger back beneath.

"I agree. Thank you for your time and help. It is much appreciated." Joseph offered his hand, Moseley shook it.

"Glad to have been of service."

Joseph left, unsure what all this meant. However, more pieces of the puzzle were surfacing. Bit by bit, he would move them into place, hoping that the picture they revealed would show his boy innocent of any wrongdoing.

"Excuse me, sir, are you Master Crockett?"

Joseph jumped from his inner reverie. "Aye, I am Joseph Crockett."

"My name is Eleazar Ferguson."

His name and reputation preceded him, and not in a good way. "May I help you?"

The man sort of smiled, lacking a better word. It was almost a grimace, oily and off-putting. "It is I who wants to be of service to you. I understand you are searching for the daughter of that tragic Daniel O'Malley."

"Among other things." Joseph felt dirty just standing near the man, though he looked bathed and groomed.

"I, too, am searching for the lass. Her father, God rest his soul, had mentioned his concern for her. What she must be enduring, all alone in the world." He *tsked*. "I wish only to help her. If you learn of anything, where she might be found, or what she might need, please allow me the courtesy of coming to her aid. In honor of her father, of course."

"Of course." Joseph nodded. "I know nothing yet. Anything I learn must be disclosed to the Justice of the Peace and the constable before I can share with anyone else."

"I see." His face tightened and then relaxed. "Very well. Should you need anything, do not hesitate to contact me. My house is off the square."

Joseph nodded, not agreeing to contact the man, but in acknowledgment of knowing where the man's house was located. He didn't want to even use his voice in the conversation anymore.

After a pause, Eleazar Ferguson, repealed his smile and turned on his heel toward his home. It was a lovely home, one of the more fashionable ones in town. However, Joseph did not understand where the man got his money to afford such splendor.

New to the town, Eleazar Ferguson, purchased the land and quickly put up the house. The strange part was, the land hadn't been for sale. It had been in the Burrow family since the founding of the town. They'd had a lovely home on the property for years, but then it suddenly burned to the ground. From a lightning storm, if he remembered correctly. Master Burrows shared how he planned to rebuild, had even started the framing, when he and the family disappeared without a goodbye.

Within a day or two, this new person, Eleazar Ferguson, continued the building project and moved in upon completion. It all seemed above board. It was plausible that the Burrows family changed their minds. The summer months with the humidity and mosquitoes could make the less hardy pull up stakes.

Joseph turned toward home, shoving the Burrows family puzzle to another part of his brain. He needed to work on the one that might concern his son.

And he needed to find the next piece sooner rather than later.

Chapter Six

The next morning, Maybe had her turn at top. She'd climbed to the platform yesterday with only the thought of doing whatever it would take to stay on board. Now she stared at where she needed to go as tingles ran down the back of her legs.

She closed her eyes, imagining Eleazar Ferguson chased her. That was incentive enough. Fingers clenching the Jacob's ladder, she threw herself into getting to the top at an impressive speed.

"You there, boy, don't set yourself up for an accident. You've won the job, you don't have to win it again." Boatswain Johnson called up while following her to the top. Once there, he stood on the platform beside her. "Getting up here is half the battle. You must make adjustments to the shrouds from here as needed. We'll talk you through until you can do it, but you must be strong. It takes strength and balance to tend the shrouds while sailing." He showed her where the adjustments would be made and gave her an idea of what she would be doing.

Those tingles up the back of her legs started jumping around in her belly. Could she do this? Not just the job, but stay up there and keep her balance and not run away in fear?

Boatswain Johnson must have read her thoughts. "Don't

worry. I'll see you are well trained. In the meantime, how much can you read and write?"

What answer would work best? "Some, I guess. Do I need to know?"

He chuckled. "No, but I was wondering if you might assist me by taking notes. I have to keep track of the financial logs and the other ship's logs for this voyage along with overseeing the crew for the master."

"I think I can help you."

"Good. You stay here. I will send Mr. Swain up. He will train you for up here. When you come down, find me and I will show you what I need. It will help me with keeping the logs."

She nodded, and he went down the ladder to the deck.

Alone, Maybe gave more scrutiny to where she was. The top was a round platform surrounding the mast up about a third of the way. It had a rail about it, so it wasn't completely unsafe. But glancing over the edge didn't exactly foster security. This high up, each wave that crashed against the side caused swaying. Of course, there was movement on deck as the ship sailed through the water. However, from where she stood, it was more than a little movement. She would not be sick. She must not be sick. Her feet stepped backward until she felt the mast at her back, where she could slide down and sit on the platform, her legs sticking straight in front of her. Her feet came to the edge. She wasn't sure she could stand again, but at least her stomach flopped less.

Maybe reminded herself that as frightening as this might seem, it was nothing compared to what belonging to Eleazar Ferguson would be. She was alive and unharmed, had a place to sleep, and food to eat. She also had Willie. He was becoming a good friend.

She shook her head. What brought that thought? Well, he was handsome and funny and caring. Aye, a good friend. But make that the extent of it.

❦

Boatswain Sam Johnson was a praying man, and something about that new boy, Maybe, called him to pray. Perhaps it was he understood having no people. Or, it could have been his expression as the wind whipped through his hair. But whatever, as he watched Maybe up top he knew that boy needed prayer. Something was different about him. He behaved older than the twelve or thirteen years he claimed, displaying a type of maturity. Did it come about because of having to make his way in the world from such a young age? But Sam noticed something else. Nothing he could name, but given more time, he'd figure it out. The boy still had a vulnerability too. Funny how life had not hardened him.

That Stewart lad, Willie, was protective of the boy. That relationship was strange.

However, if it did not affect the crew or the job, then it was none of his concern. But if it did, as boatswain he would be swift in remedying the problem.

❦

Willie received a lesson on using the chip log. Mr. Cox showed how to toss the log into the water and let out the log line while counting the knots. Boatswain Johnson kept note, plugging in the time from the sand glass and working the equation to figure how many knots of speed they moved. By keeping a consistent record, they knew how far they had traveled and about how soon to expect to arrive in New York harbor. It generally took one week, but if the prevailing winds were in their favor, they might make it in six or six and a half days.

Willie couldn't remember New York. He'd been born right before his family arrived in New Rochelle, but all his memories were of the south. The thought of seeing some place different excited him.

He caught Boatswain Johnson watching, so he returned his attention to his lesson with the chip log, this time, on how to roll the knotted line back up and stow it until next use.

It had been nearly twenty-four hours since they left port in Beaufort. Five to six more days like this until New York. When he looked forward, his excitement grew. When he remembered what he left, all the buoyancy of the trip was sucked from him. Would he ever be able to just enjoy living his dream? One thing was clear, this sailing life was more than he imagined. And he loved every minute.

As long as he quit remembering.

Cookie came looking for Maybe that afternoon, after Boatswain Johnson dismissed her. "Feel like peeling potatoes again, boy?"

It wasn't a request. But Maybe didn't mind. It was something she knew how to do, posing little danger other than the razor-sharp knives in Cookie's arsenal. Again, it was a quiet job until she caught Cookie making sideways glances at her.

"Did I grow another nose, Cookie?"

He coughed and shook his head. The silence continued until she thought he'd pop. "Who taught you to peel potatoes? Never seen a boy so skilled." His cheeks had turned to crimson.

Maybe searched her brain for a plausible story. "Back home, Ireland, sometimes the only food to find were potatoes. Ye learnt to peel them with care so as to have more to eat."

Cookie nodded, satisfied.

Maybe wanted to sigh with relief but feared not appearing manly.

It was something of which she needed to be constantly aware. So far, she'd managed to relieve herself in privacy. Willie stayed close most of the time, so she slept without too much fear. Those little things they hadn't considered gave her the most pause. What might happen when her monthly visitor arrived? Could she keep that from giving her away?

"That be the last potato, Cookie. How else can I help?"

"Nothing else, boy. You did good. Now run along." The scruffy curmudgeon waved her on.

Maybe didn't give him time to change his mind. As she came back on deck, she found Willie. Funny how her heart beat a tad faster at the sight of him. She wasn't sure she liked that. It made her tingle all peculiar. She considered going the other direction when he spotted her and waved. She waved back, her heart picking up its pounding pace.

"Ho there, Maybe! What do you think? It looks like we could be in New York in five to six days! Can you imagine?" There was something genuine and open about his excitement. He loved being on this ship.

She was happy for him, though for her, this was something necessary, a situation to be tolerated for a greater good. Sure, she enjoyed it some, but not like Willie. Pasting a smile on her face, she tried to join in his excitement. "Only five to six days? That is amazing."

"I'm learning more about this ship. Already did my turn at the wheel, and I helped Mr. Cox with the chip log. Oh, there's much to learn, and when I'm trained, there'll be lots of work to do. They say it is a hard life, but what I'm seeing is that it isn't hard when it is a joy. Do you know what I mean?" He turned his face to her, his blue eyes pulling her into his view of their adventure.

That's what it was for him, an adventure. She understood that. "Aye, Willie, I ken yer meaning." She turned away before she revealed more than she should.

MAYBE TURNED AWAY, BUT AS SHE DID, WILLIE NEARLY

gasped at the ocean depth in her eyes. He could drown in those eyes.

What did that mean? He'd never be able to explain it. Something akin to having the breath ripped from his lungs. A sudden urge to run his fingers through her hair made his hand curl into a fist at his side before he forced his palm open. The memory of the raven locks he sliced away crashed on his brain. No matter how hard he tried, he would always see Maybe as a young woman.

"Willie, what is it ye plan on doing once we get to Ireland and England? Will ye return with the ship to Beaufort?"

That was a good question. He hadn't planned that far ahead. If he went back to Beaufort, would his father let him leave again? "I don't know. What about you? Will you stay until England or leave before then?"

"I might go to Ireland. At least I know people there."

Willie nodded. He hadn't considered that she might not want to keep sailing. Of course, she wouldn't. It would mean never being herself again. He tried for a moment to consider what it was like to constantly behave as someone completely foreign to oneself. It was nothing he could do. "Maybe, I am here. I'll help you all I can. You can depend on me."

She chuckled. "What do ye think I've been doing? I thank ye, Willie, for all ye've done. Ye dinna have to help me, and it has cost ye dear to do so. I'm grateful to ye." Her eyes, full of deep purple storms, turned on him and it took everything he had not to pull her into his arms, where he might protect her, hold her, make her his own.

"Let's walk. I want to see if one of the mates can show me how to tie more knots." He held her elbow, directing her.

She didn't fight him but walked alongside. Why had he worried she'd fight? Willie was more confused than he'd ever been, and no help was in sight.

Sam Johnson watched from his perch on the top platform. Something was odd between Maybe and the Stewart boy. Something he wasn't seeing, no matter how hard he looked. What could it be? Both had done everything asked of them. They showed good attitudes, followed all the rules. They learned about every task given, no matter how menial. In fact, he'd have been hard pressed to find two better new crew members. But, when the two were together... Stewart seemed to take on an elder brother role, a protector presence. Perhaps that's what he saw.

Sam tried to convince himself, and he was close to success.

Close, but not quite.

※

Joseph left the third establishment feeling dirty. It was a possible O'Malley place of entertainment. He shook his head. Joseph wasn't an innocent and had his own memories of places that sold liquor and encouraged male bonding. But he had not frequented such places since he and Sarah had been together. However, the tavern back home was nothing like the places in Beaufort. In Beaufort they were located down by the docks to attract the lonely sailor and other travelers, plus they were more elaborate than mere planks and crates. At least some were. But the result was the same. Men paid money to buy whiskey or ale or rum. Some were satisfied with a friendly drink. Some didn't know when to stop.

One other thing was the same, at least in Beaufort. They all had met Daniel O'Malley and none of them liked him or mourned him.

Joseph paused, trying to decide where to go next.

"Psst! Crockett!"

Joseph looked to find who whispered his name. "Aye?"

"Quiet man! Over here."

Glancing about, he spotted the speaker peeking from behind

a white oak and headed in his direction. "You want a word with me?"

Now that Joseph saw the man, he spotted how nervous, even a little agitated he appeared. Small of stature and slight, the man was dressed in worn clothing and blond stringy hair swung beneath his work cap. He seemed in constant motion though he didn't go anywhere. "Aye, that I do. Ye be askin' about ol' Daniel O'Malley, God rest his soul, 'tis true?"

"Aye." Joseph nodded.

The man scanned the surroundings before lowering his gravelly voice even more. "Wells, me 'n' Danny, we was mates. As much as either of us had a mate. He needed money real bad. Someone was after him to pay up and this someone ye just don't cross. Danny tol' me he had an idea on how to work a deal with this 'ere someone, so everything should 'ave been good. I dinna know what happened to ol' Danny boy, but I'm thinkin' that that someone oughta."

"Who might that someone be?"

"First, ye gotta keep me name out of this. I don't want no one knowin' I spoke with ye. That could be me death, and well I know it."

Joseph coughed to cover a wry chuckle. "You haven't told me your name so there is no way I could share it with anyone."

The man smiled at that, but again grew serious. "True enough. We best keep it that way, if ye don't mind."

"If that is what you wish. But tell me who was after your mate to pay up."

The man sighed. "Master Crockett, I heered ye was a good man, a trustworthy man. All right, I will tell ye the name, but I will deny I ever breathed it in your presence." He paused. "Eleazar Ferguson."

Joseph wasn't surprised and perhaps that was a disappointment to the man as he repeated. "It's Eleazar Ferguson wot wanted Danny to pay up. Ye won't catch him doin' the deed, though. He has men do that for him. 'Tis Eleazar Ferguson."

"Thank you. I will not reveal that the information came from you. But I thank you for your help."

"God bless ye, sir. God bless ye." He tipped his hat and started off for the docks at a rapid pace.

Now he had the name, but no proof. However, his instinct told him this was true. What did he do with his information? What could he do with it? Another puzzle piece not ready to be added. So, what was his next move?

❧

ELIZABETH STOOD ON THE DOCK, THE SHIP SAILING AWAY. SHE had missed it. Her mother waved to her from the deck. She called to her mother, but no sound came out. Then, a grip on her arm. Her stepfather. He dragged her away. She tried to scream, but her voice wouldn't work.

She nearly pried herself free, but he threw her to the ground and motioned to someone before turning his back on her. A large shadow fell across Elizabeth. Terror mounted in her stomach and rode its way up her throat. No, no, don't go!

She turned. Eleazar Ferguson stood over her. He reached out to her, but she jumped to her feet and ran as if the devil himself gave chase. Into the town she ran. People walked and stopped to chat all around her, but no one paid her any heed. She tried to get their attention. She tugged at their arms. She pointed to Eleazar Ferguson who menacingly walked her way. It was as if they didn't see her. Her voice still silenced, she couldn't make herself known. She had no help, no one to save her.

Eleazar Ferguson now changed his form, his clothing grew scaly, his face changing into that of a snake. And bit by bit, his form slid to the ground and turned into a slithering giant. Still no one on the crowded street took note. The snake slithered closer and closer.

Elizabeth froze. The snake wrapped its body about her legs. It was cold, slimy. Her chest grew tight, she couldn't breathe. This was the end. The snake raised its head to strike!

"Maybe, sh-sh, it's all right."

Willie! Willie had her. She was safe. She was not alone. Exhaling, she leaned into him, unable to stop shaking.

"Hey, it's safe now. Only a bad dream. I'm here. Just lay back." He helped her recline on her bunk.

She grabbed his hand. "Don't leave me. Please."

"I won't leave you. Now go to sleep."

He spoke as if it were easy. But sleep would not keep her company the rest of the night.

WHAT TERRIFIED HER SO? WILLIE GLANCED ABOUT THE room where other sailors slept. Either everyone was too exhausted to wake or too uninterested to care. No one looked their way. He let out his breath. Whew, good. Maybe would ask come morning. Come morning, she would return to worrying about those things.

But now he was awake. So many things rushed through his mind, his emotions. He wanted to protect her, keep at bay anything that might bring on terror. And protect her he would. He now realized that was what he'd signed on for when he first offered his help.

His other emotion was difficult to discern. It was the fluttery race of his heart when she threw herself into his arms. He enjoyed holding her. He could do that all night and day.

If it wouldn't put her in danger.

So, to protect her, he must not fall in love with her.

That would prove a difficult job. He already had one foot off the edge.

Chapter Seven

The night terrors continued to attack, but somehow Willie seemed to sense something was coming in time to grab her hand. His touch chased the terrors away, making Maybe more secure than she had been since her father left, or rather died. It was the same thing really. Both meant he was gone.

Yet Willie was here. Her irrational fears weren't driving him away. For that she was grateful.

The days flew. Maybe became proficient at manning the top, doing what they needed with the shrouds as they sailed. She also enjoyed following Boatswain Johnson, keeping notes of things he wanted to remember. On purpose she made her spelling rough, so he wouldn't think she'd had an education, but clear enough that he might decipher her writing. She was understanding why Willie loved this life. It had its fascinating moments. She especially enjoyed spotting the whale from her post on the platform their fourth day out. It was majestic and graceful and oh, so big! A memory she would cherish.

But now they were fast approaching the port of New York.

"Make ready the lines!"

Each person knew his job, what was expected. From her

vantage point above, they appeared like busy little dolls. Aye, Willie was right. This was fun.

In under an hour, the ship was secure, the last piece of cargo unloaded. After which, they had leave, as long as they maintained a level of discipline and didn't get soused.

Willie was the one most excited about leave. Maybe merely wanted to be off the ship for a bit. She had no curiosity about New York. It seemed a little like Beaufort, only bigger with a cloudier sky. Made everything a little gloomier. However, she imagined it was much cooler in the summer than any port in the Carolinas. And it was a change.

"Come on, Maybe. Let's go!" Willie stood at the gangplank.

She shrugged at Boatswain Johnson, who smiled and shook his head, before she bounded after Willie.

It didn't matter. She and Willie could be themselves if they got away from the rest of the crew. It was difficult to remain mindful to behave as a boy.

"Where shall we go?" She had to nearly run to keep up with his long-legged strides. Her sea legs made it even harder. How did he do that?

"I want to see everything! Go everywhere!" Willie spread his arms as if to embrace the whole city. "Let's go this way." He loped toward a walkway in front of several shops.

"I've not seen so many merchants!" Maybe scanned sign after handmade sign depicting designs and symbols informing the shopper what goods the store carried. No words or numbers graced the storefronts. "Willie, we haven't enough money to spend."

"True. Pay will come once we're in England. But I want to experience it all."

Maybe scanned her surroundings. Her ears took in vocal noises that sounded like conversation, but none of the words made sense. The people talked fast and rushed about. "It's so busy!"

"Aye!" Willie fed on the haste that flowed through the

streets, increasing his normal exuberance. His eyes were wide and round, taking in every sight while his talk was clipped and quick. Maybe's gut twinged with danger.

"We might find the commons and view the trees." That would be free. And peaceful.

"Oh, Maybe, there's excitement in the air. Can't you feel it?" His smile faded; she'd let him down.

"Aye, Willie. I'm glad to be off the ship for a bit. But wouldn't it be fine to go someplace where we may be ourselves? Where we might talk and not worry that someone might over-hear? Someplace where we... where I dinna have to pretend to be what I'm not?"

His exuberance mellowed. Perhaps it was a disappointment, she didn't know for sure. But he slowed and smiled at her. "I understand. Aye. Let's go to the commons." He walked beside her now, seeming more aware of her presence.

Part of her was relieved, but now part felt guilty. He'd been so happy. Now he did this for her.

Willie stopped a man who didn't rush as fast and asked directions.

"It's the triangle between Chambers, Broadway, and Park Row. Keep going in this direction, you will find it." For a moment Maybe thought he might tip his hat. Instead, he tipped his head to the side, gave her a funny look, and then moved on.

"Guess we're headed in the right direction." Willie shrugged before starting again.

It took half an hour, but they found the place. Giant elms sprouted inviting Maybe to climb their branches. She couldn't resist and swung up into the closest one. "Come on up, Willie!"

"You climb all day aboard ship. This is what you want to do?"

"No one can see me here, Willie. I can be meself."

A moment later he joined her amidst the leaves and laughed. "Aye, I understand. You want a place to be a girl."

"I am a girl."

His voice grew soft. "Aye, that you are."

She imagined for a moment he might kiss her, and to her surprise, she hoped he would.

But he didn't.

"Willie, what will happen to us?" The question was out before she considered it.

"What do you mean?"

"I mean... we're friends?"

"Aye, we're friends."

"When I return to Ireland, where will you go?"

"With the ship, of course."

Of course. "Then will I ever see you again?"

She could feel him distance himself. He ran his hand through his hair. "Aye, we will see each other, I mean... I can sail back to you, ah, come visit you."

And once more, she was alone. On her own. The tear dropped before she could stop it, but she wouldn't let another fall.

"Ho, what's this? Maybe, I won't let anything happen to you. I will get you to Ireland and you will be safe. You can even be a girl again." He smiled at that, attempting to tease her from her aloneness. Did he even understand aloneness?

"I am a woman, Willie. Ye canna ken. Do not try."

He became quiet and his silence enveloped them. There was a comfort in it, yet the desire to break free was strong. She wanted everything in the open, a rebellion against the secrecy she must keep aboard ship.

His hand found its way over hers. "Maybe, I know. Believe me, I know. But, for your safety, that can't cross my mind."

She turned to study his face. His eyes were heavy-lidded but soft and gentle making her heart thud against her ribs. It revealed more than she imagined about them both. Nodding, she slipped her hand away.

"I mustn't ever forget that the world believes you are a boy. That's what keeps you hidden in plain sight."

"I know." She sighed. "It's not that I can't pretend to be a boy, I'm doing that. But inside, I'm not male. I am me. I am a woman. Physically and emotionally. Each day I walk a cliff. Will I slip and fall today? What about tomorrow? It is hard to find the joy you have in this adventure when I am a mere gesture or slip of the tongue away from discovery."

"You won't be discovered. I'll make sure of that."

"How? How will you make sure?" How could he make such a guarantee?

He shrugged. "I just will, that's all. Maybe, trust me. Please?"

Trust him and let him go. He had nothing to lose. He'd get her to Ireland and then it would be all done. His duty complete. But he thought of it as a duty, didn't he? He'd made a bargain and would keep his end. She nodded. "I trust you, Willie."

And she would. Until he walked out of her life.

⁂

THIS WAS MUCH TOO HARD. WILLIE HAD COUNTED ON THIS day and all its wonders. He hadn't counted on just sitting up in a tree. And he certainly hadn't counted on all the feelings flooding through him. Why was life so hard?

Under other circumstances, he would have taken her in his arms. He had little experience with women, girls, other than his sisters and mother. One couldn't take them into one's arms to do what he wanted to do with Maybe.

These were new, exciting, dangerous, and just plain stupid thoughts. And feelings.

He must put his mind, and Maybe's, on another subject. He stood on a thick branch. "Ho, Maybe, over yonder. You can see the ship from here! There's your perch, you can see it from this perch. Ha!"

She turned and stood on a different branch, scanning where he pointed. "Oh, tis so high up there! Tis halfway to the top of the mast."

"Aye, it is! I couldn't climb up there like you, Maybe. Yet you do it every day."

"You climbed this tree. You could do it. It really isn't that hard. You've been able to learn all the other jobs on board. I am amazed at how you accomplish everything that is expected of you."

Her eyes held such an open, kind gaze. If she only knew the things he couldn't do, no matter how hard he tried. He turned away. "I wonder what else we can see from here."

They took turns pointing out sights. The brick homes, the busy streets, the people in various modes of race and dress. It wasn't as if they had never seen or even interacted with people of another color in their southern colony, but the busyness seemed to stir up a mix different from anything they'd seen.

Maybe's stomach growled loud enough for him to hear, reminding Willie that they had not eaten since they broke their fast that morning. "Ready to be a boy again? I think I have enough to buy us a couple pasties down by the docks."

She didn't answer right away. Instead he noticed she stared out to sea, out towards Ireland. Did she wonder what she'd find there? Did she still have family there? He realized there was much of her story he had yet to learn.

"What will you do in Ireland? Where will you go?"

She turned to face him. "I left me sister there. I dinna know if she still lives or not. At least there I will know people. Me mother and I left because me stepfather insisted. Me sister became ill and could not go with us, so she stayed behind. Then me mother died soon after we landed."

"What about your father? What happened to him?"

"He died. Pirates attacked his ship on the way back to Bantry Bay. Me stepfather was the only survivor. He said me father died begging him to take care of me mother and we girls." She hung her head. "That must be the only reason me mother would marry the ogre. He didn't behave as an ogre before they married, but it dinna take him long to show his true self." She shuddered.

"Then I will help you find your sister. I can catch another ship. We'll find her together." The promise eased his guilt. He wouldn't be leaving her all alone. She'd have her family or what was left of it. That would make things much easier.

The eyes she turned on him gave the same expression his mother used to give when he'd promise never to do that again, for the hundredth time. She wanted to believe but would not pin her hopes on his word.

Well, he wasn't just saying things. He would find her sister. He would make sure she was settled. He would.

Before he left her and returned to the sea.

⊗

"Aphra, my tea." Eleazar Ferguson leaned back into his chair and closed his eyes. This tedium of locating his property was becoming a nuisance. It was also stirring his wrath as nothing before had.

In the past, if there was something disagreeable, he had it removed with a mere wave. But this disagreeable feeling seemed to corner him, making him the caged animal. It was not a position he had experience, nor was it one he enjoyed.

When the shoe was on the other foot, that was enjoyment. To see the fear, the terror, to hear the groveling and bargaining from those who didn't jump to obey his command was an elixir. It all proved he was lord and master of everything his hand touched. His finger stroked the silk armrest on his chair. But he had yet to touch the O'Malley girl. That was both displeasing and disagreeable. She must be taught a severe lesson once he had her in hand.

At first, he'd had hopes that the Crockett man might help if he thought it a good cause. But time showed him to be a nose-in-the-Holy Book type, not living in the real world where only the wiliest survived.

Perhaps he could be bought?

No, Eleazar Ferguson had seen it before. His scruples came at too high a price.

"Aphra!" Where was the slut?

The clumsy thing entered carrying a tray that clattered so hard he was sure she would tip it on him. "Set it down, before you burn someone!"

And then the idea dawned. "Aphra, dear, what do you know of laundry?"

Her eyes darted about the room and her fingers danced together in front of her. "Ah, sir, I learnt a bit from me ma. She were a washer woman before the fever took her."

"Good. Then that is what you will do." He rubbed his hands together as the glee of his plan formed.

"Yer turning me out, sir?"

He should slap the stupid thing, but that would not help his cause. He needed her to be on his side. "No, child. I wish you to do something for me. There is a family here. I understand it is large and the mistress might use some help. I would like for you to offer your services to her. And then you return home, keep me apprised of what goes on in the house."

"Yer wantin' me to spy?"

"Oh, heavens, no, child. I want to be of service to them. They're so helpful in the community but never ask for anything. They are very self-sufficient. If you were to help there, you might help me learn how to be of service to them."

He watched her consider it. That she even thought about it made him realize she was more stupid than he imagined.

"Aye, sir. What do ye need me to do?"

"You must go to the Crockett home. Let them know you are starting a laundry service. Tell them you are alone and must start a business. Ask if they would allow you to do their laundry for a small fee. I will even let you keep half of what you earn. How is that? So simple and you will receive a profit. You know where the home is?"

She nodded. "When shall I go?"

"As soon as you have cleaned up from tea."

The sooner the better. He could almost touch his goal. There must be something in that house to give him information, something to extract information from Crockett. He would find that O'Malley girl, and she would be his.

❧

THEY WALKED BACK TO THE DOCK. MAYBE COULD FEEL Willie's hand so close. She wanted to reach over and grasp it, letting his confidence flow from his fingers to hers. But they were back where someone might see, so she made do with him walking beside her.

They were among the first to return, coming aboard and greeting the guard. He waved them through, and they retired to their bunks.

A few hours later, loud voices and thuds woke Maybe.

Willie leaned up on his elbow. "What's that all about?"

She shrugged.

They both went topside where Boatswain Johnson and an inebriated Mr. Cox stood nose to nose.

"You know the rule, Mr. Cox. No returning to the ship inebriated."

"I'm a growd man, I am, s-sir, an' iffen I imbibe, then that's wha' I d-do."

Boatswain Johnson let out a breath. "Mr. Hawkins, put him to bed. We will deal with this in the morning when he is sober."

"Aye, sir. C'mon, matey, let's put ye to bed."

Mr. Cox tripped over his own feet and had to be helped. Once, righted, Mr. Hawkins took him below and put him on his cot. The man was asleep before his feet were lifted on to his bed.

"Wonder what he faces in the morning?" Maybe was afraid to imagine.

"I'm not sure, and I don't think he'll want to find out."

She and Willie returned to their cots.

This time, the terrors didn't come. They couldn't. Maybe couldn't sleep all night.

At first light, she was on deck. Not that she was eager to see what would happen, rather she needed to get to the open air, away from her thoughts. Willie still slept.

It surprised her that she told him about her sister and how Daniel O'Malley had come into their lives. She still recalled that knock. If it had not been an issue of survival, she dinna believe her mother would have married the man, no matter how pretty his manners. But he was all flowers and songs and sweetness, saying he'd made this promise to a dying man and he needed to fulfill it. Every day he appeared, doing things, caring for things. A totally different man than the one who stepped off the ship in Beaufort, North Carolina.

Her father, her true father, had been a good man. A God-fearing man. But God hadn't helped him or heard any of her prayers. And she'd prayed many. Prayers for her father's safe return. Prayers for her sister's health. Urgent prayers for her mother. That's when she stopped praying. When God took her mother and left her with Daniel O'Malley. That was awful enough, but he sold her. She trembled at the thought.

A shadow fell over her, and a scream clenched in her throat. It was only Willie, coming up to join her at the rail.

"You enjoy watching the water. I see you at the rail so often."

"Aye, I do. There's something about the water, like it washes the confusion of me thoughts and leaves me a bit of peace."

Willie turned his back to the water to focus on her. "It's the opposite for me. The water stirs up adventure and mystery. It excites me to my toes."

Maybe chuckled. That made sense, for sure.

A noise behind her made her turn. Willie followed her gaze.

Two men brought Mr. Cox up from below. He appeared to still be groggy, though he walked under his own power. The crew formed a circle about him and the boatswain.

"Mr. Cox. You have been accused of breaking the inebriation rule. You were aware of such a rule?"

Mr. Cox nodded slowly.

"Speak up, man."

"Aye, sir."

"And you understand the penalty for the infraction?"

"Aye, sir."

"Have you any defense?"

Mr. Cox opened his mouth and then closed it. His head hung forward, his focus on the deck at his feet. "No, sir."

"Mr. Hawkins, help Mr. Cox to remove his shirt."

Mr. Hawkins pulled the shirt from over Mr. Cox's head. Then, without a fight, Mr. Cox walked to the mast and grabbed hold of the iron ring attached to the pole about a foot above his head. He widened his stance and put his forehead against the mast.

Boatswain Johnson unrolled a length of line while the crew widened the circle.

Maybe had seen nothing like this. She was confused. But, with the first crack of the line, she understood. She turned her head.

Boatswain Johnson let out only five lashes before having Mr. Hawkins help Mr. Cox back to his cot. He also summoned the surgeon to follow before returning to the wheelhouse.

Cookie sidled up beside them. "Don't look so shocked, boy. Mr. Cox knew what he was doin'. On any other ship, his shirt would've been torn away, his hands tied to the ring, and he'd have gotten forty lashes with a cat-o'-nine-tails. And they wouldn't have waited until morning or given him a chance to say anything. The boatswain is a fair man. Some people must learn the hard way."

Still, Maybe had seen drunks. She'd even tended to her stepfather more than once. Mr. Cox was never mean like Daniel O'Malley. Why not let him sleep it off?

"Ye still dinna ken? That wasn't just for Mr. Cox. That was for the crew. Now they believe the boatswain is a man of his word and, God-willin', he won't need to do that again."

Maybe nodded. She understood. But once was enough.

Chapter Eight

Sarah sent Janie to answer the door while she finished going over Jason's essay.

"Mama, someone needs to talk with you."

Sarah put down her pencil with a sigh and rose to see. The girl was a wee lass. When was the last time she ate? "Might I help ye?"

"Aye, Missus." She curtsied. "I'm lookin' to begin a laundry service an' hoped ye might be in the market for some help."

Sarah was about to dismiss her when the look in her eyes, a silent plea that said she was frightened and desperate, changed Sarah's mind. "Come in. We can talk. Perhaps you can help." Guiding her to the big room, Sarah motioned for the girl to take a seat, then dismissed Jason and the younger girls to take a break from studies. "Might ye take some tea with us? I have oat cakes too."

The girl appeared even more nervous. "Ah, Missus, ye dinna have to do that."

"'Tis no trouble." Sarah asked Beth to bring the tea with a plate of oatcakes. While her daughter was out of the room, Sarah sat next to the girl. "First, what should I be callin' ye?"

"Aphra. Missus. Me name is Aphra White."

"Aphra, is it? That's a lovely name. And where are yer people, Aphra?"

The girl's hands began to shake. Sarah could see she tried to control it by clasping them together. "Me family is gone. Me mither, she were a washer woman, now she's gone too. 'Tis all I know to do. I have me mither's mangle."

"I am so sorry, Aphra."

Beth came in with the tray and placed it in front of Sarah, who poured. The first cup was passed to the poor unfortunate. "Here ye are, lass. Drink up."

The cup clattered against the saucer. Sarah had a flash of worry that the china might break. It was her mother's china, so carefully packed and sent from Ireland. But more important was this child. The washer woman's life was difficult indeed.

Sarah used washer women occasionally, but generally she cared for the laundry herself with the help of her girls. However, if this child was any good at doing the laundry, it would certainly free her. Perhaps Sarah could help her in return.

"Missus, I dinna want to take yer time." Aphra eyed the oat cakes but had yet to reach for one.

"Dunna worry about that. Me children are glad to have the respite from their studies. Do try an oat cake. Me Beth made them herself." Sarah put one in the girl's hand to prove it was acceptable.

The child ate it as is she'd been starved for a year. Sarah gave her another.

"Aphra, I will need to discuss this with my husband. But I might use yer help. Where can I reach ya?"

Aphra gasped, coughing and choking.

"Oh, my!" Both Sarah and Beth jumped to the girl's aid, pounding on her back, raising her arms over above her head, giving her a sip of tea.

As she calmed, Sarah rubbed her back. "Are you all right now? Oh, how frightful!"

Aphra nodded as she pulled away, her eyes moist and as wide as the teacup's saucer.

"Perhaps you should rest a bit. Here, we'll make you comfortable on the settee. You can stay until my husband returns."

Sarah didn't believe the child's eyes could grow any bigger, but they did.

"There is no need to worry. I'll speak with Master Crockett when he returns and let you know what he says. While you wait, just relax. Would you like more tea and oat cakes?"

Aphra nodded, a barely perceptible nod.

Sarah patted her knee and took the tray to the kitchen, leaving Beth to give the child some company. As timid as Beth was, she was also very sensitive and kind. Aphra might be more comfortable with her daughter.

The more she thought about it, the more her heart tendered for the child. If Joseph would agree, she would have the girl move in with them. It would relieve Aphra of room and board, and she could do the laundry that much easier. Sarah had thought it through when Joseph arrived.

She met him at the door, wrapping her arms about his neck and soundly kissing him. "I am so glad yer home."

He kissed her back and untangled her arms from about him. "I am glad to be home." He hung up his hat.

"Come with me, love. We need to talk." She brushed a kiss against his cheek and crooked her finger to get him to follow her to the kitchen. Once there, she explained to him about the waif who came knocking. "So, I'm thinkin' we should have her come live with us. She would be a great help and Beth might enjoy havin' a quiet friend. What think ye?"

"You are the one in charge of this house, love. You know what you need. I trust your judgment and that tender heart of yours. If we can help this child, then by all means, let us help her."

She grabbed his hand. "Good! Then come meet Miss Aphra,

our new laundress." She pulled him to the big room and opened the door. Aphra and Beth sat together talking so quietly that it couldn't be heard across the room. The movement of their heads and hands gave away that they were in conversation.

Beth glanced up first. "Da!" She came to Joseph and gave him an embrace. This eldest daughter of theirs had enchanted her father from her first breath, Sarah knew.

However, Aphra now grew terrified, appearing to melt into the settee. Beth took Joseph's hand and led him to the girl. "Aphra, may I present my father, Master Joseph Crockett. Da, this is my new friend, Aphra."

Sarah's jaw dropped. That was more words than Beth ever said in front of someone outside the family.

Joseph glanced over his shoulder or Sarah would have thought he'd missed the importance. However, he conducted himself as if it were the most natural thing. "Miss Aphra, it is my pleasure." He bowed to the girl.

Aphra fainted.

❦

A FEW HOURS AFTER MR. COX WAS DISCIPLINED, THEY were out of the harbor and on their way to Boston. Willie's stomach turned when Boatswain Johnson gave the lash, but the expression on Maybe's face was etched in his brain. She lost all color, and he feared she might pass out. Cookie talking with her seemed to help, but that episode of the trip would be seared into her memory. His too.

But that was all behind them now. In two days, they would approach Boston Harbor.

It was his turn at the wheel. They didn't let him have his turn if they were coming into or leaving port, but when it was open water like this, he got plenty of practice. If his father could see him now. Would he still think he couldn't do it? That he was incapable of working on a ship? Aye, if he could see him, he would know. Willie was meant for this life. It felt natural, fun.

"Pirates, astern, off starboard."

A jolt passed through his body.

Boatswain Johnson appeared at his side. "Ninety degrees starboard, lad." And then he was gone, shouting commands to the crew to man the starboard cannons.

Maybe! What was she doing? Had she been up on the top? Had she been the one to spot the pirates? He should check on her, but there was no leaving his post. What would his father do? Pray, of course.

Willie prayed and turned the ship, exposing the right side guns to the enemy. He prayed and waited to see what to do next.

The boatswain came back to the wheelhouse. "Go, help with the main deck's third cannon."

Willie didn't hesitate. He took off for the main deck and glanced up. Maybe worked the shrouds on the top. He must focus and not worry about her. He spotted the third cannon, manned by Mr. Cox and Mr. Hawkins. It didn't appear they needed the help, though Willie had only heard quick instructions. Four days ago. What did he know?

He took his place, and Mr. Hawkins shoved him aside.

"Never there. Yer own gun'll kill ye." He continued to ready the cannon.

The gun fired, recoiling to where Willie had been standing.

Chagrined, Willie now remembered that piece of advice from the practice. Stupid! He tried to recall the order of what needed to be done. As Mr. Hawkins grabbed the next ball, Willie added the powder. Mr. Cox tended the wick. Soon they had a rhythm and had perfected their angle. Their last cannon ball met its mark, landing against the port side near the poop deck.

"Cease fire!" The call was sudden. Glancing out the hole, Willie spotted the reason. A navy sloop rose over the horizon, heading straight for the pirate vessel. Their enemy's only recourse was to outrun it, and that meant letting the *Frances Pearl* go in peace.

The last hour caught up to Willie. The men broke out into cheers. He joined in, as electricity soared through his veins, tingling out through his fingers. His breath came hard, fast, as if he'd run from Beaufort to Charlestown. It was the most exhilarating thing he'd experienced in his life! He whooped with the men, pounding on their backs as they returned the pound.

Today he was a man.

⚜

THE ONLY THING THAT KEPT MAYBE FROM SHRIEKING IN terror and fleeing her post was remaining steadfast to her duty with the shrouds. When she tended to them, she had less time to think of the fear. But once the cease fire rang out and the pirates changed course, the busyness slowed and fear had room to move. What if they had been taken? What would have happened to the crew? What would have happened to Willie?

What would have happened to her?

Would she've been discovered? The fear became so palpable she tasted it—bitter, acidic.

She could not wait to disembark.

Everywhere she went the rest of the day, members of the crew discussed, explained, and elaborated on their exploits against the menacing pirate ship that tried but could not win. There was no mention of the navy vessel or the dire possibilities if it hadn't appeared on the horizon. That manly swagger oozing from all directions was laughable if not for the actual danger they'd escaped. But her disdain only meant she must keep a tighter lid on her feminine emotions.

"Cookie, I dunna ken why the men talk so crazy. Instead of tellin' bolder an' bolder lies, why aren't they amazed at how close we came to meetin' our Maker on the bottom of the Atlantic?"

"Ah, laddie, that is how they cope with the fear. They

conquer it over an' over, smashin' it 'neath their feet with their words."

She nodded. It made sense. In a male sort of way.

"Ye'll learn, laddie. Men aren't s'posed to be afeared, but we're all human. This chatterin' on brings it out into the light o' day and plants courage for another."

Cookie was wiser than he looked. "How did ye learn all this, Cookie?"

"Spent me life aboard ship. Canna remember doing anythin' else. As I prepare the food, the crew treats me better. As I listen more than I talk, I hear things. I like it this way." He winked at her.

She returned a smile, along with a wink. They set about getting dinner ready for the men.

Soon they'd be landing at Boston. Next stop, Ireland. She'd be off this ship and herself once again.

But she would miss Cookie, that's for sure.

❧

"Aphra? Miss Aphra?" Joseph picked the girl up and put her back onto the settee before stepping out of the way for Sarah to work. What was wrong? Sarah had an instinct about her. She seemed to sense when one of the children was becoming ill. Perhaps her idea of this girl moving in with them stemmed from that instinct.

Bethy brought a basin of water and a cloth for her mother and then moved to stand beside him. She leaned in. "Da, she told me she feared men. I told her you were safe, but she must have been more afraid than I thought."

Afraid of men? Afraid of him? What was there to fear from him? He was just a husband and father.

Bethy linked her arm in his.

A wave of gratitude for this lovely daughter flowed through his heart. At least she didn't fear him.

"She's coming around." Sarah spoke over her shoulder before turning back to her patient. "Ye need some food and rest to put you right. Master Crockett and I are in agreement, we want you to move in here and help take care of the laundry. We'll give ye yer room and board and a stipend—we can discuss how much and when you start when you are better. There now. Ye rest yerself, and I'll get ye more tea and cakes." She stood and linked her arm through Joseph's on her way past him, leading him to the kitchen.

"Joseph love, there's somethin' very wrong with that lass. She needs more help than just work." She'd begun pouring more tea and setting additional oat cakes on the tray.

"Aye. Bethy whispered to me. Said the child is afraid of men."

That stopped Sarah mid reach. "Afraid of men, is it? A wee lass like she dunna fear men without cause. Oh, Joseph, what can we do to help her?"

Joseph loved how every notion in his wife's head registered across her face. He read her like a poster. Her thoughts were kind, loving, full of charity. "I do not understand, love. But doubtless you will figure it out. For now, I will keep my distance and add her to my prayers."

She cupped his cheek as she took the tray back to the other room. Her touch still sent tingles through him, making him smile.

Beth entered carrying the basin of water and the rag. "Da, you would never hurt her. You are too kind." His sensitive little girl, almost a woman. Her words now confirmed that she'd noted her whisper surprised him and now worried for him.

"I am glad you believe that, sweet one. Though someone has hurt her, or she would not be this frightened. She must feel safe speaking with you. If you learn something, would you tell me, please? If there is a need to protect her or if having her here puts you and your sisters in danger, I need to be aware." That last thought appeared as he spoke. What if this child's presence put his daughters in danger? Could he turn her away?

The answer was plain. No, he could not.

Beth nodded. "Aye, Da. I'll tell you. She hasn't told me much. Only that she feared meeting you, you being a man."

"In that case, I will give her time to get over her fear of me."

His daughter smiled, that lovely smile that made her look like her mother at that age. "She will get over being afraid of you, Da. Trust me. She'll see you are good and kind to us. Then she will know."

"Know what?

"That you are safe. And so is she." Beth came and hugged him. She might hate being put on the spot or talking in front of several people, but she had a way of seeing into a person's heart and revealing her own.

He hugged her back.

⬥

She should have returned by now. The girl wouldn't run away from Eleazar Ferguson. She was too frightened to cross him. And she knew the penalty if she even considered it. So, what was keeping her?

He paced to the window and scanned the street. Still no sign of her.

This was not a scenario he'd considered. He'd had no doubt she'd be back, but now... He needed answers. If he knocked on the Crockett home, would that give things away? Would it appear too forward? What pretext could he use?

Stupid, stupid girl. He shook his head. Such a simple task. What could have gone wrong?

He muttered a curse, as he pulled on his hat, tugged at his cuffs, and stormed out the door, his slam rattling his expensive glass windows.

Two minutes into his walk, it was plain he needed to calm

himself or the result would throw all his plans to naught. Reducing his speed, he breathed in and out, slow and steady. He remembered who he was. He made the rules. The rules did not apply to him. He was not that pedestrian. He decided what happened, when it happened, and how it happened. This was who he was. The rest had better understand, remove themselves from his path, or be crushed.

Ten minutes more, and he made it to the house. This was a better plan than going to the Crockett home. He rapped with his walking stick.

The door pulled open to show an elderly woman. "Aye, may I help you?"

"I wish to speak with the Master. Tell him Master Ferguson is here to see him."

"Aye, I'll tell him." And she closed the door on him.

Stunned, Eleazar choked on his rage. Who did she think she was, leaving him standing on the front porch? She belonged in the pillory at the very least. What type of hospitable greeting was that? He began to imagine just how he would see to her demise.

By the time the master opened the door to usher him in, Eleazar had the woman tarred, feathered, and boiling in oil. "How dare she keep me waiting out there!"

"My sincerest apologies, Master Ferguson. I am so sorry. Ever since we found the remains of that O'Malley man, she has been terrified of a murderer. Please, come in, make yourself at home. Can I get you anything? Tea?"

Eleazar took a breath. He must remain calm. "No, thank you. I understand how she feels. It has been a bit of a fright since then, hasn't it?"

"That is the truth of it. Aye. I'm aware you are a busy man. How can I be of service to you, sir?"

Eleazar smiled. That was the proper way to speak. "I have a bit of a problem. I am attempting to find my laundress. She seems to have disappeared. Normally I wouldn't worry so much. These washer women come and go, but she's just a girl and I've an interest... much like an uncle or guardian. And I am concerned for her welfare, what with that unfortunate episode concerning Master O'Malley. Might you make inquiries? Her name is Aphra."

Constable Thomas Miller stood and offered his hand. "You have come to the right place. I will see to her whereabouts post haste."

Eleazar looked at the proffered hand and forced himself to shake it. "I know that you will. I'll await your findings. Thank you, Constable." With that, he took his leave.

⁂

SARAH CHECKED IN ON APHRA, AGAIN WONDERING WHAT secrets the girl kept that made her so terrified. She'd thought it best to let her rest on the settee instead of moving her upstairs for now. No need adding more strangeness. The child had trouble enough handling the new surroundings of the parlor. Sarah turned to tiptoe to the kitchen.

"Mistress Crockett?"

She just caught the soft voice and returned to the girl. "Aye, Miss Aphra? May I get you anything?"

She shook her head. "No, but I thank ye. But might I speak with ye a moment?"

"Aye, child. What is it?"

Aphra scooted so she was sitting more than lying, her hands trembling on her lap. "Ye've been so kind to me."

"Oh, no, ye needed help. And ye offered yer services, for which I am grateful. Do not worry."

The girl kept her eyes glued to her hands as if they might fly away, leaving her arms without their tools.

"Is there something else?"

"Aye, Mistress. I—"

A door slammed. "Mama! Where are you?" Jason burst into the room. "Mama, I need to talk with you."

"Jason, we have a guest, and yer being rude. Please, wait for me in the kitchen."

"But..."

"No argument. Go!"

He blew out a big breath, yet obeyed.

Sarah looked back to Aphra. The child had turned to her side, pulled her knees up to her chin, and her arms clasped her legs. She buried her face in her skirt and trembled like a leaf in a hurricane.

Sarah must wait to hear what she planned to say.

Chapter Nine

Bits and pieces of the bravado floated back to Maybe as the ship pulled into Boston Harbor. Oh, the men did their jobs, probably at a faster pace, but the talk still ran high. She wondered how long before things returned to normal. She also wondered if they faced another encounter with pirates, would there be anyone alive to talk so brave?

What had been her father's thoughts as the pirates seized his ship, the ship he had last sailed? Had he been frightened, like her? Did he suffer? She shuddered and turned her attention back to the shrouds.

The cargo bound for Boston soon would be unloaded and shore leave granted to the crew within an hour. She wanted off the ship, but she didn't want to celebrate with the crew. Willie wanted to be with them, though. Was there a compromise?

She mulled that thought and decided to slip him a note. He might meet her at the commons, like in New York. Perhaps spend time together after he'd had fun with the men. If he met her late afternoon, she could find the location and indulge in some time to herself. The boatswain often left extra pieces of scrap paper with her and a pencil nub or two. She found them and crafted a quick note. Now to find Willie.

He was laughing with Mr. Cox and Mr. Swain when she approached.

"About ready to go, Maybe?"

"Not yet, but ye can go. I can meet ye later. Here." She handed him the note. He opened it, a queer expression passing over his face.

"Is there a problem?"

"No, no problem." He refolded the paper and tucked it in his pocket. "I will see you later?"

"Aye. Later."

He smiled and nodded as she turned to go. But she could hear him talking with the men before she'd taken five steps.

◈

A NOTE? WHY DID SHE GIVE HIM A NOTE? IF HE questioned it, it would raise suspicions. If he didn't… well, he'd have to do his best. He was going with the men. Be one of them. Where would they go?

Willie imagined this moment, but reality would be different. He couldn't wait.

"C'mon, lad, it's time to raise a ruckus. Yer mates are gonna show ye how." Mr. Swain put his arm across Willie's shoulder. "I know of a brewery where we can have our tankards filled. A wee bit nicer than the places along the docks. Let's go."

Willie's gut tingled. He'd never known his father to take hard spirits, but he wouldn't turn down an offer of a tankard of ale would he? This was Willie's first time. If he were a man, he should be about manly things. And men drank ale occasionally with friends.

Between the rationalizing and anticipation, he hoped he wouldn't throw up all over himself.

The Adams Brewery was an average sized, based on the bit of knowledge Willie possessed about such places. He sat at the table with Mr. Swain while Mr. Cox ordered for them. It took a moment to realize that the other patrons were deep into political and religious conversations. Was this what went on back home in taverns? His father would have thoughts on these subjects, but he'd never known his father to go to such places. Perhaps he didn't realize this was what happened?

The men two tables away got louder. The bartender called a boy. "Sammy, go fetch your father."

The boy raced out, returning behind a large man. Authority seeped into his every step. "I could hear you out to the street. Debate all you want, but no yelling and no fighting. You know the rules."

Both men appeared chagrined. "Aye, Master Adams."

Adams. Willie leaned in and whispered to the men at his table. "Is he the owner?"

They both nodded. "He keeps this place respectable. He's a deacon in his church, and his wife is a practicing Puritan. There won't be any trouble here. That's why I chose this place."

Willie nodded and took a sip of the ale. It wasn't what he expected. Maybe he needed to build a liking for it. That must be it, otherwise it made no sense why men drank the stuff.

Mr. Cox laughed. "Yer first taste, aye, boy. Well, here's to many more." He raised his tankard as did Mr. Swain.

Willie raised his, then tried another sip. Still horrid, but he would not let his face betray him.

An hour later, he excused himself to go find the necessary. When he stood, things wobbled. He paused to see if the wobbling stopped. It merely slowed, so he used the chair backs and walls to find his way out. After taking care of his business, he remembered Maybe's note and pulled it from his pocket. He opened it, the words jumbled and tumbled. It was no use. He couldn't read it. He'd have to apologize to her later. He was good at that. Apologizing. He had a lot of practice.

William the Apologizing Oaf.

William the Idiot Oaf.

William the Never-Will-Get-It-Right Oaf.

He sighed and returned to his friends.

❧

Maybe found the commons with ease and chose her tree. Her arms had gained strength from all the climbing she did aboard ship. The elm was tall and majestic, with many limbs strong enough to offer level after level of height. Maybe took full advantage of the offer and climbed higher than she ever had. There, alone with her thoughts, she allowed her mind to go where she hadn't allowed since leaving Beaufort. What happened to her stepfather when she wasn't found? She felt some guilt, knowing that it was not a good thing. She didn't have compassion so much as guilt that her actions caused the problem. Still, she wouldn't change her decision to leave rather than submit.

She thought of her sister, Eliza. Would she find her still alive? She wanted to pray that she would, but she'd forgotten how to pray. How did one approach the God of the universe when one had turned her back on Him? She wasn't as angry at Him now since she was relatively safe. That made her realize that as uncomfortable as her charade was, and at times it felt heart-poundingly dangerous, it afforded her safety. And isn't that what she'd prayed for when she ran away? A plan of safety?

So, maybe God had listened. He had a strange way of helping.

Maybe glanced about, hoping to glimpse Willie coming onto the green. Still no sign. She knew he knew she expected him. He'd read the note in her presence. Had he gotten so carried away with the men that he forgot about her?

She watched from her perch in the sky as the sun meandered toward the western horizon. With summer so close, the days were longer. But even longer days could not keep back the night. If she were to make it to the ship before dark, she'd have to leave now.

She shimmied back to the ground, dropping the last foot

onto an old root that turned her ankle. Ouch! She rubbed it and tested her weight. Well, she had no other choice. There was no one to help her. She'd must make her way back. It would be a slower going, though.

Maybe limped along, through the streets, heading back for the dock when a familiar voice filled the night air. Willie!

Only it was slurred and sing-songy like her stepfather's used to get when he was on a drunk. Now she understood why he hadn't come. It made no sense he that he'd drunk so much.

And then he spotted her. "Maybe! Iz Maybe!"

Mr. Cox and Mr. Swain walked on either side of him. They didn't appear any worse for wear.

"So ye let him do all the drinkin' did ye?"

"Ah, no, Maybe. 'Tisn't like that 'tall. No, he had one tankard of ale. One." Mr. Cox held up one finger and giggled. "He just can't handle his liquor."

She wanted to doubt them. Something told her they spoke a part of the truth. There must be more. And why didn't he search for her? Perhaps he plain couldn't. Perhaps he didn't realize one tankard would do this. All the power seeped from her anger. Willie looked at her, and the last of her peeve vanished.

"So, what do we do now? He can't go back on board like this, and he's nowhere to go for tonight."

"We was just talkin' about that. What if we keep the night guard busy? We can get his attention to the other side and you can sneak him on board. Might put him under one of the jolly boats off the davit. Just keep 'm quiet 'til he falls asleep. Then come mornin' we'll get 'm out when no one's about."

"Why not take him to his bunk? He can sleep it off there?"

"Not a good ideare, boy. Should the boatswain make a walk through and see him before he goes to sleep, or catch him casting up his accounts, it would be just as bad."

Willie clearly didn't comprehend what was being said around him. He just smiled and lolled his head.

"Can ye do it, lad?" Mr. Cox didn't have to remind her of what might happen. None of them wanted that for Willie.

Maybe nodded, following them to the dock. Down from the *Frances Pearl,* they stopped and leaned Willie against her. She might as well hold up the mast.

"All right, Maybe, stay here 'til ye see me signal. Then make for the stern and the jolly boat. Ye should be able to slip him inside as it's tipped on edge."

She nodded and took a deep breath. "Oh, Willie. Ye put life aside to help me. I reckon it is me turn to do the same for ye."

Waiting while holding up the lanky, sleepy form of her friend was more difficult than she would have thought. A thank you for all the hard work she'd put in building her muscles on the top was in order. A month ago she'd never been able to do it.

Mr. Swain gave the signal. The guard went in another direction.

"C'mon, Willie, ye got to give me some help here. Just keep walkin'." She steered him up the gangplank to the back of the ship. There a jolly boat rested against the stern. Now to get him behind it.

She got him to his hands and knees with a lot of coaxing. "Wha' kinda game we playin', Maybe?"

"Shush! Willie, just go. No talking, please!"

Maybe pushed from behind, getting his big, fat boots into hiding when she heard the guard coming back. No place to hide. And if he saw her, he might want an explanation. An investigation would ruin everything. There was no choice. She followed Willie behind the jolly boat.

"Wa zis?"

"Shut up, Willie." She tried putting her hand over his mouth.

"Wha' ya doin'?"

"Ye must hush, now!" Footfalls sounded, heading toward the stern.

"Bu—"

She didn't ponder it. She did the only thing that came to her brain. She kissed him, hard on the mouth.

That shut him up. And aroused him. He returned the kiss, stirring up more passion within her than she'd ever known.

This was a mistake. But it was what she'd longed to do. She closed her eyes and her mind to the warning.

Somewhere she heard a call, the steps receded. She could stop now.

Except she didn't.

Willie's hands began to caress her, drawing a craving from her, one she knew she'd regret.

Now she could not stop.

And neither did he.

☙❧

WILLIE TRIED TO ROLL TO HIS SIDE BUT WAS STUCK. HE opened one eye, then both. It didn't help. It was dark. He started to sit and banged his head. Ow! Was he buried alive? Terror flooded. He tried to raise his arms, but his right was pinned beneath something.

Maneuvering his left hand across his body, he explored for what held him prisoner. Something warm, something alive! He gasped. The something moved.

"Willie, be still. Let me check if the coast is clear." Maybe's voice.

His heart rate slowed.

She didn't move right away but did something he didn't understand. Finally, he felt her moving down his body, past his feet. "All right, roll to yer stomach and scoot backwards. Be quiet about it."

He did as she said, though his head seemed too large to slip out of the opening his feet just used. He must have hit his head harder than he imagined.

Once out, he started to stand, but Maybe pulled him down

again. "Wait until I see where the guard is." She crouched and moved out before coming back. "We're clear. Now, quietly go below to yer cot. I'll meet ye there in a few minutes."

He nodded and wished he hadn't. His bearings gathered, he headed below as Maybe instructed. Somehow, he was missing something, though for the life of him he couldn't think what.

That was it. He couldn't think. What had happened to him? He went over the past day. He remembered going to the brewery with Mr. Cox and Mr. Swain. He even remembered his first taste of ale. It wasn't a pleasant memory.

Somewhere along the line, Maybe had appeared. He remembered a game she wanted to play, but she kept shushing him… something else. It was there, just beneath the surface. He lay back on his cot and closed his eyes.

And he knew. It wasn't anything he saw in his mind, it was impressions. The touch of her lips on his, the warmth of her skin, how she… oh, what had he done?

◈

When Maybe got below to her cot, Willie's back was to her. She hoped he was asleep and that this would be the end.

But it wouldn't be the end. How would she face him? How can they stay friends? Why did she let this happen?

Just when she started to believe things would get better, she threw away the one thing she treasured, the one thing she'd refused to let her stepfather sell.

Would Willie even remember? How would he see her come morning?

She wanted to be angry with him, to hate him for what he took. But he didn't just take it. She allowed it. She could have stopped, but she hadn't wanted to stop. Feeling his kiss, his touch, falling asleep in his arms, that should've been wonderful. If he were her husband, it would've been. She knew this because she knew something else.

She was in love with Willie.

But in love or not, this was wrong. If God allowed such misery when she'd been as good as she knew to be, what grief awaited now that she had done this?

And there was no way to undo it.

Chapter Ten

Sarah brought a bowl of chicken soup to Aphra who still occupied settee. The child was much too thin. If Sarah could get enough nourishment into her, she might feel more like sharing her story.

Though reclined, the girl was more alert. She had slept two hours.

Joseph left without disturbing her to see if he could find information from the constable. That left Sarah to care for Aphra.

"Are ye ready to talk?" She stroked a stray tendril from the girl's face.

Aphra nodded and sat. "'Tisn't a pretty story, Mistress. Me father took sick and died when I were a wee bit. Me mither became a washerwoman to keep us alive. Then she took sick. Me plan was to take over her duties, but I found a job as a maid for a gent here in town. He offered room and board, so I took the job. I dinna understand all that it would require."

"Was the work too difficult? Did he not feed ye, child?

"Comin' here was the first time he let me leave the house. He says I am his property to do with as he pleases. Now he pleases to learn about yer home. I dunno know why."

The child's words wiped away every sane thought in her brain. She shook her head, then stared hard at the lass. "He said ye were his property?"

Aphra nodded.

"What does he do with his property?" Though afraid to ask, Sarah was more fearful of not knowing.

"Whatever he pleases." The words sounded dead, matter of fact.

Her mother instinct kicked in. Sarah pulled the child into an embrace, rocking her in her arms. "Don't ye worry none. Ye are safe here. We'll not let anything happen to ye, I promise ye that."

The child pulled back, tears glistening. "Ye canna make such promises. Ye do not ken the power he wields. If I stay or if ye tell anyone else what I said, it will go hard on me and yer family."

"No, Aphra, no, ye canna go back to the beast. We will care for ye. Have no worry." She pulled the child close again.

Aphra melted into her arms. "I want to believe ye, Mistress. Oh, I want to."

ॐ

JOSEPH ARRIVED AT THE CONSTABLE'S HOUSE JUST AS HE was coming out the front door. "Ho, Thomas Miller, might I have a word?"

"To what is it in regard, Master Crockett? Have you learnt more about the O'Malley fellow?"

Joseph stopped at the steps to the porch. "Aye, but I've come for a different reason. There's a young lass who came by my house this morning. She's hoping to be a washerwoman—"

"Washerwoman, you say?" At once he focused. "There was someone else here just a bit ago asking about his washerwoman. Said she'd gone missing. A young girl, answers to the name of Aphra."

"Aye, that is the girl."

Constable Miller moved faster than Joseph had ever seen, his arms flapping about. "Where is she?"

"Aye, that is what I tell you. She is at my home. Something is wrong with the child. My wife is with her now, attempting to learn the truth. The poor thing is terrified of men."

The constable froze and stared. "Terrified of men? What do you mean?"

"I mean, when I or my son walk into the room, she panics and curls into a ball. Something happened causing this child to be so timid. My Beth is shy. This is different. It is fear." Joseph was sure he made himself clear. What kept the man from doing something?

"What shall I do about it?"

Do? Your job! "I want you to come to my home. You can see her reaction. You can also hear from my wife anything she has learned in my absence."

The man sighed. "Oh, all right. Shall we?" He motioned for Joseph to lead the way.

Ten minutes later, they came in the door. Sarah left the parlor to greet him. "Hello, Constable. Welcome." She curtsied and turned to her husband. "Might I have a word in the kitchen, Joseph?"

He nodded, excused himself and followed her to the other room.

"I'm glad yer here, love. It is worse than I could have ever dreamed."

"What have you learned?"

Sarah paused and glanced about before leaning in. "After her mither died, she took a position as a maid to a man here in town. He provided bed and board and then told her she was his property to do with as he pleased. What she has gone through, it yanks the thoughts from my brain. Oh, Joseph, we must—"

A scream rang from the front room.

Sarah ran back, Joseph on her heels. The door to the front room stood open, and the constable held his hand to Aphra, who continued to scream.

Sarah pushed past the man to the girl and held her in her arms.

"Dunna let him take me, Mistress! Dunna let him touch me!"

"Sh-sh, it's all right, Aphra. It's all right. He won't take you."

Constable Miller, wide eyed, stuttered at Joseph. "But I must, you see. I must take her. Master Ferguson is waiting for her. He's been searching for her."

"No!" Aphra clung to Sarah.

Joseph put the pieces together. "What do you mean, Thomas, you must?"

"Why he came worried for her. He asked me to find her for him."

Aphra shook her head. "No! He works for him. I told ye he has power. The constable takes a wage from him."

Thomas Miller's shook his head, over and over, terror in his widened eyes. "Ah, no. You can't believe a girl like that. She'll say anything."

Sarah faced Joseph. He could read her thoughts, knew she would die trying to save this child.

She wouldn't have to. No one would die here today. "Constable, we pay you your wage, our citizenry. It is to them you owe your allegiance. You will not take this child anywhere. You will, however, go with me to find our Justice of the Peace so that together we might arrest Eleazar Ferguson."

"On what charge?" The man's voice squeaked.

"What do you mean, what charge? He has kept this poor child a prisoner, forced himself upon her, and misused her!" Joseph had more than lost his patience.

"She is not his wife. She cannot claim wife beating." Could the weasel hear himself?

Sarah reared tall, her voice menacing. "Ye mean to tell me that she must be wed to the beast before it is illegal to beat her? He forced himself on her. That is rape."

Now the constable's face turned so white, it was possible no blood flowed to his brain. "Rape?"

"Aye, rape. She is a child. He did not marry her. He kept her a prisoner. What would you call it?"

Constable Miller cleared his throat. "Might we speak in the hall?"

Joseph glanced at Sarah who waved him away. They moved to the hall.

"You do not understand what you are stirring, sir. Master Ferguson is a powerful man. It is best to do as he wishes. The results are not pleasant." The mouse trembled.

"You can live with yourself, knowing what that man did, and allow him to continue after seeing that child in there?" Why must he point this out? *Open your eyes!*

"When it puts my entire family at risk, aye, that I can."

Joseph stared, unable to grasp the depth of this man's cowardice. "How can you live this way? How will your children think of you? You must stand for right. They will never learn unless they see you. Think, man. This is the job you agreed to. You must do it."

The constable stared at the floor, shaking. "You think me a coward. I think the same. But I know the danger. You don't know what you ask."

"I am not asking. Let's go." Joseph shoved him out the door.

The man sputtered the whole walk to Master Waddington's home. Did he think to change Joseph's mind? There was no other recourse. They must stop this villain.

Once at the house of the Justice of the Peace, Constable Miller caved. His shoulders slumped, his gaze remained downcast. Joseph gave him a moment to knock, but when it didn't happen, he did it himself.

The maid answered, leading them to the parlor. "I'll get the master."

Joseph thanked her and, after she left the room, took a seat. The wait was but a moment. Henry Waddington entered, smiling as if he didn't mind the intrusion.

"Ho, Joseph, Thomas, to what do I owe the pleasure?"

"Hallo to you, Henry. I wish we were here on something of pleasure. Unfortunately, we are not." Joseph stood when Henry walked into the room, Thomas had yet to take a seat.

Henry motioned for them to resume sitting as he chose a chair. "Have you learned the details of that O'Malley incident?"

Joseph shook his head. "No, it is another matter. We would like your backing to arrest Eleazar Ferguson." Joseph scrutinized the man's reaction at the mention of the name. If Henry took bribes too, this would be a tougher challenge.

"Eleazar Ferguson? I'm acquainted with the name. What has he done?"

"A young girl came to us today, asking to be our laundress. After spending time with my wife, she told her that Eleazar Ferguson had kept her locked in his house. She'd accepted a maid's position, but he's claimed her as property and misused her."

The justice raised his chin and narrowed his eyes. "Misused? How?"

"She says rape."

Henry Waddington's features changed from passive to crimson and angry. "Rape? Are you sure? That is a serious charge."

"Quite sure, sir. She is terrified of all males, even boys as young as my Jason. Her fear is real. Something has frightened her. Ferguson searched for her. He already approached the constable here to search for her and bring her back. Master Miller did not know about the claim before he agreed to do so." Joseph glanced at Thomas. The man's color improved. One could only hope that was true. The other possibility was far worse for him.

"Then let us be done with this. I will get my hat, and we will go arrest this beast."

Now a weight lifted from Joseph. He didn't want to think ill of Master Waddington, hoping the man was above bribery.

Joseph stood, motioned for Thomas to precede him, as they followed the Justice of the Peace out of his home.

⁂

ELEAZAR FERGUSON RANG THE BELL FOR TEA. HIS housekeeper didn't do as good a job with it as Aphra, but soon the girl would be back. Maybe he would keep her on, just to make his tea. That is unless the O'Malley girl brewed a good cuppa.

But, Aphra knew things. And that she hadn't returned to him right away only proved she could not be trusted. He must get rid of her.

Hopefully that stupid constable would bring her back. He'd been vague enough, and generous enough, that the man should get the meaning without having a prick of conscience to bother him. After pulling out his watch, he decided to give the man one hour more before he encouraged his progress.

A knock sounded at the front door. No need to rise, his housekeeper would handle it.

"Sir, there are some gentlemen here to see you."

"Show them in, show them in."

Eleazar stood, tugging his cuffs, a ready smile to greet his visitors. Few came unannounced. Not many dared. But the way his housekeeper said "gentlemen," he wondered if it might be a social call.

The parlor door opened to the constable and justice of the peace.

Eleazar's smile increased.

Then Master Crockett brought up the rear.

Eleazar's smile vanished. It was not a social call, he knew. Still, he could play the part. "To what do I owe the honor, sirs?

The constable's face betrayed him as he appeared to fade behind the justice. This was not good.

Justice Waddington stepped forward. "We are here because charges have been made against you, Master Ferguson."

"Charges? Against me? What charges might those be?"

"Do you know a girl who goes by the name Aphra?" The justice was all business. He was not to be dissuaded.

"Aye, I do. I'm concerned for her well-being. She said she was looking for customers, that she wanted to expand her laundry business. But then she did not return. I began to fret, I confess. So, I asked Constable Miller to investigate. Has he found her?" His heart pounded in his chest, but he was not about to give them the satisfaction of showing fear. He did not show fear.

"Aye, she's been found. Please come with us."

Now he was confused. Had something really happened to the girl? Was she dead? Did they blame him? "Why? Why do you need me to come? Where?"

"Master Eleazar Ferguson, you are under arrest for the rape and abduction of the girl Aphra."

The blood left his face. She had told. How much did she say? He couldn't afford to go to jail. They might learn everything. Then a darker thought hit him. They wouldn't have to learn more. Rape was a capital offense.

No, he wouldn't hang, not for that piece of trash. "I will go with you. May I get my hat?"

The justice nodded.

Eleazar moved to the hall, put his hat on his head and picked up his walking stick. He could feel the men's presence behind him, following him from the room. Turning, he called over his shoulder. "Mary, put the tea on hold—"

He swung out with his stick, dropped it, and raced through the door. At the first step he was tackled from behind, knocked down the porch stairs. The other person held him fast.

Everything in his nature clawed, swung, punched, kicked. He must get away. He heard a *whuff* as his assailant's breath was knocked from him.

Eleazar grabbed his opportunity. Scrambling to his feet, one step, two, someone yanked his leg from behind, pulling him flat to the ground. He landed face first. A weight smashed his back.

"Constable, do you have anything to bind your prisoner?" It was the voice of that Crockett man, puffing as he spoke.

"Aye. A set of manacles."

Moments later Eleazar felt the metal clamping his wrists before they dragged him to his feet.

"Let us to the jail." Master Waddington slapped Eleazar's hat on his head and led the way. Masters Miller and Crockett walked on either side, lugging him.

Jail. What was he to do? It wasn't the first time he'd faced death, but this was the tightest situation he'd met. He must think fast, starting now.

⁂

"Och! What happened to ye?" The shock of seeing Joseph with a split lip and swelling eye brought Sarah running. "Oh, love, does it hurt?" She touched his cheekbone.

He winced. "Aye, it hurts."

She pulled him to the kitchen, making him sit on the stool while she gathered a rag and basin of water.

He chuckled until she put the damp rag to his lip. "Ow!"

She stopped, rag in the air. "What happened, Joseph?"

"Aphra won't need to worry about Eleazar Ferguson. He was arrested and taken to jail."

Sarah exhaled and sat on his lap. "So, she's safe."

"For now. He still goes to trial. She will need to testify."

No! She hopped up. "Oh, Joseph, I don't think she can." Shaking her head, she imagined the look of terror on the poor child's face. "What will happen if she canna testify?"

He took her hands in his. "She must testify. If she refuses, he goes free."

Chapter Eleven

The winds blew strong enough the boatswain made Maybe stand down. She used her time to watch the waves from the rail. Might she jump in?

How was she so stupid? All she had to do was stop him. He was drunk. Drunk differs from sober. She didn't hold it against Willie.

Still, he hadn't bothered to speak with her all morning. He was up before she. Strange. Coupled with his drinking, that was stranger still. She'd overheard Mr. Cox and Mr. Swain teasing him about holding his liquor. He must be too embarrassed to talk with her.

Well, that made two of them. She wasn't eager to look him in the face yet either.

She'd hoped Cookie would call her to help, but he hadn't.

So, she watched the waves, imagining them washing her clean again.

"You are quiet today, Maybe."

She startled. The boatswain arrived without a sound.

"Not really. I'm only watching the water."

"Oh. What do you see?"

She glanced back at him. Was this a test? "Water. I ken there's life in it, but right now it's churnin'. Like wind from beneath blowin' around."

He smiled. "Aye, me too. Reminds me of my faith. I know God is there, even when I can't see Him. That gives me strength to go on."

She cocked her head and mulled his words. "Ye sometimes dunna want to go on?"

"Everyone gets that way some time. It is what you do with the feeling that counts. Me, I believe I was put here for a purpose. It isn't my job to decide when it is over or even what it is. So, when I'm discouraged, I remember the water."

It made sense. When one was on speaking terms with the Almighty. But what if one made an unchangeable mistake? "I thank ye. It is somethin' to think on."

He patted the rail, appearing as if he wanted to say more. Then, shaking his head, he pushed away and moved on.

Maybe liked Boatswain Johnson. There was something fatherly in his ways. If he had been her stepfather, none of this would have happened. It made her wish she might come clean and tell him her secret, or at least the one that got her onto the ship.

The other one she couldn't reveal to anyone. Ever.

❧

IT WAS WILLIE'S TURN AT THE WHEEL. AS A RULE HE LIKED this part, but today the sea foamed and frothed. Mr. Cox had made more than one check with the chip log, and Boatswain Johnson had double checked the numbers and his compass. Something told Willie change was coming.

He'd developed a skill early on which served him in embarrassing situations. He deflected remarks, firing out retorts that made the other person the butt of the joke. A skill at which he excelled. Only today, nothing witty came to him.

Today he must take it. Every elbow, every twitter.

Because they had no clue just how badly he had messed up.

And he could never tell without betraying Maybe.

But then, isn't that what he did?

"Mr. Stewart, we're heading for Port Royal."

"Nova Scotia, sir?"

"Aye. This water isn't stirred just by the depths. A storm's on the way. A bad one. We need to make for Port Royal. Change course, port forty degrees."

"Aye, sir." Willie made the change while the boatswain went out to supervise the sails.

Port Royal. How long before they got there? How long would they stay? Maybe wanted to get to Ireland.

Oh, now his mind was concerned for what she wanted. He should've remembered that when it meant something. What a dolt he was! He needed to talk to her, tell her he was sorry. Yet a part of him wasn't sorry. That was what was so awful. His feelings for her ran deep. If things were different, he might court her. But he had no right to do what he did. He stole from her. How could he face her?

Still, that was what he must do. He must tell her.

There was no private place aboard this ship—unless you counted the jolly boats, and he would never do that again. If he wrote her a note, she would know. He needed to speak to her. Privately. Would she even trust him enough to be alone with him?

A wave splashed over the deck. He watched the sea growing chaotic. Just like his life. Well, at least if he were busy helping keep the ship afloat, he wouldn't have his mind on Maybe. He shook his head and tried to put his focus back on the wheel.

The top priority now was to get to Port Royal. Then they might go walking, talk. At the nine knots they were sailing, they'd be there sometime tomorrow.

Now he needed to pray they would make it.

"Sir, don't you want me up top to help with the shrouds?" Maybe had done her part with the pirates. Surely he trusted her work now. She was needed.

"No, I want you below to help Cookie with the galley. If the seas get any more rough before we reach the port, he'll need your help." Boatswain Johnson pursed his lips before turning back to the rigging.

She made her way to the galley. Cookie, at least, appeared happy to see her.

"Ho, laddie, we're in for a ride an' that's a fact."

"Do ye think it'll get worse, Cookie?"

"I've seen it get worse. and I've seen it calm out of the blue. There's no way to tell until it happens, so we'll just prepare for the worst and hope for the best." Though he waxed philosophical, he summed up her life. Hoping things improved, but worrying about what might go wrong. Because the go-wrong part always won.

She sighed. "What would ye have me do?"

"Start o'er there. Seal and weight the bins."

Maybe got to work. Once she completed one job, there was another. She and Cookie worked to protect the stores and prepare food for the men. The crew ate their meals in shifts, coming in groups of two or three.

After awhile, Willie arrived at the galley. She portioned out his serving, handing it over without letting their gazes meet. But then his hand touched hers. She had to look.

"Willie…"

He leaned close to her ear. "I know. We need to talk. We're heading for Port Royal, should be there no later than midday tomorrow—maybe even sooner with this wind. We'll talk there. I promise."

She nodded. Afraid to use her voice, she ran her sleeve over her face and got busy with the next meal.

He wanted to talk. Perhaps that was good, if he loved her that was. Perhaps it wasn't, if he thought her loose. Had he decided she wasn't worth his efforts?

There were too many hours between now and Port Royal. The clock needed to move a lot faster.

⁂

Sam Johnson felt things in his bones. It was more than just an impression. Some days he knew something would go wrong on board or he sensed the weather about to change. This time his bones whispered about Maybe. That something was wrong.

He watched the exchange from the doorway. Aye. Whatever bothered Maybe had to do with that Stewart fellow. He was too far to hear what they said and couldn't get a good view without revealing himself, but how their heads came together, the spoken words lasting more than a quick "thanks" told him he was on to something.

That boy tugged at his heart. If he ever settled down, he'd want a son like him, one brave enough to prove his worth when the odds were against him. Maybe had no family or even a recollection of one, yet he didn't let it hold him back. Cookie called him the best help he'd ever had in the galley.

If the lad weren't so close to the Stewart boy, he'd offer him a chance to stay on and learn from him. Perhaps even make him his ward. Funny, it had never crossed his mind before with anyone.

Should he reveal his hand, ask Maybe if he was all right? Would the boy confide in him if there were a problem?

Something unsettled him about this whole relationship. The Stewart boy worked hard, and he was affable enough. He even learned so fast that Sam wondered more than once if the boy had previous ship experience. Most men needed several attempts to learn a task. Not Willie Stewart. Sam had nothing against him. Yet when Willie met with Maybe, Sam's mind saw puzzles. He'd encountered nothing like it in all his years at sea.

In the meantime, something bothered Maybe. Should he push the boy to talk? Was it enough to say he'd listen anytime? Until his bones told him different, that was the best he could do.

A large wave crashed on the deck, sending water down the hold. Sam needed to get his mind off puzzles and back onto getting the ship to Port Royal. That was the priority. Nothing else mattered until they made safe harbor. He shook his mind free of everything else and returned to the deck.

❧

WILLIE PRAYED. THERE WOULD BE NO SLEEPING TONIGHT. Well, a wink or two in shifts perhaps, but the crew couldn't afford more. The North Star hid from the boatswain as he searched for reckoning. At this point, they were outrunning the worst of the storm, hoping to find the port by daylight. If they stayed ahead of it, they might make a safe harbor.

So Willie prayed. What else could he to do, other than his job, of course? Yet there was no guarantee God heard his prayer.

Mama would argue with that, he knew. She would remind him that God always heard our prayers, no matter what we'd done, no matter where we were. When we turned our hearts to God, in desperation or gratitude, He heard. We might not like His answer or timing, but He heard. Her voice whispered in Willie's ear.

The wind howled. Willie prayed harder. The image of Jesus waking in the boat when everyone cried doomed splashed across his mind. Oh, ye of little faith. Was his faith so small? Mama often reminded him that one only needed the faith of a mustard seed—a tiny seed. That was all he had, a tiny seed of faith. But he offered it all.

The storm didn't quiet completely, but it sure quieted

immensely. It stunned Willie, tempering the fury of emotions inside him. It was what he'd prayed for, yet it surprised him. Shocked him was more like it. God listened to him, answered him. Others must have prayed. In fact, he would bet hard money on the fact that his mother prayed right this minute. She didn't know what he experienced or how dire the straits, but she would pray. She would also realize when her prayer was answered, no matter whether she saw the answer. That was more than mustard-seed faith. That was the faith Willie needed. And he needed it now.

MORNING DAWNED GRAY AND OVERCAST. OUTRUNNING THE storm propelled the ship in the right direction. Praise God. Sam called for them to heave to and use the sounding lead. The tallow-encrusted drop found the shelf, just a tad less than the full one hundred fathom line. When they pulled it up from the bottom, the fine sand sticking to the tallow told him exactly where they were and what he needed to know.

Mr. Stewart helped raise the anchor and, once underway, assisted Mr. Cox with the chip log. Between his charts, the figures he got from the chip log and the magnetic compass, Port Royal was only a few hours away. They could wait out the storm there and God willing, it would be a short wait. The longer it took to get the merchandise to its destination, the less pay awaited. But, reaching the destination was more important than the speed, he reminded himself. Sam took responsibility for every life aboard ship, in prayer, on his knees. He put his trust in the Almighty, doing everything in his power to make it work. He prayed that was enough.

"Land, ho!"

Maybe fluttered with a twinge of excitement at hearing those words. It meant they'd nearly made it to port, safely. Soon she and Willie would have their conversation. Truth was, she dreaded it as much as she anticipated it. She had little time to dwell on that since the boatswain gave her permission to resume her duties on top. She'd increased her skill with the shrouds, adjusting, pinning, unpinning as needed, to get the ship into the harbor. It would keep her busy until they moored and Willie was free to disembark with her.

Pulling into port, they docked the *Frances Pearl*, making her secure. A surge would do real damage. However, the storm had abated. Maybe hoped this was a short stop. She descended the Jacob's ladder, keeping clear of the men making secure. She'd be out of the way in the galley. Perhaps Cookie needed items from the town while they were in port.

"Kind of ye to ask, boy, but I canna think of a thing right now. Me head's apoundin'. I might catch forty winks while the ship's quiet."

"Hope ye feel right as rain soon, Cookie. Perhaps a nap is the answer. It was quite the night."

"Aye, laddie, that it was. Now off with ye."

Maybe waved and returned on deck.

Willie headed her way. "Are you ready? Want to go walk about the town?"

She nodded. Her voice, in his presence, evaporated inside of her.

Some men called, asking if he wanted to join them. He declined without explanation, hurrying her down the gangplank.

They walked in silence. Willie pointed out a copse on the edge of town. "Let go in there. Get lost in the trees." He smiled.

He was trying. There was kindness in him, making her love him more.

She nodded and followed.

Once a stone's throw inside the grove, he slowed. "Take your pick, Maybe. Which one looks like climbing?"

She wandered to the nearest one with the lowest hanging branches. "This will do." She pulled herself up and made her way high among the leaves. A moment later, Willie sat on a branch at her feet.

He said they would talk. He must start. She didn't know how. She swung her legs. "So?"

He glanced at her and then back at his lap. "So… I am sorry, Maybe. I don't know what to say. I—" He cleared his throat. "I had no right. Couldn't blame you if you never trusted me again."

She hadn't expected that. Air escaped her, leaving her heart thumping in her ears. She shook her head. "It was my fault, Willie. I only wanted ye to shut yer mouth so ye wouldn't be discovered. Nothing else worked. So I kissed ye. I could've told ye to stop. I should've."

"Why didn't you?"

She looked away. How could he ask that? "Willie…"

"I shouldn't have asked. You were honest. But it is my fault. If I had just gone with you."

"Why dinna ye jist meet me, Willie?"

⚜

WILLIE CLOSED HIS EYES TIGHT. NOT EVEN HIS SISTERS knew. Nor did Jason. His parents had covered for him his whole life. James was told only because his help was needed for them to attend college.

How did he tell her? How would she react? After what he'd done to her, though, she deserved the truth. He coughed away the tickle. "Maybe, I can't read."

Her eyes bored into him. She didn't believe him.

"I don't understand why, but when I try to read, the letters on the page all dance around."

"But you wrote a note to yer parents. Ye told them in a note yer going to sea. How?"

"If you ask me how to spell something, I can tell you. I have memorized so many words. I can see things in my head, and if I memorize it, it is with me forever."

She shook her head, staring off into the distance.

"My parents thought since I could memorize so well, I should be able to go to college. They sent me to William and Mary, but to help, they sent my brother James too. He was to read the assignments to me, and we would take the same classes. But it was harder than we imagined. He had to study so hard he didn't have time to read to me. I couldn't tell my parents. He wasn't trying to cause a problem, and I hated being cooped up there, anyway. So, I left school, told my parents it wasn't for me."

"I'm sorry, Willie. I convinced myself you just didn't want to meet me."

"Don't feel sorry for me. I do that well enough myself. I had never tasted liquor, plus I had not eaten all day. It didn't take much to get me drunk as Davy's sow. I only had one tankard. Didn't like it much either."

She laughed. "Mr. Cox said it was only one tankard, but I was sure he'd tried to make it less than what it was."

"At least I know my limit, now. One sip! Ha! The stuff tastes so awful. I didn't want them thinking I was…" How was he to admit this?

"That you were less of a man?" So, she understood.

"Aye. Some man. I've a lot of growing to do."

She put her hand over his. "Ye are a man, Willie. A good one. Not every man would come talk. Ye've taken good care of me on this trip. I'm beholden to ye."

Anyone else, including himself, would regard him as a thief. Why not her? "Maybe, I stole from you, put you in danger, all because I can't hold my liquor and wanted to be a man. If we were home, if I could do this over, I would ask permission to court you. I care about you, very much, very deeply. You are more gracious than I deserve." He squeezed her hand as something warm and wet plopped. "Don't cry, Maybe. I can't take that."

"I care about ye, too, Willie Crockett. Very much, very deeply." She sniffed and wiped her forearm across her eyes. "Let's just sit here. We've done enough talkin' fer now."

Willie agreed.

Chapter Twelve

Aphra grew stronger each day. Sarah had grown to care for the girl as one of her own. Aphra pitched in with chores and helped with the younger girls, though she still avoided the males in the family.

Sarah and Joseph went back and forth concerning how to tell her she needed to speak in court. Joseph agreed to wait until the Sabbath since they couldn't start a trial before then. But Monday morning, the trial would begin, with or without her. Joseph stressed that without Aphra's testimony, they would release the man.

Now Sarah must figure the best way to approach this. She took a deep breath and called the child. Patting the settee, she offered a seat. "Aphra, I want to thank you for all the help ye've been giving the past couple days."

"Oh, no, missus, tis me who ought to be thankin' ye. I dunna ken what woulda become of me if he hadn't made me to go spyin' on yer family."

"Spyin? I dinna realize that was the plan. Do ye ken why ye were to spy?"

"No, missus. He never told me. Jist says to listen an' tell 'im what I hear an' see."

That was a new development. She would have to tell Joseph. "Aphra, the man is in jail and canna bother ye more. Unless he gets out."

Her back straightened, and her fingers danced together as fear shone through her eyes. "How would he get out, missus?"

Deep breath. Patience. "He would get out if they do not convict him at his trial."

"When is the trial?"

"On the morrow, in the morning."

Aphra trembled. "Oh, he mustn't, they can never allow him out. He will hunt me down an' kill me. He canna get out, missus."

Sarah took the girl's hands in hers. "I understand. There's one way to ensure he doesn't get out. One way. But only ye can do it."

The girl shuddered. "What must I do?"

"Ye must testify in court to what he did."

The child's eyes grew wide. Her intake of breath broke the silence of the room. "Ye mean, I must tell me story in a court? In front o' everyone? Or live me life knowing he can kill me any time? What choice is that?" She jumped up from the settee, her eyes wild as she paced.

It took everything in Sarah to sit quiet, let Aphra work through the information.

"I know what I must do, I just dunna think I can. Oh, missus! Please help me!"

Sarah opened her arms, the girl threw herself into the embrace. "Yer not alone, Aphra. We're here for ye. Yer not alone." Sarah swayed, rocking the child. At least she was considering what she knew she must do.

THE DAY DAWNED HUMID AND HUMORLESS. JOSEPH KNEW

this would be a day he'd remember. The question was, would he remember it as a victory or tragedy?

Sarah told him at bedtime that Aphra decided to testify though it terrified her. Her determination might be gone by the time they left for court.

They'd held each other, praying for the girl all night. Every time he woke, he sent up another prayer. Now the morn arrived. Ready or not.

The children readied the morning table as if an ordinary day. Aphra sat next to the end near Sarah with Janie across from her and Beth at her side. He'd noticed Jason kept his distance and was thankful for that. When all had eaten and the table was cleared, Joseph pulled out his Bible and read the story God placed on his heart.

He read Second Kings chapter six starting at verse eight, recounting the story of how the king of Aram wanted to kill the prophet Elisha. The prophet's servant could only see the king's army surrounding them, but Elisha prayed that God would open the eyes of the servant to see who stood with them—the angel army. He prayed that Aphra would trust that an angel army surrounded her with protection.

Then Sarah helped the girl get ready. When they left the house, they walked arm in arm a few strides ahead of Joseph so he could protect them without Aphra watching at his back.

The knot in his stomach grew. There was the need to get this animal off the street and away from young women—Joseph's girls each passed before his mind's eye. Bile rose in his throat. Nothing must happen to them.

Then there was Joseph's reputation. If the verdict did not find the monster guilty, this village might not trust him again. It wasn't so much that he would be seen in a bad light, but it could affect his livelihood, which would impact his family. Would they have to leave everything behind to start again? What if Willie returned to find them gone? What would happen? How would he get word to him?

So much depended on the child's testimony. Yet if she were brave enough to speak in court, would it be enough for the judge to believe her and find Eleazar Ferguson guilty?

Upon arrival, Joseph came to his wife's side to get the door for the women. Aphra quavered, and his heart went out to her. He couldn't imagine putting his sweet Beth through this. He offered her a smile as her gaze darted his way. Did she return the smile? If so, it was quick. Perhaps she trusted him, a little. He hoped he'd made some ground.

Joseph guided Aphra and Sarah to their seats, taking his on the other side of his wife so as not to frighten the girl. She was on the end so no one else could sit next to her.

A few minutes later, the prisoner was led in, wearing chains and appearing ragged. Jail had not been comfortable. His waistcoat was wrinkled, and the seam at the top of his sleeve had ripped open a few inches. His breeches were soiled, ratty, and dry mud covered his shoes. It was not the same impression Joseph received at their first meeting, however, it felt more like the man's true self. Dirty.

Joseph caught the prisoner glancing about, figuring he searched for Aphra. He stood, moving to block the view.

Judge Gibson chose that moment to enter.

Everyone stood, Joseph remaining in front of Aphra. He had no idea what to do once required to sit, but he'd protect her as long as he could.

Court was called to order, all taking their seats. Joseph glanced back at Sarah. She'd read his mind, instructing the child to stare at the floor.

"We are present to hear the case against one Eleazar Ferguson on the charge of rape. Will the prisoner stand? How plead you?"

Eleazar stood. "I am innocent, Your Honor."

Though not surprised, Joseph wanted to vomit at the atrocious lie. He had no doubt of Ferguson's guilt. In this and more. It was the *more* part he could not prove.

"The prosecution may call its first witness."

Joseph was named. As Sarah's husband, he was expected to testify to what she knew. Only in an extreme case would they call Sarah herself. Joseph shared how the child had come to his home, how his wife and daughter had learned of her fear of men, and how he saw this for himself when he met her. He told how they offered her a place to stay as she was terrified to return to her place of residence. It wasn't until later, when alone with his wife, that the girl revealed that Eleazar Ferguson had held her captive, misusing and abusing her.

At that point, the defense attorney rose. It disturbed Joseph that Alexander Thornton would deal with the monster, but it was important everyone have access to a defense. There was wrongful prosecution. But nothing was wrongful in this case. So deep was the evil that it felt as if snakes slithered near his feet.

"Master Crockett, you would have us to believe that you have no ulterior motives with your charges?" Where had Thornton arrived with that?

"What ulterior motives might I have?"

"Your son has gone missing, is this true?"

Joseph glanced at Sarah. She looked as stunned as he. "My son has gone to sea."

"Alone?"

What was the man saying? "No one goes to sea alone. It takes a crew to handle a ship."

"I mean, did he sign on alone?"

"To my knowledge, yes, he signed on alone."

The man paced a few steps until he lined himself up in front of the judge. "Didn't his departure coincide with the disappearance of a young girl?"

What did he imply? "I know nothing of anything coinciding."

Now he spun on his heel, pointing at Joseph. "I believe you do! I believe your son attacked and killed the daughter of Daniel O'Malley. And when you found that she was not his only victim, you convinced the girl Aphra White to name a philanthropic gentleman of means, whose only crime was caring for the unfortunate, as the monster. I believe you know the real monster is your son!"

Air ripped from Joseph's lungs; he gasped for breath. His son a monster? This man had not only besmirched his son's good name, but that of the entire family! He grabbed hold of the chair arms to keep himself from flying out at the man. Closing his eyes, he prayed *help*. Breath returned. "You are mistaken. I take umbrage at your accusation and will bring in as many witnesses against—"

"No more questions. You are dismissed." Thornton waved his hand as if batting a mosquito.

Joseph glanced from the judge to the prosecuting attorney. No one would meet his gaze. They should be ashamed. He stood and walked to his chair. If the defense attacked him like this, what would they do to poor Aphra?

❧

SARAH LONGED TO EMBRACE JOSEPH, REMIND HIM THAT none of that was true, that their friends would never believe such nonsense. Instead, she offered her hand. He squeezed it, proof he understood her meaning.

The prosecution lawyer stood. "We call Miss Aphra White to the stand."

The clerk called out, "Miss Aphra White."

But the child didn't stand. Sarah gently rubbed the girl's shoulder.

Aphra caught her gaze, fear freezing her.

"If ye stand, I'll stand with ye. Keep yer eyes on me." Sarah stood, Aphra did the same focused on Sarah.

"Now, we take a few steps. Just a few. Walk with me."

Aphra followed Sarah until they were next to the witness stand.

"Go ahead, sit in the chair. I'm right here, love." Sarah moved to block Eleazar's view so that the child would not have to lay eyes on him.

The defense attorney objected.

Sarah leaned in to speak with the judge. "Your Honor, if ye want to know her story, I must be here. Ye can see I'll not do anything wrong. But the child canna speak here without me. She needs to hold my hand, keep watch of me. Ye can, too, if yer afraid I will do something improper."

The judge thought for a moment. Just as Sarah feared he would send her back to her seat, he gave his decision. "I see no harm in Mistress Crockett standing and holding the child's hand. Your objection is overruled."

The defense lawyer sat, loud enough to shout he was unhappy.

The prosecution lawyer stood. "Miss Aphra, I will stay back here. I will not come close. I ask you to tell us, in your own words, what happened between you and Master Ferguson."

Aphra's eyes darted from the prosecution lawyer to Sarah and back several times. Finally, she opened her mouth, but her voice was less than a whisper. "I hears of a position of maid at—"

"Speak up, child." The judge sounded kind, but Sarah knew he needed to hear this story.

She nodded to Aphra, squeezed her hand and mouthed, "Go on."

The girl cleared her throat. She was louder this time. "I went to his house to ask about a maid's position. Me father died long ago an' me mither had just passed, so's I needed work. He was nice an' hired me. He had me take a room in his house. The first night he came to me room..." Aphra's eyes were growing larger.

Sarah turned to the judge. "This is very hard for her. Please be patient."

Turning back to Aphra, she again squeezed her hand and nodded.

Aphra nodded back. "That were the first night. After that he came most every night. He… hurt me. He burnt his letters on me back with a brand. He often raised his hand to me jist to make me scream. I runned away once, but he sent men to find me. They broke me fingers. They tol' me it would be worse if I ever did that again."

No wonder the child always clutched her hands.

"Last week he says he wants me to be a washerwoman for the Crockett family. He told me to go watch and listen and report to him. But I was too afeared to return." Suddenly, she pleaded to the judge. "Please, do not let him kill me. If ye let him go, he will kill me." She started to sob repeating her plea.

Sarah pulled the girl into her arms as the court murmurs grew. "Shush, ye did good, love. Ye did good."

The judge pounded his gavel, and the courtroom noises subsided. "Does the defense have questions?"

"I have several, but there's no point in asking as the witness is being coached and is too hysterical to give a truthful answer."

"How dare ye!" She wanted to slap his silly face.

The judge pounded harder. Joseph rushed to Sarah's side. "Shush, now. It is all right." He rubbed his hand up and down her back. It soothed, putting her focus back on the child in her arms.

"Order. Order in the court. Master Thornton, you may question this young lady, however, I believe she has been honest. I find her testimony credible."

❧

Eleazar wilted. The slut had done him in. There had to be something to do.

His lawyer leaned in and whispered.

It was a possibility. That old clause could be his loophole. Slim, but it was better than hanging.

"Does the defendant wish to make a statement before I pronounce my verdict?"

Alexander Thornton stood and motioned for Eleazar to join him. "Your Honor, it is evident that you have decided. This is a capital offense; there is but one sentence. One, but for this exception." He met Eleazar's gaze and nodded. All he had to do was read the Latin. And not get struck down by some invisible hand.

"I request the Benefit of Clergy, your honor."

The room gasped as if one giant person inhaled all at once. Had the tears swayed everyone? What was he saving his life to?

The judge repeated, "Benefit of Clergy? Then you may come forth. Bailiff, bring the Bible, opened to the passage."

The bailiff brought the book, opened to Psalm 51, and stood beside him. His hands were manacled so Eleazar had to use both as he guided his fingers under the words. He read aloud in Latin. "*Miserere mei, Deus, secundum misericordiam tuam.*" Be gracious to me, O God, according to Your lovingkindness.

At the close, the judge pounded his gavel. Eleazar glared at the man who so proudly sat in judgment over him. How did he dare to sit there? What right had he to sit there? He was only one of the little creatures, fortunate enough to breathe the same air as himself. No one was in the position to sit in judgment over him. This was a farce.

"Defense attorney, join your client at the bench."

Eleazar waited for Alexander Thornton to join him, his stomach roiling, his rage mounting with each pulse.

"This court finds you guilty of rape. This is a capital offense, punishable by hanging. However, as you have requested Benefit of Clergy and proved your request, you will not be hanged."

His attorney patted him on the back. The toady touched him. He shrugged.

"Instead, you will be placed in the pillory for one month. You'll be released to the jail at night. And you will be branded with R on your right cheek as this is the only time you may claim Benefit of Clergy."

Rage exploded from Eleazar's belly to his hands. He lunged

for the judge. Though tentacles grabbed at his arms and legs, he kept striving for the man's neck. He would kill him. He would kill him. "Leave me go! I will kill him!"

JOSEPH STOOD BETWEEN THE WOMEN AND THE MAD ANIMAL dragged from the courtroom. If anyone entertained a doubt concerning this monster's guilt, Eleazar Ferguson's actions now wiped the doubt clean. Joseph remained vigilant until the cries came from outside the building. Then he turned to see how Sarah and Aphra fared.

Sarah held Aphra in her arms. They both cried.

Aphra lifted her face. "They'll not be hanging him?"

Sarah wiped tears from the girl's cheeks. "No, they canna as he claimed Benefit of Clergy, the old law to save him from death. God dinna strike him down when he read the Holy Word when he asked for God to be gracious, so he canna be hung this time. But he can only make the claim once, that is why the branding. I dunna understand how he can still be living after such blasphemy—those holy words in that vile mouth, but he'll not be coming for you ever again. Yer safe with us."

Joseph expected her to return to Sarah's embrace. Instead, she lifted her gaze to him. "Thank ye, sir, for believin' me."

He barely heard her words, only but a breath, but he knew the healing had started. Perhaps one day she could speak with him like his daughters because, as he now realized, he felt protective enough to be her father.

Chapter Thirteen

aybe and Willie returned to the ship. They'd been gone a few hours, so she checked in on Cookie, hoping his headache had subsided.

The galley remained neat and tidy, just the way he kept it, but she found no sign of the sweet old man. Maybe remembered that he kept his pallet with the stores "to keep precious food portions from landing in some gluttonous bellies." She made her way to the larder. He slept on his cot.

She thought to leave him to his snores, but something stopped her. She felt his head and pulled back. He was feverish. Nearly on fire.

She raced to find Willie. "Go get the surgeon and the boatswain. Cookie is sick." Then to the galley where she grabbed a basin of water and rags. The water was cool, less than room temperature. *Please let it help.* She dabbed Cookie's neck and face.

He moaned; his eyes fluttered. "Och, 'tis ye, boy. Whatcha doin'?"

"Ye've got a fever, Cookie."

He started to sit but grabbed his head and lay back.

"Jist stay still. I'll take care o' ye."

He didn't like that idea but was too weak to fight. She continued applying the cool water and watched him close his eyes, drifting again.

"What's the problem here?"

The surgeon and boatswain arrived, the former pushing his way to Cookie's bedside. "What are you dabbing on him?"

"Water, sir."

"Good. Now let me see what's what."

The surgeon woke Cookie and made him open his mouth. Using a candle with a reflector, he looked in, shaking his head. "Your throat's mighty sore, isn't it, Cookie?"

The old man nodded his head.

Turning to Maybe, he changed his tone. "Have you had the chicken pox?"

"Aye, when I was little."

"Then you can stay and care for him. Boatswain, we need to quarantine the ship. We can't let this get off. Expect it to go through the crew. Anyone who has not had the chicken pox will get it. If they were with Cookie when he was exposed, they'll be showing up with symptoms in the next few hours. Those who were not exposed and never had them, will experience the fever in approximately a fortnight. You must be making plans. The older a person is, the worse the consequences are. Children generally get over it, but folks like Cookie can have a hard time. You mustn't sail until this is done. They must stay out of the sun." He patted the boatswain's arm. "I'll see what I have for his pain. The spots should pop in the next twenty-four hours." He left the room.

The boatswain appeared stricken.

Cookie moaned.

Maybe resumed dabbing him with the wet rag.

CHICKEN POX? HOW WAS THE SURGEON SO SURE? SAM

Johnson's head swam with all the possibilities, none good. What if it were smallpox? Had the whole crew been exposed? Meanwhile, how did he feed the crew? Quarantine the whole ship? That part just sank in. For more than a month? He turned to the door. The Stewart lad stood, having heard the whole thing. He grabbed him by the shoulder. "Mr. Stewart, have you had the chicken pox?"

The boy shook his head.

Great. "Then you must leave this room. Go. Do not tell anyone. They'll all be finding out soon enough, but we do not want a panic before we form a plan. Do you understand?"

He nodded, his eyes a little too big.

"Your friend will be fine. He's already had chicken pox. You can only get them once. It's the ones who haven't that need our concern. While you are helping, start praying."

"Aye, sir." He paused. "I've already been exposed. And I know nothing about cooking, though I'm willing to help. What if I help with Cookie? Maybe is most experienced in the galley. Could... could he cook and I help here?"

Sam glanced from Maybe at Cookie's bedside and back to the boy. "You're a good man, Mr. Stewart. Thank you. We may need to accept your offer but not at this moment. Let me talk with the master and the surgeon first. You can wait on deck." He guided the boy up the hatch.

Before making his way to the master, Sam went to his cabin. There he knelt by his bed. He had prayed for this voyage, prayed for each onboard. He prayed for every voyage. And he'd pray for this one again.

But he'd never had to pray so hard on a voyage in all his born days.

❧

WILLIE STOOD BY THE RAIL, SENDING PRAYERS OUT INTO the cloudy sky and waiting to hear what to do. The plan scared him. He did not want to get sick. Plus, the boatswain's face told him something more. If he were only concerned about a childhood malady, he wouldn't have appeared so… grimly frightened. That was it, grimly frightened. Did he not believe the surgeon?

Plus, how could the surgeon diagnose chicken pox without spots? What if it wasn't chicken pox? What if Maybe was exposed? Perhaps the surgeon knew she'd already been exposed and figured she'd be less worried about something she'd experienced.

He didn't want Maybe sick. She'd suffered enough at his hands. Relieving her at Cookie's bedside not only made sense for all concerned, he owed her that. And if he got sick, well, he deserved it.

❧

SAM JOHNSON AND THE SURGEON GATHERED IN THE master's quarters. Listening again, as the surgeon explained, Sam had to ask. "How do you know it's not smallpox?"

"I don't."

"What do you mean?" The master had a growl to his voice that matched the one Sam held at bay.

"I mean, I'm preparing for the worst and hoping for the best. The worst is it turns out to be smallpox. I'll quarantine us on this ship for the next month and a half until it's run its course. The best case is chicken pox. If the rest of the crew has had it and Cookie improves, we'll be underway in about two weeks. There are several varying possibilities between these two scenarios. Part of the good news is I had chicken pox as a boy, so I won't get it again. If that is what we fight, I can treat the crew without becoming ill, and you will not lose a surgeon. Have either of you had the chicken pox?"

The master nodded, but Sam shook his head.

"Then, Boatswain Johnson, you have things to prepare. You'll want someone who has had the chicken pox and train him to do your job until you are better." The surgeon began to pace —four steps out, four steps back. "The worst, if it is chicken pox, will run its course in about a week once it hits, but you must stay out of the sun another week, or until the scabs dry and no pox erupt." He sighed. "If it is smallpox, we must be vigilant so as not to expose the town. I suggest going out a mile to sea, using a jolly boat to go to shore if the need arises. I'll work a plan with the town. They can leave needed supplies at the dock." He paused, capturing their gazes. "Understand, with either possibility, there's likely to be deaths."

"With chicken pox?" Sam's pulse increased.

"Aye, it is easier on children, but on older adults chicken pox can be brutal. There are many complications to consider. You may need new crew members before this is over. If we stay quarantined, staying from the town not only keeps them safe, it should remove the fear of getting the disease because of joining the crew once this is over."

"You've given us plenty to think about."

"And do," Sam added.

The surgeon stopped pacing. "It is a lot. Things come to mind even now. But you'll want to prepare the crew. I'll leave it in your hands. I must go to my patient before I've more." With that, he left Sam with the hardest part of the ordeal to date— telling the crew.

❧

WILLIE SPELLED MAYBE AN HOUR AFTER THE SURGEON left. She worried that he was unnecessarily exposing himself, but he assured her it was the boatswain's orders. They needed her in the galley. No one else knew Cookie's business.

So, now she was the cook.

She'd not imagined the voyage like this. But what she imagined had little in common with reality.

She realized something—she mustn't cook as well as Cookie.

The crew needed to eat, but they must want Cookie to return. Otherwise someone might wonder why she cooked like a girl. The leap was too easy.

So, she planned based on the stores available. When Cookie was lucid, she questioned him, but tried not to bother the old man too much.

The first meal, dinner, turned out acceptable. Maybe felt she'd passed some examination. The next meal came easier. Soon, the men accepted her.

In the meantime, more crew succumbed with the fever. A few days after spots appeared. The surgeon confirmed it was chicken pox, not smallpox. A lightness lifted the spirits of sick and well members alike. There was less fear, only annoyance.

Then Cookie took a turn.

He hadn't been improving like the others. Though he didn't improve, he hadn't gotten worse. Until the end of the second week.

Willie had no signs, keeping a constant vigil with the old man. Maybe loved him more for that.

Whenever there was a moment, she'd steal away to check on Cookie and find Willie keeping him as comfortable as possible. This day something was different. Cookie's fever spiked, his spots appeared angry and red. "Has the surgeon seen him, Willie?"

Willie shook his head and then pinched the bridge of his nose. "Ah, no. He comes a little later."

"I think he needs to see this. She laid her hand on Willie's shoulder only to pull back. The heat told her he'd caught it. "Oh, Willie. Ye should've said something."

"What was there to say? We all knew what was coming. Cookie needs me. I can't get him any sicker."

"But ye can get sicker. Ye will. I'm getting the surgeon."

She heard him try to restrain her, but his weak attempt only made her hurry that much faster.

※

WILLIE'S HEAD HURT LIKE NEVER BEFORE. HE COULDN'T remember having a sniffle, let alone a childhood malady. So this was how sick felt.

Heat emanated off him, but his body shivered as if he were in a snowstorm. His eyes burned, his head pounded, and his throat was raw. Still, he wouldn't leave Cookie. The old man was in worse shape. It had been awhile since Cookie opened his eyes and recognized who sat with him. For two weeks, Willie bathed him in cool water, cleaned his cot, sponged his pox, keeping him as comfortable as he knew how. And for two weeks, Cookie had thanked him, scolded him, and shared secrets of his life. Willie had grown to love the curmudgeon. He wouldn't give up on him now.

Standing, he grabbed the basin. With more water, he might bathe Cookie's fever, possibly lower it. He managed two steps toward the galley when the world began to spin. Willie reached for the doorway, but his hand missed. He sensed himself falling, falling, then—

※

MAYBE RETURNED WITH THE SURGEON TO FIND WILLIE unconscious, blocking the door. She knelt next to him. Who did she help first? Willie needed immediate help, but Cookie might be dying.

The surgeon touched Willie's head, *tsked,* and stepped over him to Cookie.

Maybe remained with him. The basin lay under his body. She tugged it free and filled it. The tepid water felt cold next to the heat projecting off Willie.

He appeared so long just lying there, though he'd filled out from all the work he'd done. Willie was a tall man. She couldn't move him, so she stooped and bathed his head and neck where he was.

His eyes fluttered. "Maybe? What happened?"

"I dunno. Found you like this."

He tried to move, but his hands grasped to his head. "Never had a headache like this."

The surgeon noticed him moving. "Stay where you are. We'll get you help. First, we need to help Cookie. Maybe, I need you over here."

She stepped past Willie to the surgeon.

He leaned in, his voice low next to Maybe's ear. "Cookie won't be with us much longer. His spots are infected; it is in his blood. There isn't anything I can do. Can you stay with him? I'll get help to carry Mr. Stewart to his bunk."

Maybe nodded. No, not Cookie. He had been so kind to her, helping her to understand when things were strange. Giving her a place to belong. Next to losing her mother, father, and sister, this was the hardest parting. She wiped her sleeve across her eyes.

The surgeon patted her shoulder. "It's never easy." He went for help for Willie.

Three hours later, Cookie was gone. Mr. Cox and Mr. Hawkins came to wrap his body and remove it. Since the crew was quarantined, they had the burial at sea that evening. Any of the crew not stuck in bed attended, as sunlight had faded to twilight by then.

Two days later, Mr. Swain was given the same service as Cookie.

Of the original thirty-five crew members, only twelve had never had the chicken pox. Of those twelve, they buried four. Maybe cried for the first two, Cookie and Mr. Swain. Then, she had no more tears. Plus she was too worried about Willie to think. His fever spiked more than once until the spots appeared. If his fever broke, and he could keep from scratching, he should come through.

Maybe prayed. A part of her felt guilty, not worthy to bring a plea before the God of the universe. But she didn't care what happened to her. Every time she placed another wet rag on his head, she prayed. Every time she gave him broth or a drink, she prayed. Perhaps she wasn't worthy enough to be heard, but she determined to be persistent enough not to be ignored.

Within a day after his fever broke, Willie was sitting up on his cot and being his old self, or a weaker version. He was ravenous. Maybe saved extra for him as she continued to cook for the men. In five days, he returned to normal, except for her reminding him not to scratch. His expression reflected how badly he wanted to. She remembered the dreadful itching and could only imagine how much worse it was for a grown man. He took over duties below deck as he was still to stay out of the sun until the spots had finished scabbing.

Several days later, Maybe found him talking with two men. They whispered. Something serious from what Maybe could tell. It came to a stop as she wandered up to them.

The others sauntered off.

"What was that all about?"

He shook his head. "Ah, not anything to worry about. They've got an idea. It's just not a good one."

"An idea about what?"

Willie scanned their surroundings as if making sure they were alone. "They think since we are down four men, we need to impress from the town before we sail."

Impress? "Oh, Willie, yer not goin' along with that, are ye?"

"No! Of course not. But we need the hands. We were just making it work with who we had. To be short four is not good."

"What's Boatswain Johnson say?"

Willie looked at the floor, twisting his toe on the floorboard. "He doesn't know. You know how sick he was, just now pulling though and staying in his quarters out of the sun. I doubt the men even brought it up to him. I'm sure he would not approve. He's not that type of man."

"On that we agree. We need to tell him."

He grabbed her arm. "We can't! Think about it. If they are the kind to impress someone, they won't hesitate to take it out on anyone who gets them in trouble. You can imagine what Boatswain Johnson would do for punishment."

She pulled free. "If ye won't, I will."

"Maybe, you can't. They will know it was you. Promise me you won't go up there."

She clamped her mouth shut.

"Maybe, I know what I'm talking about. Promise me, for your own good."

She stared at the floor, hoping he wouldn't get too technical. "I won't go up there."

He relaxed, accepting her word.

She hoped he wouldn't be too angry when he found out what she planned.

❧

MR. HAWKINS BROUGHT HIS DINNER. SMELLED PRETTY good. Maybe did well with today's catch.

Sam told Mr. Hawkins to set the tray on the bureau and thanked him. A moment later he was alone.

He felt like his old self, but the surgeon insisted he stay out of the sun until every spot scabbed and no more showed. Other than wanting to scratch himself to death, he was fine. Well, the sun would eventually set. Come nightfall he'd go on deck, see how things progressed. A reflex, he caught himself, hand raised to scratch his chin, and grunted. At least he could pick at his food without fuss.

He moved his plate and noticed a folded piece of foolscap. Opening it, he recognized the handwriting. Maybe's.

A few crew members are talking impressment.

So, some think they know better, huh? Well, that tears it. He would definitely have a talk with the crew. They hadn't thoroughly considered it or they would understand impressment would not work. Maybe was too young to understand. Or perhaps it was fear of the word. But he was a good lad.

Aye, he would talk with the crew, but with care. Maybe delivered the message in secret. No one would find out.

AT TWILIGHT, WORD PASSED AMONG THE CREW FOR everyone to meet on the main deck. No one was feverish or bedfast. All could attend. Willie joined the men standing around the master and boatswain.

He spotted Maybe across from him, not making eye contact. Had she done something? He told her not to, and she promised!

"Men, according to the surgeon, we should be able to resume our voyage in three more days. That will give time for me to go with Mr. Hawkins to town by jolly boat to make arrangements for new crew members. We will speak with those interested and choose the best. As we've been cautious in our dealings with the town to keep them from getting the chicken pox, they've sent their appreciation. Perhaps you were unaware of extra food stores we were allowed to purchase. Because we have been fair, they are treating us fair."

Willie was now sure she'd talked to Boatswain Johnson, but he never said the word "impress."

"What if no one signs? What do we do then?" It was one of the men who'd been talking to him that afternoon.

"I don't believe we have a problem. Are you worried?" So, the boatswain would make someone else say the word.

"Aye, we're worried. Why all the fuss? Why not just grab the ones we want and bring 'em along?"

The boatswain cleared his throat. "Not only is it wrong, it's foolish. We don't work that way on the *Frances Pearl*. Anyone brought forcibly abroad will be returned to their port, even if it means losing time and money. This ship does not impress. Is that clear?"

The "aye, sirs" floated around the circle. Willie caught Maybe's glance. So, she was behind it. He could see it in her eyes.

She lied to him.

"Dismissed."

The crew went in various directions. Willie made a beeline to Maybe, dragging her to the rail. "So, your promise doesn't mean a thing, huh?"

She pulled her arm from him. "Willie, I promised I would not go up to see him. I didn't go."

He sighed. "Then what did you do?"

"I sent a note."

Chapter Fourteen

Eleazar Ferguson stared at the closed drapes darkening his parlor. The pain and humiliation of the past month repeatedly played through his mind. He heard every jeer as he stood helpless in the pillory, felt every piece of refuse that smacked him in the face—the face that now bore the brand of the rapist on his right cheekbone. Sometimes at night he woke himself screaming, still smelling the burnt flesh. His cheek remained tender. The R prominently visible in his mirror. The mirror he shattered moments after returning home.

Not one person in that courtroom had the right to stand in judgment of him. That girl was his property. He could do with her as he pleased. He'd paid for her, given her a home and food. She owed him. She did this. His hand crept his face, lightly tracing the rough scar tissue protruding from the hated brand.

What good were fine clothes and money and power when everyone could see his mangled face and judge him, without cause?

He rose to his feet and paced. Even his faithful cook and housekeeper took to the hills. Once he was convicted, she was sure everyone would think her virtue besmirched as well. Ha! Like he'd even go near the cow. The only reason he'd kept her on was that she did her job. Now he had to fend for himself. Who would cook his meals? Bring his tea? Clean his house? Do his laundry?

Who cared about him?

Oh, he'd make them care. They would care about what they had done to Eleazar Ferguson.

They would wish they cared sooner.

❧

THE THUNDERING AT THE DOOR COINCIDED WITH THE BIG bell in the center of town clanging.

"Stay here, love. I'll go."

Joseph's mind was a fog, having been roused from a deep sleep. Why the clamor?

He left Sarah in their bed and pulled on his breeches, tucking in his nightshirt while stubbing his toe on the way to the stairs. Bethy peeked out of the girls' room. "Stay there, girl. I'm going."

At the door, he pulled it open. Thomas Miller stood, frantic, fist poised mid pound. "Fire! At Judge Gibson's home! Gathering all the help we can get!"

"Let me get my boys. Go to the next house. We're on our way."

Joseph ran back upstairs for his shoes. As he passed, he pounded on the door for the boys. Jason opened the door. "Wake John. Then go to Joseph Louis's house and get him. There's a fire at the judge's house."

Sarah was up, her wrapper tied about her. "I'll get the girls. We can help."

"No, stay here. We may need you to feed and house people, depending on how bad this gets. The Gibson's have several close neighbors. The fire might spread. I've got to leave." He brushed a token kiss across her forehead and ran out the bedroom door. "Boys, let's go!" Tearing down the stairs, he heard Jason and

John fast behind him. He didn't turn back, trusting them to follow.

Flames climbed into the night sky. He raced harder, spotting the constable on his way. "Did everyone get out?"

"No idea. They may be gone somewhere, no one has seen anyone."

Joseph covered his mouth, holding in his thoughts. Then another thought took hold. "The neighbors, they are all out of their homes?"

"Aye, they are safe, though it looks as if the Turners may be needing a place to stay until they can rebuild."

Joseph and his sons joined the fight to save as many homes as possible. The Gibson and Turner homes were a total loss. Two other homes had minor damage but were repairable. The sun shone bright as they stomped the last spark.

He glanced around at the tired, dirty men. Each wore a mask of dread at the next job, searching through the remains of the Gibson home. But it must be done.

Joseph stretched his back, then pulled his sons close. "I don't want you in there. I don't know what we'll find. Perhaps nothing, but if we find someone I don't want you with us. Understand? Go home, tell your mother that the Turners will be needing a place to stay. She might find room for the boys at our house."

His sons nodded. Jason opened his mouth like he might argue, but John put his arm across the boy's shoulder and turned him toward home.

Henry Waddington, looking nothing like his tidy self, and Thomas Miller led the small group of men into the charred remains. Wood was the quickest way to build; it was plentiful. But it was susceptible to fire. A shiver ran up Joseph's spine. He should have used the more expensive bricks to build his home.

Nearly everything inside the home was combustible, leaving very little to look through. The bricks from the chimney still stood. Wrought iron and copper kitchen items lay about with broken crockery and cracked china. The fire had burned the floorboards and ceiling so that the second story crashed on the first. Charred bedroom furniture lay scattered amidst the first floor living quarters. Things that might have been parts of beds also lay broken and burnt, without signs of bodies.

Until they found the scorched remnants of a large brass bed. "Over here."

Joseph followed the voice. He didn't want to see what he knew he would.

A charred body reclined just under the bars of the headboard.

The late Judge Robert Gibson.

He didn't know whether to cry or vomit.

❧

SARAH DIVIDED THE GIRLS INTO GROUPS. BETH AND MARY worked on getting the boys' room aired with fresh linens on the beds. Martha and Janie helped her in the kitchen, making enough food to feed a British battalion. What was not needed at her house to feed guests might be taken to help others. Besides, Janie and Martha were due for another cooking lesson. If she focused on that, she would not worry so much about her men or her neighbors. Worry. She wasn't supposed to do that. She sent up a prayer and kept busy.

A little before noon, Jason and John came home.

"Where's yer father?"

They each kissed her cheek.

John snatched a honey cake. "He's fine, Mama. The fire is out, but the Turners lost their home too. They all got out, though. Da says to make a place for their boys, that they can stay with us."

Sarah smacked his hand as he reached for a second treat. "Leave some for the others. What about the Gibson family? Are they all right?"

Jason stared at the honey cakes. "There's been no sign of them. Da is hoping no one was home. They planned to search what was left of the house. That's why he sent us home."

"Oh, how awful. I hope they were all away. Well, go ahead, Jason, ye can have one. Bet ye boys could use a good meal. Go wash up, and I'll set ye some plates."

They grunted their male sounds and grabbed the towel on their way out to the well. She still thought of John as her little boy, but blond and stocky, he was more man than boy now. He'd been spending time at the home of a girl from church. He didn't like to speak of it, most likely due to the teasing he'd get, but she was sure he was courting the lass.

Thinking of the girl brought her back to the fire and the Gibson family. They were also friends from church. So terrible! They might have died in such a horrific way. How did the fire start? If no one was home, what could have sparked it? The last storm was two weeks ago.

She shook her head and returned to work. Joseph would be along shortly, probably bringing guests. She needed to be ready.

AFTER LOCATING THE JUDGE, JOSEPH AND THE MEN DOUBLE checked the ruins for anyone else. Only Judge Gibson was home when the fire took hold. Most likely he died in his sleep. Joseph prayed it was true.

It took time to remove the body, as carefully as possible, and to make arrangements. Someone needed to locate the rest of the Gibson family and break the news. Someone needed to find housing for them on their return. And someone needed to find lodging for the Turner family while they decided if to rebuild. Joseph volunteered to take in the Turner sons. The Turners were good friends. They could take the whole family if his boys slept in the parlor on the floor. But before he made the offer, other neighbors stepped up. Helping lessened the pain.

Joseph headed for home, with the two teens in tow. Their ages fell between John and Jason, so it worked well. Sarah would have food ready for them, and his boys would see that the Turner lads felt welcomed.

As they entered, that little voice in his heart reminded him how blessed he was. Everything was as he predicted. The food was ready, and his boys showed their guests where to get cleaned, giving him a moment to take Sarah in his arms, hold her like he never had to let her go.

She didn't fight him. Instead she held on, sending strength and love to him, refilling him with what had been drained.

He kissed the top of her head. "I am filthy and need to bathe. It was… oh, love, it was not good." He shook his head, remembering. "I had to send the boys home. I couldn't allow them stuck with that vision in their minds for the rest of their days."

She pulled back. "Then ye found the Gibsons?" She shuddered speaking the words.

"Only Robert. He was home alone and asleep. He never knew what happened."

"What did happen, Joseph? How did the fire start? We haven't had a lightning storm in over two weeks. I can't understand."

Joseph had been so busy putting out the fire and looking for… he hadn't gotten to that point. He released her, starting to mull her words. "I don't know if we'll ever know. The damage is extensive; who can tell where it started? Perhaps the cat knocked something over, or Robert smoked his pipe in bed. He was alone in the house. He might have tried that without his wife to tell him no."

Sarah chewed her lip. That meant she gnawed on an idea. He let her put it together without interruption.

She walked away a few steps, then faced him. "What if it was not an accident? What if it were deliberately set?"

"Murder?"

She nodded. "Aye, only perhaps it was arson. And the arsonist thought everyone out of the house?"

Joseph shook his head. "I can't believe we have someone in our community who would do such a thing." Yet the thought wouldn't shake from his brain.

"Joseph, our community isn't the most likely place to find the person. We have the area by the docks. People there who've been on the wrong side of Judge Gibson's rulings. I don't want to blame anyone without proof. But I would keep my eyes and ears open."

He hated it, but Sarah could be right. Yet who?

❦

IT WAS THE FIRST RESTFUL SLEEP HE'D HAD IN OVER A month. Oh, he'd heard the clang, but it only brought him a smile, and he went back to sleep.

Waking, he stretched in his bed, the reality of living without assistance falling on him like bricks.

But he'd have his revenge.

Eleazar Ferguson sat on the edge of his bed and reached for the pencil and the book on his nightstand. Perusing the journal page, he found the name Judge Robert Gibson and drew a line through it and smiled. Some weight of the bricks fell away. They would learn the price of crossing Eleazar Ferguson.

He inhaled the new day and stood. Might as well get the morning underway.

Downstairs, he started the hot water for his tea. He was civilized when left to his own devices. Tea, a bun, a leisurely morning stroll. His hand made its way to his right cheek. No, no more morning strolls. At least not leisurely.

The lack of food in the pantry reminded him he needed to purchase more. That required going into the world. He was willing to pay someone to make his purchases, but there was no one willing to take his money. Even minions like the O'Malley creature avoided him. And fear was losing its touch. Now it put distance between them and a branded rapist.

The bricks returned heavier than before.

There was nothing else to do about his food situation. He must go out. Would the shopkeeps sell to him?

He pulled his suit out and gave it a thorough brushing before getting dressed. Next he located a linen scarf and wrapped it around his face, tying it under his chin. Though it would be a warm day, he would cover his cheek.

Downstairs, he topped it off with his hat and carried his walking stick. At the door, he paused. He was Eleazar Ferguson. These people, these creatures, should feel privileged to serve him. He had money and power. Well, perhaps his power was tarnished at the moment, but it would return. He would see to it. Anyone getting in his way would learn firsthand. He would not grovel. He'd done that once as a boy and learned the hard way. The feeble of the earth are steppingstones for the powerful to tread.

And he was powerful. He would show them.

Eleazer Ferguson pulled open the door, tugged at his cuffs, and stepped into reality. No bricks toppled him. He strode for the market.

❧

Beth climbed the bluff and found a place under the sweet gum. The house was too full of maleness. She needed a quiet place to be alone.

Funny, she'd forgotten how boisterous it could be with five brothers under the roof. Bringing the Gibson lads into their home made her miss her brothers who were gone. Joseph Louis still came by, but he was married now. Even with his wife as a new sister, it was different. They were starting their own family. James, away at school, rarely even remembered to send a letter. He always kept his nose in a book. But the one she missed the most was Willie. Not that she loved him best, but they were the closest. He understood and never pushed her.

Perhaps that's why she enjoyed coming here so much, his place. He told her when he stood on the bluff, the wind cleared his head of everything demanding his attention. Then he could come back, more focused.

For her, though, it wasn't a matter of focus or too many things vying for attention. She inhaled the peace of the place. Watching the birds, finding cloud pictures, listening to the stories told by the breeze. Peace.

It brought her closer to Willie.

She tried to imagine his life at this moment. What did he look like now? Had he filled out, becoming more manly? Did he have a beard, and was it as curly and wild as his hair? She laughed at that one. "Oh, Willie. I sure miss you. Come home soon, brother. It's not the same without you."

Her laugh turned to a solitary tear.

Please come home, Willie.

Chapter Fifteen

True to his word, the boatswain got the new crew members on board. They resumed their voyage toward Ireland. One of the new crew was an experienced cook, making Maybe grateful. He wasn't as grandfatherly as Cookie, but a good cook, and he allowed Maybe to help. But something about the rolling of the ship, different from sitting at anchor, made her stomach want to roll along.

She excused herself to the deck to stand at the rail. The wind in her face helped. Did she pick up the chicken pox even though she'd had them?

She shook her head. No, not likely. She'd be busted out with spots by now. She was merely worn from the draining work while quarantined. Now lifted, life went back to normal so her body relaxed.

True, she didn't sleep well. Willie pouted, still put out with her for sending the note. She only promised to not go to the boatswain's cabin. She kept her word. Well, perhaps not in the spirit he intended, but what should she have done? And no repercussions.

Or had she missed seeing any? Would he tell her if she did?

Every time they had an understanding, something made her

bubble burst. He said that if they were back home, he'd be asking to court her. On her part, she'd say yes. She loved him. At times she could still taste his kiss, feel his touch. It wasn't fair that it was wrong. She wanted him. She wanted to be his wife. She desired that more than returning to Ireland.

Should she stay on with the crew? Now that was a foolhardy thought. She'd have to continue pretending to be a boy. Eventually something would give her away.

In truth, she was surprised she'd lasted this long. She thanked Willie for that. He was great at keeping her secret, helping her when needed.

When needed. Something about that phrase made her think. Something she'd forgotten? Something she should have done? Something…

Then she knew. She knew what hadn't happened.

Oh, no! Oh, please, Dear God, no! Not that! Oh, no!

She wrapped her arms about her waist and vomited over the rail.

⁂

WILLIE ARRIVED ON DECK IN TIME TO SEE MAYBE lose her breakfast over the side. He was still angry with her for not keeping her word, though she would argue that point. But he didn't want her to be ill.

He raced to her side. "Maybe, let me help." He pushed her hair off her face, then glanced about to make sure they weren't seen. It's wasn't exactly the thing men did for each other.

When she was done, he guided her to a barrel, had her sit while he went for a cup of water. Then he wiped her face with his sleeve while she sipped. "What's the matter? Have you gotten the chicken pox? Didn't you already have them?"

She shook her head and stared at her feet. "No, not that." She sighed. "I lost me sea legs while at anchor too long. Just give me a wee bit, I'll be right as rain."

It was possible she told the truth. Nah, there was more to it. Perhaps she'd worked too hard during the quarantine and needed to rest. Provided no more storms, they should reach Ireland in two months. That wasn't long. She could rest and be herself there. And he'd find her sister, like he promised. He might even stay beyond that.

That was a strange thought. He'd never considered staying beyond what it took to find Maybe's sister.

Yet saying goodbye was not a notion he wanted to ponder. His hand tucked her hair behind her ears, unbidden. No, he couldn't say goodbye to her. They may disagree at times, but he'd rather disagree with her than anyone else in the world.

❧

THE DAYS FLEW BY TO BECOME WEEKS, AND THE WEEKS added up to a month. Now they'd neared the two-month stage. Ireland was but a few days away. Maybe's heart pounded with each second it took to draw closer to home. Not only because she longed for Bantry Bay but also because she knew her body was changing. If she could tell, how long before someone else noticed?

She scanned the horizon for anything resembling land from her perch high above the deck.

She'd been able to resume her duties at top once the new cook was employed. She still missed Cookie, but he'd have been the first to notice her secret. Would he have told on her or protected her? Would he have judged her?

So many questions filled her brain. She hadn't told Willie. She wasn't sure she would. He wanted to go back to sea. He only promised to help find her sister so she wouldn't be alone. She had no idea what he would do if her sister were dead.

No idea what she would do, either.

That was a possibility. No, she couldn't go there. Not unless there was no choice. Her sister was her only hope. Without other proof, she believed her sister lived.

A swell raised the bow of the ship and brought it down making her stomach jump into her throat. She gripped the rail and hung on for the ride. Things swayed so much more up here. It was a random occurrence and the smooth sailing resumed, but Maybe felt a tad swoonish. She backed up to the mast and slid down, putting her head between her knees.

The sensation passed, and she returned to her job, adjusting as the boatswain called out, waiting for directions as needed. An hour later, her turn was finished. Time to come down. She'd done her shift and, after another touch of lightheadedness, she was ready to be on something sturdier. If she slipped off to her bunk for a few minutes, that might help. If she got caught, though, she'd be branded as lazy. But if she didn't get a wee bit of rest, she'd—"Oh!"

Woozy again, she missed a step on the Jacob ladder. Panicked, she grabbed at the wet rope. She missed, swinging headfirst.

Then everything went black.

⚜

WILLIE CAME OUT OF THE WHEELHOUSE AND SPOTTED Maybe. She hung upside down from the Jacob's ladder. Her right foot remained tangled in the rope. She swung helpless. His heart raced as he ran to her, sure she'd smacked her head on the mast. She appeared unconscious.

He shimmied the ladder to her, turning her body and right foot in the opening so he could put her over his shoulder. Once he had her there, he freed her foot and brought her down, laying her on the deck. Was she alive? Yes, she breathed. He did too.

"Bring him to my cabin." The boatswain stood over Willie's shoulder.

He scooped her in his arms, carrying her to the boatswain's

room and placed her on the bed. Seconds later, the surgeon pushed him out of the way.

Willie backed into a corner, watching as terror crept up his throat. Was she all right? Would she be all right? What if the surgeon's examination revealed—

"Clear the room."

The surgeon saw something.

Willie's pulse pounded at his temple.

The boatswain shoved the crewmen out, closing the door before returning to the bed.

"You can move over there, Sam." The surgeon pointed over by Willie as he pulled a blanket over Maybe.

The boatswain moved. "Why? What's going on?"

The surgeon glanced up. "We have a young lady here." Then his eyes bored into Willie. "But I think you already knew that, didn't you, Mr. Stewart?"

Boatswain Johnson glanced from the surgeon to Willie. "What do you mean?"

"I mean crewman Maybe is a female. Not only that, she is with child."

Willie watched the boatswain's face changed colors from white to red to purple as something dawned in his own brain. Clarity and confusion fought inside him as he tried to put meaning into the words.

Suddenly the boatswain gripped Willie by the throat, shoving him into the wall. "You did this! What have you done? I should kill you!"

Willie struggled for breath. The thought that Maybe carried his baby sank in. He was ready to let the boatswain have his way. He deserved to die.

Spots formed in front of his eyes. His hands slapped the wall —he couldn't raise them.

"Stop! Don't hurt him!" Maybe's voice.

The blockage lifted, air flowed to Willie's lungs while he slid down the wall. Someone lifted his chin, the surgeon's face came into focus. "You'll live, though you might regret it."

The surgeon stepped aside.

Boatswain Johnson stood by the door, his hand on the knob. "I will flog you within an inch of your miserable life!"

"No! Don't! Please!"

Maybe, let him, I deserve it.

"And why not?"

"Because everyone will know me secret if you do."

❦

SAM JOHNSON PEERED AT MAYBE, NOW REALIZING WHAT stared him in the face this whole time. Not a boy, but a young woman. "What would you have me do? He took advantage of you."

"Might I speak privately with you, sir?" He… she looked so small, fragile.

Sam glanced over at the surgeon who nodded and helped Mr. Stewart to his feet before guiding him out the door.

Sam waited until it closed. "What do you need to tell me?" He stood by the bed.

She sighed. "You mustn't blame Willie. It was as much my fault as his, probably even more mine. He… didn't know about the baby. Might I tell you what happened? How we ended up aboard ship?"

Sam nodded.

The whole story came out, from her father's death to her stepfather selling her to Willie rescuing her and keeping her safe, even how he had given her the name Maybe. She explained about that night, her trying to keep him from being flogged for only one tankard of ale—to which Sam figured Mr. Cox and Mr. Swain filled the tankard with something other than ale. Irish whiskey most likely. He could understand. Even show a bit of sympathy. But the girl was with child. Something must be done.

"What is your true name?"

"Elizabeth Boulay."

Boulay? He once met a seaman named Boulay. He was a good man. If this girl was that Boulay's daughter, he owed it to him to set things right.

He patted her hand. "You rest now. He won't be flogged."

She relaxed.

Sam left to find Mr. Stewart.

It wasn't a hard task. He waited outside the door. The stricken expression he wore softened Sam's ire against him. Especially now that she explained the whole story.

"Do whatever you want to me, sir. I deserve it. But please take care of Maybe. It's not her fault."

"You two are a pair. I should have seen it from the beginning. She's in there begging me not hurt you, and here you are worried about her. You *are* worried about her, correct?" Sam watched the man's eyes.

"Aye! I swear I didn't know she was with child. She never said."

"Do you love her?"

Mr. Stewart nodded. "I haven't told her, but I do. More every day."

"Then I'll get the master. You will marry that girl, right now."

❧

Marry? He was about to become a married man? With a baby on the way? Willie grappled with this new reality. Did Maybe want to marry him? But the baby. She'd want a father for her baby.

Father? He hadn't a clue how to be a father. He didn't know how to be a husband, either.

But Maybe deserved both a husband and father for her baby.

It was his baby too. And he loved Maybe. Why shouldn't they get married?

Because he was an idiot. Maybe didn't deserve an idiot for a husband. She deserved so much better than he.

His thoughts swirled. Stupid! *She's waiting, just open that door!* He hesitated a moment and went in.

Maybe lay with her eyes closed. Her raven hair splayed about the pillow and her face, oh that lovely face, looking peaceful, serene. He hated to disturb such beauty.

Her eyelids fluttered before he saw those violet orbs that so dangerously drew him in. "Willie." Neither surprise nor disapproval. Simply his name on her lips.

"Aye. So… you didn't tell me."

"What would ye have done? We're on a ship in the middle of the Atlantic. No one is supposed to suspect I'm a girl. What could ye do?"

He came near the bed and enveloped her hand in his. "I could've shared your secret so you wouldn't have been alone. It would have been our secret until we got to Ireland."

"And what then? After we find my sister, you are off to sea again." She pulled her hand back.

"No, you don't understand. I—"

The door opened. The master and boatswain entered, closing the door behind them. "I hear we have a wedding to perform."

Maybe pushed herself up, staring at each man's face.

Suddenly Willie wasn't sure getting married was the right idea.

"What do ye mean, a wedding? Sir, I confided in ye. Are ye sharing my secret with others?"

Boatswain Johnson stepped to the bed, so Willie stepped away. "I told one person, someone with the ability to make things right. The master can perform the ceremony. You will be married."

"And what if I don't want to marry Willie?" She straightened her back, tipping her chin a tad.

The master paled.

Willie froze, stunned.

But the boatswain chuckled. "You are telling me you do not love this lout?"

Maybe's cheeks pinked. "He's not a lout." She stared at the bedclothes, picking at the blanket. "Aye, I love him." Turning her gaze to Willie, she added, "But how do I know he loves me?"

"You know because anyone with a brain can see it." The boatswain turned to Willie. "Tell her, man. Tell her what you told me."

"Ye told him? But not me?" Maybe's eyes glistened.

"It's what I was trying to say when they came in." Willie glanced at the other men and then swallowed his pride. Private would've been better, but he'd say it from the top of the main. "Aye, I love you, Maybe. Like I've loved no one else. I love you and am asking you to marry me."

"Are ye now?" She sniffed and swiped a hand over her eyes. "Then I guess I'm saying aye. I will marry ye, William Crockett."

The boatswain and master both peered at him.

"If my secret is out, then so is yers. And I'll not be marrying ye with a made-up name. Elizabeth Boulay is marrying William Crockett or there will be no wedding."

This was silly. The chuckle erupted like laughter in church. The men stared as if he'd lost his mind, but Maybe understood. "Aye, lass, William Crockett the Oaf is marrying Miss Elizabeth Boulay. I'm not about to let another man marry my Maybe girl."

She held out her hands, he wrapped them with his own.

The master came near the bed and the ceremony began. No pomp. No sermon. Nothing but a few questions followed by a chaste kiss. But he was now a married man. Married to a lovely lass.

Married. She was married to Willie. The wonder of

it left unfathomable thoughts whirling through her brain. What about the rest of the trip? How could she have a wedding night and the crew not discover she was a girl… woman? A married woman.

The master cleared his throat and nodded toward the door. Boatswain Johnson nodded back, and they stepped out, leaving her alone with Willie. Her new husband.

A shyness shrouded her, she pulled the bedclothes higher.

"No worries, wife. I'll not be forcing myself on you."

She glanced at him. Willie wore a pained look. Did he do it for the others?

He must have noticed something in her face because he reached for her hand. "We will figure this out together. This isn't what we would've planned, but the result, being married, is what I wanted. Is it what you wanted?"

She nodded, not trusting her voice.

"Are you worried that the rest of the crew will learn our secret?"

He said "our." The shyness, the fear, evaporated with that one little word. "I was."

"I will say nothing unless you want it said. I believe the others won't either. It makes it a little difficult for a wedding night." His cheeks grew ruddier, and she loved him even more.

"Ireland isn't that much farther. Can we wait for there?"

He nodded. "Aye. We'll wait for as long as you say. I love you, Maybe."

Oh, he made her smile. "I could do with another kiss, though." She grabbed a handful of his shirt and pulled him closer.

He obliged.

Chapter Sixteen

No one else had uttered the word arson, but the way the justice of the peace and the constable kept the investigation going, Joseph was sure the idea had crossed their minds. Another neighbor shared information on the whereabouts of the judge's family. Joseph had been willing to take the news, but the reverend volunteered. A much better idea, and it lifted a load off Joseph's shoulders. Willing was one thing, wanting to do it was another.

The Turner boys fit in well, though it was obvious they missed being with their family. Joseph, along with his sons and the guests, joined with the rest of the men in the community to remove the damage and reframe the Turner's new home. Within a week, the biggest part of the job was complete.

In two weeks, the Turners were in their home. Yet, there was still much to do. Community members donated everyday house-keeping things—pots, pans, utensils, linens, even furniture. It reminded Joseph of how the early church worked together, and it spoke to his heart.

A few days after their guests left, Henry Waddington and Thomas Miller stopped by the house.

Joseph was coming from his workshop and spotted them

speaking with Sarah at the door. "Good day, gentlemen. How can I help you?"

"Ah, Master Crockett, just the man we need to see. Might we have a word?" The justice of the peace took charge. By all appearances, Thomas was not there on his own accord. Oh, well.

Sarah allowed the men to pass. "Come in, come in. Ye can talk in the parlor."

They followed her. Joseph brought up the rear, closing the door. Sarah offered tea, but the men declined. "Then I will leave ye to speak in private." She curtsied and left.

Joseph motioned to the chairs. "Please sit, tell me what's on your mind."

Thomas continued to glance about the room. Did he recall his last trip here?

Henry cleared his throat. "You are aware we are making investigations into the fire?"

"Aye."

"Joseph, let me get to the point. I have an uneasiness, there's more to this than the judge falling asleep with his pipe. It makes no sense. He was too careful. We had no storms in the area, no lightning to cause the fire. I, um, I hate to voice this without proof, but my rumbling stomach says the fire was deliberate."

"But you have no proof."

"That is correct." Henry's hands didn't want to settle anywhere. First, they rubbed his breeches, then folded together, then slapped his knees. "But it roils in my gut, and you understand."

Joseph nodded. "I've had an ugly feeling about this since the first day. But, like you, I have no proof."

"I don't want to make an unfounded accusation. So I'm at a loss on how to proceed." Henry rose and paced. "Have you an idea?"

"Possibly, but it's not a good one."

Henry stopped pacing and stared him down. "Well, go on, man, what is it?"

"First, are we on the same page? Who might be behind this? Do you have someone in mind?"

Thomas harrumphed. "You might as well spit it out. You know good and well that you think Eleazar Ferguson is behind this." He looked from Joseph to Henry and back. "It's true."

Henry nodded. "Aye, it's true. The man is having difficulties getting even his basic needs met. No one will do business with him. A new community won't help because of the brand. If he starves, it's as good as if we'd hung him and less kind. A slow death."

"But that's not the whole reason." Joseph wasn't about to add his thoughts without knowing what they'd learned.

"No, that's not all. You were there in the courtroom. Remember what he tried to do before they took him to the pillory? He screamed bloody murder that he'd get the judge, see him dead."

"That would make him the perfect scapegoat for the crime, if someone else had planned it, wouldn't it?" Though Thomas was the one to point it out, it also occurred to Joseph.

"Aye, that is true. You understand why this situation so difficult."

"Then we have two problems. First, we need to learn if the fire was deliberate and two, somehow we need to meet Master Ferguson's basic needs. It's understandable why people won't do business with him, but we cannot allow him to starve."

Plopping in the chair again, Henry rested his hands on his knees. "So, what do you propose?"

"He won't take charity from you or me, and I doubt there's a money problem. Perhaps if, as part of your job as constable, Thomas, you stopped to look in on him. You could volunteer to check that stores are delivered to his door—if you had a boy take them and bring you the money? Could you get him to agree to such an arrangement?"

The constable shrugged. "I do not know. But what would people be saying about me if they see me associating with him?

This job is thankless enough. I don't need to be making enemies."

"If it's part of your job, it's not anyone's business to judge. The welfare of the community is your responsibility. If the man starves or, when the temperatures drop, gets too cold and commits a crime to stay alive, what would they say? You are keeping a community member safe. And, by extension, the rest of the community. If he has his basic needs, he's less likely to do anything drastic—such as stealing out of desperation." Joseph couldn't believe the man was that dense.

Henry sat back, looking less worried. "That sounds like a good plan. And Thomas, should you learn anything while you are there, you are to share that information with us."

"Spy? Me? I can do the good deed, but I draw the line at spying."

Joseph shook his head. "We're not asking you to spy. Your job is straight forward welfare. Should you, while doing your job, notice anything, you can tell us. But that's not the reason for this assignment."

Henry cleared his throat. "But don't forget your first responsibility is to protect this community. Do not let something slip past you because you're worried about offense."

Thomas grimaced, looking trapped. Joseph almost felt sorry for him. If he wasn't such a coward, perhaps he would. But he asked for much of the troubles he received.

"So, do we have a plan?" Joseph wanted the men gone. This was his home. He didn't need his daughters walking in on such a discussion.

"Aye." Henry stood, signaling Thomas to his feet.

Joseph rose. "This is too important to rush ahead. I do not think the judge ever considered letting the man starve when he made his judgment. Thomas, it's obvious you are not pleased with this plan. If you have a better one, we'll listen."

The constable, hands shoved into his pockets, shook his head while staring at the floor. "No, no other idea."

Henry took charge again. "Then we'll be going. Thank you, Joseph."

The men shook hands, he walked them to the door. Joseph was glad to be done with the ugliness. He watched them walk away and closed his mind to the questions.

Rubbing the bridge of his nose, he took a moment. The more he tried to protect his family, the more he got drawn into things. None of this happened before Willie left. So he couldn't have anything to do with this. He wasn't even here. But something about his leaving triggered something. All he had were puzzle pieces. Nothing fit together. *Oh, Willie, when will you be home?*

⊱❦⊰

Eleazar Ferguson heard the sound and had to remind himself what it was. Someone knocked. Who would dare? He peeked between the closed draperies and spotted that dotty constable on his step.

A chill went down his spine. Did he suspect?

No, the man was a cretin. He couldn't conjure his own thoughts.

But had someone sent him?

He let out his breath. The only way to find out required acknowledging the man. He could handle just that one man, if he must. Perhaps it wouldn't come to that.

Eleazar pulled open the door. He remained silent, though, not giving him any help in his mission, whatever it may be.

Thomas Miller looked shocked. Perhaps he didn't think the door would open to him. Well, normally it wouldn't, but Eleazar wasn't in the mood for more problems.

"Uh, Master Ferguson, sir. You're home."

"Where else would I be?"

"Right. I, um, might you use some food stores?" He indicated a crate in his hands.

Eleazar stared. Perhaps he misjudged the idiot, but that was doubtful. There was more to this. He must proceed with caution, and there was no reason to make it easy. "Why?"

"Well, I just thought…" The constable shrugged and turned to go.

"Wait." Might he use the creature?

"Aye?"

Too much interest would tip him off, but if the fool had a reason to keep him coming back… "Would you be interested in a business deal?"

"What type deal?" Already his eyes glanced to and fro.

"Nothing wrong, I assure you. I would pay you if you would bring necessities on a regular basis? I'll pay for the supplies and for your time. It is rather difficult to leave here these days." The bitterness had to come out, it refused to be stopped.

The constable nodded. "Aye, that would be acceptable."

Eleazar was sure it would be. "Perhaps I should check what you brought and then let you know what I still need? I'm happy to pay you for this delivery. Would you like to come in?"

The twit shook his head a bit too quick. Apparently, he wasn't completely altruistic and still worried about his own reputation. No matter.

"Perhaps another time." When no one might see him. "Let me take this crate inside. I'll be back in a thrice." Eleazar closed the door and took the food stuffs to his very empty larder. Nothing seemed left out at the moment. Besides, if he sent the creature away, he would have more time to ponder, to plan, to work this in his favor. A satisfied sigh escaped. Aye, he would turn this, and no one would see what he had planned until too late.

❧

Later that night, as Joseph held her, Sarah sensed the tightness in his muscles. Earlier she noticed those little lines between his brows were deeper. Something worried him. She stroked the insistent curl that always claimed his forehead back into place and let her fingers glide along his temple and jaw. "Won't ye tell me what has you so worried, love?"

His sigh warmed her neck. "I don't want to burden you with my imaginings."

She pushed back from him. "Since when do we not share our burdens? I can tell when you worry, and my imagination is good enough to construct worse things than what might be happening."

His chuckle told her he was ready to open up to her. "Aye, you do have an imagination, love." He pulled her close. "I am struggling with my thoughts. I have no proof but I think Eleazar Ferguson set the fire. I don't know how to get proof. And if I am wrong, I cannot take it back. Already the man has become a pariah. No one will do business with him. He cannot even buy food. So, the meeting today was to figure out what to do. Thomas Miller will make it an official part of his business to see that the man won't starve. I have no doubt of his guilt from the trial, but it almost would have been kinder to hang him rather than put him through all this."

"But if he didn't set the fire, and God uses this trial to save his soul, wouldn't that be better?"

His nod brushed her cheek. "Aye, love. You would remind me of that. Sometimes God must get us into the struggle where there's no hope without His intervention. He used the Benefit of Clergy and could read the Scripture without pause."

"But it is a struggle in ye, I can feel it."

"Aye. If that had been Beth, I would have torn him apart. And now that Aphra is part of our household, I could do it for her. There's a war inside me, that is sure. To do what is right, to show mercy after what he did. But I cannot stand by and let him starve to death." His voice quavered.

"Yer a good man, Joseph Louis Crockett, Sr. I love ye for it, and I trust yer heart. Yer a godly man, one who listens. Ye will hear and obey. I'm sure."

He kissed the top of her head and soon relaxed in her arms. Before long his breathing changed, telling her he slept. She lay there, fully awake, aware of the weight of his burden.

In truth, she didn't know if she would be as charitable as her husband. She'd seen the physical scars from where Eleazar had beat and burned Aphra. The girl had come out of her shell only to revert back once he was sent home from the pillory. She still jumped at any strange sound, and it was Aphra who first made her consider arson as more than a fleeting thought. The girl was sure Eleazar Ferguson was behind the whole thing.

There was some good coming out of having the girl stay with them. Beth also made strides at coming out of her shell. In fact, Beth was very protective of Aphra, treating her in much the same way as Willie used to treat Beth. Sarah smiled in the dark as her heart warmed.

She must trust Joseph. He would do what was right for all concerned. She just hoped it wouldn't cost them too dearly if he erred too well on the side of mercy.

Chapter Seventeen

S tuck in bed with a twisted ankle, Maybe reminded herself to be thankful it wasn't broken. The memory of setting her stepfather's arm rushed back while the surgeon wrapped her injured foot and calf—something he'd waited to do until after the ceremony—setting off a whirlwind of thoughts. She'd experienced enough these last four months to last a lifetime.

And now she was married.

And carrying a baby.

Who was she anyway? Maybe had no answer.

As far as the crew were concerned, she was still the boy who shimmied up the Jacob's ladder faster than anyone else and who, in a pinch, filled their bellies with a passable meal. At least that is what she hoped.

Besides the surgeon daily checking on her, Boatswain Johnson stopped by his cabin, which she'd taken over, several times a day to learn how she fared—she discovered he slept with the crew in her bunk.

And then there was Willie, who looked so befuddled at times, he must wonder why he bothered to help that mad girl in the tree. Speak of the devil—no, no devil came to visit her. He was her husband who made her heart flutter as he peeked in around the door.

"You are awake. That's good. How do you fare?"

Had these men no other question? "I'm as fine as can be expected. Confined here in this bed. Secretly married. Secretly a woman about to have a baby."

Willie looked like a kicked puppy. "I'm sorry, Maybe. I'm concerned, but I imagine we have asked you that a lot more than you care to answer."

Her heart softened. She wasn't angry at him. "I'm sorry, too, Willie. I'm glad to see ye, and as puzzled as anyone how my moods can change like the winds. Right now I'm frustrated and sick of this bed. It's been two days. Why canna I not try me legs?"

He sat on the edge of the bed. "The surgeon is concerned about you falling again. He doesn't want to risk the baby. And we're getting very close to Ireland now, might dock at Bare Haven in Bantry Bay in less than a day. You'll need to be up by then to disembark." His cheeks pinked, his thoughts splashed across his face.

In truth, hers drifted that direction as well. Her stomach churned. It wasn't from the baby. Waiting was hard. Anticipation needled her, filling her with excitement and fear. What if he realized he didn't want her? What if he only married her because of the baby? Would they spend their time growing cold, living a routine of emptiness? Oh, she wanted to believe he loved her and would have married her under other conditions. She wanted to, so badly.

"Willie, will we make it?"

He cocked his head to the side, his eyes narrowing a bit. "We're less than a day from port. We'll make it. Don't worry about that. You're safe."

She shook her head, sad that he didn't understand her question and not sure she could explain. Biting her lip, she considered her words. "I mean the two of us, Willie, as husband and wife, as parents to this baby. We didn't start the right way. Can we do this?"

Willie took her hands in his. His work-worn hands felt secure and warm. "Maybe girl, I do not know what tomorrow brings. I can only promise to be here with you, and will do everything I know to do. I love you, my wife. I didn't marry you to escape anything. I married you because I love you. You believe that, don't you?"

She wanted to. She wanted to hold on to his words until they became part of her being, lifting them to say to her doubts, "See, he loves me and you are wrong."

But her name was Maybe. Maybe was the best she could answer. She smiled and accepted his kiss.

Time would tell.

☙❧

WILLIE KISSED HIS WIFE GOODBYE AND HEADED FOR THE wheelhouse. It was his turn.

Wife. His wife.

The words floated through his mind as if a foreign language. And how did he get used to the sound when he mustn't use the words aloud?

Up in the wheelhouse, it remained quiet, granting him plenty of time to ponder such things. He needed to keep his eye on the horizon, but he could think and watch at the same time —he might have trouble reading a simple note, but this he could do.

The old guilt started eating at his gut. He enjoyed sailing, what he'd wanted to do his whole existence. But he had no right to pursue his dream anymore. He had a family to consider. Adult responsibilities. His mother might not be proud of him for how he got here, but she'd jump for joy that he finally behaved as an adult.

So this was adulthood. Putting aside one's own dreams and pursuits to become responsible for meeting the needs of another. Not too horrible, though getting to married life should make it better. He felt a smile spread. He longed to take his wife into his arms and convince her of his love. She needed convincing. He'd seen it in her eyes.

It was his own fault. Why didn't he declare himself before he learned about the baby? But if he had, she would have been in more danger. A relationship where they might slip up, making her secret known. The touch of a hand, a stolen kiss, any of that caught would be dire for her. He thought he protected her by keeping his feelings to himself. His gut twisted. Even in his attempts to do the right thing, he was an idiot.

He turned his thoughts to Bantry Bay. His parents lived there before he was born, in Bare Haven. Might he find people who remembered his family? It could be fun to look them up, tell his folks about them when he returned.

When he returned. What made that idea pop in his brain? Would Maybe want to return? What if she found her sister and wanted to stay? In the back of his mind he'd always planned to go home again, at least to visit. His heart stopped beating a moment. Never go home ever? Never again see his family?

Adulthood was so much harder than his mother had let on.

"Sir, might I have a word?"

Sam stopped mid-sentence in his directions to Mr. Cox when the surgeon called out to him. "Aye." He turned back to the seaman. "We'll discuss it more in a few minutes. I need to take care of this." Dismissing the man, he turned his attention to the surgeon as he approached.

"We need to fashion a crutch for that young lady before she

leaves the ship tomorrow. Who might accomplish this quick and well?"

Sam's stomach clenched. The surgeon had not waited to close the gap between them before he started talking. He glanced about. Mr. Cox still lingered, but perhaps he did not hear. Taking a few strides in the surgeon's direction, Sam waited until they were next to each other before saying more. "Aye, Mr. Hawkins would be the man. I should ask him, though, as we still do not want the crew to know her secret."

"Oh, aye. You take care of that, then. She'll be needing a bit of practice with it before we dock."

Sam clapped the man on the back, assuring him it would be done. As the surgeon left in another direction, Sam glanced over his shoulder. Mr. Cox was just leaving the deck. But when the crewman met his glance, something in Sam's clenched gut told him the secret was out.

⬥

THE SUN WAS MAKING ITS WAY HIGH IN THE SKY WHEN Maybe heard the words called out. "Land ho!" Ireland was in sight. She'd be out of this bed and onto her home soil before the day was out. The thrill made her sit higher. She longed to swing her legs over the side and step out onto the floor, but she had promised she would obey the surgeon's orders. But it shouldn't hurt to dangle her legs a bit, should it? She took the chance.

Until now, the only real movement had been making use of the chamber pot. An adventure in frustration and humiliation. Not the way she'd wanted her new husband to get to know her. But he'd never complained, at least around her. She needed to show him there was more to a married life than this type of duty.

The door opened and Willie entered, a big grin spread across his face. "I suppose you heard."

"Aye. We're close. My heart can feel the pull of home." She patted the bed for him to sit with her.

"I brought you something." She hadn't noticed until now how he kept his hand behind his back. When he brought it out, he held a crutch in his hand.

"Oh! Do ye mean I can get up now?"

He nodded, his grin growing wider. He handed her the crutch. "The surgeon wants you to get a little practice before you walk down the gangplank."

She put the crutch under her arm and stood on her good leg. Finally! With the weight on the good side, she moved the crutch a step. She leaned on that while moving her good leg out. Step by step, she crossed the room. The ship gave a little lurch just before her hand hit the wall and she lost her balance. Instantly she was in Willie's arms. He was there for her, like he promised. His closeness made her heart race, her breath raw.

"I've got you, Maybe. I've got you."

"Aye, ye do, Willie. That ye do." She looked up into those gentle eyes. Were they green or blue? It was like they couldn't decide, and it pulled her in. At once, she was in his arms being kissed like she'd never been kissed but had always wanted to be. Slow and gentle, building as he pulled her closer, almost as if he asked permission with his actions and she granted it. Her arms held him secure around his neck while her fingers entwined themselves in his hair.

His lips moved to her ear, whispering her name as if it came from deep inside his soul. "Maybe, my Maybe." He groaned, his hands roaming up, his fingers threading through her hair. He pulled her back to gaze into her eyes. "You have no idea how much I want this to continue dear wife, but not here. I will find the right place and soon. I promise."

Maybe licked her lips, the taste of him filling her with desires she never knew she possessed. As though under water, she nodded, the sense of drowning in passion for him overwhelming her.

He was a good man. The thought slipped into her consciousness, and she knew it to be true as she tried to catch her breath. She nodded and took the crutch as he handed it back to her. A good man. A man of honor.

So much honor that he would do the right thing whether or not he loved her?

Oh, she must let those thoughts go! He said he loved her, and he was ready to prove it. He had already proved it. She needed to just trust it.

Turning, she made her way back to the bed. "Let me try again. It's wonderful to be out of that bed."

Willie was at her side as she made two more practice turns. A knock sounded as she completed the third time.

"Come in."

Boatswain Johnson appeared. "Looks like you are getting your pins back under you. Good on you, Maybe."

"She's walked to the wall and back three times now. She will do well with the crutch." Willie beamed as if she had learned a new trick.

"Well, I wanted to say we have fair winds and are moving at about ten knots so we should be docked in less than two hours. Do you have anything below deck you want brought up here?"

She shook her head. Willie had already brought her the bit of money she had and her da's fiddle. There was nothing else but memories. And Willie. That was all she had.

"In that case, I should pay you now for your services. You both worked hard and earned your keep." He brought out a small leather pouch and handed it to Willie. "I put the pay for you both in here. Perhaps it will be enough to get you started on your life together." The boatswain rubbed his face and ducked out the door.

Willie weighed the pouch in his hand, and his eyes grew rounder. He opened it and poured several gold sovereigns into his palm. "That's just the start! Oh, Maybe, he's overpaid us. We can't accept all this!"

Maybe limped over to him and peeked in the pouch. Her mouth went dry. This money meant buying a house or building one. They would be safe. And he wanted to give it back? "The boatswain knows what he put into the pouch, what he gave us. We need not give any back."

Willie still stared at it, but he shook his head. "No, this isn't right."

"Willie?"

"No." He headed out the door before she could stop him.

Maybe started to stomp her foot but caught herself in time, a jolt of pain rising from her ankle at the thought. She loved that he was good and honorable, but couldn't he look the other way just this once?

She sank back onto the bed, more frustrated than she'd been before he walked in the door.

It wasn't as if they were stealing. The man gave them the money. He wanted them to have it. This was for their future.

The worst part was, she could see Willie's side of it. Oh, why was it always difficult?

She propped the crutch next to the bed and flopped back on the pillow, running her hands through her hair and winced when she touched the spot where her head had hit the mast. If this was married life, did she really want it?

Closing her eyes, she willed herself into a nap. Anything to make the time go faster. Another knock jolted her. "Come in."

It was the surgeon. "I hoped to see you before you leave to make sure everything has been done."

She smiled at him. He was the first to discover her secret, and he never judged her. "Thank you. Ye've taken very good care of me. I am grateful."

"I'll tell you a wee secret. I've worked on these sea dogs for so many years, patching their wounds, treating their ailments, and in extreme cases, saving them from appendages that have turned on them. But treating a young mother is a joy and an honor. May this baby bring you much love and happiness."

Maybe bit her lip and blinked several times. Her emotions ran amok with her enough. She would not cry right now. "May I ask ye a question?"

He laughed. "Aye, you just did, but you may ask another if you wish."

And clever too. "Might you tell me your name? No one has said it. We call you the surgeon. What is your Christian name?"

He smiled and sighed. "I've always preferred it that way. If they know my name, they'd want to learn more about my life. But for you, young mother, I will tell you. My name is Josiah Featherfield. I am trusting you with my secret."

"Doctor Featherfield, you have my word." Another secret kept.

"In that case, let me look at your ankle. Have you practiced with the crutch?" He sat on the edge of the bed and began to unwrap her leg.

"Aye." She told him of her trips back and forth across the room.

He murmured "good" and began pressing places on her ankle. "How does that feel?"

She was fine until he hit one spot. She gasped and thought her body would send her through the roof.

"You've bruised the muscles here, most likely when you dangled from the ladder. You can soak it in cold water if you notice swelling. Also, keep it propped up whenever you can. You must get your rest. Once the baby comes, rest will be a thing of the past." He rewrapped her ankle and patted her knee. "Miss Maybe, it has been a pleasure treating you and working together on the *Frances Pearl*. I wish you the best."

Maybe shook his hand and he left, giving her more time to watch the ceiling, count the minutes and second-guess every decision she'd ever made. She'd thought Willie would be back, but when the ship's motion changed as it pulled into dock, she remembered he must do his part. She only hoped he'd not returned the money or at least the boatswain assured him he meant for them to keep it.

An hour later, Willie knocked at the door—something in the rhythm gave him away. He helped her from the bed and stepped ahead of her to get the door.

She longed to ask what happened with the money but couldn't bring herself to do so.

He held the door for her as she stepped through. Step by step, he stayed with her as she made it to the main deck and headed to the gangplank. She stopped for a breath and raised her head. All along the gangway, the crew had lined up, their heads bare, hats in their hands. She glanced at Willie, heat rising in her cheeks.

He shook his head. His expression assured her he knew nothing about it. The slip had not come from him.

She swallowed the lump forming in her throat and continued.

Mr. Cox stepped forward. "Maybe, we just learnt, and we think yer the best at riding the top there is. Ye can sail with us anytime, even if ye are a girl."

Then Mr. Hawkins stepped forward. "Maybe, I was going to give these to me wife, but I'll have time to make more. Won't ye take 'em to help ye remember yer sailing friends?" He shoved an intricate bouquet of wooden flowers into her hands, each one carved with precision.

Maybe's throat constricted, and her eyes burned. They didn't judge her. Instead they spoke in kind words, thoughtful gestures. Her legs failed her. She froze as her soul was moved more than she could handle.

Boatswain Johnson put his hand on Willie's shoulder. "Take care of our Maybe."

Willie nodded, as choked up as she.

"You both are always welcomed on the *Frances Pearl.*"

Maybe's knees grew rubbery. There was nowhere to sit. Just as she met Willie's gaze, he scooped her into his arms.

He carried her down the gangplank as if she weighed no more than a farthing. Turning back to the men, he grinned while they all cheered.

She buried her head in his shoulder. For now she'd let her husband take care of her.

Chapter Eighteen

illie carried his wife, trudging up from the dock, into the village and to the first place that resembled an inn—an older home with a picture sign in the yard. She clung to him, her crutch, fiddle, and wooden bouquet over his shoulder the whole way, her head still buried in his neck. The lightness of his load surprised and delighted him. He moved much heavier things aboard ship. That he could do this with ease only made it easier. He shifted her in his arms.

"Ye can put me down now."

He fumbled at the door. "What?"

"I said, ye can put me down."

Indignance colored her voice, confusing him, but he did as requested. "We need a room. After, if you want, we can inquire about your sister." She looked too tiny, almost frail, standing there with her crutch under one arm and cradling the carved flowers and fiddle with her other.

"I would like to get clean and then find some female clothing before I see her." She still had that shy look. How she could traverse between indignant and shy so quick, he did not understand.

Then comprehension dawned. "Of course! Let's get a room and, well, let's start with a room."

He held the door for her and then led her to a table with a bell. A robust woman, perhaps in her mid-forties, appeared, taking in the scene. He stepped forward, sheltering Maybe from the woman's scrutiny, and asked for a room.

"Jist one?"

"Aye. And a bath, too, if you please."

There was something about the smile she gave when she nodded that made Willie feel like he was doing something… wrong. He shook it off and thanked her.

She slid him the key and gave directions. "I'll have me son up to fill yer bath in a twinklin'."

"Thank you." He guided Maybe toward the stairs. Should he scoop her up or let her negotiate them on her own?

"I can do it, Willie."

So he stayed behind her, ready to protect her from falling.

At the landing, she stopped and glanced in both directions. Rooms appeared both ways.

"She said to the right, room three."

Maybe nodded and launched herself down the hall to the door.

Willie used the key and allowed her to enter first before following.

The room was small, crowded. Barely a place to put a tub for bathing. But it was clean, and they would sleep on clean sheets after getting themselves clean. It had been so long.

"Would you prefer to sit in the chair or on the bed?" A wooden chair sat tucked next to a small desk in the corner.

"The chair, please."

Willie pulled it out for her.

She took the seat and eyed him. "Ye know ye need not coddle me. I can pull out chairs and do things for meself."

"I know. You are my wife. I want to take care of you."

"I thank ye kindly, Willie. Ye always take good care of me. But I canna have ye smothering me. We need to find a balance."

She didn't want him to take care of her?

"Ye look confused. I'm sorry. It is confusin' fer me too. Yer a good man, Willie Crockett. Please, jist let me be meself. It has been too long since I was meself. Do ye ken?" Her brogue had thickened since crossing the threshold.

Threshold! He hadn't carried her over it! Ack! Again, he could do nothing right!

"What is the matter? What did I say?"

He hung his head. "I was supposed to carry you over the threshold. I made a mess of things again."

She laughed.

He looked at her. Had she lost her mind?

Her laugh continued until tears rolled down her cheeks.

Willie's face grew hot. He not only messed things up, he'd humiliated himself with his honesty.

Maybe stood and hobbled to him without her crutch. "Ye are a sweet oaf, my Willie. Ye carried me all the way from the ship. That should count for somethin'." Her arms twined around his neck and she pulled his face to hers. "Ye are my sweet oaf, and I wouldn't have it any other way, William Crockett." Her kiss punctuated her words, warming him from his toes all the way to his senses.

As he was about to scoop her up and place her on the bed, someone knocked at the door. It took every ounce of will power to untangle himself to answer.

"Ye ordered a bath, sir?"

"Aye." Willie stood aside, allowing the boy to bring in the tub. Two more boys followed carrying large jugs of hot water.

This began the parade of boys and jugs and hot water until the tub was filled. Willie flipped them each a coin and closed the door.

"Do you want help to get into the tub?"

"Yer hopin' I say aye, that ye are." She smiled, then ducked her gaze. "No, I can manage. If ye can go find me some lady things, that would be a great help. Put the towels and soap where I can reach them, and then I'll be right as rain."

Willie nodded, not wanting to make more of this. They needed to find their way, and he had promised not to force himself on her.

Stupid promise. Stupid thought!

He did as she asked and left her to her privacy.

ONCE WILLIE LEFT, MAYBE'S HEART SETTLED BACK TO A normal beat. She undressed. Months in the same clothing with only the occasional sponge bath when no one was looking left her feeling very dirty. She could not understand how Willie even wanted to be near her in her present state. But she would make the wait worth it.

Unwrapping her ankle proved the most revealing—she hadn't had a good look at it since the accident. The human body turned so many colors! Now naked, she tried balancing on one leg while putting in the other. That worked halfway, but balancing on her injured foot was not going to happen. Then she remembered her crutch and got herself in, submerging as much as the tub allowed. Oh, sweet thunderation! The hot water opened every pore, releasing more than dirt. Anxiety, fears, even anger seeped from her body. She scrunched more, ducking her head under, holding her breath and letting memories of good and clean and safe flood over her. If she held her breath long enough, she might stay in that place forever.

But she couldn't. Popping up with a gasp, Maybe surveyed about her. She was in Ireland, in a clean room, getting clean for the first time in four months. And she was with a darlin' man who loved her and gave her his name. Perhaps good and clean and safe lived right here in these four walls.

She grabbed the soap, wet it, and gave it a rub before putting it under her nose and inhaling. Ah, it had been too long.

Twenty minutes later, she decided she was clean. Besides Willie would be back soon, and she wanted to be out and at least wrapped in a towel before he returned. She had nothing else to wear. The thought brought heat to her face. She'd have to get over that. She was married.

Getting out was harder than getting in, but with her crutch, she maneuvered herself on to the edge of the bed while wrapped in the towel. Just as she debated whether she could rewrap her ankle, there was a knock followed by Willie's voice.

Her heartbeat increased, she caught herself smiling. "Aye. Come in."

He carried a bundle. "I'm hoping I got this right. There was a small shop in the village, and I had to make guesses."

"Would ye come help me wrap me ankle?" She held the bandages out to him.

"Of course!" He dropped the bundle on the bed and knelt before her, beginning the rewrapping process. In less than a minute, he had it completed, never once causing her the least twinge of pain, though his touch sent tingles throughout her entire clean body.

"Would ye like help dressing or prefer me to step out?"

"I canna tell if ye are that hopeful or that helpful, Willie Crockett."

He started to protest, but she put her fingers to his lips.

"Jist give me a bit more time. I am getting there. I promise. I know what I want, but I'm not quite ready to be that brazen."

He smiled at that and winked. "Then I'll step out. Call me if you need me. I'll be outside the door." His hand caressed her cheek before he exited.

Maybe dropped the towel and perused what he'd brought in the bundle. As she held up a yellow linen dress to herself, her hand brushed against the life forming within her belly. She put the dress back on the bed and caressed where the baby caused her stomach to pooch. Her baby. Willie's baby and her baby. She'd been hiding from him, but already he intimately knew her.

Would he act this shy around her, if roles were reversed? He'd be needing a bath once she dressed. She needed to get clothes for him.

Then she examined the rest of what he brought. He'd bought for himself too. She smiled. He didn't want her to have to go alone and shop for him. Instinctively, she realized that was his reasoning. It was his way.

She got into her chemise and stopped. By decent society, she was still undressed, but at least covered enough for her husband to enter. "Ye may come in now."

Willie looked surprised. "Do you need help with your stays?"

She nodded. "I will, but not now. It is yer turn. Ye need a bath too. I'll turn me back as I shouldn't be goin' into the hall like this. When yer in, I'll scrub yer back for ye."

His eyes twinkled. "Oh, will you now. What if I'm not ready for that?"

"Master Crockett, I do believe ye are tryin' to tease me. Here I am offerin' to help, and yer turnin' me down?"

He laughed. "Who said anything about turning ye down, Mistress Crockett? Now, ye be turning yer back, and I'll get into the tub." He sounded more Irish than when they arrived. He did it on purpose.

She covered her face and turned her back. "Tell me when yer ready."

Listening, she heard clothing drop to the floor, a few steps, and then the sound of water displaced. "Ready."

Maybe spun around and parted her fingers.

He sat with his back to her, though she could see his knees sticking from the water like two pale mountains. Where the sun had repeatedly kissed his skin while aboard ship, he was tanned, almost bronze. But the areas where the sun missed—his back and knees—were without color but for the freckles that liberally peppered. "Ye need to get yer hair wet too. I'll scrub it for ye."

He glanced over his shoulder. "I think I might grow to like this."

"Oh, ye do, do ye?" She pushed his head under, and he came up sputtering, shaking his great curly mane and beard. "Enough! Yer getting me wet!"

"Then take off your shift and join me."

Did he think she would? Her heart pounded. Was she ready? This was her husband. He already knew her. Was she afraid? Of Willie?

He might as well see what he'd acquired. She gathered her skirt in her hands and pulled the chemise over her head, tossing it on the bed.

Willie reached for her, lifting her into the tub, ankle bandage and all. "You are very beautiful, my wife."

"Go on with ye, me husband." His wet skin warmed her deeper than her own.

He threaded his fingers through her clean hair and kissed her.

❦

Something kept Willie from moving. He cracked open his eyes. Maybe lay curled against him, over his arm. Still in his embrace. Fast asleep. He might as well drown in a vat of honey, the sweetness that overwhelmed him took his breath. Her raven hair, getting a bit longer each day, now silky and damp, still called to his fingers, though he feared his touch might wake her. Even her lashes lay dark against her face looking soft enough to want to stroke with his fingertip. Her skin, warm against his body and fragrant of roses, felt as soft as a newborn's.

Newborn. There would be a newborn for them. The power of the thought choked him. He was barely a husband. How was he to be a father? He knew nothing of being a father, and the one he could ask for advice was on the other side of the world. The flutter of sweet love turned to waves of panic in his gut. He was in over his head drowning before the wee one could arrive.

The sooner they found her sister, the sooner they might find a ship and sail back to North Carolina.

Willie slowly tried to slip his arm free, but she opened her eyes, those violet eyes that made his heart go all erratic—stopping and then pounding out of his chest.

She smiled. "Hello."

He ran a finger down the side of her face. "Hello."

She snuggled closer, her fingers playing at his chest. "What shall we do now?"

"We might get dressed and find a bite to eat before we look for your sister."

Maybe bit her bottom lip, insecurity mounting in her eyes as she glanced away. "If that is what ye want."

He pulled her closer yet, whispering in her ear. "I am looking forward to tonight, though. Just so you know, dear wife." Kissing her temple, he hoped he'd eased her fears. He didn't know how else to reassure her that this was a commitment of love, not duty.

She nodded and rolled to her side of the bed, wrapping bedclothes about her. Had he gotten through?

His side banked against the wall, so he scooted to the foot of the bed. The new clothing lay scattered across the floor. After handing her the chemise, he picked up the other items, shook them and handed Maybe hers while putting his on the chair.

He noticed she followed his movements with her eyes when it hit him: he was naked. The room became very warm. Was it possible for his entire body to blush? "Guess I should put on some pants." The nervous laugh that came out sounded nothing like him.

She slid the chemise over her head and laid the bedclothes aside. "Willie, might ye help with my stays?"

"Of course!" He pulled on his breeches and buttoned them before coming to her aid. "How does this work over the baby?"

"Jist dunna pull too tight. I will be fine that way."

He adjusted as best he could and tied the bow. Another first. He'd never helped his sisters with any of this. He blew out a breath. This wasn't merely Ireland, it was a whole new world.

Willie fastened her dress for her and helped her into her new shoes. In between he'd pulled on his shirt and waistcoat. Last of all, Maybe tucked her hair up under her mobcap. No one would see it had been cut, and she definitely resembled a girl again. No, he corrected himself, she looked like a woman.

He offered her his arm, then realized that was silly since she'd need to use her crutch. She smiled at his oaf-ness and waited while he got the door. Then it was back to negotiating the steps. "Will you please let me take you to the first floor?"

After the first two treads and nearly falling, Maybe agreed.

Willie scooped her in his arms and had them downstairs in seconds where he put her back on her feet.

"Thank ye." She pinked, looking away.

He shook his head.

The lady who'd given them the key was still in the sitting room. She glanced up and her eyes widened. "Why glory be, 'tis a girl with ye!"

"No, mistress, no girl. This is my wife." Willie smiled as charmingly as possible, hoping to put the nosy woman in her place, but nicely.

"Aye, so it is, so it is. Would ye be wantin' a wee bite?"

"That would be kind. Thank you."

She led the way to the dining room.

Willie waited to let Maybe go next before he brought up the rear. He held her chair before taking his own.

"It has been a long time since someone held a chair for me." Maybe whispered, almost wistfully.

"Well, it won't be a long time anymore." He put his hand over hers.

"Excuse me, mistress, sir, might I get you some tea?"

Maybe's hand fisted beneath his, and he glanced, first at her, and then at the face of the speaker.

Her chair tipped back, and Maybe jumped to her feet, embracing the girl. "Eliza! Eliza!"

"Elizabeth?" The girl dropped the tea pot. It shattered in a million tiny pieces like islands in a hot brown puddle. "Elizabeth!"

The lady of the house rushed in with the crash. "Eliza! What have you done?"

"Willie, Willie, this is Eliza! This is my sister!"

Chapter Nineteen

❧

Could it be so simple? Maybe hugged her sister, pulled back and gaze at her, followed by another hug and gaze. Right here, all the time. The tears refused to stop. Maybe wasn't about to let go of her for fear she'd disappear.

Over her shoulder she heard Willie dealing with the woman, paying her for the teapot, and offering explanation. But nothing was here but her sister. "I feared ye had died. I dinna know what we would find."

"Daniel O'Malley sent me word that ye and Mama had died, and no one was left to bring me over. Is Mama truly dead?"

Maybe's heart squeezed in a vice, the day rushed back. "Aye. It were soon after we landed."

"What happened? Did she get sick from me?" Eliza's eyes filled with even more tears and now fear.

"No, oh, no, darlin' girl." Maybe paused for a breath. Until this moment, she'd never told Willie what happened. "We were out walking. It was early spring, and the flowers were just bloomin'. I heard the noise but paid no heed. Just a part of nature. Mama swiped her hand in the air, and I noticed the bee. It wouldn't leave her alone, and she kept waving her hand at it. She clapped her hands together. 'There, it will not bother me again,' she said. Then a moment later she grabbed at my hand. Her face looked queer— like she dinna ken what happened— and her eyes grew, full of fear. She tried to speak but her tongue seemed thick, she made sounds but not words. Her hands went to her throat, and she dropped to her knees." The memory of the day poured over her, weighing on her. She felt Willie's arms around her. "I couldn't do anything for her. I cried for help, but by the time anyone came… she was gone." Turning, she cried against Willie. He held her, rubbing his hand up and down her back.

When she breathed enough to control her sobs, she lifted her head. His eyes stared back with understanding. "Now ye ken why I was so terrified."

He nodded.

Eliza shyly stood at her side.

Maybe pulled the girl into the embrace. Now they were three. She would never leave her sister again.

❧

IT TOOK A FEW QUESTIONS, BUT SOMEONE FINALLY remembered the place where the pirates attacked twenty years ago. Willie hiked in that direction, finding a tower house and the ruins of what might have been a house on a bluff. Memories of the stories his mother and father told him, how she helped fight off the pirates who wanted to take the tower house, how his father returned from a trip to find the home where he left his wife and sons obliterated. Now a married man and soon-to-be-father, these stories held a deeper meaning for Willie. Even apart, his parents worked together, loved each other, and cared for each other. He hoped for that with Maybe.

Willie stood on the bluff, gazing out at the scene that must have filled his mother's eyes more than once as she watched for her husband's ship to arrive. No wonder he found solace standing in such a place when his mind filled with dancing thoughts.

The young girl who served them turning out to be Maybe's sister? How simple was that? Now to get them all aboard a westbound ship. Perhaps they could still make the season before the seas were too rough to transverse.

No, common sense told him they needed to wait for spring. By then the baby would have arrived, he would be a father, responsible for one more person. Could he convince Maybe to travel back with a newborn? She'd have her sister with her, so it wouldn't be so awful.

It would be dangerous for a newborn to travel across the ocean, though. Would the money hold out that long? If they sailed now, he had enough for the passage. If they must live on the money for six months… Willie shook his head.

The money situation aside, what if Eliza didn't want to leave Ireland? What then? What would Maybe say? That was the real question, and there was only one way to learn that answer.

❧

"Yer very deep in thought." She found him, right where she'd figured he'd be. Maybe crested the bluff on her crutch, hoping to find a boulder on which to rest before the return trip.

Willie startled at her voice. "How'd you get here? You didn't climb by yourself, did you?"

"Ye worry too much, Willie. I took me time, I was careful. So what brought ye here?"

He returned to the view of the bay. "I just needed to work on some things."

"Are ye worried about something?"

"Nothing more than usual." He flashed her a smile over his shoulder before resuming bay-gazing.

"Then are ye fearful of something?" When Willie pulled

away to be alone, something was wrong or he needed to sort things in his head. Now that they were married, shouldn't he be sharing this with her?

She saw his shoulders droop. This was something unpleasant.

He guided her to a large rock near an oak and lifted her up on it. "Too bad we can't go climbing. We always seem to have our best talks up in a tree."

"Do we need to have a talk?"

He nodded. "Aye."

"Then, spit it out, Willie. The not knowin' is making me crazy."

"Maybe, it is nothing bad. I love you, and I am so grateful you married this oaf. But…" He paused, and she wanted to shake him. "I miss my family. You understand, you've missed your sister so much. I'm… nervous, anxious about becoming a father. I'd like to ask my father questions." He grew silent, kicking at a stone on the ground.

"Ye want to go back?"

"Aye. I want to go home."

Home? This was home, with her sister, not that faraway place where Daniel O'Malley sold her to someone who still looked for her. "I dunna ken what to say."

"I know, I've sprung this on you. You need not worry. I've counted the cost. We would bring Eliza with us. You'll never be separated again. We've enough money for three passages now, but it might be too late. As much as I love the stories of it, I don't want our baby born at sea like me. That leaves spring, right after the baby comes. If we are careful, we might stretch the money until March. Our baby born in Ireland and your sister with you the whole way, what do you say, Maybe? Could we go back?"

"Yer forgetting the reason we left. What about Eleazar Ferguson?"

"You'd not be going back as yourself. You are now Mistress Maybe Crockett. Who can say where we met or when we married? You'll be a mother and wife. No one will make the connection."

She had to admit. He had a point. She'd be relatively safe. And she'd have him to protect her. "May I think on it?"

"Of course, love. And talk it over with Eliza. See what she says. Perhaps she wants to get away."

She chuckled. He had no idea. "We talked some before her employer made her go back to work. After we sailed, Eliza got better, but then the letter from our stepfather arrived saying both Mama and I were dead, the money ran out, and the couple we'd left her with both became ill and died. Then she found this job. I don't believe she is treated kindly, so we must get her away from that position."

"So you'll speak with her? You'll think about it?"

He'd done so much for her. "Aye, I will ask her. But I want to stay until the baby comes. I want our baby born on Irish soil."

He stepped and then turned. "You know, this spot is special in our family. See those ruins over there?"

She nodded.

"My father built that house. Pirates destroyed it. My mother and brothers were safe in the tower house behind you. She helped fight them off."

Stories Maybe had heard as a child began to dance in her memory. She'd been told of a family who once lived in a fine house where the ruins now stood. They'd left for the colonies. "That was your family?"

"Aye. My father came home to find nothing but rubble. He didn't know what had happened to her or my brothers. He pounded on the door of the tower house, panicked, and found everyone safe. I understand it was soon after that they left for the colonies. I could have had my start here on this bluff." He chuckled.

Maybe didn't chuckle, though she tried to give him a smile. Instead she wondered if all this were possibly true.

❦

WILLIE HELPED MAYBE OFF THE ROCK, AND THEY TRUDGED back to the village together. Near to the house, Willie heard a shout.

"Ho, Willie boy, Maybe!"

Mr. Cox waved, coming from the pier.

Willie waved and trotted to the man. "So, you have yet to sail."

The man clapped Willie on the back as if he hadn't seen him in ages. "Aye, the boatswain said we're starting fresh this trip, so we might as well stretch our pins on land. Unloaded the last of the cargo here at Bare Haven, so we're not going to England. We'll sail tomorrow for Bermuda and then Charlestown."

Maybe hobbled up. Mr. Cox viewed her with new eyes. "Maybe, you really are a girl. And a pretty one at that."

That brought a smile to his wife's face.

"Aye, she's that."

Now she peeked up at Willie, a sweet blush climbing her cheeks. She smacked his arm.

"Only stating the obvious, and I'm not alone in my opinion, wife."

"Go on with ye, then. I'll leave you lads to yer tall tales and wait for ye back at the room, Willie. It was grand to see ye again, Mr. Cox and have the chance to say thank you." She hesitated a moment then gave the man a quick hug before hobbling off toward the village.

Mr. Cox stood, a surprised expression etched on his face.

Willie burst out laughing. "Once you see the girl, it's hard to miss."

"Aye. You've got someone pretty special. So what are your plans?"

"Well, our first plan was to find Maybe's sister. We did that within hours of arriving. So, I guess we wait for the baby to arrive and then go back home to Beaufort come spring."

"You're going to take a new mother and child on one of those fetid passenger ships?"

Willie registered the concern in his friend's voice, but was he overreacting? "My mother gave birth to me on the trip over. I just don't want Maybe to be on board during her confinement. She wants the baby to be born here."

The man sighed. "I understand, but you don't know how bad those tubs are. Boatswain Johnson and the master keep a ship with a very high standard. It is clean, the water fresh from each port, and they expect the crew to keep things clean as well. On those other ships, if the water doesn't make you sick, the maggots in the food or the lice in your bed will. The *Frances Pearl* isn't perfect, but she's so much cleaner than the others, you are in for a shock."

Shock was the word. Willie couldn't find his voice. Instead he shook his head.

Mr. Cox clapped him on the shoulder. "Not what you hoped, I can tell."

"No, no it isn't. What do I do? I need to get them home, and I can't put them in that kind of danger."

Mr. Cox grew quiet and then snapped his fingers. "I know, let's go talk with the boatswain. He might know a good ship."

Willie let the man guide him toward the *Frances Pearl*. There was something familiar yet weird about returning aboard. He'd spent so much time there, but never imagined he'd be aboard again.

Boatswain Johnson met him at the top of the gangplank. "Ho, Mr. Stewart, er, Mr. Crockett. I thought we'd gotten rid of you." The man's smile and handshake took any sting from his words.

"I thought you had as well, but Mr. Cox said you might be of help. I've a bit of a dilemma." Willie explained what he needed to do and what Mr. Cox had shared. "So, what do you think?"

The boatswain scratched his head. "I have an idea. Wait here a minute."

Willie shrugged, not sure what to say. He glanced at Mr. Cox who sported a grin. What were they plotting?

Five minutes later the boatswain returned. "I needed to get the master's approval, it was but a formality. Your family will sail with us on the morrow. The ladies will take my cabin. You and I will bunk with the crew. If you want to work, I can pay you. I have yet to replace you on the roll. Won't let Maybe, rather Elizabeth, work, though, or her sister for that matter." He stated a price for the fare far below what Willie had heard other ships advertise. They would still have part of their money when they arrived home.

Willie choked on his emotions. "I cannot thank you enough."

"Remember we leave tomorrow. Be here by nine in the morning."

"Aye, sir. Thank you, sir." Willie shook the boatswain's hand and Mr. Cox's hand and then shook each man's hand again. "I'd better go tell Maybe." Maybe! Oh, what was he going to tell her?

❧

MAYBE LISTENED ONE MORE TIME TO HIS WORDS, NOT believing he would break his promise so quickly.

"I'm sorry you think I'm breaking my word, but if you'd heard what I did, you'd realize this is the best solution. I can't put you and the baby in danger. There's a surgeon on board the *Frances Pearl* who knows you and can take care of you. Plus, you will have Eliza with you and the two of you will have your own cabin. I can work and earn more money for us—"

"Is that what it is, Willie? The money? Or the chance to sail again?"

He stared at her as if she'd spoken in another language, then shook his head. "Why can't you just believe I'm doing the best I can for you and the baby? Back home we'll have my family for support, to help us raise this baby the right way. The *Frances Pearl* will get us there in a safer, healthier way. You will have your sister, away from unkind treatment and with you. I don't understand."

What he said was true. But all that glared back was his broken promise. The baby was to be born here in her homeland. Couldn't he understand that was important to her? And he didn't even discuss it. He just made the plans. No discussing it. How could she trust what he said to her anymore? What if… no, oh no. A lead weight dropped into her stomach. She sank to the floor. "How can I ever trust your word, Willie?"

He stooped in front of her and tried to pull her up.

She batted him away. The last person she wanted to see right now was William Crockett the Lying Oaf.

He stood. "I'll tell them downstairs that Eliza is leaving with us in the morning and make sure she gets paid."

"Going after her money too?" She knew it was too much the instant the words were out of her mouth. Willie would never take money that wasn't his.

He slammed the door before she could take it back.

She jumped at the jolt. She'd never seen him this angry, and it was her fault. He was right. It would be safer to sail with the *Frances Pearl*. But her dreams—of her baby being born here in her homeland, a place she never thought she'd see again—lay broken and shattered about her like shards of sparkling glass. They sliced up her heart into thin ribbons.

And even if he did it for her good, he broke his promise to do it. Would she ever trust him again? Her head told her she overreacted and tried to remind her of all the times he had come through for her even when it cost him. But her battered heart screamed her fears over the quiet common sense that should be her guide.

Maybe rolled into a ball on the floor and cried herself to dreamless sleep. The next thing she knew, she was scooped up.

She tried to fight until she realized Willie carried her to the bed. She kept her eyes closed.

Gently placing her on the sheets, he covered her with a blanket, kissed her forehead and went back out.

Why did he do that? She wanted to stay angry with him. And here he was kind to her. Again. She brushed her hand over her eyes and pulled the blanket to her chin. With so much right in her life—the baby, finding her sister safe, and a good man like Willie as her husband—she should be elated, or at least grateful. Instead she was curled in a ball feeling sorry for herself.

Well, no more. She threw the blanket off and hobbled for her crutch, stopping long enough to find the mirror. The girl blinking back was a mess, but at least her eyes showed a spark of intelligence. She tucked a wayward strand of hair beneath her cap and headed out to find her husband.

He was downstairs in the dining room, having a cup of tea and a biscuit. Eliza stood next to him, laughing.

"Willie?"

He turned her way.

She didn't know if he was happy to see her or too hurt to want to. She tried to smile. "Willie, what time should we be ready tomorrow?"

Chapter Twenty

The chill from the ocean breeze made Sarah pull her shawl a tad closer. She hated sealing up the house for winter too soon, but November brought an extra chill. She entered the boys' room, not sure why she bothered. Jason was the only one to sleep there now, what with John newly married and James still at school and William— She felt the familiar catch in her heart when she thought of her Willie— where was he now? Was he warm and well fed? Did he want for anything? Was he safe?

Was he alive?

Yes, until she knew for sure otherwise, Willie was alive. She sat on the edge of the bed he had shared with James until he got it to himself, for that short bit of time. It brought her peace. It was how she coped. Joseph walked to the docks every day, asking anyone who might answer if they'd seen Willie somewhere in their travels. The answer was always no. Yet he never gave up. It was where he was now. He always came home trying to put a brave face on it for her. But the disappointment took a toll.

"Mama! Mama! Come look!" Janie grabbed her by the hand, pulling her to the girls' room. The window in there viewed the ocean. "Over there, Mama! Do you see?"

"Who is with your da… OH!"

Sarah ran from the room, down the stairs, out the front door. She ran along the walkway to the lane, toward her husband, running as she had as a girl in Donegal. She ran without stopping until she wrapped her arms around her tall son with the wild red mane and a full beard.

"Willie!"

He picked her up and spun her around, just as Joseph used to do. "Mama! Oh, it is good to see you." He squeezed her as tight as she squeezed him and then set her on her feet.

That was when she noticed they were not alone. Two young women stood just behind him, huddled together, eyeing the exuberance.

Willie reached for the arm of one of the girls, who was… Oh! Obviously with child. "Mama, I want you to meet Maybe. My wife. Maybe, this is my mother, Sarah Crockett."

So much to take in. Sarah's brain froze until she realized she stared. "Oh, married." She blinked a few times and took a breath. "Maybe is it? That's an unusual name." She wiped her hands on her apron. "Oh, this is silly. Welcome to the family Maybe!" Sarah pulled the girl into an embrace.

She could tell it caught Maybe off guard, as she felt the tension in the girl's arms. It must be strange for her too.

"Please come in." She glanced at the other girl who remained behind, a trembling smile beneath wide eyes. "And you are—"

"Oh, this is Maybe's sister, Eliza. Ladies, we are home. And you've just started to meet the family." Willie linked his arm with Maybe's and his other with her. "What is for dinner, Mama? I have missed your cooking." He gave her a peck on the cheek.

But it did nothing to sort out the crazy emotions coursing through her brain.

Just as she thought she might go mad, a small voice in her heart whispered. *He's home. Willie is home. He's alive, and he is home. The rest will work out. He is home.*

Joseph caught her hand and held her back, while Willie led the girls to the house. She could hear the squeals of his sisters, each wanting to greet him and welcome him home. Joseph pulled her into an embrace. "He's home. Our prayers have been answered."

Sarah lay her ear against his chest, listening to the faithful beat of his heart. "Yer right, my love. Our boy is home. But I think he is a boy no longer."

"Jason, I need to speak with ye." This could prove to be a difficult conversation. Jason must move into the tiny guest room, adjacent the girls' room, and give his room to Willie and Maybe. Eliza could sleep with the girls, though that room was getting crowded now with two additions and no one leaving. Of course, the girls were too young to be leaving. Sarah's mind jumped from one thing to the next. "Jason!"

"Aye, Mama, what do you need?"

Sarah jumped. "Oh, I dinna hear ye come in, love." She took a breath. "I'm sorry, but I canna think of another way. Ye need to move into the guest room."

"I figured that would be the case. My things are in there already."

"Already?" She grew misty-eyed. How sweet and understanding this boy had become. She grabbed him in a quick hug and kissed his cheek.

"Aww, Mama. Please don't make a spectacle. It only made sense."

"Well, I thank ye anyway."

"And Mama, I am glad Willie is home. I missed him."

She smiled. "I know, love." One less worry. Now to discover the answers to her other prayers.

WILLIE LED MAYBE UPSTAIRS TO THEIR ROOM. THE brother—Jason, if she remembered right—helped his father move a bed out of the room into another.

"They need another bed in the girls' room, and we won't need it."

Willie's whisper startled her. She hadn't felt so out-of-place when she pretended to be a boy aboard the *Frances Pearl*. Did they all stare, or was it her imagination?

He guided her through the doorway, set their meager luggage in the corner, and kissed her cheek. "I will see if they need help with the bed. Why don't you rest? Perhaps I can bring a new pitcher of water so you can clean up before dinner."

"Won't yer mother expect me to help cook?" Her hands shook as images of going down there and doing the wrong thing raced through her brain.

"Not until you are ready, love. You'll be helping Mama soon enough. It is fine. Take a nap."

She nodded, not wanting him to worry or keep him from what he needed to do. But the dread of not knowing what was expected and the worry that they could judge her as wanton, unfit for their son, never left her mind. Slipping out of her cape, she laid it across the bags and sat on the edge of the bed. Unbidden, she started to bounce and caught herself smiling. The bed was friendly enough.

She lay back on the pillow and knew nothing more until a sound roused her. Glancing around, she spotted her mother-in-law setting a pitcher on the bureau. "Oh, I dinna ken I'd fallen asleep."

"I dinna mean to wake ye. I'm so sorry, it's just in case you might want this when ye woke."

Maybe raised herself. "No, it is fine, thoughtful. Thank ye very much."

Mistress Crockett smiled and backed to the door. "Let me know if ye need anything." She was out the room before Maybe's brain conjured a reply.

Perhaps the family was clueless concerning what to say, just as she? Or had the judgment already started.

Maybe stretched and got up. She'd been lazy enough. On the bureau she found fresh towels next to the basin, so she slipped down to her stays and petticoat and did a sponge bath. Her stays were becoming tight again. She'd have to have Eliza help her loosen them more. A clothing brush lay on the bureau top, too, so she used it to freshen her dress before re-donning it. Last, she ran a comb through her hair before adjusting her mobcap. Her hair was growing though nowhere near the length it had been. But it was also thicker than she'd ever known it to be. For a moment she felt Willie's fingers as they wound their way through her tresses. She warmed at the memory.

It was time. Maybe opened the door and went downstairs. Her ankle still pained her occasionally, but other than a slight limp when she wearied, no one else could tell. It only crossed her mind because of a twinge as she reached the last step.

"Is there a problem, love?" Willie must have seen her face reflect the twinge.

"No." She shook her head then wondered if she protested too much. "It's nothing. I thought I'd see how I can help."

"There's nothing to do now. Come watch." Willie led her to the kitchen room. Each of the girls had a job. It resembled a flock of birds as they danced in the sky, not bumping into one another, but moving in and out as if they had choreographed it. "One minute."

He left her side and, with his brother, moved the table into place and added the chairs around the table. They accomplished it as if made to do this job.

The only hitch Maybe noticed in the whole procedure was a young girl who flinched and moved to great lengths to keep away from Willie. No one explained her behavior. Had she been the only one to notice? Perhaps she misinterpreted what she saw.

The girls placed the food on the table and stood behind their chairs. Maybe glanced about, wondering where she should go—

her sister appeared to have found her place between two of the older girls.

Her mother-in-law understood. "Maybe, might you take the seat on Willie's right?" She indicated with a nod the next to the last chair as she stood by the one on the end.

The brother held the chair for his mother, and Willie held one for Maybe. The girls sat and then the men. All very proper, but so seamless. Each claimed the hands next to them, making a circle around the table. Willie's father blessed the food, and everyone chimed, "Amen."

Then everything changed to a cacophony of voices and clinks and passing sounds as food and thoughts were exchanged. Everyone wanted to hear from Willie, and he relished the attention. Laughs and gasps punctuated his stories. Maybe squeezed his hand as he chose them with care. He said nothing about her nor revealed anything that pointed to what actually happened. Not that he lied, but he redirected the stories from dangerous topics.

As things quieted, her mother-in-law glanced her way. "Maybe, I detect a lilt from me homeland in yer voice. From where in Ireland do ye hail?"

Maybe swallowed though she hadn't taken a bite, while her stomach fluttered. She knew there'd be questions. "Bantry Bay, Mistress."

"No! Bantry Bay? Joseph did ye hear? Did Willie tell ye that's where Joseph and I lived after we married?"

Maybe nodded. "Aye. He showed me the tower house and ruins, though I'd seen it my whole life growing up there."

"What was yer family name?"

"Boulay." Eliza blurted before Maybe came up with an answer.

"Boulay? Oh, now yer foolin' me. We knew a lad there, a David Boulay. In fact, he married a lovely lass not long after the pirate attack. He'd helped fend off the brutes and after said he couldn't waste another moment of this life without her. I was there when Reverend Fontaine married them."

Maybe could hardly speak. "That was me father."

"Oh, my. And ye've traveled all this way for us to meet. How are yer parents? I remember them with fondness."

The quiet pounded in Maybe's ears. They waited her answer, only her voice didn't want to say the hated words.

Willie put his arm about her shoulder. "They have passed, Mama."

Her new mother-in-law reached out and covered Maybe's hand. "I am sorry. They were caring people, very kind."

When Maybe glanced up, Willie's mother had a tear on her cheek. No wonder Willie was a good man.

"Doesn't anyone want to know what we learned today?" The little voice shifted focus from Maybe, and gratitude overflowed her heart for the child's kindness.

"Aye, Janie, what did you learn today?" Willie understood.

"I learned that God answers my prayers, even when it takes a long time."

"What did you pray for, little one?"

"I prayed for you, Willie. I prayed you'd come home safe, and you did."

It was slight, but Maybe could sense the change in the muscle tension from the arm Willie still draped over her shoulders. It was as if it merged with her, and they were together. His voice became husky too. "Thank you, Janie. Thank you all. It is good to be home."

This wasn't home yet. There were too many ugly memories associated with Beaufort. But sitting here with Willie's family, she understood why this was home for him. It was a place of love. If it was a place of acceptance, too, then it could be her home.

WILLIE REALIZED MAYBE WAS MORE THAN QUIET. THEY'D returned to their room, so conversation was free. "Were we a little overwhelming? Or was mentioning your parents too much?"

"Ye've a lovely family, Willie."

He came to her, taking her hand. "They are your family, now too."

"Perhaps soon, but we dunna ken each other enough yet." She sat on the edge of the bed. "But yer parents remember me parents. Do ye think if they'd never left, ye and me, perhaps we would've met there? And things would've been the way they should've been?"

Willie sat next to her. He'd been pondering something similar. "It's possible. I would have enjoyed courting you in Ireland. There's something romantic about that." He chuckled.

She ducked her head, but he noted the slight smile. "Aye, that is what I wish. But some things canna be prayed away."

"Prayed away?"

"What if yer family won't accept me or our baby? What if they condemn me? I canna blame them. I condemn meself."

Willie put a hand beneath her chin, guiding her gaze to meet his. "I don't condemn you. I love you. I love our baby. Mama often says God makes beauty from ashes. You just need to trust my love. Can you do that?"

She searched his eyes. "Aye, I will trust yer love, Willie. If yer with me, that is enough."

Pulling her to him, he held her close and whispered in her ear. "I love you, Maybe. I will never leave you. If anything ever separates us, I will fight my way back to you. Believe that."

☙❦❧

MAYBE WOKE THE NEXT MORNING TO FIND WILLIE ALREADY gone. They'd not had but two nights—three counting last night —together as man and wife though sleeping next to him was easy and full of comfort. She stretched until the thought of what her new mother-in-law might think about her lazy ways spurred her from the bed. After a quick wash, she dressed and hurried down to the kitchen.

Mistress Crockett was at the fireplace while the girls set the table. "Good day, Maybe. How did ye sleep?"

"Well, thank ye. How can I help?" She desired to be part of this amazing kitchen dance.

Her mother-in-law seemed to understand. "Ye can help me with the sausages."

Maybe sighed with relief. Something she could do. Her breathing returned to near normal. She took the spatula and began rolling the little meat logs about in the skillet.

Willie came in. He greeted his mother and sisters before planting a kiss on her cheek and trying to swipe a tidbit of sausage.

Maybe smacked his hand with the spatula, laughing. Something so comfortable and easy. This was what she'd dreamed married life would be. She found herself believing Willie's words.

One girl, the one who seemed uncomfortable around Willie last night, gasped and raced from the room as Willie left. Maybe heard footfalls on the stairs.

She glanced over at Willie's mother who nodded to another girl, the eldest one, who followed the other girl. "Is something wrong?"

Willie's mother called. "Lettie, Mary, please take over here? I must speak with Maybe a moment." The girls came at once, one smiled and held out her hand for the spatula.

Maybe handed it over and followed Mistress Crockett out the back door.

The crisp November air nipped at her nose causing it to drip. She sniffed and continued to follow to a carved bench where she was invited to sit and join her hostess.

"I need to explain about Aphra. And if I explain, I need to tell you something else."

Maybe's stomach began to make knots.

"Aphra is here because she had nowhere else to go. A man cruelly abused her. Now all men terrify her. It has taken time, but she is used to Joseph and Jason. But Willie is new to her, so she is afraid."

That wasn't so awful. Well, it was horrible for Aphra, and Maybe's heart went out to her, but it wasn't what she feared would be said.

"The reason I brought ye out here to tell ye is because we, Joseph and me, know who ye are."

They know who I am? The knots began in earnest.

Mistress Crockett took her hand. "When we found Willie's note, Joseph began to investigate. Yer… Daniel O'Malley's body was found the evening Willie left. No one knows if he was murdered or what happened. There was no proof. The neighbors informed the constable he had a daughter. Then our lasses discovered some young lady clothes up on Willie's hill and some strands of long black hair. Plus Jason noticed some of his older clothes were missing. It made us wonder if Willie was with a girl who wanted to look like a boy, but we dinna ken. As Joseph investigated, he learned more. One, that O'Malley's daughter was not his daughter, she was a stepdaughter named Elizabeth Boulay and that a man named Eleazar Ferguson was very interested in finding her."

The blood drained from Maybe's face. She froze. "Ye have said nothing?"

"Oh! We would never say anything. When Aphra came to us, we not only saw how abused she'd been, we learned who abused her. It was Eleazar Ferguson. We turned him in to the authorities and they found him guilty… of rape."

Maybe couldn't breathe, couldn't voice the question she needed to ask.

"They found him guilty, but he saved himself from the gallows by claiming Benefit of Clergy. He passed the test, so they put him into the pillory for a month and branded him a rapist.

Now he has nowhere to go, no one will do business with him. Joseph had to work with the constable and justice of the peace to keep him from starvation. He doesn't leave his house, and no one will work for him. The brand on his face identifies him." Mistress Crockett scooted closer and put her arm around Maybe. "We dinna understand everything when Willie left, but we know our son. He is good and kind. He has brought you here, and we will help him keep you safe."

Air forced itself into Maybe's lungs, and a cry wrung itself from her, unbidden. She leaned into her mother-in-law's arms.

Her new mother rocked her back and forth, patiently holding, caring, protecting her. She was home.

Chapter Twenty-One

December blew into the Carolinas with gusto. Willie peeked in the kitchen from the back and a chorus yelled, "Shut the door!"

"Aye!" He laughed, closed the door, and slipped next to Maybe, taking her by the hand and whispering, "Come with me." He led her to their room where he closed another door. "I have an idea."

Maybe didn't appear as excited as he felt. Well, of course he'd yet to tell her, but it was perfect and the answer to everything. She sat on the edge of the bed, gazing at him.

"Do you remember the exact words from that receipt your stepfather had?"

Now she looked stunned. "Aye, I'll never forget. 'One girl, seventeen years of age, four and a half stones. Sold to Eleazar Ferguson in lieu of the thirty-pound debt. Delivery expected the twentieth of May in the year of our Lord 1730. Debt paid in full upon delivery of girl.' Why?"

He took a breath. She'd love this. "We write another note. I'll include thirty-five pounds, so he even comes out ahead. And then he has no legal recourse with you." Willie grinned, waiting for her to get excited.

She didn't.

"What's the matter? The biggest problem is the legal part. We can protect you on everything else but until we correct the legal part, you cannot be yourself."

She tipped her head back and sighed. "Oh, Willie, there are so many questions. Where will we get the money? How do we get this to him without him knowing who sent it? And I am yer wife, why must ye pay for what I willingly give to ye?"

He was stunned. Didn't she understand? No court in the land would want to give her to that madman, but if he should produce the receipt, they would be legally bound. He sat next to her. "We have the money. Boatswain Johnson paid me for the work I did on the return trip. I only want you safe, Maybe."

She stroked his cheek. "I know, Willie. Yer heart is in the right place. But I think it's more of a problem than a help. Besides, we need that money when we build our house in the spring."

"So you don't want me to do it?"

"No, Willie, I dunna want ye to do it. Now I need to get back downstairs and help get dinner ready." She kissed his cheek. "But I love that ye were thinking of me."

He captured her face between his hands and thoroughly kissed her before letting her go. "Then back to the kitchen with you."

Her expression told him she was weighing her options. "Ye dunna play fair Willie Crockett."

"I know. I play to win." He winked at her. "I will see you downstairs, wife."

"As ye wish, husband." And she left the room.

Willie lay back on the bed. It was a great idea. She should trust him to do it. How many times had she said she wanted to be herself? Once they paid the madman, she could be herself without fear of anyone sending the law to collect her. He worked his jaw back and forth, as the idea argued with Maybe's comments in his brain. This was too important. He hopped up and dug into the top drawer of the bureau for the writing desk he'd taken to college and brought back nearly new. Once opened, he took out the little used quill, a clean sheet of paper, and the glass ink well. After mixing up the ink, he dipped the quill and then put it down. He needed to practice the words first. If Maybe had agreed, she could have written it for him but since she didn't, he needed to do it himself. He found a pencil and practiced the words. Once he thought he had them, he traced them with ink. And left a big smear. Great, he must do it again.

He crumpled the first try, tossing it in the corner, and started again with a pencil. Then with great care, he traced it. Once it was dry, he sealed it up with three ten-pound notes and one five-pound note. There'd be no claim they'd cheated him.

Beth called up the stairs to say dinner was ready just as he put the writing desk away.

"Coming!" He slipped the note into his pocket. Half the battle was over. Now to get it to Eleazar Ferguson.

❧

"I'm going for a walk, love, while you help here. I'll be back." Willie kissed her cheek and slipped out before Maybe could speak.

Her hand traced the place on her face while she stared after him. How odd. Confused, she shook her head and returned to putting the room to rights. It was quick and easy. *Many hands made light work.* That was her mother's voice in her head. She would appreciate this.

It still amazed her to watch the wonderful management her mother-in-law—no, Mother Sarah put in place. Maybe hoped she would someday be as skilled. Of course, she first must give birth to an army of children, as Mother did, though this once was adventure enough. She put the cleaning rag away, rubbed her growing belly, and smiled.

Since Willie was out, she wandered into the sitting room to see what the family was doing. Mother sat knitting something small while helping Janie with her math. The child was becoming proficient with multiplication facts. Lettie and Mary sat with perfect posture on the settee embroidering samplers while Martha and Beth wound yarn and spelled words to each other. Aphra and Eliza played a game of whist in the room's corner. Everyone was busy. Everyone had a place. What was her place?

Mother raised her head. "Do ye need something, Maybe?"

She shook her head, sorry to have disturbed things.

Mother patted the chair next to her. "Do ye ken how to knit?"

Maybe took the seat. "A wee bit. I'm no good at it, though."

"Then let me help you. Making baby things is the perfect practice. Here, I have some extra yarn and needles. Do ye ken casting on?"

"Aye. Thank ye." Maybe tried her hand. It had been some-time since she'd tried to knit, and as she'd never been skilled with the craft, it was tough to get started.

Mother set her project down and showed Maybe and then handed it back, giving her a chance to try. "There ye go, lass. Now do that about a hundred more times and ye can start a blanket for yer wee one." She smiled. "And by doing it that many times, yer hands will remember."

Maybe had no doubt they would.

❧

Eleazar had surveyed the tall man who paced back and forth in front of his house. He'd made a small opening in his draperies that allowed him to peek at the world without being seen. It amazed him the things one could view when no one knew they were under scrutiny. He'd walked to the door but never knocked. When past twilight and the man long gone,

Eleazar opened his door. At first he saw nothing. But then he spotted an envelope. It stuck out along the hinge side of the door. He brought it in and stared at it for over an hour, trying to be analytical. Why would someone leave him an envelope? Was there something dangerous about it? Did one of his former assistants send him a message? He dismissed that idea as none of them were that tall.

His curiosity grew, but the fear churning in his gut cried out for caution. Finally, his bed won out as curiosity and fear were at a stalemate.

❧

MAYBE HAD KNIT THREE ROWS, AS NEAT AS SHE COULD, BY the time Willie returned. "Look what yer mother taught me to do." She held up her needles with the small bit of yellow yarn. "Can ye see what it is?"

His eyes squinted, and he scratched his head. "A very long baby scarf?"

"No, silly man, 'tis a baby blanket." She smacked his arm.

He grabbed at his injury as if mortally wounded. "Ow! That was my second guess, honest!"

The women laughed. It was Willie being Willie. Maybe loved this playful side of him.

"May I take this to our room, Mother?"

"Of course, love. Sweet dreams to ye both."

Maybe kissed her cheek, and Willie followed suit before entwining his fingers with hers. His touch still sent tingles everywhere. She returned a squeeze before letting him lead her to their private place. He still wanted her, desired her, even though she was growing rounder with each passing day. It was a miracle. She wanted to wrap it up like a precious gift and hang on to it forever. Because she knew, this was too good.

Something would happen and ruin it.

But, if she just sealed this good into her memory, she might still remember that once she held happiness in her arms and it loved her back.

◈

COME MORNING, ELEAZAR WASHED AND DRESSED, TUGGED on his long sleeves, dusted off his shiny boots, and polished the crystal of his pocket watch before coming back downstairs. The envelope still waited. Well, it could continue to wait until after his coffee and whatever foods the constable supplied for breaking his fast.

Finally, he finished putting it off. His curiosity won. He lifted the seal and first noted the money. Thirty-five pounds. Who would give him money?

He returned to the letter, but that left him more puzzled. It appeared as if a child wrote the note. Not the giant oaf who delivered it last night. Inspecting, he worked out the gist of the words. When the meaning became clear, he drew in a breath. Someone knew about the sale with O'Malley. What else did they know? Who was this?

And then it hit him.

Whoever wrote the note had information on where to find her. Money or no money, he earned that girl. None of this humiliation would have happened if she hadn't run. She belonged to him, and he would find her if it was the last thing he did.

◈

WILLIE NOTICED THE MEN ENTER THE SHOP BEFORE HIS father did, so he went to offer his help. "Welcome, how can we be of service?"

Of the two, the first assumed charge, the other remained quiet. "Well, we've got this grab chain hook here that won't last the trip to Puerto Rico, so we were wondering if you could fix it or fashion another."

Willie held out his hand. "Let me see."

The quiet man handed it to him.

Willie recognized the piece. "You say you're headed to the Caribbean?"

"Aye."

Willie continued to turn it over in his hand, memories of being at sea splashing over his brain. "Then you want this fixed. We can do it. Off the mizzen or the main?"

"Mizzen. You know ships?"

"Some. Sailed on the *Frances Pearl* to Ireland and back."

"You did now. Sam Johnson's the boatswain on her, right? Word is he runs a tight ship."

"Aye. He's firm but fair. A good man."

"That's what I heard too. Well, if you were good enough to sail with Sam Johnson, you're good enough to sail with us. I need another crewman to fill the roster. What do you say, laddie? Tired yet of being a landlubber?"

Willie laughed, and for a brief instant he thought about the wind and manning the wheel. But then he saw Maybe, standing at the rail, stunning even dressed as a boy. She was here. So was his heart. "No, sorry, I'm not interested. I have a wife, and she's expecting. I'm staying put."

"If you change your mind, you can tell us when we come back for the part. When will it be ready?"

Tossing the part in his hand, Willie put the last of his sea dreams away. "I can have it ready this afternoon. Say three o'clock?"

"Done. We'll be back then."

Willie waved as they left. Funny, he hadn't thought about going to sea once since they came home. Not something he would choose again. However, if there was no Maybe, would he do it? Willie shook his head. He didn't want to know.

MAYBE STRAIGHTENED THEIR ROOM, MADE THE BED. Standing in the doorway, she saw something crumpled in the corner. A piece of paper.

She picked it up, thinking to toss in the trash, when her curiosity got the better of her. She pulled it open. Childish scrawl, with ink over pencil, stared back. Why would the younger girls…? Her breath came hard as she deciphered the words.

Mastr Fergsn, plese find enclsd the pris of therty ponds for one grl purchsed from Danel O'Maly plus anther five punds for yor trubl.

She sank on the bed. He did it. She said no, but he did it. What was she to do now?

MAYBE REPLACED THE LAST POT ON THE SHELF, WIPED HER hands on her apron, and went in search of Eliza. They didn't talk as much as she thought they would. Coming over on the ship, they had caught up with each other's lives, though Maybe had lied, saying she and Willie married secretly in New York but had to hide it from the crew. She couldn't face telling her sister the truth.

But somehow, the lie became a wedge between them. Maybe feared saying too much in case she exposed her lie. Now Eliza even seemed to prefer Aphra's company to hers. Well, they were close in age.

But today she needed to talk with her sister. There was no one else. It wouldn't be fair to burden Mother, she was really Willie's mother. Even if it meant telling Eliza more than she wanted to tell her, she needed to find her sister. She needed someone to help her know what to say to Willie.

Eliza wasn't in the sitting room or kitchen. Upstairs, Maybe knocked on the girls' door and marched in without waiting.

Aphra was alone, washing at the basin. She gasped, spun around and grabbed her dress, holding it in front of her.

"I'm sorry, Aphra. Was just looking for Eliza. Sorry." Maybe retreated to her own room. Though Aphra had turned to face her, covering herself with her dress, she wasn't quick enough. The scars on her back, arms and chest—from burns and cuts— glared at her. All places modest dress would cover, but when revealed told the story of the tortures she endured at the hands of Eleazar Ferguson.

That could be her.

Maybe grabbed the chamber pot and lost her lunch.

⁂

Maybe was quieter than usual throughout supper. Willie tried teasing, whispering in her ear, but she pushed him away. He hoped no one else noticed, but he knew. Something was wrong.

After things were clean and put away, she didn't wait for him but went straight upstairs. He followed and closed their door behind him. "Would you like to tell me what's wrong? I feel you are angry with me."

"Guess you're not as stupid as I thought."

Stupid? She thought him stupid? His heart dropped to his gut. Had she always? "Why do you say that?"

"Dinna I say no to sending that note? Just yesterday, dinna I say no?"

Oh, no. How had she found out? Then he wanted to call himself stupid. The messed-up page. He'd left it on the floor. "I know you said no, but I had to fix this. We have everything else taken care of, but if the law becomes involved, I don't know what might happen."

"What did your father say?"

Willie stared at his feet, willing them to send up the right words.

"Ye dinna ask him, did ye? We come back here so ye can learn from yer father, and when the most important thing we have to deal with at the moment rises, ye try out yer own idea without asking his opinion?"

He sighed. "You are right. It was a stupid thing to do. I'm sorry."

Her hands straddled what was left of her hips. She still seemed angry.

"Maybe, I really am sorry. Honest. Even when I mess up, I'm trying to do the right thing. Please." He tried giving her the look that got him out of trouble with his mother. Not that Maybe was like his mother, but at this point he was willing to try whatever it took. "Come on, can't you forgive your oaf?"

She sighed. "Ye really are an oaf some days, Willie Crockett. But ye are my oaf."

"So you aren't angry?"

"Oh, aye, I am angry, just not as much."

He could live with that. "I say let's change the subject. What shall we talk about?" He took a step in her direction.

She didn't move, so he took another. Three more steps and he had closed the gap between them. Standing behind her, he wrapped his arms about her disappearing waist. "What did you do today wife?"

"Besides the usual of helping with meals and lessons and working on the baby blanket?"

He nuzzled her ear while his hands wandered to her growing belly, waiting for the little flutter. "Um"

"Suppose ye tell me about yer day."

By now he was trailing kisses down her neck. "I was offered a position on a ship sailing for the Caribbean tomorrow."

She spun in his arms and pushed him away. "What?"

"I said I was—"

"I heard ye, I jist canna believe it? What of yer promises?

What about ye would never leave me? Was that jist until another ship docked?"

He stared at her. There were no words he could form. How did she jump to the conclusion that he took the job? The walls closed in more than they had since they'd returned. He shook his head and headed out the door.

"Then away with ye! Go sail your ship! See if I care!"

Each word stabbed him deeper. "Perhaps I will!" He headed outside for air.

◈

Sarah grabbed Joseph's hand as the angry voices floated past, followed by the sound of two slamming doors. He understood. He squeezed her hand and followed his son.

Catching up before he turned toward the bluff, Joseph touched the boy's shoulder. "Slow down a mite, son. Let's walk to the commons."

Willie returned a brief nod and slowed his pace, moving in the direction Joseph suggested.

Flashes of memory, recalling the last time they had made this walk, sparked in Joseph's mind causing him to consider his words. He still thought he could have kept his son from running off to sea if he'd framed his advice different. Perhaps not, considering what he'd learned of Maybe's situation. If he'd kept his son from the sea, what would have become of that young woman? Too many questions to answer. Tonight the ones to focus on now had to do with how to help his son and daughter-in-law.

Joseph found the large rock he'd used for a seat the last time and sat watching Willie pace, as per his nature, and kick about oyster shells. Patience was his friend. He needed to stay patient until Willie was ready to talk.

The pacing stopped. Willie ran a hand through his hair. "I'm lost, Da. I try and try to do things the right way, to protect her, to help her. She must realize that I love her, am here for her. Just when I start to get through, something always happens."

"Want to tell me about it?"

"No. And yes. I need to explain, tell you stuff I don't want to say. So you can understand. You won't like me much. I don't like myself much when I remember." He ground the toe of his boot into the dirt.

Joseph could guess, though he didn't want to think of his son like that. It was too late for recriminations, though, so he remained silent.

"Maybe told me you and Mama know who she is. What you don't know is that O'Malley sold her to pay his debts. He sold her to Eleazar Ferguson. She found out and ran away. I found her, or rather she found me, up on the bluff. I wanted to help her, Da. So I came up with this idea. We dressed her as a boy, and I cut her hair. Then we signed on to the *Frances Pearl* and left. The plan was to get her to Ireland where I'd help her find her sister, and then leave, go back to sea. Only things happened. I guess I fell in love with her. But I realized if I acted on it, things would be more dangerous for her. No one could recognize she wasn't a boy."

He began pacing again, his hands more expansive. "Then one night we went ashore in Boston. It is a long story, but I assumed I was man enough to try some ale. I learned later my friends substituted whiskey without my knowledge. It didn't take much. I wasn't used to it." Even in the moonlight, Willie's cheeks had more color, and it wasn't from the chilly December air. "Maybe found me and my companions. There was a rule about coming aboard drunk. She didn't want me flogged, so she hid me. From what they told me, I was pretty loud. There's much I don't remember. She kept trying to shut me up and as a last resort, she kissed me."

Joseph scooted over and made room to share his seat on the rock. "You don't have to tell me.

Willie plopped next to him. "I need to. You need to understand it is my fault. Come morning, when I tried to remember, the memories came back. It shocked me. I'd let my guard down, knowing I couldn't get involved with her if I was protecting her. Then I took advantage. I was so ashamed." He had yet to meet Joseph's gaze.

"Later we talked, and I apologized. I had already told her I'd stay until she found her sister, but in my head I planned to court her once in Ireland, and ask for her hand. Make things right, for her. While on ship, that was impossible." He kicked a shell. "Well, we had some delays getting to Ireland, a few months in fact. Then Maybe fell from the Jacobs ladder. When the surgeon checked her, he discovered she was a girl and with child." For the first time, Willie caught Joseph's gaze. "I swear, I didn't know until that moment."

"I believe you, son." And he did.

"The boatswain agreed to keep things quiet, for Maybe's sake, but had the master of the ship marry us right then. We were less than two days from landing at Bantry Bay. Ever since I have done everything I can imagine doing, Da."

"Such as?"

"I tell her how much I love her. I do everything to protect her, care for her. I even sent a note and paid Eleazar Ferguson thirty-five pounds so he has no legal recourse. She tells me she just wants to be herself. If she doesn't have to hide from him anymore, that should help, right?"

Joseph stood, grabbing his son by the shoulders. "You did what?" He could shake that boy.

"I paid Eleazar thirty-five pounds and wrote him a note."

"Oh, William. That man has no regard for legality. You have only told him she is hiding somewhere in the community. What if he saw you?" For the first time since Willie came home, Joseph felt worry gnawing in his belly.

"Maybe asked if I had talked to you about the idea. She didn't like it and told me not to, but I thought it was the best way to protect her."

"Who wrote the note for you?" How many others now knew about this?

"I wrote it. Da, I know my writing it terrible, but I was careful. I wrote in pencil and then traced with quill and ink. I got a splotch on the first try so wadded it up and tossed it aside, planning to get rid of it later, but Maybe found it. That's what started the fight. But I thought we had it worked out, that she forgave me."

Joseph sighed. There was more? "What happened?"

"We began talking about our day. I told her some men offered me a position on a ship heading to the Caribbean, but before I could say I turned it down, she assumed I was leaving her. She yelled and screamed, saying she thinks I'm stupid. I guess I am, but I wouldn't lie to her. I promised her I'd never leave her, I don't want to leave her. Why can't she just trust me?"

Joseph shook his head. His son needed to hear some hard facts. "Willie, there is something I need to share with you that all expectant fathers should understand. Mothers-to-be carry two lives, sometimes more. That changes more than just their figures. It changes how they see the world, how they see themselves. It questions everything they ever took for granted. A woman runs a gamut of emotions that would make a man go mad. Yet, for the gift of a child, she does it." He wrapped his arm about his son's shoulders. "Maybe isn't doing this on purpose. She feels out of control and scared, and in all that she's terrified you will leave and needs reassurance of your love."

Willie nodded. "That sounds like Maybe."

"Remember, you weren't given much time to be a husband and wife before needing to be parents too. This will be harder in some ways. But, be patient. What she misses with your words, let her see the proof of in your actions."

"Aye, Da. I should have come to you sooner."

Joseph blew out a breath. They'd deal with the note thing. If it came up. The rest, he'd pray for guidance for Willie and Maybe. "Let's go home."

"You go. I want to mull over your advice. Get it into my brain. I also want to give her a chance to cool down before she throws something at me—she's got a good aim." He laughed.

"Aye, I will see you at home, then. Don't take too long, son."

"I won't." They embraced. "Thank you, Da."

"One last thing. Something important that my father used to tell us. He said it came from the Proverbs. 'Make sure you are right, then go ahead.' Think about it, son. That advice has helped me more than I can say." He paused, emotion constricting his words. "Son, my father would have enjoyed you." He wanted to say more, but thoughts of his father brought moisture to his eyes and closed his throat.

He hugged his son once more and headed back to the house.

Chapter Twenty-Two

S arah tapped at the door.

Maybe threw it open, her fist raised in the air. Her gusto deflated, and she dropped her fist. "Oh, I'm sorry. I thought it were Willie."

And ye would hit him? Sarah bit her tongue, remembering what it was like to have her emotions whirl within when she carried one of her babes. She also remembered more than once when she'd wanted to strike Joseph. "Might I come in?"

"Of course." Maybe held the door and stepped aside.

"How can I help, darlin' girl?"

Maybe appeared to crumble in front of her.

Sarah wrapped her arms about the girl and helped her to the chair. "Oh, child, this is just one bump in the road. When ye both are calm, ye can talk it all out."

Maybe grabbed a piece of paper off the table and thrust it as Sarah. "Look at this! Look what he did! How can I go hiding when he's telling the villain I'm here?"

Sarah opened the wrinkled page and her breath caught in her throat. There was no missing her son's writing or misspelling. *Willie, what were ye thinkin'?* "He shouldn't have done this. But perhaps he was trying to protect you?"

Maybe stared at her shoes. "Yer right. He's always tryin' to protect me, even when I tell him not to do it."

"Ye told him not to do this?"

"Aye, and he did it anyway. And then he found himself a position on another ship."

"What?" Sarah's blood turned to ice, and her knees went weak. She reached for the bed and lowered herself to sit. "Why would he do this?"

"Because he loves the sea more than he loves me or our baby." Tears traversed Maybe's cheeks.

"Och, no, I canna believe such a thing. Oh, no. There must be another reason. He loves you with all his heart. There must be more to this."

Maybe sniffed. "He was telling me about his day and said he someone offered a position aboard a ship heading for the Caribbean."

"They offered him. What did he say?"

"What else could he say? Someone dangles his favorite thing in front of him, he's bound to grasp at it."

Sarah's heart began to return to a normal beat. "Ah, but he didn't tell you he agreed, did he?"

Maybe met Sarah's gaze. She could see understanding dawning in the girl's eyes. "Oh, he dinna say!" Then her face grew fearful. "He dinna say because I never gave him the chance! I just yelled at him as if he said aye. What have I done?" Her hands covered her face, and new sobs filled the air.

Sarah came to her, kneeling in front of her. "Oh, lovey, it will be fine. Do not worry. Willie will be back in a thrice. Ye can tell him yer sorry and listen to what he has to say. He wouldn't leave ye. He loves ye."

Maybe threw her arms about Sarah and sobbed harder. "It is worse than that. I called him stupid. I know he isn't. But I also know that is something that hurts him. I wanted to hurt him right then. What have I done? He won't want to come home to me now."

There was nothing left to do but hold her new daughter in her arms and rock her back and forth until Joseph brought Willie home.

Twenty minutes later, Sarah heard the front door open and close and breathed a sigh of relief. Maybe had calmed, but she needed to see Willie. They needed to talk this out. At least things were on the mend.

Joseph peeked in.

"Where's Willie?"

"He'll be along. He wanted time to think before returning. I'm guessing he walked to the bluff. He will be back."

Maybe lifted her head. "But he's coming back?"

"Aye, lass. He's coming back. Have no fear."

The girl's muscles relaxed. A moment later she pulled back and wiped her face.

Sarah tucked a curl behind Maybe's ear. "I think we should let ye wash yer face and straighten yer cap before he gets here. Joseph, let's go to our room." She reached for his hand reveling in the strength he sent her.

Joseph nodded. "Aye, we'll be in our room if you need anything."

"Thank ye, Mother, for listening and setting me straight."

Sarah blew a kiss to her and let Joseph lead her.

WILLIE THOUGHT OF WALKING TO THE BLUFF, THEN changed his mind. Maybe was right concerning one thing: he loved the sea. The freedom he felt while sailing compared to nothing he'd ever experienced. Without planning, his feet led him toward the docks. Even this late, a few sailors and strangers walked about. He glanced at the faces and spotted a common denominator. Too many looked lonely. He would be lonely, too, without Maybe. He might have planned to rescue her, but if he were honest, she rescued him. And as much as he loved sailing, he one hundred times more loved holding her in his arms, viewing their future in her amazing eyes, and caressing her soft skin before allowing her kiss to sail him high above the clouds. It was no contest. His life was with Maybe. He wanted no other.

Shoving his hands in his pockets, he turned his steps toward home, toward Maybe and their family.

Then all went black.

❧

SARAH WOKE AND DRESSED. THOUGH STILL DARK, SHE needed to get the fires banked and the kitchen ready for cooking. Upon opening the door, she noted a shadow at the top of the stairs. A step closer, she could see Maybe sat on the top step, her head resting against the wall.

"Maybe, love, what are ye doin' here?"

"He didn't come home, Mother. Willie didn't come home."

"Joseph!" Sarah sat next to her, holding on to the girl who looked like she might faint. She'd been here all night? How had she kept from falling headfirst down the stairs?

Joseph emerged a moment later.

"Carry her to her bed. I'll stay with her while ye find yer son."

"My son?" He scooped Maybe in his arms.

"He's yers when he doesn't come home all night and leaves this poor child worried sick." She followed him to Maybe and Willie's door. "I'll have Beth and the girls start breakfast." Knocking first, she opened the girls' door and told them to get things started. She returned to Maybe as Joseph left their bedroom. "Please find him, love. I had such peace last night, but this morning I fear something is wrong."

He kissed her forehead and went downstairs. Seconds later she heard the front door. She lifted a prayer for her son and returned to Maybe.

WILLIE LISTENED TO A FAMILIAR SOUND BUT AT FIRST couldn't place it. Then it came to him, lapping water. He was aboard a ship. He sat as panic convulsed in his muscles. It was dark but for a few overhead cracks seeping lines of gray light. He was in the hold.

Feeling around, he got to his feet. His hands found no cargo in front of him, so he took a few steps. And tripped. He fell, landing on his right side, smacking his elbow against something. What had he tripped over? Moving to his hands and knees, he heard a moan. He used his hands to investigate in that direction, finding a body, a man based on his clothing. And alive, if the moan were any indication. He found the man's shoulder and shook it. "Hey, are you all right? Hey!"

The man moaned again and tried to roll from him. Willie grabbed him and shook hard.

"Stop. Ow, me head. Stop shaking. Where am I?"

"That's what I'd like to know." Willie ran his fingers through his hair, finding a very tender spot. Ow! He dropped next to the man as understanding clobbered him. "I'm not sure, mate, but I think we've been impressed."

JOSEPH WANDERED NEAR THE DOCKS. HE'D FOUND nothing to give him a clue up on Willie's hill so he tried here. He wasn't alone. Another man was there with a woman. They asked questions about a missing brother who didn't come home last night.

"You too? My son is missing."

"Aye, Andy only went out for a wee bit last evening. Wanted to stretch his legs a mite, he said. He didn't come back. We've been asking questions for over an hour."

"Have you learned anything?"

"Only one word. Impressed. I'm praying that's not it, but if yer son is missing, too, then I think we know what happened." The man put his arm about his sister as she dabbed her eyes with a handkerchief. He turned her away from the docks and toward the town.

"What do you intend to do?" Joseph called after them. This couldn't be all.

The man paused and glanced over his shoulder. "Go home and pray. That is all that is left."

Joseph had been praying, ever since before he left the house. He needed to do something. He needed to bring his boy home. He needed to find his son. Now.

He turned back to the dock. The sun teetered on the eastern horizon, the area buzzed with people going about their business. It overwhelmed him. How could life appear so normal when men went missing?

Where did he start? Where should he look? There was no giving up on his boy.

Where to begin? What was the starting point in all this busyness?

If Willie had been impressed, that ship would have already left port. Something inside left him in that instant. He had no power, no control, no say. This had happened, and he had no strength to change it.

The man was right. There was nothing to do but go home and pray. Helplessness weighted his steps. How did he tell Sarah and Maybe that Willie had been taken?

He needed to pray before returning home.

❧

"Ho, you there, down in the hold. Come to the ladder."

Willie helped the man up, a boy really, called Andrew Ryan.

They felt their way towards the ladder by the light from the above opening.

"Climb on up here."

Willie followed instructions with Andrew coming behind him.

Daylight blinded him after so long in the dark hold. He scrubbed his eyes with his palms and surveyed his surroundings. They were out to sea. Land was a tiny speck aft in the distance.

It was also his first chance to view Andrew. He was young, maybe sixteen and scared. The scared part registered the loudest.

They were prodded from behind to move closer to the bow. "Stand over there."

Willie moved where indicated, still working out in his brain how this ship was run. If he could get an idea of that, he might plan the best way to extricate himself from this situation. Something he would have time to think on since land behind them was shrinking fast.

The crew made a semi-circle around them with one more man standing on the bowsprit, a coiled whip in his hand. He appeared to be in charge, though Willie wasn't sure yet if he was a boatswain or a master. The ship appeared to be a sloop, a smaller ship than the *Frances Pearl*. It looked to be a crew of twelve, far scruffier than his former mates.

The man up front raised his fist, the crew grew silent. "Mates, we have new men on the *Saucy Sally*. We want to help them feel right at home, learn the rules of our ship. So mates, who is the boss?"

"Declan Stryker!" They sang out in unison.

"Who makes the rules?"

"Declan Stryker!"

"And if you don't agree, who's right?"

"Declan Stryker!"

"One last question. Who is Declan Blackheart Stryker?"

"You are!"

The man jumped down and walked to Willie and Andrew, tucking the whip under their chins. It assured attention and intimidation all in one move. It worked well with Andrew who trembled.

"You're not afraid of me, are you." It was a statement, not a question.

"Am I supposed to be, sir?" He wasn't about to show it, that was for sure.

The man chuckled. "Nice touch. Polite arrogance." He moved to Andrew. "Now this one, he's terrified. That is fine. He'll do as he's told." Then back to Willie. "But you, I'm not sure you know how to be obedient." He lowered his hand with the whip. "I could wait and see, but we don't have that luxury." He turned to the crew. "Take him!"

Three men grabbed Willie.

The instant they started to drag him, he knew what was about to happen. And it would only happen when he couldn't fight them anymore.

Willie kicked and thrashed and bit. He yanked his arm free and punched. They might get him there, but they would pay for doing it.

It took eight of the crew, but they dragged him to the mast. Someone tore his waistcoat off him, buttons popping and flying. Then someone else ripped open the back of his shirt while others tied his hands to the metal ring on the mast and bound his feet together. They ran the line from his hands, through the ring, and down to his boots and pulled it taut.

The first crack of the whip never touched him. It was for effect, to make him anticipate and fear. It nearly worked as there was a sudden need to urinate. Willie gritted his teeth. *I will not call out. I will not make a sound.*

The next crack made contact. He gasped but refused to cry out. Another crack, another tongue of fire down his back. He set his jaw.

By the fifth crack, his knees grew weak, but he would not give satisfaction. He put his mind on Maybe. He saw her smile, he touched her face, he kissed her lips. He knew nothing more.

❦

Maybe held onto Mother's hand, terrified that she would be alone if she let go. Together they waited for the sound of the front door opening. "What if he canna find him? What if he changed his mind?"

"Hush now, lovey, he dinna change his mind. I dunna ken why he isn't here, but I know Willie. If he told his father he would come back, then that was his plan."

What if something happened to him? The blood drained from her face. What if he was in danger because she chased him out of the house? "Oh, tis all my fault! What if…?" The awful things she imagined were too awful to put into words.

"'Tis not yer fault. He said he'd be back, he'll be back. Ye've got to have faith, lovey. Faith in yer husband but more important, faith in yer God. He not only loves ye, He loves Willie and will help him. God will bring him home to us."

"I dunna have any faith left. At least not in God. It has been one thing after another—me father, me mother, now Willie." She feared closing her eyes, afraid she would imagine a lifeless picture of him in her mind. It sent a chill down her spine.

"Willie is not dead. I'll have no talk like that. And ye've got the baby to consider. Ye want to remain strong to bring Willie's babe into the world. What if he walks in and sees you like this? What would he say?"

Right now she wasn't as worried about what he would say as she was terrified he couldn't come through the front door. She needed him. *Oh, God, please don't take Willie too!* A little faith? That was all she had, but she put every bit into her plea and prayed God heard her.

The front door opened and closed. Mother helped her sit up and wiped her face as footfalls sounded on the stairs.

Then her father-in-law stood in the doorway. Alone.

Mother rose, facing him, but his eyes remained on Maybe. Was it the December winds or had he been crying?

"I'm sorry, Maybe. I should have insisted he come home with me."

"Joseph, where is he? Where did he go?"

He stood there, his mouth working like he wanted to speak, but his voice refused. He swallowed. "They've impressed him."

Maybe couldn't breathe. Air would not go in or out. The room swirled before everything went dark.

❧

"Why'd he hit him so hard? Now we've got to lug him around."

"Y' know Declan cannot abide someone who won't submit. If he'd just hollered a bit, it would have been better for him."

"He's coming around. Hey, hey you."

Willie tried to bat the hand away. Air caught in his chest. It hurt to breathe, let alone move. All the surrounding voices drew him from the dark, making him more aware of his pain. "What?"

"Hey, you sure made Declan angry. You might want to not do that."

"I'll try to remember that. What are you doing with me?" How long had he been out?

"We're trying to get you to your bunk. If you lay still, we can put some bandages across your back."

Willie wasn't sold on the idea. He'd seen how clean the ship wasn't and remembered what infection had done to Cookie. "I'll be fine. Where is my waistcoat? That will cover my back."

"I doubt you'll see your waistcoat again, unless Declan decides to wear it. He's got your boots too."

Willie rubbed one bare foot against the other and inspected the men. They were both in their forties, perhaps, and about the same size and weight—short and wiry. But that was where the similarities ended. The one doing most of the talking, and emphasizing that Declan (whoever that was) didn't like him, had dark hair and a touch of scruff. The other, the one more concerned about tending his wounds, had dirty blond hair and a full beard. "Do you have names?"

"Aye. I'm called Long John." That was the dark one.

"Long John?"

"Well, me Christian name is Georgy Galloway, but who goes by their Christian name out here?"

"And I'm Bucktooth. Or Benjamin Spade."

"Bucktooth?"

The blond one smiled. Bucktooth.

"So who are you?"

Willie started to give his name, then thought better. If there was a way for Declan or anyone to use it against him, he would not make it easy. His brain whirled with ideas they might accept. "Rusty. Rusty Samson." He better understood how the Old Testament hero felt.

"Rusty Samson. Good to meet ya. What should we do about your back?"

Back when he helped the surgeon on the *Francis Pearl*, they used ocean water instead of drinking water. The surgeon thought the salt properties helped prevent infection. But it would hurt, he knew. Better to hurt than die of infection. "I need some ocean water. Either something to pour over me, or on strips of cloth. Better to pour over me. I need to rinse my breeches."

The men gaped and nodded. Bucktooth jumped up to go fetch.

Long John just shook his head. "I wonder who will win between you and Declan. Much more, and I might be putting my money on you."

"What is the problem with Declan? Why does he feel such animosity toward me?"

"Oh, Bucko, you haven't seen animosity. Declan is just

trying to fill the britches of our former captain. Now, ol' Silas Keel, he was one hard one, that's for sure. He'd have had you keelhauled. That's how he got his name, Silas Keel. Never knew his Christian name, don't supposed he had one. But now that Declan is in charge, he wants to show he's just as mean. He could be, but he's still got a streak of fear. That was something ol' Silas never had. Caution, aye, but fear, never."

Chapter Twenty-Three

Sarah knew, better than her name, that if she didn't care for Maybe and the baby, she would fall apart this very instant. But taking care of her new daughter meant caring for her spiritual needs as well as any others, and in doing so, she opened her own heart to let the Holy Spirit care for her.

Maybe refused to eat or drink unless reminded of the baby. Then she only took nourishment and rolled over in bed. She would lose her physical strength if this continued. Sarah was at a loss, but remained by her side, reading from her Bible while Maybe slept. Daily, verses spoke to her, strengthening her, giving her hope. Still she hesitated to read aloud to Maybe. If she forced the issue before the girl was ready, she could not only turn her away from the one hope they had, she could crush any tiny hope to which Maybe still clung.

Sarah closed her eyes and began praying the verses she'd read that day. *You are my strong tower. You are my hope. You never leave nor forsake me.* She prayed for Willie, over and over, that he would recall what they had poured into him since birth. That God's Word that was hidden in his heart would come forth as a sword to bring him victory and bring him home. She prayed for

Joseph who blamed himself and struggled to lead now. Sarah prayed as she had never prayed before.

"Yer praying. Again. Do ye think He hears?"

Sarah opened her eyes to see Maybe watching her.

"Aye, I do."

Maybe closed her eyes. "I prayed, too, but I dunna ken why He'd listen to me."

Sarah knelt by the bed and took Maybe's hand in hers. "Oh dear heart, you are His precious child. Why would He not listen?"

"Because I'm not worth it. Even when I was… even when I tried to do what was right, He still dinna hear my prayers. And now, Mother, ye dunna ken just how bad I am."

"Do ye want to tell me?" She stroked the hair back from Maybe's forehead.

"Ye will not like me if I do, ye will not want me to call ye Mother."

Sarah smiled. "I doubt that, but ye can try."

"Our baby is a punishment from God."

Sarah stifled the gasp fighting to escape. She was under no illusion the baby came before marriage, but why point it out? They were married and loved each other. No one else would guess when they married. But to view this sweet gift as punishment? "Maybe love, a baby is a gift, not a punishment. And only more proof that God loves ye. He offered ye this gift to love and care for. It shows His trust in ye."

"But, but we… we had relations before we married."

"I've had a few babies of my own. I can count."

"And ye dinna say anything?"

"What was there to say? Ye love Willie; Willie loves ye. Ye are married and planning a family. Ye might have gotten started off on the wrong foot, but ye found yer way."

"And ye dunna condemn me?"

"Why would I do that now? Yer my daughter. I love ye like one of me own."

Maybe started to sob.

Sarah took her in her arms and rocked her. This child needed mothering before she became a mother.

In fifteen minutes, Maybe had drifted to sleep so Sarah tiptoed downstairs to get her something to eat for when she woke. The kitchen was in perfect order. She had taught her daughters, and with the help of her extra girls, they were doing a wonderful job. It relieved Sarah of that worry.

Beth had made more oatcakes, so she put them on a plate. She picked up a crumb and popped it in her mouth. The child was becoming skilled at this. She added a few more to the plate for herself.

Sarah was just ready to put the hot water in the teapot when she glanced up. Maybe stood in the doorway. "What are ye doing out of bed? I can bring this up to ye."

She shook her head. "I've had enough of wallowing. I need another view."

Perhaps this was good, the beginning of an answered prayer. "Fine, let's repair to the sitting room." Sarah added two cups to the tray and led the way.

The children were in there, quietly working on schoolwork. Each of the older ones had a younger one to assist—Jason helped Mary, Beth helped Martha, Eliza helped Lettie, and Alpha helped Janie. Sarah blinked back tears. Beth raised her head, so she mouthed, "Thank you."

"We might be in the way." She smiled. "Let's go to the kitchen. I'll take down some chairs." Sarah retraced her steps with Maybe following her.

Once they were comfortable at the table, Sarah poured. "I'm glad to see you come down here."

Maybe stared into her cup. "I had to. My staying in bed won't bring him back. I've been terrified of what ye'd say if ye knew. I…"

Sarah watched the girl and waited. Things were coming out,

things that blocked her faith. Well, let them come, be dealt with, and gone.

"The day Willie and I had that argument, I wanted to tell Eliza everything. She doesn't know the truth. I went looking for her. Someone said they thought she was with Aphra upstairs. So I opened the door." She shook her head and her voice dropped. "I walked in on Aphra as she bathed."

Sarah was aware of what she'd seen. It was shocking, disturbing. That was why the girl bathed when she thought no one might see her. She still physically hid herself from the other girls. No one but Sarah had seen the scars until now.

"It made me ill. And then all I could think was that could be me. That's the real reason I became so furious with Willie. I was terror struck I would end up like that."

How did Sarah respond to that? Was it selfish to fear something so vile? No, and it didn't mean she had no pity for what Aphra endured. "Aphra has come a long way since she arrived at our home. There are times I want to take all those bad memories from her and bury them far away. But I can't say I'd be brave enough to endure what she has gone through in her place. I'm not that brave. I am that flawed." Sarah took a breath and weighed her words. "Ye were a target of that mad man. It is natural that ye would fear. And I can see how Willie's note would make it even worse. Ye know that Jesus understood what the punishment for sin was. He knew what He would face on the way to the cross. His flesh, the part of Him that was human, begged the Father for a different plan. But there was no other way. He took our punishment. Every strike, every jab, every humiliation. Even the pain, the agony, all the way to the cross, all the way to death. He took it all. That is why when ye ask forgiveness in His name, the Father hears and yer sins are gone. Jesus took them."

"I ken, I just…"

"So yer sins are special and need something other than Jesus?"

Maybe's eyes grew wide. "No, I dunna think that."

"Well, that's what I'm hearing. When He said all, He means all. Why not yers?" Sarah's heart pounded. She hadn't expected to say all that. Was it too much?

Maybe continued to stare into her cup, having yet to take a sip. "What should I do?"

Praise God! "Ye might start by praying and telling God ye are sorry for yer sins. Ask Him to come into yer heart and help ye to be the person He created ye to be."

"Will ye pray with me?"

"Aye, sweet girl, aye." And she did.

When they raised their heads, Sarah saw something new in Maybe's eyes. Hope.

❦

"Rusty, ho, Rusty, we gotta go up on deck. Declan calling." Long John sounded eager.

No matter, the chance to stand in the sun was a gift. Willie got stuck below deck with every menial and demeaning job Declan could find. Obviously, the boss wanted to break him, but Willie was as determined not to be broken.

The sun gleamed up on deck, the refection off the water blinding him at first. But the warmth of its rays caressed his skin, and the air above smelled much cleaner. A week of being enclosed below was worse than going through the quarantine for chicken pox.

The crew formed a circle, and one stood in the center. Declan stood at his makeshift podium, waiting for everyone to arrive topside. He searched the crowd, and when he spotted Willie, a slow grin cracked his face.

Willie counted the crew as they came, joining the circle. Twelve men, including the one in the middle. Where was Andrew? He glanced about but didn't spot him.

Declan raised his fist. "Crew, it is that special day we wait for all week. Fight day!"

The crew cheered as if it were a birthday celebration.

"Today we have a new contestant to take on our champion Rook Teague."

Great. Willie knew he was about to hear his name, or rather his pseudonym.

"Puddle Jim, come to the center."

What? And then Willie understood. This man thrived on growing fear in others. He thought watching the champion fight would plant a seed in him. Well, it might. But Willie had another plan.

❦

MAYBE WORKED THE DOUGH. WILLIE'S CAPTORS WERE ON the table in front of her, and she kneaded them into submission with her bare hands. At least in her mind. As far as the dough was concerned, it was well worked. She plopped it into a greased bowl and covered it before washing her fingers. "Mother, tell me a story about Willie when he was a child."

"Let's see. I have many. He wasn't one to go unnoticed." She chuckled at that. "But he always wanted to help. And he has this knack for quickly learning something, especially if it is physical."

"I saw that on the ship. Every time the boatswain gave him a job, he picked it up as if born to it. I attributed it to his love of sailing."

"Oh, I'm sure that had something to do with it, but he understands how his body moves. He sees things, how they are done, and then he does it like he's been doing it his whole life. I remember this day. I took the children to the river for a picnic. Joseph worked, and Janie, me wee babe, was perhaps a month old. The day sweltered. Too hot to keep their wee minds on their studies. So we planned a grand picnic. After we ate, I fed Janie, and the boys played pirates, jumping off rocks and pretending to sword fight. Beth wandered over and tried to do what they were doing. She climbed up on a rock and jumped. But she lost her balance. She landed and rolled into the river."

Maybe gasped and her hand went to her belly. "What did ye do?"

"Nothing I could do. By the time I laid Janie down somewhere safe, Willie had already jumped into the river and had grabbed her. I don't know how he managed to get her to shore, but when he got pulled out by his brothers, I grabbed him and shook him. 'What were ye thinkin' lad? Do ye think I need to lose two children?'"

Maybe leaned forward, captivated. This was her Willie! He'd done this! "What did he say?"

Sarah chuckled again. "He said, 'I dinna think ye'd want to lose any.'"

Maybe covered her mouth with her hand and laughed. "That sounds like Willie."

"But hear this. Willie hadn't learned to swim."

"What?"

"I know. We'd not taught him yet. So I asked him where he learned to do that. He told me he'd seen some boys doing it the day before. He watched what they did and practiced in his mind. Then, when he needed to do it, he didn't have time to be afraid, he just did it and it worked."

"He just did what he'd practiced in his mind?"

"Aye."

That man was far from stupid. Anyone can have a bad idea, but that dinna make one stupid. It's a smart man who does what Willie did. Right there, Maybe prayed Willie could use his brain to get out of this mess.

Long John and Bucktooth dragged Puddle Jim out of the center of the circle. Rook hadn't even bothered to use his hands. Instead, he kicked the man until he couldn't get up again. It had startled Willie to see Rook's foot come flying. But as he watched, he learned a couple things. The man blinked before he kicked out his foot. And he kicked so that his body came around in a counterclockwise circle, with a small jump in the air and landing so that his back was partially to his opponent. He must be pretty certain he had time to be in that position before the next kick. That meant the man had arrogance.

Willie filed it all in his mind, seeing the kick unwind and make contact. Was there a vulnerable moment? Could someone beat Rook at his own game? He'd had a lot of practice.

Words his parents had spoken over him as he grew materialized from out of nowhere. It was as if he could hear them saying them in his ear. *For it is He who delivers you from the snare of the trapper.*

"Rusty Samson!"

Willie glanced toward the voice. Declan called his name.

"Your turn with our champion."

I will fear no evil.

Willie took a breath, wiped his hand over his dry mouth, and thought the shortest prayer he'd ever prayed, all while walking to the center.

The sun was higher in the sky, but he now realized why Rook faced the way he did. Willie walked the inside of the circle until he forced Rook to peer into the sun's light. He stopped moving and waited.

Rook glared back. The man was solid, tall, menacing.

Willie refused to flinch. As long as Rook thought he was part of a staring contest, it was safe.

But then Rook blinked.

His foot came up and his body turned, all in one fluid motion.

Willie saw the foot coming his way. He grabbed it and twisted.

Rook hit the deck headfirst. It took a minute for what

happened to register on his face. But when it did, he roared and charged.

Willie took the brunt of it in his gut, the force causing him to vomit all over Rook's back. He gasped for air and pulled himself up by the rail.

Rook shook his shaggy head and roared again. And blinked.

Willie looked in time to spot a foot coming toward his face. Once more, he grabbed it, though not as fast, nor with the same twist. Instead he raised the foot higher in the air.

Rook landed on his back, banging his head onto the deck. He didn't get up.

"C'mon, Rook, Get up! Don't let him beat you!"

Declan Stryker was a sore loser.

THE FAMILIAR TAP AT THE DOOR SOUNDED. ELEAZAR COULD set a clock to it. Every Wednesday evening, at seven, the constable came, tapping the same timid knock. Soft, for fear someone might spot him at the evil one's door. But Eleazar knew this man's weakness. With a touch of encouragement, he might get him to help. He only needed make it sound innocent and put the correct amount of incentive in the envelope.

He rubbed his hands, tugged at his cuffs, and opened the door. "Thank you, constable. I appreciate you remembering me."

"You pay for it. It's my job." The man's voice dripped with sullenness. However, if he did what was needed, he could sound anyway he wanted.

"Well, I still thank you. I have the new list and money here, but I was wondering, if you would do me one other little favor."

"That depends." He glanced about.

"I miss knowing what happens in our little village. The newspaper doesn't tell near enough. I understand. You prefer not to enter or be seen here. But if you took notes concerning things that occur. Just those everyday comings and goings that make life normal. I would be grateful, so grateful. Perhaps ten pounds a week grateful?"

Eleazar studied the man's eyes. They'd stopped darting. A view into the man's brain would see him tallying up a profit that his present position had no chance of matching. At any moment, saliva might spill from the corner of the creature's bulbous lips.

"I think that will work. Ten pounds you say?"

"Aye, ten pounds." The deal was struck. No questions concerning the source of his money. That was fine, Eleazar would never tell. But it would cut into what he'd hidden away if he didn't get answers soon.

No, he would ferret out the answer. Then he would make them all pay.

Chapter Twenty-Four

The fight on deck happened weeks ago. Declan hadn't called for a fight day since. Rook healed but was none too happy with Willie. Though Declan enjoyed making life miserable by throwing the worst of the worst jobs at him, Willie got the impression that he'd also put out word that no one was to touch him—which made him wonder what Declan planned next. Rook made guttural noises every time they were in close quarters, but never made a move. Long John and Bucktooth remained friendly, though Willie wasn't about to trust them with his life. Still, it was better than being alone.

Declan would never trust him. Willie didn't bother to convince the man otherwise. No pearls before swine. Instead, he observed the comings and goings the few times they allowed him on deck.

He eventually located Andrew, seasick and full of fear. Until recently, Declan systematically frightened and isolated the boy, but in the last few days he'd started a campaign of kindness toward the lad. It was the second part of getting Andrew under his spell. Willie saw where this was going. He also could figure that the third step in Declan's plan was to turn Andrew against Willie.

One thing about Declan, he was as smart as he was devious.

And the truth of the matter was, Willie had enough on his plate trying to save himself. Could he save himself and someone who, soon, might not want to be saved?

Still Willie kept his eyes open. If the chance presented itself, it would be a one-time thing. He'd better be ready. So he took every opportunity to study the sloop and the crew. He was getting most acquainted with the cook.

Declan enjoyed assigning Willie to galley duty. The old cook reminded him of Cookie until he opened his mouth. Then it was foul language and foul odor. Pegleg Pete had little in common with the other gentleman. Instead of quiet wisdom, Pegleg was gruff and crude. He did his job. Not that he did it well, mind you, but he did cook the meals.

The stores were spoiled and disgusting, reminding Willie of what Mr. Cox had said about passengers ship he might've booked in the spring to bring Maybe and the baby to Beaufort. And then some. Moldy and mildewed grains, maggots in the flour, and rats populating the larder. It whittled Willie's appetite to nothing—he ate only when he had to and what was the cleanest he could find. Still, it was disgusting.

More than once he overheard the cook telling Declan that they needed more stores. That would mean contact with another ship or port. Willie never mentioned it, even with Long John and Bucktooth, but he continued to listen and keep alert. This might be his only chance.

But even that played to Willie's advantage. Coming back from the larder with a load of flour, he noted Declan getting an earful from Pegleg and stepped to the shadows.

"You'd best be finding a port or another ship if you want any more meals after this week. There's not enough left, and I can't feed this scurvy crew with air, you know."

Declan spewed a few choice expletives. "I'll see what I can do."

"You'll do more if you want to eat."

"Don't threaten me, Pete."

"Declan, I don't have to threaten, I'm giving you the facts. You can stick 'em—"

"I said I'd do what I can. Now get to work!"

Pegleg turned away, whipping up a new string of profanities. Willie retreated to the larder.

Declan walked past without a notice, and Willie breathed a sigh of relief. If they went to port, he'd be off the ship, one way or another. If they captured another ship… He pushed that thought away. The British Navy rarely checked with a pirate crew to distinguish between guilty and guilt by forced association before hanging.

◈

MAYBE HAD AN OVERWHELMING URGE TO PRAY FOR WILLIE. She often prayed for him throughout the day. Today was no different. Except now. The urge burned within, and it had to do with his safety. She lay aside the baby blanket she was knitting and bowed her head. An icy tingle slithered her spine that had nothing to do with the January chill. Willie needed her prayers. Now. She was sure of it.

Each time she thought she'd finished, another wave flooded over her, insisting, urging, and she'd begin again. She prayed with everything she had, tears streaming over her cheeks, her mind calling up every conceivable need.

Something touched her. She jumped.

Mother stood beside her. "Are ye all right, lovey?"

"Aye, I just felt the need to pray for Willie." Maybe wiped her wrist across her eyes.

"Then I will join ye, if ye do not mind." Mother pulled up a chair next to her and they clasped hands.

They began to pray together. They prayed for his strength, his endurance, his wisdom, his safety, his life… though it always came back to his safety. The air was so thick with emotion.

Maybe could hardly choke out a word. She didn't recognize her own voice, but she couldn't stop. The need to pray was strong.

And then there was a release. As if the burden to pray melted into the floor beneath her feet. Air flowed in her lungs again. Her throat was no longer constricted. A blanket of peace dropped over her shoulders and she sighed.

She opened her eyes as Mother did the same.

Mother patted her hands, wiped her face with her apron, and returned the chair to its place. "Whatever the need, it is now met." She went back to working on her spinning wheel.

Maybe nodded and smiled as the baby kicked. She let out a breath as if she'd been holding it for hours, rubbed the growing bulge in her belly, and picked up her knitting. Her baby needed some attention too.

⁂

Though stuck below deck, Willie felt the ship slow its course. Every fiber of his being became taut and alert. Was this it?

Long John and Bucktooth entered the galley. "Declan needs you."

Willie wiped his hands across his breeches and followed them to the corridor. Long John let him slip past, so they moved single file with Willie sandwiched in the middle. That alone raised suspicions. His heart pounded harder, but he couldn't let them know. They must believe they had the upper hand.

They led him to a small room in the hold, too tiny for a cot. Bucktooth opened the door and Long John shoved him from behind. The door slammed, and a key turned.

Willie pounded on the door. "Hey! Hey! What's going on here? Why did you lock me in?"

"Pipe down. We're doing you a favor. Declan wanted us to hit you and knock you out. This way you don't get hurt."

"But why? What have I done?" He needed to keep them talking. Any information would help.

"It's not what you did. Declan's worried about what you might do. He hates to lose crewmen. I don't think he's through with you, anyway. I think he has plans." Long John was the most talkative.

"Hush, John. Rusty, don't worry about it. Relax, we'll come back in a bit to let you out."

"Come back? You're leaving me?"

"Don't worry. It's all going to work out. Now just sit quiet, matey, and we'll be back later."

Willie did just that. He sat on the floor and leaned back against the wall until the footfalls faded. A dim beam of light filtered in through the bars in the wooden door. It wasn't much, but more than when he'd first been taken. The hold at the other end was pitch black. He studied the door. The hinges were on the other side. So much for taking them apart. He felt around for anything to use as a tool. Nothing but dirt and some wood splinters.

He examined the wood on the door and noticed one board, closest to the hinges, was rotting at the bottom. He also peeked through the keyhole, but it was blocked. Just as he hoped.

Willie kicked at the rotted board until he heard some cracking. He then worked his fingers under and pulled it toward him. It broke off just below where the cross piece attached a foot or so from the base. He couldn't help but smile. This might work, but he hadn't much time.

Next he slid the rotten piece under the door until only the last of it remained for pulling back. Then he used the longest splinter he found and worked it into the keyhole, twisting and pushing until he felt the key moving out on the other side. One last push and it dropped. Onto the piece of rotted wood. Now to slide it under the door.

It wouldn't go. The key on top made it too tall. Willie paused and sighed. Then another thought gave him hope. He pulled the board back in, knowing it would knock the key to the floor. That was fine. He used the board and pushed it back next to the key, then made a sweeping motion and dragged it over to where the gap was from the missing rotted part. Now he could reach out and grab the key.

He stood, freedom in hand, and fitted it into the hole. With a pounding heart, he took a breath and turned it—the door unlocked.

Tingles pulsed through his veins. As quiet as he could manage, he made it to the stairs going to the upper deck. On impulse, he grabbed a crate and hoisted it to his shoulder, hoping it would hide his face.

Once on deck, he noticed Rook and several others forward, near the gangplank. He wasn't going that way. Glancing around, he spotted a rope ladder and dropped it over the side. He slipped a belaying pin in his waistband, took one last glance and then slipped over the side, too, hustling down the ladder into the bay.

The frigid water sent a shock through his body, but he swam for the pier. A minute later he found the wooden ladder and pulled himself onto it. Before getting all the way up, he scanned the ship. No one paid attention in his direction, so he finished the job. He wanted to stretch out and catch his breath, but he knew better. He might be missed or spotted at any moment, so he ran toward land.

Five yards more. Then he spotted trouble. His hand went to the belaying pin just as Declan stepped on the pier, spotting him.

The pirate was talking, his hands animated, when recognition flashed across his face. He reached for his knife. The person behind him, the audience of all the talk, stepped into view. Andrew.

Willie didn't want to hurt the boy, but nothing would stop him.

"So, you got off. Where do you think you're going?" The

expression on Declan's face shouted anticipation. But his eyes told Willie it was bravado.

"Andrew, I don't want to hurt you, but I am getting off this ship here."

Declan laughed. "You belong to me. I will let you know when I am done with you."

"Do you hear him, Andrew? Is that the life you want?"

The laughing stopped. "Tell him Westy. Tell him you are one of us."

"Are you Andrew? Has he changed your name so you will forget who you are?"

"Shut up!" Declan widened his stance and leaned in, tossing his knife from hand to hand.

"Have you forgotten your family? Are they waiting for you? Will you leave them not knowing what happened to you?"

"I said shut up!" Declan lunged.

Willie was too intent on reaching Andrew. He moved just in time, the knife leaving a red slice on his upper arm. It only grazed.

Declan froze, appearing uncertain.

But Willie knew his next move. He pulled the belaying pin free and slapped the club end in his other palm. "We don't have to do this Declan. You can let me pass."

"Can't do that, Rusty. Now I have to kill you." He charged with his knife fisted over his head.

Willie grasped the pin with both hands and swung.

Declan landed on his stomach, skidding along the weathered pier.

Willie didn't wait to see more. He took two steps.

Andrew stood in front of him, a boarding pike brandished in his hands.

"Don't do this, Andrew. I don't want to fight you, but I'm going home."

Andrew remained quiet but grasped the pike tighter.

"Andrew, don't—"

"Agh!" The boy ran past Willie.

Declan staggered to his feet.

Andrew plowed into the pirate, knocking Declan Blackheart Stryker into the bay. "My name is Andrew! You do not own me! If you come near me again, I will kill you!"

Willie put his arm over the boy's shoulders. "C'mon, let's get out of here before anyone else comes."

Andrew glanced at him and dropped the boarding pike.

Willie pointed with his head toward the beach. "Let's go."

They ran and never looked back.

❧

JOSEPH WANDERED INTO THE KITCHEN, THE DELICIOUS scents soothing his soul the tiniest bit. Sarah never blamed him, but he blamed himself. Even Maybe behaved as if he were guilt-free. But he wasn't. His boy was out there, in danger, because he hadn't insisted he come home.

This blaming himself put a wedge between him and God. It was hard to lead his family in Scripture reading and prayer when he could see his failing, a sackcloth cloak he couldn't remove. Trying to hide it from Sarah was as useful as trying to hide it from God. They both knew how he saw himself.

So he took long walks down by the docks, praying and searching and hoping. The January winds blew him back home, with no change but for a drive to keep going for his family. He plastered a smile on his face and greeted the bevy of females working to put the evening meal together.

Sarah left the oven to embrace him. She never doubted, never wavered in her faith. Instead, she pulled him into her circle of belief that Willie would be home, one day soon. It crushed him to tell her that today was not the day. Instead, he buried his face in her mobcap and shook his head.

She squeezed him tighter, kissed his cheek, and then let him go. "I'm glad yer home, love." She returned to the oven. His brother Robert went hunting with his sons and brought back several wild turkeys. Sarah basted one of them in the oven now. Even expecting the great meal did little for his outlook.

"Father, might I speak with ye?"

He turned to see Maybe behind him. "Of course, Maybe. Let's go to the sitting room."

She followed him and took a seat on the settee.

He pulled up a chair. "What can I do for you?"

"Ye can stop blaming yerself."

He sat back. He didn't realize she'd noticed. "I'm sorry, child. For so much. But it is my fault. I should have made him come back. It wouldn't have happened if I had."

She took a breath, and Joseph got the impression she'd practiced her words. "Ye've ken me husband longer than I. And even I ken he would need that time alone. It is who he is. That is how he pulls his thoughts together, in that alone time. If ye'd pressed, ye'd had an argument on yer hands. How were ye to predict he'd been in danger? No, this is not yer fault. But I believe God can use it to make things better."

Her faith had grown in her time with Sarah. He could almost hear his wife's wisdom coming from her. "Thank you, Maybe." Not that it changed things. Or not much.

"Consider it, Father. If my stepfather had not sold me, I wouldn't have run away. If Willie had not left school when he did, he wouldn't have been where I would meet him, he wouldn't have helped me, we wouldn't have found my sister or fallen in love or be about to give ye this grandchild. I know that we made the wrong choices more than once, but God can bring beauty from ashes. He has done that a lot lately, and He's not done yet, I'm sure. We canna change the past, but we can watch for what He will do next."

She was not making it easy to argue. "I'll think on what you've said. I know you are speaking the truth."

"If ye feel that ye've committed a mortal sin, then ask for forgiveness. Didn't Jesus already pay for it?"

He sighed. Why was she so right? Nodding, he smiled at her earnest face. "You are right. Perhaps I need to go spend some time alone. Call me for supper?"

"Aye, of course."

"You are a Crockett female. They all seem to be praying women with a lot of wisdom. Someday I might tell you about my mother. You remind me of her, a little." He stood and tweaked her chin. It was time to take this burden where it needed to go.

Chapter Twenty-Five

"To be honest, Andrew, I'm not even sure where we are." Willie and Andrew ran to a village. But it was the outskirts of a larger city. Not hearing English, Willie didn't panic. At least the signs were in pictures instead of words. Those made sense.

"Declan spoke of St. Thomas, though I don't know if he was talking about here or going there."

Willie remembered St. Thomas from his geography lessons —God bless his mother. It was a Danish island colony in the Caribbean. No wonder the words sounded strange. "We've got to do something. Either find someone who knows English or learn to speak their language. We need clothing and food, most importantly food. Then shelter. If we might get work, we could save for a trip home. It'll take time, but we can do this."

"What if Declan comes for us?"

"It isn't worth his time to comb this whole place. If this is St. Thomas, the Danes have a fort on that hill. See there? Burning the city to find us would not be in his favor. He needs this port. Don't worry about him anymore. He'll be angry, and the next ones he impresses will have a harder time of it, but he's not coming after us."

"Are you sure?"

Willie nodded. He was mostly sure. Some of his words were for his own security too. Perhaps getting more into the city he'd find someone who spoke English and might help.

Before long, they were among bigger buildings and people, though few resembled them. The white population dressed quite proper and appeared to be more affluent. The poorer population comprised African slaves or freed men, and they looked as poor as Willie and Andrew. They needed work. But why hire? Slaves did the work. Without the work, there was no income. Without income, there was no money. No going home.

Willie's shoulders slumped. He searched for a place to just sit and think. For the first time, he wanted to give up. He'd worked so hard to get free, but to what end?

Thwack! Willie was so lost in thought, he walked into a man. "Oh, pardon me. I am sorry."

"Not at all." The man's accent was German, though he spoke in English. He moved a few steps and then turned. "May I do something for you?"

What should he say? "We're new to this area and are lost. Could you direct us?"

"But of course! You appear to need a meal too. Let me buy you one."

Every fiber in Willie's body wanted to refuse the charity. But without something to eat, they were in dire need. What they'd had on the ship had been barely enough to keep them alive. Without that, they would starve unless they accepted the charity. "Thank you. Perhaps we can be of service in return for your generosity."

"Perhaps." The man smiled. "My name is Johann, Johann Dober. With whom have I the pleasure?"

"I'm…" Willie had to stop a moment. In the past year he'd been Willie Stewart and Rusty Samson. Finally, he understood Maybe a little more. He just wanted to be himself. "I'm William Crockett. Willie."

"I'm Andrew Ryan." The boy stayed near Willie.

"Willie, Andrew, it is nice to meet with you. Let me see about some food. We could eat here in the sunshine. Wouldn't that be nice?"

The man omitted that no respectable place would admit them dressed and smelling as they did.

"That is a good idea. We can find a spot, can't we Andrew? And wait while you bring the food."

Johann smiled and bowed before walking three doors down and going inside.

"Willie, what if he doesn't return? Or he brings the constable?"

The idea had crossed Willie's mind. "We'd be no worse off. Even in jail, we're better off than aboard the *Saucy Sally*. At least there we'd get some food and a roof over our heads."

Andrew shrugged his shoulders.

Willie headed to a small patch of grass with a few trees and colorful flowers in a garden. The fragrance of the foliage was such a sweet change from the stench of the ship. Willie sat on the ground and leaned his head back, breathing in the ambrosia.

"Are you worried?"

"Andrew, what good is worry? What do we worry about? Let's wait a bit and see what happens." He closed his eyes again, imagining Maybe in a garden of flowers. It made his heart ache, but it gave him stamina to keep going.

"Ho, what's going on here? I was told there were vagrants. Is that you two men?"

Willie hopped to his feet, praying he had a word or two to keep from trouble, when he heard a voice behind the officer. "Pardon me, sir, but these men are my guests. I asked them to wait here for me."

The officer tipped his hat. "So it is you, again, Brother Dober. Well, if you can vouch for them, then I will leave you to whatever it is you are doing." He went on his way.

"Brother Dober? You are a monk?"

Johann shook his head. "No, not I. I belong to the Moravian brotherhood. We are missionaries to the slaves. I almost did not stop when we bumped. But the Holy Spirit urged me to speak. I believe someone is praying for you."

Willie laughed. A weight dropped from him. He still didn't know what to do or how to get home. But now he had hope. "You must know my mother."

"No, but I bet we know the same Savior."

"I believe you must, Johann. And thank you for being an answer to prayer."

⁂

THE NEW YEAR HAD ARRIVED WITH A CHILL, WINDY January, but February brought storms. Maybe and the rest of the family hunkered in the house, venturing out only per necessity. The baby blanket became three baby blankets, with plenty of time to knit. She now had one in yellow, one in green, and one in a creamy white. She'd also done some sewing, as had Mother and the girls. Each gave her a gift for the baby. In fact, she was as ready as she could be. The only thing missing was Willie.

The last night of February, with a full moon rising, Maybe noticed the first twinge. She shook her head, ignored it and climbed into bed. Twenty minutes later, it happened again. This time she rubbed her belly. "Sweet baby of mine, yer father isn't home yet. Ye must wait a bit longer. He'll be home as soon as he can. Just stay put a while longer, love."

Another twenty minutes of twinges and a tight belly, though, it was obvious that this baby would be a willful child. Painfully obvious.

The contractions remained twenty minutes apart for several hours. Maybe hated to bother Mother too early, but then they moved to ten minutes apart. It was still dark out. Mother would be sleeping. A call to her would also rouse Father. She didn't want to be a bother, but now fear grappled with her intentions.

The next contraction came, harder and stronger than before, and it hadn't taken but five minutes.

Now Maybe wasn't sure she could make it to Mother's door to knock, but she had to try. She tossed the covers back and slipped out of bed, waddling as far as her door when the next pain came. She grabbed the post with both hands and leaned in, waiting for it to pass. Instead, it grew in intensity until there was a little pop and something warm and wet rolled down her legs. She got the door open and called, "Mother!"

Doors flew open. Mother came running but so did Eliza and Beth. The fear melted into the pool of water at Maybe's feet.

Mother sent them for hot water and the strips of linen that were all ready and waiting. Then she helped Maybe back into her bed. She crawled in as another contraction wrapped about her middle. This time the baby made known it was on its way.

"Hold on, lovey. Yer baby is in a hurry." Mother got Maybe's legs and knees into position and checked. "Aye, this one is in a big hurry, like his father." She shook her head but smiled.

Since Mother was here, Maybe had less fear. Yet, what if something happened before Willie returned? No, she mustn't think that way. She had to trust. She had to—"OH!"

"Push, darlin', just push. It will be all right soon."

Maybe grabbed the leather straps on her bed posts and pushed. The contraction let off.

"Take a breath, darlin' girl. Yer just getting started."

Just as she got her breath, the next one was on its way.

"Push. Ye can do this. Come on, little one, ye've a whole family excited to meet ye!"

Maybe gripped the leather straps, pulling them to her as she pushed, tucking her chin into her chest. If this little one didn't arrive soon, she'd have nothing left.

"Stop, dunna push!" Mother was doing something.

Panic rose in her throat and her heart pounded in her ears. "What is it? What is the matter? Is the baby all right?"

Eliza wiped her forehead and made little shushing sounds.

Maybe wanted to slap her. "What is the matter with me baby?"

"Nothing, darlin', nothing. I need to make sure the cord isn't around its wee neck."

She started to say something, but the next contraction took her breath. She bore down, pulling the straps and pushing with everything she had. Then all at once something swooshed between her legs.

"Aye! Welcome to the world, wee one." Mother held the crying baby up for her to see. "Ye have a fine strapping laddie with his daddy's long limbs and yer beautiful dark hair."

Maybe dropped the straps and held out her arms. She had no voice, as her tears came too fast to let her speak. She had to wait while Mother cut the cord and tied it off before her baby lay in her arms, her arms that had ached with loneliness for so long.

"Oh, Willie. I miss Willie, Mother. He has a son."

"That he does, lovey, that he does." Mother sat on the bed. "Ye ken we need to clean him. But I'll be swift, and he will be in yer arms in minutes." She took the baby back and laid him at the foot of the bed. After unwrapping him, she bathed the newborn with soft cloths and warm water from the basin.

Maybe watched every move, wanting to wrestle him away.

Mother wrapped him up again and gave him back.

Sighing, Maybe relaxed. She traced her finger around his tiny, perfect ear and down his downy cheek. When she brushed her knuckle over his lips, he began to suckle.

"Ye ken what he's wanting. Time to feed the laddie."

Mother helped her get into position on her side, with the tiny bundle in the crook of her arm. It was awkward and then painful at first but soon he was getting his first meal. The tears returned. "I canna understand why I keep crying. I want to stop, but then a fresh wave comes."

"That's normal, lovey girl. Dunna give it a thought. Just enjoy yer wee one." Mother stared at the baby while she spoke.

Maybe realized it must bring back thoughts of Willie for her too.

"Thank ye, Mother. Ye are a grandmother now."

"Aye. Oh, if yer ready, I think there is more family wanting to see the wee one. One new grandfather I'm sure is eager to come in, if yer up to it."

Maybe checked that she was covered and nodded.

Mother returned with Father. Others followed them into the room to catch a glimpse of the new arrival.

"I hear we have another Crockett lad."

"Aye, Father. Would ye like to hold yer grandson?"

Father's face beamed. "Are you sure?"

She handed the baby to him, watching the moisture form in his eyes. He didn't have to say it aloud, Maybe understood. They all felt it. The bittersweetness of the miracle without Willie here. "He'll be back, Father. I can feel it. He promised me that if we were ever separated, he would fight his way back to me. It is taking longer than I want, but he will be back. Then together we can name this baby. He will be back."

Mother reached for her hand and squeezed.

Father stared into the baby's eyes. "Aye, he will be back. I believe it too."

❧

Johann wiped his mouth. "What do you plan to do here in St. Thomas?"

Willie reached for another chunk of bread, then tore off only half. He didn't want to appear greedy, but now that he'd gotten some decent food, he couldn't get enough. "My plan is to go home. But that means I need to earn enough money to go home. So we need jobs, shelter." He tugged at the knee of his breeches. "Different clothes would help too. We're willing to work hard, but we haven't figured out where or how to start."

"Hmm." Johann leaned back in the grass. "I might help. I

am here with a friend. He must leave soon to return home. He is a carpenter and might use the help. Do you know anything about carpentry?"

Andrew shrugged.

"I've helped my father. He's a carpenter and also works with metal. He's taught me, but I'm nowhere as skilled as he is." Just mentioning his father increased his yearning for home.

"Then let's pack up our picnic. I will take you to where we are staying. I think you are to come help us and that we are to help you. Yes, I think that is right." Johann let out a breath, stood and began picking up the remnants.

Willie did the same, as did Andrew. *What did he mean that we're to help them and they are to help us?* It felt mystical, for lack of a better word. But if helping them would get him home, that was fine with him. He followed Johann out of the park, down the road, and out of the city.

It wasn't long before fields of tobacco and sugar cane ushered the road. Slaves dotted the fields, and activity whirled around Willie and the others.

"Where are we going?" Andrew was nervous.

Perhaps he had a right, but Willie found no reason to distrust Johann. At least not yet.

"We are going to where I am staying with my friend. We want to be where our African brothers and sisters can quickly find us when they have those few minutes without work. It makes sharing our Lord with them that much easier for all."

A few minutes later and they arrived at a lane. Johann turned there and pointed. "Our home here on St. Thomas." He pointed to a structure, little more than a shack. But Willie recalled that he only requested shelter, not a mansion.

When they got closer, Willie heard hammering but didn't see anyone. "They are working out in back." Johann brought them through the front and out back where two men hammered in rhythm. One man hammered the way Da always did, but the other kept his left arm straight at his side, working only with his right. There was trust between them as the first man held the boards for them both.

"I've brought us help. Come meet our new friends." At Johann's voice, both men stopped and raised their heads. The first man smiled, shaking hands with Willie and Andrew.

"William, Andrew, this is my friend and brother, David Nitschmann. And our other friend is also a David."

The second David didn't offer a handshake. Instead he withdrew, peering at his feet and turning his body as if to hide his left side.

"It is nice to meet you both. Johann rescued us. What shall we call you so we don't get you confused?"

David Nitschmann pointed to himself. "Call me Brother David and my friend is just David. I know, it can become complicated." He laughed.

"Then, Brother David, how can we help here? We are eager to be of use." The sooner they could get started, the sooner he could get home. He'd work without food or sleep if it would get him home any sooner.

"Let me show you what we're building here, and then I'll put you to work."

Willie glanced back at Andrew. The boy still appeared scared, but at least he was trying. He smiled, wishing to give the lad more hope. They were a step closer. It would be many steps, but each taken brought them that much closer to home.

Chapter Twenty-Six

W illie, Andrew, I think I've found something for you."

Willie laid aside his saw and followed the voice. Johann was inside the shack, holding up some breeches. More clothes lay on the bed.

He handed Willie the pants and waved his arm over the other items. "I cannot guarantee the fit, but you will be more properly dressed."

"That is no worry. I'm grateful to have something decent to wear besides these rags. I miss my boots, though. Declan took those first thing, along with my waistcoat."

Johann patted Willie's arm. "Let him keep them. You are heading home. Now you are another step closer." Then he held up a pair of worn boots. "Again, the size might not be perfect, but then you won't want to wear footwear until you are headed home."

Willie grasped them, a bit too fast, and sat on the bed. "Thank you! I want to try them on, though you are right about saving them for the trip."

Andrew came through the door about then.

"See what Brother Johann found for us!" Willie held up the second boot.

"Why?"

Willie turned and stared at the boy. What had come over him? "What do you mean 'why'?"

"Why is he being nice to us? What is he planning to do? What will this cost us? Why?"

Stunned, Willie dropped the boot. Had Declan messed the boy's mind so much that he couldn't tell the difference between kindness and manipulation?

"I'm sorry if you don't understand. I can well imagine that it is hard to trust after what you experienced. I've no conditions on these gifts. I give as my Savior directs. You need clothing, do you not?"

Johann didn't seem to take the wariness personally, for which Willie was grateful. He'd never met a more humble or generous man. It made sense that Johann was called to share the gospel in St. Thomas. No one else could do the job.

"Johann, perhaps I should talk with Andrew alone. We appreciate your kindness, more that I can say. Thank you."

Johann nodded and left the room.

"Why don't you ever question anything he does? He could be as evil as Declan."

Willie started to stand but decided that might be too confrontational, so he remained on the edge of the bed. "You don't trust yourself either, do you?"

"What do you mean?"

"I mean you don't trust your instincts to tell you who is genuine and who is false."

Andrew stared at the floor. "No, I don't. I let Declan's kindness fool me. I'll not be the fool again."

"Well, treating Johann that way pretty much makes you a fool."

Andrew raised his head, his eyes sparking anger. Good. He got through to the boy.

"Listen, some people manipulate and have nothing but evil on their minds. They will pervert kindness to get their own way hoping you will do what they want out of loyalty, without question. But Johann and Brother David are genuine. When you spend time with them, you can see it. Can you imagine anyone would come here to live where they live and to work as hard as they work just to bring the gospel to the African slaves with an ulterior motive? What other reason could they have?" He ran his hand through his hair. "Listen, Andrew. You are insulting a good man. Instead, why not try to get better acquainted with him?" Willie took the one boot off and set it with the other. "I'm going to work. You can try some clothes or ponder what I said. But if you are smart, you'll find Johann and apologize." He left, closing the door behind him.

David, the other one, was back and working with Brother David. Willie noticed that he kept an eye on him, watching where he went. Perhaps Andrew wasn't the only one with trust issues.

An hour or so later, Johann arrived with a tray of food— plenty of fresh tropical fruits, some bread and some black beans.

Willie and the Davids put down their tools and came to where Johann set the food between two sawhorses. They waited while Johann blessed the meal and then helped themselves.

A reddish orange fruit caught Willie's eye.

When he picked it up, Johann pulled out a knife. "You will need this. Let me show you." He sliced a second one into four long parts, leaving a core—a single large seed. "Now, score through each part like this." He cut the flesh on each piece to resemble a checkerboard. Then he bent the rind back on itself and began eating the flesh while juice dripped down his chin. "Try it!"

Willie did as he was shown, even to letting the juice drip. It was sweet and light and cool and tasty. Like nothing he'd ever eaten. He wiped a hand across his mouth. "What is this called?"

"A mango." It was the first word Willie heard David speak.

"A mango, huh? It is the best thing I've eaten in a long time." He picked up another slice and checker boarded it before eating, this time with some satisfying grunts. Oh, it was delicious! After finishing off the mango, he thought he'd try something else. Perhaps David would explain that too. He reached for an elongated yellow thing. "What is this called?"

"A banana fig."

"How do I eat it?"

David picked one up and pinched the end, the peel split. He pulled the peel away to reveal a soft yellow fruit. "Like this." He bit the fruit in half, chewed, swallowed and then ate the other half.

Willie chuckled and tried it. This fruit wasn't drippy but had a thicker consistency, though very soft. The flavor was delicate too. A great contrast to the mango. "Now I don't know which one I like more."

"Dunna worry about it. After a while, ye'll tire of the taste and long fer what ye miss." David rose. "Excuse me. I'll be getting back to my place now."

Willie watched him walk away. "Where does he stay?"

Johann began cleaning up. "He lives down the lane."

"What is his story?" Willie wanted to retrieve the words. It was none of his business. But he wondered about the man. Something painful hindered him, and not just his arm.

"I think David will tell you his story when he is ready. He spoke to you today. That is a step for him. Give him a little more time."

He could do that. A little more time. But if it took longer, he'd have to leave for home without knowing. Nothing would stop him when it came time to leave.

"Why don't you tell me your story, Willie."

"I did. We were impressed by pirates and escaped here on St. Thomas."

Johann shook his head. "Yes, but there is more. Where is home? Who waits for you? You told me a little about your mother, that she prays, and your father who works with metal and wood. But what about you? Who are you, William Crockett?"

That was a good question. He rubbed his eyes and sighed. "A very tired man who longs to go home."

"But to what?"

Maybe's face floated in his mind's eye. "To my wife and our baby, who most likely has entered this world without waiting for me to get there. I hope they have not given up on me."

"Why would they?"

He rubbed his hands over his eyes and cleared his throat. "The night I was taken, we'd had an argument. It was a bad one. My father came after me, and we talked it out. I was returning to apologize when I was knocked out. I awoke on the ship. I don't know if my wife believes I'm coming home. I don't know what to expect. I just need to get there."

Johann came to him, placing his hand on Willie's shoulder. "We could pray about it."

He was in earnest. But the man didn't understand what he asked. He was grateful others prayed for him, he was sure his mother and father did. But he and God only spoke when things were crucial. When all else failed. He wasn't worthy of praying when things weren't about to fall apart. "Thanks, but that's all right."

"You don't want God to help you?"

This was getting too personal. "I would love any help God wants to give, but I don't think I have the right to ask for it right now."

"Oh, Willie, when will you understand? Look to God first. When will you not rely on your parents' faith and find some of your own?"

It was as if he heard his mother. She'd said the same thing. That it was time he found his own faith in God. Perhaps she and Johann were right. "I've got a lot that I'm sorry for. I need to deal with that before I go asking for favors."

"Then let's pray. I can pray with you, if you want, or leave you to have a private time."

"Stay. I could use a friend."

Johann knelt on the floor, and Willie knelt beside him. It was strange at first, talking to God, telling Him what He already knew. But finally, finally he dropped the burden. All the shame and unworthiness rolled away. More than ever, he was himself, who God created him to be. Even if he couldn't read or write well, he had abilities, God-given abilities, and with God's help he would get back home and be the husband and father God called him to be.

As they finished, Johann turned to him. "What is your wife's name? I want to pray for her too."

"Maybe. Rather, her real name is Elizabeth. Elizabeth Boulay Crockett. I've called her Maybe, though, since the first day we met. It was a little joke and then became her name out of necessity."

Johann's eyes grew wider, and he cocked his head to the side. "What necessity?"

"Someone wanted to do her harm, so I helped her hide aboard a ship as a boy, another member of the crew. We sailed to Ireland and found her sister and then came back home. That has been another worry, but I know my parents are taking care of her."

"You found her sister in Ireland?"

Now the questions sounded strange. "Aye. What are you getting at?"

"I need to go for a walk. Please tell Brother David I will be back." And he left, almost at a run.

Willie shook his head. The past hour had been strange and wonderful and freeing. The time in prayer left him assured, deep inside, he would return to Maybe. And soon. But he must trust God. That he would do.

MARCH CAME IN LIKE A LION BUT WAS MOVING OUT LIKE A lamb with gentle, warmer breezes. Spring called Maybe to come take a breath. She longed to be in the fresh air, seeing other faces. Oh, the faces in the house had become quite dear, but a small change of scenery after several weeks of confinement would do her spirits good. She was in the kitchen with Mother when the idea struck. "Mother, I desire a new dress. I want to find something special for when Willie arrives. Do ye think ye could watch the babe while I go to the mercantile? Perhaps Eliza or Beth or Aphra might want to go along?"

Mother brightened. "I think that's a splendid idea! I'm happy to rock the wee one and play with his toes until you get back." She was already tickling a foot that had worked its way out of the blanket.

"So, Eliza, Beth, Aphra, would any of you like to come along?"

Neither Beth nor Aphra wanted to go, but Eliza was more than happy. The girls checked their clothing and hats before getting shawls and heading toward the center of town.

Maybe had avoided going out for the longest time, feeling fearful before her little one was born, and then after, when she stopped living in fear, she was prevented by her time of confinement. Now with both excuses gone, she breathed in the air of freedom and began to show her sister parts of the town of Beaufort.

"Here we are. The mercantile. Shall we go in?" Maybe led the way, while a little bell tinkled welcome.

"Good morning, ladies. How can I help you today?" Miss Fuller was all smiles at a possible sale.

"Good morning, Miss Fuller. I wish to make a new dress. What might you show me in the way of blue linen, in a medium hue?"

Miss Fuller fluttered to her linen section and pulled out a bolt in shimmery sea blue. "This arrived only yesterday from the ship. It came from Portugal."

Maybe rubbed a corner in her hand, imagining the dress she could make and how Willie's eyes would light. "Aye, this is the one."

Miss Fuller cut the fabric before wrapping it in a small package.

Maybe and Eliza perused the shop wandering in different directions.

The doorbell tinkled again, noting another customer.

Miss Fuller called from the back. "Be with you momentarily."

"No hurry. I'm just looking today." The customer turned her attention to Maybe.

It took a moment, but she remembered where she'd seen the woman. She'd been the next-door neighbor who was always yelling at her stepfather for being a lout and a drunk. It was all true, but why advertise it? The memory still called heat to her cheeks.

The woman stared at Maybe. "Excuse me, dearie, aren't you Miss O'Malley? The daughter of that poor soul, Daniel O'Malley?"

"No, sorry, I am not Daniel O'Malley's daughter." She never was, never would claim to be his daughter.

"My, I am sure I've seen you before. You could be twins. She disappeared, you know, about the same time her father met his demise."

"I am Mistress Crockett. My husband is William Crockett. My name was never O'Malley."

Mistress Attwater's face bloomed in color. "My apologies my dear. I can't get over the resemblance. Oh, dear, I am sorry."

Poor thing, no need to make her feel awkward. "That's quite all right. Do not think a thing about it."

"Elizabeth, you should see what I just found!" Eliza popped up at her side just as Miss Fuller returned from the back.

She handed Maybe the package, neatly tied. "Thank you and come again. I hope to see you in the dress."

Maybe took the package, noting Mistress Attwater's scrutiny. "Thank you. I will stop by. Good day!" She linked arms with her sister and nearly dragged her away from the place. It most likely meant nothing, but a little danger alert pinged in her brain. She would mention it to Father and then put it out of her mind. Mistress Attwater was the queen of gossip in town, but she was done with being afraid.

❧

JOHANN RETURNED WITH DAVID IN TOW. "WILLIE, MAY WE speak with you a moment?"

David muttered something to Johann. The man shook his head, standing firm concerning something on which the two disagreed.

Willie shrugged and followed where Johann led, back into the shack.

"I think I have news for both of you. You are family. I may be wrong, but if you talk about it, you might find you share more interests than you realize."

Willie gave David more scrutiny, searching his face, his physique, his mannerisms for something familiar. He was short, stocky with salt and pepper hair. But his eyes, eyes that radiated distrust, so he'd only given a passing glance. Now he saw it, those eyes, with a deep color so dark they gleamed violet. His heart pounded. Hard. He could barely breathe. There stood Maybe's father!

"You are my father-in-law."

David shook his head. "No. It's not possible." He didn't seem in disbelief, only denying the possibility.

"But I can see it. You are my wife's father."

"I can't be. Don't you understand? Me wife married another man believing me dead. If I go back, it would be horrendous for her. I can't do that to her." He dropped to the edge of the bed. Then he gazed at Willie, his eyes, so like Maybe's, pleading with him. "Please. You canna tell them that I'm alive. It will ruin their lives."

"You don't understand. Your wife—" He glanced over at Brother Johann. This would be so hard. Kneeling in front of the man, he chose his words. "I'm sorry. Your wife died more than a year ago from a bee sting. Maybe, I mean Elizabeth and I went to Ireland and found Eliza. She had been ill and was to follow when she got better, but her stepfather sent word that both your wife and Elizabeth died so she never came. When we found her, we brought her back home to Beaufort with us. They are with my parents, they would love to know you are alive."

David broke at that point. Brother Johann motioned for Willie to step out.

At the door, he took one last glance at his father-in-law. A broken man held together by one of God's servants. They would talk later. For now, Willie would pray for his new family member.

Chapter Twenty-Seven

Willie returned to work, but the idea of Maybe's father being alive still left him stupefied. There had to be a story. The man must trust him enough first. What happened? Where had he been all this time? Here? Why not go home? How did he learn his wife remarried? So many questions.

It also brought up other questions. Did Maybe wait for him? Did she believe he would come home to her? Would she want him home? A stitch in his chest at the mere idea made him put down his saw. It was a valid question. What would he do if he got home, and she didn't want him?

The desire to get back to her was all that kept him going through the *Saucy Sally* ordeal. Now that he knew he would get back, the question, the fear of what awaited wracked at his brain.

There is no fear in love. Perfect love drives out fear.

He heard his mother's words as if she were beside him. Fear was not the answer. He gave that burden to God. He would not fear. God would make a way. That is what he would believe. He would not fear.

Johann came out of the shack and motioned to Willie. "He wants to tell you his story. It is difficult. It may take some time."

Willie hugged the man. "If I can bring Maybe's father back to her, then all this is worth it."

"This may be the reason God allowed it to happen. His ways are higher, but His love is perfect." Johann clapped him on the back and pulled away. "Go in. I'll help Brother David."

Inside, Willie spotted David still sitting on the edge of the bed. "You wanted to see me?"

"I need ye to understand what happened. I dinna desert me family."

Willie sat cross-legged on the floor, ready to listen.

"Me last voyage we were not far off Bantry Bay, perhaps another day or so and I'd have been home. I couldn't wait. I love me family. They understood sailing was what I did. I'd done it since before I married me wife." He paused for a breath.

Willie wanted to tell him then that his mother attended their wedding but thought it better not to interrupt.

"Pirates attacked. What I dinna know, none of us did, was one of the crew, a new member, work for the pirates. He had a signaling device, a mirror or something, and they had worked out a code. That meant when we were attacked, we had the most cargo, were the most vulnerable, and least expected it.

"The pirate, Silas Keel, ordered that all be killed. But the traitor on board had heard me speak of me wife and had seen her when he first signed on. When he was to kill me, he put a mini ball into my arm instead. After he fired, he told me that he was going back to Bantry Bay to take the news that all had perished save him. He planned to tell my wife that we were the best of friends, that he was with me when I died, and that my dying wish was for him to care for me family. He told me that while I bled to death, I could imagine him with my wife."

Willie's blood turned icy. He knew who the traitor was. Daniel O'Malley.

"I held onto a piece of wreckage for days, not sure how

many, but the British Navy rescued me. They were fine to nurse me back to health, as much as possible. Nothing could be done about me arm or they might have impressed me. By the time I returned to Bantry Bay I learnt me wife had remarried, and they had left for the colonies. No one told me Eliza was still there, though I probably wouldn't have seen her. I couldn't let anyone call me wife a bigamist, I love—loved—her too much for that. I still can't fathom she's gone." He shook his head, his voice softer. "I have been so filled with anger. Now, I want me daughters. I also want to kill the monster who caused this. Daniel O'Malley."

"He's already dead."

"What?"

Willie nodded. "No one knows for sure if he died because of his drinking or if he was murdered, but they found his body. Your girls are protected with my folks. You only need to come home with me."

David looked at Willie. "'Tis that easy? Just come home?"

"Aye, come home with me. We have someone to meet there, you and I. Maybe, I mean Elizabeth was to have a baby by the end of February or early March. I'll be greeting my child. You can meet your grandchild."

"Grandchild? I have a grandchild?"

"Aye. Another reason I want to get home. It is about time I learn if I'm the father of a boy or girl."

David's laugh burst like a ray of sunshine through a cloudy day. "Aye, Willie me boy, let's get home to our family."

❦

BACK OUTSIDE, WILLIE AND DAVID'S SMILES TOLD BROTHER Johann and Brother David all they needed to know. Andrew wasn't sure how to take the news, but Willie understood. He knew the boy feared he'd be left off the boat in favor of Willie's newfound family member. "Andrew, we started this voyage together, we will finish it together."

"And, because you have brought that up, Brother David has some news." Johann stepped aside so all could focus on Brother David.

"I was not supposed to stay on like Brother Johann. My job was to help get this work started and go home. We have raised enough money through the things we've built to pay for all of you to go with me on the ship next week. All those things we've built, Brother Johann took them to the city. The well-to-do enjoy feeling as though they help the poor. It is easier to throw money at it than to get dirty and help. But that is fine with us."

Guilt gnawed at Willie's gut. "We can't take money away from your mission here."

"Oh, but you can. A worker is due his wages, and as the price I asked as quite high, the money will stretch far. If I'd put a small price on the items, they would have thought them cheap and worthless. I put a high price on them, and they were fighting each other to purchase. There is enough to get you three home along with Brother David."

Home. He was going home. Next week and he'd board the ship home.

"Willie, how long will the trip take?" Andrew was getting excited too.

"That is a good question. It depends on what stops we make between here and there."

Brother David smiled. "We stop in Charlestown and then Beaufort, working our way up to Boston before we cross to Oslo and Copenhagen where I disembark. From there I will travel overland to home." A wistful sigh escaped.

Willie and Andrew weren't the only ones homesick. But soon, he would be home. Soon.

"Then, Andrew, with fair winds and no storms, we might be home in two weeks." Even as he said it, Willie rechecked his math. Three weeks until Maybe would be in his arms. He would hold his child. The reality took his breath away.

THE DRESS WASN'T FINISHED, BUT DONE ENOUGH FOR Maybe to try it. A tuck here, a pin there. Her figure was coming back, but not fast enough to suit her. Hopefully she would take the dress in more soon.

"Eliza, love, will Willie like this?" She turned in front of the mirror, letting the skirt sway back and forth.

"Of course, though I doubt he will notice it. His eyes will be on ye." She giggled while playing with the baby who lay in the middle of Maybe's bed, then paused. "Elizabeth, ye've never told me why we had to leave the shop so fast. What happened?"

Maybe set the pincushion on the bureau. "I haven't told you many things. I didn't want you to hurt more than you have." She took off the dress and set it aside. "After Mama died, Daniel's true colors came out. He was a gambler and would spend faster than I could replace it. I sold Mama's books to eat. I had to hide money or he would take it. An evil man lives in this town. Folks whisper about him, but no one had any proof, so he did what he pleased." Maybe sat on the bed next to her sister. "Daniel sold me to him to pay off his debts. That's when Willie found me and helped me run away."

Eliza wrapped her arms about Maybe. "I'm sorry. I had hard things happen, but ye had it worse I'm thinkin'."

"That woman at the shop? She was our neighbor. She is also a gossip. If word gets back to Eleazar Ferguson that I am here, he might come for me. He is pure evil. I've seen what he can do."

Eliza's mouth worked with little *ohs*, as if she couldn't find the words to say.

Maybe put her arm about her sister and pulled her close. "Dunna worry, love. I'm done with worry. I will not be afraid. Me God has a plan, and He is me sword and shield."

"Yer not afraid?" Eliza pulled back and stared at her, searching her face.

"Sometimes I feel afraid, then I remember Who is in

control. I tell Him, and He takes me fear. I will not let Eleazar Ferguson terrorize me."

"Ye are much braver than I, Elizabeth. And I am glad ye are me sister." Eliza hugged her again, then went downstairs.

Should she have told her? Was it too much? Should she have said more? Her sister needed protection. The baby started to cry, reminding her he needed protection too.

WILLIE TOOK ONE LAST GAZE AT THE SHACK. NO, IT WASN'T a mansion, but he'd been blessed at this little place. Others would be blessed, too, while Brother Johann shared the gift of grace to those in need. But now, home filled his focus. In two weeks, plus or minus some days, he would be with his family. He would see his child, he would hold his Maybe. No, she was his Elizabeth. An amazing woman he called his wife.

"Fair winds and safe travels, friends." Johann hugged each one leaving. "Brother David has your passes. May God bless and keep you. May His face shine upon you and be gracious unto you. May He lift His countenance upon you and grant you His peace. Go with God, my friends. I will never forget you."

Willie returned his hug. "And I will never forget you, Johann. You are a true friend and brother in Christ. God's blessings on you and this endeavor, my friend."

He didn't think it would be this hard to leave. Even after traveling down the lane to the main road, he glanced back several times. Brother Johann smiled and waved.

"I will miss him." Andrew wiped his arm under his nose.

Willie shook his head. Their stay had forever changed him. Andrew too.

He slowed to walk with David. During the last week he got to know his father-in-law. The man remembered the young wife staying with the Fontaine family who attended his wedding. Learning that it was Willie's mother came as a surprise. But that was only the start. When he and his bride married, that young wife was with child. Simple math proved that child was Willie. They had a good laugh over that while Johann pointed out that God planned it all long before anyone could imagine.

Willie longed to hear more about the pirate attack. A part of him needed to know Long John and Bucktooth weren't a part of that crew, though they had sailed with Declan and Silas Keel for a long time. He didn't want to think of them as murderers as they had broken orders so as not to hurt him.

But there was time for talk. They had two weeks of sailing, perhaps a tad less. It all depended on the wind and weather. God willing, they would have the fair winds Johann wished for them and fair weather. No matter what, though, Willie was counting the days.

THE KNOCK NO LONGER MADE ELEAZAR JUMP. IT WAS SO precise that he should set a clock by it. However, this week the knock had an insistent quality. Annoyed, he rose from his chair where he'd been waiting, and struggled to put an amiable face over his true feelings. A deep breath and then he opened the door. "Good evening, constable. And how fare you this fine day?"

"Well, sir. And you?"

He should have been more direct, less polite. This tiresome creature would drag it all out and he'd never be rid of him. "I am well." For one who was subjected to this hellish existence.

"I have your goods, and I've written the latest news from about town." He appeared anxious and not in the usual sense. As if he had something to share.

"You've written it all down?"

"Aye, sir. You will find items of interest on the page."

"I thank you for doing that. I have your money right here, along with the money for next week's stores."

The creature's eyes lit as the envelope came into view. "Happy to help. Let me know how else I can be of assistance."

"I will. And good night to you, sir."

"Good night." He tipped his cap and looked a little disappointed. Perhaps he wanted to watch while Eleazar read the note. Pity.

Eleazar could not close the door fast enough. He took the crate to his sitting room and dug around until he found the folded sheet, tucked under a bag of flour. His hand began to tremble. What if it had nothing to do with what was important? He must open the note to know. He unfolded the paper. Only one scrawled sentence.

Mistress Attwater swears that Daniel O'Malley's daughter has returned to town calling herself Mistress William Crockett.

His breath came slowly, with much control. So the minx was back. His mind considered what to do first. There were so many things. And he wanted to do them all. He must plan with care, take his time. He considered how much fear he wanted to see in her eyes. This was important. She must be afraid. And scream. She needed to scream. How loud did he want her to scream? That didn't matter. She might scream as loud as she wanted. And she would scream. Scream until the end. There was nothing anyone could do.

Because it would be the last thing either of them would ever do.

Chapter Twenty-Eight

The ship docked in Beaufort thirteen days after leaving St. Thomas. Now that they'd moored, Willie could not leave fast enough. "Brother David, thank you. I will never forget you."

"Go. You have waited for this moment. All is well. Go with God, my friend." The missionary patted Willie on the back and gave him a push. He did the same for Andrew but brought his friend David into an embrace. "You are through the dark night. Let your joy shine, my friend."

Willie's father-in-law nodded.

"C'mon, David, you have a grandchild to meet!" Willie grabbed David's good arm and pulled him through the throng trying to exit the ship. Since he was taller than most, he viewed over heads, maneuvering through the crowd. A glance back assured him that Andrew had linked arms with David, so they were still together. "Pardon us. Excuse us. Pardon." All the way to the bottom of the gangplank. Willie was certain no one in the history of sailing had desired more than he to arrive at his destination.

Once through the crowd, the three stopped. Reality dropped over them like a fog. They were in Beaufort. Just a bit of walking and they would be with their families. The excitement of docking now quivered throughout Willie's being. But he needed to say goodbye to Andrew. He ended his responsibility for him. It was as though he said goodbye to his son.

Andrew seemed to sense something. "I would never have made it home if it weren't for you. You are a good man, William Crockett. I am proud to call you my friend." He held out his hand.

"A handshake is for strangers. It's not enough for us." He pulled the boy into an embrace. "You are home, now, Andrew. Go find your family and Godspeed." He thumped him on the back and then pushed him toward his house. "We will see each other again. Beaufort is not that big a place."

Andrew took a few steps then broke into a sprint. Running backward, he waved to Willie and David. "We're really home!" Then he turned, disappearing at the road's bend.

Willie wiped his eyes and turned to David. "Well, friend, are you ready?"

A familiar voice yelled his name.

"Willie!"

He turned.

His father raced to him, wrapping his arms about him, weeping.

Willie embraced his father. He couldn't stop the tears. "Da! I'm home! Now I'm home!"

"I knew you would come home. I knew you would."

Willie pulled back, ran his sleeve across his face. "Da! This is—"

"David! I remember you from the Fontaines'. You are Maybe's father! Praise God!" Da didn't hold back. He released Willie, he embraced David. "Oh, I can't figure who will receive more attention. Willie, your wife will love you forever for finding her father."

David returned the embrace. "Good to be here, Joseph. I cannot thank ye enough for caring for me daughters."

"Your daughters are strong, courageous young women. You can be proud of them."

"Aye, that I am. That I am."

Da clapped David on the back once more and squeezed Willie shoulder. "There's more at home who long to greet you. We must get there and put their minds to ease."

Home. They were almost home.

⚜

"Janie, would ye please help Aphra while I rock the babe? She's getting more nappies ready for him." Maybe kissed the top of the little one's head, then held him against her cheek, relishing the warm scent of clean baby.

"I'd be glad to." That girl, so full of energy and joy, lit up a room with her smile. Plus, she helped keep hope alive, reminding everyone that today might be the day Willie came home. She never showed disappointment, only hope in the next day because she knew he would walk through the door one day.

Maybe cradled the baby in her arms and rocked, watching his sweet eyes stare into hers. Soon his blinks came more often until his wee eyes closed. She kissed his forehead and stood. His cradle stayed in the sitting room so she was able to watch him while she sewed.

Crash!

Maybe jumped. That sounded like a plate splintering on the floor. She put the baby in his cradle and hurried to the kitchen.

"He's here! Willie's here!" Janie ran outdoors.

"NO!" Aphra's face blanched white. She hadn't seen Willie in a while—

Aphra grabbed Maybe's arm. "No, not Willie. HIM!"

Cold swept over Maybe. She knew without asking. "No! Janie!" She ran out the door after her.

There in the twilight, she saw a tall figure struggling with something—Janie! What to do? She ran behind, grabbed the figure's collar, and pulled hard and fast. His sleeves constricted his arms. "Janie, run!" She paused to assure the child got away.

He turned, blocking her retreat to the house. The only direction to run was toward the bluff.

She grabbed her skirts and ran as if the devil chased. The evil in his presence nauseated. She continued to run. Even when the stitch in her side burned. No glance over her shoulder. She ran.

At the bluff, she searched for a hiding place. Her tree. It called to her, beckoning safety. No time to hook her skirts, no time for ladylike niceties. She scrambled into the branches and froze, praying for invisibility.

❧

"DA! DA! HE'S GOT MAYBE!"

Janie ran from the house, panting and shouting. Then she spotted Willie and threw herself at him. "Oh, Willie! He's got Maybe. That bad man, he's got Maybe!"

He pulled her away from him, stooped and held her by her shoulders. "Tell me what happened."

"I thought I saw you at the window, so I ran out. It wasn't you. That bad man grabbed me. Then Maybe came. She made him let me go, told me to run. She ran too."

Every fiber of his being pulled taut. "Where? Where did she run?"

"Toward your hill."

Willie knew where before she answered. He took off as fast as his sea legs could move. If that savage touched her…

His new used boots slipped on his feet. But he pounded on. He moved faster than he'd ever moved, praying with every footfall. *Keep her unharmed.*

He rounded the crest seeing only one silhouette, too tall, too lanky to be Maybe.

The silhouette called, pacing, searching for something. "You cannot hide from me forever. Where are you? You might as well come out. I will find you. Don't hide, lass. We have a destiny, you and me. Prolonging this will only make it worse. Come out! I tire of this cat-and-mouse game."

"I'll finish your games!" Willie grabbed him and threw him to the ground. He swung his fist at the man's head.

The man's face contorted.

Willie hit him again. And again. And again.

"Willie! No! Don't kill him!"

Maybe!

He stopped at her voice, his fist pulled to strike again.

She dropped from the tree and ran to him.

Then she was in his arms. He lifted her from the ground, holding her close. "You are safe!"

"Oh, Willie! Yer here! How did ye find me?"

He laughed. How indeed! He squeezed her tighter, sighing. "Where else would I find you?" Her cap fell free, and he buried his face in her hair. He longed to hold her like this forever, making all right with the world.

Then she pulled back. A confused expression overtaken with wonder worked her face. "Da? Da!" She dropped from his arms.

He turned as she ran to her father. David and Da had followed. How could his arms ache that fast?

While father and daughter embraced, Willie's father stooped next to the unconscious form on the ground. "It is Eleazar Ferguson. He's still alive. We need to carry him back to the house."

"I'd have killed him, Da. If she hadn't stopped me, I'd have done it. I wanted to. I still could." Willie studied the still form. Hate overwhelmed.

"She was right, son. If you had killed him, you would have to live with it. Not him. He will pay. But it is not our job to be the judge. Grab his feet. We'll carry him back to the house."

It was the right thing to do. But it left a bitter taste in his mouth.

Eleazar squinted at the light. It burned his eyes. His whole head hurt. He stuck the tip of his tongue to the corner of his mouth and tasted blood. When he tried to reach it, he realized his hands were bound. He tried to move his feet. They, too, were tied. Panic rose.

He blinked a few times, his eyes adjusting. Sounds in the background, whispered voices assaulted his ears. He turned his head to the side.

Aphra.

She stood a few feet away, her face without expression.

"Aphra child, help me. Please."

She stepped closer.

"Please child, undo my bonds."

She came closer.

"Please." He raised his wrists.

She spit in his face and ran from the room.

He tried to wipe away the spittle. It was hard enough his wrists were tied like a common thug, but when he touched his face, the pain made him gasp.

Three men entered his view. He was acquainted with the Crockett person. The tall one, with the red hair, he looked like… He was the one to leave the note and money, aye. The third, he felt he should recognize his face, but could not place him. "What do you want? Why am I trussed like some fowl for the oven?"

"Fowl? Because you are foul."

"Willie, no." Crockett shook his head. Taking charge again, it seemed.

"Who are you?" Sparks flew before his eyes when he tried to indicate the third man.

"David, this is Eleazar Ferguson."

The third man shook his head. "No, I dunna think ye ken who's in yer home, Joseph. Who ye have here is Silas Keel, the pirate. The one who took me ship, killed me crew, and let that lout O'Malley steal me family."

Eleazar's temples began to pound. "You're daft."

"Do ye deny it?"

"Aye, I deny it!"

Then the man whispered something to Crockett.

"Let me see your forearms."

"What? You have me tied up. How can I show you my forearms, even if I wanted to?"

The redhead stepped forward. "You will show your forearms." He reached for Eleazar's arm.

Eleazar swung both fists at him, connecting with his head.

The redhead landed a fist alongside Eleazar's right cheek, making his head swim.

"Step back, Willie." Crockett pulled at the tall one's arm. "Are you sure, David?"

"Not a doubt, Joseph. I know tis him."

"Then I will hold his fists while you pull back the cuffs."

Eleazar struggled, but the men overpowered him. As the cuffs rose, they revealed his tattoos.

On his right forearm, *Silas*.

On his left, *Keel*.

❧

"JASON, RUN TO MASTER WADDINGTON'S HOUSE, BRING him now. Willie, go with him. I can't lose either of you again. Stay close and vigilant. Bring the justice here."

Leave? Now? Willie didn't want to go. He didn't trust Eleazar even bound. That monster should be gagged. But he must protect his brother. Jason couldn't be impressed into some ship.

The women were told to stay in the kitchen and retold when Aphra came running from the sitting room. But Maybe ran to him. "Where are you going?" Terror made her eyes enormous.

He kissed her cheek. "Don't worry, love. We'll be right back.

I'm only going with Jason as far as the Justice of the Peace. We'll be back in minutes. I promise."

"We've not had any time. I've waited so long for ye, Willie."

He ran a finger down her cheek. "I know. I've waited for you too, love. Fifteen minutes and I will be back. I promise."

She accepted it, but did not look happy.

As soon as they were out the door, he called to Jason. "This needs to be fast. I cannot be gone long. It took too much to get home."

"I understand. And Willie, I'm glad you are home."

Willie put his arm about his brother's shoulders and gave him a squeeze. "Me too. Let's run."

And they did, all the way to Master Waddington's home. They knocked. Willie explained. The justice grabbed his hat, sent a servant to fetch the constable to the Crocketts', and followed them back to the house.

Willie doubted the man believed them until he saw it with his own eyes.

"Silas Keel? Here in your sitting room? Under our noses all this time?" He stared, shaking his head.

"I am Eleazar Ferguson. I am not Silas Keel. That man no longer exists. I am not Silas Keel." The pirate continued to scream and thrash.

No more. Being in that room brought up anger, hate, feelings Willie thought he no longer had. Feelings that kept him from his wife and baby. Robbed of time with them. To hold his child. Or do anything he'd dreamed of while gone. Evil still stole from him, swiping time he should spend loving his wife, meeting his baby, reveling in being home.

He stepped outside to his mother's garden. The blooms gave off fragrance in the dark. He closed his eyes and breathed in, allowing the sweet sent to cleanse away the rage. He remembered Brother Johann's words and the prayers he spoke over him. This was now his faith, his own. He lifted his heart to the One Who made it, fashioned it to feel and pulse and break. *Take this hate, this anger. Fill me with gratitude for Your mercy. You brought me home.*

His next breath was lighter. He was lighter. The night was lighter. He stared at the twinkling stars overhead. How vast, yet he could count each one.

"So ye come home and I find ye hiding out here?" Oh, the music in her voice. His heart began to thump with anticipation. He turned around to find beauty beyond his words, holding out her hands to him.

"I needed a moment." He couldn't explain and didn't want to challenge the mood. He was home. She was here. Nothing else mattered.

"I've missed ye, Willie. I prayed for yer safe return and never gave up hope. Oh, yer right here."

"You were always with me. I'd close my eyes and see your face, your voice whispered to my heart. I so missed you."

She stepped closer. "I think I need to be calling ye William the Conqueror. Ye saved me. Again."

He bowed. "At your service, Mistress Elizabeth Crockett."

She took another step toward him. "'Tis Elizabeth now? What became of Maybe?"

He pulled her into his arms and whispered. "There is no maybe about it, wife." Lifting her chin, he stared into those eyes that made his heart do mad flip flops. "You are my always." His mouth found hers, and he kissed her.

Epilogue

Willie sat in the rocker, his son in his arms as he had dreamed. They studied each other's faces while the world fell away. A new sensation pushed to make room in his heart, something he'd never felt. A different sort of protectiveness covered with wonder. Staring at this miracle, amazement overwhelmed him.

"He has yer temperament, always busy watching at things." Elizabeth stood beside him.

He didn't want her out of reach. He needed her touch. "What do you call him?"

"I wanted to wait for ye to come home before we named him. He's been going by 'sweet baby' until now. What do you think?" Her question flashed in his brain.

He broke the stare with his son and glanced about the room. His parents, Elizabeth's father and sister, all his siblings waited for his answer. "I need to study on this."

"Da? What will happen to that bad man?" Janie asked the question no one else wanted to voice.

"Well, Sarah Jane, he is a pirate. Pirates do not make good choices, so their end is not pretty. But we can pray for him. There's a price on his head. He hadn't garnered a pardon yet but was working on it, from what I gather. Master Waddington said that the money comes here because we captured him. But I'm thinking we couldn't have done that without help. Family, should we split the money between Aphra and David Boulay? What do you all say?" Willie caught the glance that passed between his parents. They had discussed it.

Everyone but Aphra and David called out "aye." They both protested, but no one would change their vote.

"Then it is settled."

Elizabeth stepped forward. "Da, I was able to save something. I ken you canna play anymore, but perhaps, when our son is older, you might teach him to play the fiddle?" She picked it up from the table and brought it to him.

David nodded, too overcome to speak.

Da cleared his throat. "Now we need to name the baby. Willie, what have you decided?" Again, everyone stared.

"I imagined that if I came home to a daughter, I might like the name Mercy. It seems I've had a lot of that poured over me of late. But since we have a son, I want to call him David. Do you agree, Elizabeth?"

The moisture she attempted to blink away told him he made a good choice. David. It would always remind him of his father-in-law, but also another David. One who showed kindness and love without asking for anything in return. An example for his son. One to show mercy, a willingness to serve. One to build the Crockett line with integrity, continuing the thread of faith from generation to generation.

Elizabeth kissed his temple.

He captured his son's gaze one more time. "May you be like another David—a man after God's own heart."

David Crockett smiled and grabbed his father's finger.

Cast of Characters

Bold denotes a mentioned historical figure. Italics denotes fictional characters.

*

1. **William Crockett**
2. **Sarah Jane "Janie" Crockett**
3. **Jason Spotswood Crockett**
4. **Elizabeth "Maybe" Boulay**
5. **Sarah Stewart Crockett**
6. **Mary Crockett**
7. **Joseph Louis Crockett, Sr.**
8. **John Crockett**
9. **Joseph Louis Crockett, Jr. (mentioned)**
10. **Jeanne Crockett (mentioned)**
11. **James Crockett (mentioned)**
12. **Thomas Crockett (mentioned)**
13. **Martha Crockett**
14. **Leticia "Lettie" Crockett**
15. **Elizabeth "Beth" Crockett**
16. **Anne Fontaine (mentioned)**
17. **Edward Mosely**
18. **Jacques Fontaine (mentioned)**

19. Samuel Adams, Sr.
20. Samuel Adams, Jr.
21. Eliza Boulay
22. Johann Dober
23. David Nitschmann
24. David Crockett (this is the Elder, not the famous one)
25. *Daniel O'Malley*
26. *Eleazar Ferguson/Silas Keel*
27. *The Master of The Frances Pearl*
28. *Boatswain Sam Johnson*
29. *Aphra White*
30. *Abigail Attwater*
31. *Mistress Freely*
32. *Master Freely*
33. *Thomas Miller*
34. *Henry Waddington*
35. *Smythe family*
36. *Burrows family*
37. *Cookie the cook*
38. *Mr. Cox*
39. *Nameless friend of D. O'Malley*
40. *Mr. Hawkins*
41. *The Surgeon, Josiah Featherfield*
42. *Mr. Swain*
43. *Thomas Miller's maid*
44. *Mary, Ferguson's housekeeper/cook*
45. *Judge Robert Gibson*
46. *Alexander Thornton*
47. *The Turner family*
48. *Various unnamed sailors*
49. *Andrew Ryan*
50. *Andrew's brother and sister*
51. *Declan Blackheart Stryker*
52. *"Long John" Georgie Galloway*
53. *"Bucktooth" Benjamin Spade*

Afterword

Here we are again, dear reader. I hope you've enjoyed our journey. As with all **The Crockett Chronicles**, this book is fiction *loosely* based on fact. In fact, the first fact I need to share is I can't say Joseph and Sarah ever lived in Beaufort. I know they spent time in Virginia and either admired or were friends with the lieutenant-governor, Alexander Spotswood because of Jason's middle name—Spotswood. But death certificates put them in North Carolina. So, I searched for Huguenot communities in North Carolina that were established far enough back and had an ocean view. I found Beaufort.

I also found a wonderful librarian there, Mary Taylor Creech, who answered many questions and read through an early version of the book to help me with historic and geographic accuracies. We ran into a snag. Beaufort is flat. One can see for miles. I might have caught on earlier had I been able to visit, but I couldn't, so I didn't, and now that bluff was key to the story. Therefore, in the spirit of full disclosure, Beaufort has no bluff. Just another author license. Remember, it's fiction! I hope you can forgive me and enjoy.

Something different about *The Prodigal* is I wrote the draft in two-and-a-half months. I've never written so fast in my life.

Having mulled over the idea in my head for fifteen years helped though. I lived and breathed Willie and Maybe's tale twenty-four/seven.

I ran into the same problems with *The Prodigal* that appeared with *The Sojourners*—duplicate names. Seriously, did they not think a distant progeny might write stories concerning them? So, I devised nicknames again. The biggest is connected to a bit of mystery. Maybe, or rather Elizabeth Boulay, was not even listed as a wife when I began my research fifteen years ago. But because of explosive interest in ancestry sites, some have identified her as William's wife. Or one of them. Other places have him to the altar three times. Some places have him wed to Eliza, making her the same as Elizabeth. And another I found had Elizabeth and Eliza as sisters who married brothers. I liked that best. There is no data stating Willie and Maybe went to sea or that they conceived a child before marriage. In fact, the whole idea of Elizabeth being called Maybe is solely from my imagination. Mere storytelling. Author license again.

Our other Elizabeth, Willie's sister Beth, lived almost one hundred years. To think of all she saw happen in her lifetime. Little Janie, a.k.a. Sarah Jane, might have been nicknamed Janie to differentiate from her mother Sarah. I tried to imagine that houseful of children and can believe Sarah was that amazing.

For those of you who read both *The Patriarch* and *The Sojourners*, you know that the Huguenot cross pin was key in those stories. I couldn't come up with a reason for Willie to receive it over Joseph Louis (Wee Joseph in *The Sojourners*) so I didn't mention it. I hope that was not a problem.

One fun detail I researched was the Age of Sailing. I immersed myself in stories of brave travelers taking to the sea. And the pirates! Oh, my! That was interesting. I learned when they wanted to be finished with that life, many signed agreements with the governing authorities to behave as good citizens for an expressed amount of time and then they received a pardon. (Anyone remember *Alias Smith and Jones*?) That was

Silas/Eleazar's goal, only he had bad habits. And a bit of an attitude. The brand he received was often done, especially to those who claimed Benefit of Clergy, though on the face was rare.

The Benefit of Clergy clause was dying out about then. A practice begun in medieval days, it hit its stride further north in the Puritan communities but found a calling in the other colonies. Originally it was only for entangled members of the clergy. But soon others called on the loophole which said that if they read "the neck passage," Psalm 51, in Latin and were not struck dead, they escaped the noose.

There're tons of behind-the-scenes memories from this book. It's good when an author loves what she writes, and that is true here. But I will save you from my ramblings and thank you for taking the time to read *The Crockett Chronicles*. I've no plans for more in this series but have started another I hope you will enjoy. You can look for the first in the Relentless series, *Relentless Heart*, to release this coming July (and there's a sneak peek in just a few pages!), and a novella, *Tales of the Hob Nob Annex,* to come out in May. Until then...

Abundant blessings!

Jenny

❧

If you enjoyed this book, please leave a review. Reviews can be as simple as "I couldn't put it down. I can't wait for the next one" and help raise the author's visibility and lets other readers find her.

Acknowledgments

First and always, my thanks and wonderment go to my Abba Who continues to leave me breathless with how He orchestrates it all.

To my Phil, who isn't afraid to say the hard stuff, even if it makes me mad, to get me to think and do the better. I love you, baby.

To my girls, my boys, and my grands—thank you for listening to me go on and on and…

To my dear friend and mentor, Esther Bailey. This would still be a dream on the someday list if it weren't for you. Thank you! (That goes for Wilma too!)

Several good friends and family members read the drafts of this and offered feedback. It is better because of you, Mary England, Jaime Zorich, Diana Brandmeyer, Dorothy Shields, and Christine Cain. I thank you!

Jen Crosswhite, you get a thank you all to yourself. You make me look good. And you are a wonderful friend. Love you, kiddo.

Mary Taylor Creech, I cannot thank you enough for your insights on Beaufort, for taking the time to read through for historical accuracy, and for all your kind words of praise. I have enjoyed working with you and look forward to that continuing.

When in need of a pirate name, I put out a call and was overwhelmed with response. So thank you to the following who should find their offering in the pages: Jackie Marsh, Lauren Waymire, Richard Goodell, Connie Legg, and Linda Lou Downing's grandson, AJ McGie.

To my Street Team, you know who you are, ***thank you*** for getting the word out.

To my Pit Crew—Lori Doe, Annie Oertel, Debbie Atkinson, Julie Burch—you intercessory pray-ers who keep me accountable, thank you, thank you, thank you!

Sean and Mariah, I am so glad we met. You look amazing on the cover! Love you guys!

And to Gaby and Andy with Aries 70 Studio, you did it again. Your photography is wonderful. Thank you for your patience and care to get the best poses.

And to you dear reader. Thank you. With all the books in the world, you chose to read this one. I am humbled and grateful.

Reader's Guide

1. Each book of the series ended up leaning more
   toward fiction than historical. Once you read the
   Afterword, what surprised you to learn really was
   true? What surprised you to learn was fictitious?
2. The 1730 setting fell smack dab in the period called
   The Age of Sailing. Though Jack Sparrow is fiction,
   and so is Silas Keel for that matter, there were many
   pirates during that time. What do you know about
   the pirates of that period? Were you surprised to
   learn that some worked out pardons with
   governments and became "everyday citizens"?
3. After setting the story in Beaufort, North Carolina, I
   learned there are no hills there, yet the bluff became
   an important part of the story. Would you have
   changed that to something else to bring the couple
   together? What do you feel the bluff symbolized and
   how might you get the same symbolism with a
   different idea?
4. How did you feel about Sarah and Joseph's character

growth after reading *The Prodigal*? Was it realistic that they matured in their faith as they did?

5. Joseph Louis (Wee Joseph in *The Sojourners*) never appears in this book—according to the dates he was married by then. Did that disappoint?

6. The Huguenot cross from the first two books did not show up in this book. If you were to work it into the story, how might you have done that?

7. *The Patriarch* had a theme of faith. *The Sojourners* theme was trust. How do you think those themes were built on to develop the theme of mercy for this story?

8. Who was your favorite character for this book? Who was your favorite character of the whole trilogy?

9. The David Crockett at the end of the story is the grandfather of the famous frontiersman. If you knew that his end was not good, would you still want to read his story? How do you feel about ending The Crockett Chronicles two generations away from Davy Crockett?

10. Even though the stories are fiction, they deal with life and questions and problems that happen in any time period. How did this story speak to your faith? How did the series speak to your faith?

About the Author

Jennifer Lynn Cary is a direct descendent of Davy Crockett making Antoine and Louise her ancestors as well. A retired elementary teacher, she resides in Arizona with her husband where they enjoy family time with two more generations in the Crockett linage.

You can find her at www.jenniferlynncary.com

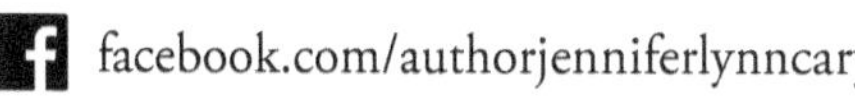
facebook.com/authorjenniferlynncary

Sneak Peek of Relentless Heart: The Relentless Book 1

May 24, 2068

"He's ready for you."

Natalia Alaniz stood. Her heart pounded as she brushed a wrinkle from her skirt. After all the strides of this twenty-first century, why had no one invented a method to keep clothes from wrinkling? Did she look professional? She brushed the thought away with one more swipe and followed the secretary.

Breathless, Natalia pinched herself. Since childhood, she had dreamed of this room. Old and new media often used the setting. Yet standing in this place bathed her in surreal almost as much as the sunlight filtering through the windows. Her eyes roved from the ornate desk to the curved walls, landing on the Seal of the United States, emblazoned on the carpet at her feet.

"Your first time, I see."

Startled, she spun to the voice as the voice in her ear spoke, "Don't be too much the fan. Remember, you're the professional."

She held out her hand. "Mr. President. Thank you for seeing me."

Mr. David Joshua Salem, President of the United States, shook her hand, guiding her to the chairs set up all rolled into one motion. Natalia's mind screamed like a teenage groupie—*I'll never wash this hand again!*—while the voice in her ear brought her back to Earth. "Breathe, smile, and make nice."

"You are correct, sir. This is my first assigned interview on-site outside of the Press Corp room. I'm sure it shows all over my face."

"Not at all. You are doing fine. You'd never believe how I behaved the first alone moment I had in here."

"Would you like to tell me about it?" She'd have an exclusive.

He shook his head and chuckled. "You are good. Almost let that secret out of the bag." He winked, taking the other chair.

"Well perhaps we can get started." She double checked her right earring. Her producer's voice came through loud and clear. Next, she touched the statement necklace that held the camera, waiting a second to hear the "looks good." Last, she handed the tie clip to President Salem. He put it on. She gave him a thumbs-up as her producer expressed approval for the wireless reception.

"We're set." She paused, ignored her thumping heart, and began. "This is Natalia Alaniz, correspondent with CBS Sunday Morning, streaming live from the Oval Office. My guest today is President Salem. Good morning, Mr. President."

He leaned back, ever so slightly. "Good morning, Ms. Alaniz."

One last glance at her bracelet of notes. For months she dreamed of, prepped for this moment. Now here it was. She took a breath. "You are concluding your first term in office and gearing up for a second. Overall, the American people seem to think they know you. Is that accurate?"

"Pretty much, yes, that is accurate. In this day and age, not much is hidden. The opposition has tried to expose my sins or faults. But, what you see is what you get. I'd say I'm fairly transparent."

"Your military career is of public record, along with the

heroic actions for which you received the Medal of Honor while serving in the Sudan War. I understand you come from a long line of warriors."

President Salem crossed his legs. "I guess you might say that. My father, grandfather, and great-grandfather all served in the military."

"How did their service impact you and your new program, Plows of Peace? How does it impact you as Commander-in-Chief?"

He chuckled. "I am who I am because of their choices as much as my own. The nucleus of Plows of Peace started many years ago in my family, eventually growing to include others from my hometown. We believed the time was ripe to present it on a bigger stage."

"Do you view Plows of Peace to be the Peace Corps of the twenty-first century? In some ways that might put you on the level with President John Kennedy, wouldn't it?"

He sat straighter. "I don't see that. I just know POP, as we affectionately call it, has served many. By championing it with a national platform, the numbers of people helped grows exponentially."

"So, what was the nucleus for POP? How did all this get started?"

He smiled. Memories twinkled in his eyes. "There was another warrior. She inspired the idea behind POP."

"Another? Who was she?"

He nodded and held out his hand. "Come, I'll show you." He led Natalia to a shelf behind his desk, taking down an old-fashioned double frame, two five-by-sevens hinged together. The left held a photo of an elderly Asian woman. Her smile tired, but gentle, nearly closed her eyes to thin lines. Small bits of her silver hair wisped about her face while the rest was pulled to the back. She appeared to be... Natalia couldn't guess. Her only thought was ancient.

The photo in the other frame included the woman, though

one could see she sat in a rolling chair—a thing they used to call a wheelchair. Now her smile was wide. A small child, perhaps preschool age, pushed the chair from behind. "This is my *Bà*." He rubbed his thumb over the wheelchair photo. "My great-grandmother." Pointing to the boy, he added, "That's my son, David Junior."

"He met his great, great-grandmother?" How could that be?

"Yes." He sighed. "She passed away not long after this. Bà lived to be 104 years old. I remember when it was taken. DJ says he remembers, too, though I'm not sure that it's her or the photo he recalls, but yes, they were great buddies."

This was something new. Excitement bubbled from her toes. And he seemed to want to talk. So she nudged. "She's lovely, very sage like."

"She was. And she was more than determined. Not ruthless or anything negative, but her faith, the way she loved, it was strong, tenacious. You could say relentless." He replaced the frames.

"How do you mean?"

President. Salem motioned to the chairs. "To understand, you must go back one hundred years to a city once called Saigon."

❧

Saigon, January 1, 1968

Hien gazed square into the eyes of the man whose hands held hers, the man whose eyes captured her heart. The heart that was about to pound out of her chest, if his eyes didn't hold her captive. If she blinked, it would all fall apart.

And so would she.

"Michael Ryan Wheaten, do you take this woman to be your lawfully wedded wife? To have and to hold from this day forth, for richer or for poorer, in sickness and in health, 'til death do you part?"

"I do."

He said I do! Heart, calm down!

"Nguyen Han Hien, do you take this man to be your lawfully wedded husband? To have and to hold from this day forth, for richer or for poorer, in sickness and in health, 'til death do you part?"

Michael squeezed her hand.

She squeezed back. "I do." A tear etched its way down her cheek, plopping in a warm, wet blob on her new red *ao dai*, the traditional Vietnamese dress she bought for today.

Tears welled in his blue eyes, too. He looked so handsome in his Air Force dress uniform.

"By the power vested in me by the United States of America, I now pronounce you man and wife. You may kiss your bride."

Michael's lips were on hers before she caught breath. But how sweet to faint in those arms. More than a peck, but not so much as to be embarrassing, they broke off the kiss together. He swept her off her feet.

"OH! Michael!"

He spun her around before planting her feet back on the ground.

Heat flooded her cheeks. Hien glanced at the man who performed the ceremony. The officer grinned. So did Michael's parents. Apparently, it was not too embarrassing.

His father, Minister Ernest Wheaten, a retired colonel, pulled her into an embrace. "Welcome to the family, Hien. You are now Hien Wheaten. Think you might get used to being a Wheaten?"

Hien nodded as she whispered her new name in her brain. Yes, she could get used to anything with Michael by her side.

His mother Melanie hugged her, not as effusively as his father, but still warmly. "We're so happy for you two!"

Then she was back in his arms.

With a new name.

And a new home.

So much new. But she could figure it all out with Michael.

❧

That evening she lay curled in Michael's arms. He tucked a few wayward strands of long hair behind her ear. "We can't tell my mom yet. Dad plans this big surprise once we get out. Brother Charlie's enlistment won't be up for a while. He's already told me he wants to reenlist. He and Lai might settle down here, with her teaching and all. They're not sure." He sighed. "I'm rattling on."

"No, Michael. I love the sound of your voice. I want to just listen. Tell me more plans." Her finger made lazy circles on his sternum.

"You sure?"

She nodded, nuzzling next to his neck. His words flowed softer than the moonlight, filtered by the cherry tree leaves, through their bedroom window. The bed in the room he kept at his parents' in the embassy villa was only a single, but she had no complaints about sharing it tonight. Or any night.

"Okay, so the farm is near a little town called Breadville in Indiana. It's a few miles away from Bunker Hill Air Force Base. Kokomo would be the nearest bigger town, I suppose. Peru's not far either. Mom and Dad came for a visit one time while I was stationed there, and we got to talking about the future. Dad has wanted to retire to a farm like where he grew up, and I suppose I've always listened to his stories, because he's got me thinking that way, too. We found this place close to some of Mom's family. The farmhouse is in good shape. It has all sorts of possibilities. My cousin has been caring for it until we can get there. He lives close by, so he said he didn't mind. It will still need work, though."

Hien nodded into Michael's shoulder. She could do anything if they could do it together.

"But here's the part you can't tell Mom." His finger made a slow trace from her temple to the base of her throat. "Dad is signing the farmhouse over to you and me as a wedding gift. He plans to build her a new house on another part of the property, but this way we won't have to inherit the farm. It'll be ours when we move back. Think you might enjoy being an Indiana farmer's wife?"

She nodded and nibbled his ear. As much as she loved his voice, it was time to stop talking.

"Morning, Hien! Glad you're back. Where've you been?" Nick Jones, a correspondent for a small newspaper in upstate New York, threw out the soliloquy as he dashed past. Hien figured out a while back that he did not want answers unless he was sure it led to a story. If he wanted answers, he would pause to give you the opportunity. No pause, no real interest.

So she called, "Morning!" after him and headed for her desk.

To call it a desk was a kind misnomer. Rather it was a disintegrating school desk with the attached seat removed. A metal pipe protruded where it once had been. However, it was perfect to stow any immediate work and a few belongings—a box of Kleenex tissues, two Bic pens, a stenographers pad, an extra tube of Slickers lip gloss (the only makeup she allowed herself because Michael liked how it tasted). Hien did not mind. Her camera stayed with her at all times. Two or three spare rolls of film hid in the Kleenex box, and that, as well as the rest of her treasures, lay stashed beneath the lift-up plywood board which served as a desktop, though it barely remained attached by the grace of one tiny hinge. Unused film disappeared faster than they could replace it, unless you had the backing of a big media outlet. Hien's photos were for the independent market. There was no telling who might buy them. So, film was a precious commodity not to be wasted. Out of habit, she felt inside the tissue box. The canisters were where she hid them. Whew!

She started with the Corp as a translator. Her English was fluent. In truth, it was extremely fluent, thanks to the Catholic school nuns who drilled the language into her and her brother. She gained a reputation for accuracy and an awareness of semantic subtleties.

One day she brought her camera to an interview and snapped a shot. No other cameras were available. The correspondent she assisted became excited for the photo. He did not care how amateurish it turned out.

It turned out better than amateurish. Hien's life changed.

Tony Bennett crooned from someone's radio, extolling that for once in his life he had love and hope. Hein understood.

Had it only been a year since she left her family in Huê? One year. She went from a daughter to a working woman, from translator to photographer, from single to married. Her two-week-old ring glittered like the candle in the little paper boat she sent sailing down the Houng River last *Tet*, filled with wishes for the new life she was about to start the following week in Saigon. The river gleamed that night with all the tiny New Year boats sailing off into the future.

Funny, in two weeks, it again would be the New Year—Tet. What would this New Year bring? Perhaps she would become a mother. She and Michael might start their family. Four more weeks and he would be done flying sorties over jungles. They would leave Vietnam. She would say goodbye to everything familiar, more than when she left Huê for Saigon, but the excitement tantalized. Her destiny lay on the other side of the ocean. She was sure.

Indiana, what a strange name! She shook her head. The things that happened in one small year.

Hien checked the schedule for the darkroom. Someone got there before her. Too much day-dreaming. She knocked, inquiring how long the wait.

Of course, she could fly to Huế. When she lived there, she built her own darkroom in the bathroom of her parents' apartment building. People knocked on the door there, too. But it was a four hour flight.

She missed that world—her family, the city, her home. Never did she expect to return to that world. Yet, her family was there.

Her family.

She sighed. Her family had not come for her wedding. They sent word that it was too dangerous to travel.

At least, that is the reason they gave.

Hien shrugged and knocked again.

"Almost done. Five minutes."

"Okay." What could she do but wait? She leaned against a table cluttered with dirty paper coffee cups, crumbs, and dried smeared something.

Mat Morrissey soldiered past to grab the schedule clipboard, grunted as he perused, and tossed it back onto the file cabinet. "Hien, you gotta let me in ahead of you. I think I've got something. Something big!"

"Like what?"

"I'm not sure. You know that niggle when you know something, but you're unsure what it is?"

Hien nodded. She did not know, but she knew Mat. He could not let go of this any more than her brother's dog could let go of a bone. "Fine, you may come in with me. I will share my time, but you must tell me what you learned."

Mat hesitated. "Deal. But I've got the scoop. Right?"

"Deal."

Mat checked his watch, then pounded on the door. "C'mon, Riley! You're holding up the show!"

The voice behind the door called back. "Gimme a sec, Morrissey! Geez Louise!" Usually the language was saltier, but

Hien was sure Steve Riley realized she was there and controlled himself.

Finally, the lock clicked, and the door opened.

"About time, man!" Mat pushed through.

"Hey, you can't rush perfection!" Steve waved a sheaf of photos. "And, you're welcome!"

"You coming, Hien?"

"Coming, Mat!" She smiled at Steve as she hurried past and shut the door. She fixed the lock which would keep others from coming in and destroying their work. The safe light was on. "Where were you shooting?"

Mat had opened the small film canisters. "I was over by Huế last evening. Just got back. There's this feel in the air. Something's not right. That city used to be so beautiful, even the atmosphere. The one place the war overlooked. Now it's like walking into the opening of a horror movie."

"What do you mean?"

He shrugged, the red glow casting eerie shadows on his face. "Like nothing is out of place, yet something is. It's a sensation I can't shake. I swear, if Alfred Hitchcock stepped out from behind a tree, I wouldn't have been surprised. Terrified, yeah, but surprised, no."

Hien's heart climbed its way up her throat. "My family is there."

"Oh, sorry." Mat's gaze met hers, and then he returned to his work. He was reconsidering his bargain.

"I remember the area well. Perhaps I can see something."

"Perhaps." He didn't raise his head.

They worked in silence until Mat had his second roll developed. "Man! I thought for sure there was something. I'm just not seeing it."

"Let me look." Hien started with the first photo hanging from the drying line. A teenage girl on a bicycle. She studied the next. Then the next. The bicycle girl was not the only human photographed, but the manner in which she showed in different places... and she was only in maybe eight shots? But Hien could see it, rather sense it, whatever it was Mat meant. But she could not put a name to it either. "The city looks weird, different." The fear she had pushed away reared.

"Yeah. There's a curfew in effect for the locals. They don't get far from home that late in the evening. This isn't even inside the Citadel. I took these in the Triangle district, just south of the river. Still, I can't shake the eeriness. What does it mean? Have they gone underground or are they following orders? And why was that girl in those places?

Hien shook her head, reviewing each shot. Hien well knew the area. It was where she grew up. It was where her mother lived. Mat developed sixty photos altogether, and only eight of the girl—a girl she had never seen—but in a different locale each time. Who was she? What happened to her beautiful city? "What is this?"

Mat searched where she showed.

The girl was doing something near a doorway. What? "Hand me a magnifying glass, please."

He grabbed one from the table.

She peered closer, pointing to a shadow in the doorway next to the girl. Was she talking with someone? Was it supposed to be secret? It made no sense. Huế was beloved by both the north and the south. Battles raged near it, but neither side wanted to desecrate the Imperial City. Plus, the cease fire for Tet was just around the corner.

She must see for herself. "Can you get me there?"

"Not a good idea."

"I must go. I need to see this."

Mat shook his head. "I can't take you there. Not without some kind of security team. Your new husband would kill me deader than dead."

"If you will not take me, I will go on my own." New husband or not, she almost added. Michael was on call for a flight today, anyway. He would not learn of this before she returned tonight.

Mat paused. His eyes gave him away before he spoke. "This is against my better judgment, but there's a guy who owes me. Let's go."

Hien returned the film canisters she had planned to develop to her purse for another time and grabbed her camera before Mat changed his mind.

"C'mon Hien, the sooner we leave, the sooner we can get back to Saigon."

⚜

The cargo hold of the C-130 Hercules allowed no room for conversation. The plane's four engines roared loud enough to silence the most talkative. That left Hien running scenarios in her mind and asking herself questions she had no information with which to answer. Mat appeared calm, from the waist up. The rhythm of his right knee bouncing the entire flight belied him.

The second they rolled to a stop, he was out of his seat, heading for the cockpit.

"When do you need to take off?"

The pilot, Juan Andrade, shrugged. "This is a turnaround flight. Just long enough to unload."

"Can you give us an hour?"

"An hour, yeah, I'll stretch it that far. But, if you're not back, I'm not waiting."

Hien grabbed Mat's arm, speaking in his ear. "Tell him not to leave us!"

"She says don't leave us."

Juan shrugged again. "Then be back in an hour." He returned his attention to the controls.

"We'd better move. I'll get a vehicle." Mat climbed out and ran for the operations shack, leaving Hien to dismount the plane on her own.

She followed, only to have him return, running with keys in hand.

"Let's go." He grabbed her elbow, steering her toward a jeep on the edge of the runway. They both jumped in, he started it up, and they were on their way into the city. Hien gave him directions to her parents' apartment building. That was the easiest place to start.

Fifteen minutes later, they pulled up in front. Everything looked the same, though different. The tree outside her old bedroom window appeared taller. The flowers in the pot beside the door bore a different color. A neighbor she did not recognize swept the stoop of the adjacent building. Her heart did a little twist. This must be the definition of bittersweet.

Clambering out, she motioned for Mat to follow, and ran to her parents' door, what used to be her door. She tried her old key, but it did not work. She reinserted it, trying again. It would not turn. Hien left the key in the lock and knocked. "*Mẹ, chính là con.*" She called to her mother. Now she could hear her brother's dog, Bao, barking from the back of the apartment. Surely someone was there. Bao grew quiet. She knocked again. "I do not understand, Mat. Mother should be here."

Mat tapped her shoulder, put his finger to his lips, and pointed down.

A small piece of paper stuck out from the threshold. The folded sheet moved, sliding further out. She stooped to retrieve and open it. Only three scrawled words.

Rời khỏi, Nguy!

To order *Relentless Heart*, click here: